Praise for Carla Buckley's
The DEEPEST SECRET

"A taut family drama . . . Smart and thrilling."

—*People* magazine

"Superb . . . The story offers the intricate suspense and surprise of a thriller, along with rich characterizations and nuanced writing. . . . [Its] suburban world is beautifully observed, its characters convincing, flawed, and sympathetic. Ultimately, Buckley delivers a **gripping read** and a memorable reflection on the conflicting imperatives of love."

—*Publishers Weekly* (starred review)

"A harrowing story."

—New York *Daily News*

"*The Deepest Secret* gets under your skin—when you're not reading it, you're thinking about it. The first fifty pages already draw you in, but then Buckley sets a hook that makes it impossible not to race to the end to find out what happens."

—#1 internationally bestselling author Linwood Barclay

"Carla Buckley masterfully portrays an ordinary family trapped in a heart-wrenching crisis. A memorable novel about how far a parent will go for her child, *The Deepest Secret* will make you count your blessings."

—William Landay,
New York Times bestselling author of *Defending Jacob*

"Carla Buckley captures the beauty and sorrow of a family about to change forever. This is an unbearably wonderful novel."

—Luanne Rice, *New York Times*
bestselling author of *Little Night*

"The dark tangled secrets of a quiet suburban neighborhood are slowly, masterfully exposed in Carla Buckley's riveting novel. *The Deepest Secret* will have you wondering what lengths you'd go to protect the people you love most, questioning your own ideas of right and wrong, and pulling your family a little closer to you each night."

—Jennifer McMahon,
New York Times bestselling author of *The Winter People*

"*The Deepest Secret* blew me away. Equal parts dark family drama and pulse-pounding thriller, it's a wrenching meditation on love in the face of mortality. This book will make you hug your children tighter. I loved it."

—Sean Chercover, bestselling author of *The Trinity Game*

"*The Deepest Secret* is a mesmerizing page turner. . . . Loved ones are not exempt from suspicion, as the devastating power of a mother's love has unimaginable consequences that kept me riveted until the very end."

—Melanie Benjamin,
New York Times bestselling author of *The Aviator's Wife*

"*The Deepest Secret* is a ferociously passionate book, and I am unabashedly obsessed with everyone populating its pages."
—Lyndsay Faye, author of *The Gods of Gotham*

"Sensational . . . an exceptionally moving and unrelentingly suspenseful yarn that grabs you tight and never lets go . . . a wonderful mix of Judith Guest's *Ordinary People*, Rosellan Brown's *Before and After* and William Landay's *Defending Jacob*. Everything a great novel, and thriller, should be."
—*The Providence Sunday Journal*

"Daring . . . Buckley takes readers into the grayest area imaginable. . . . Hearty book club discussion fodder. As winding and treacherous as a slick road, this masterful thriller will leave readers clutching their chests."

—*Shelf Awareness*

"An intense tale in which nobody's life is what it seems and nothing can remain a secret forever. These well-written characters rely on love, hope, and perseverance to get them through."
—*RT Book Review* (four stars)

By Carla Buckley

The Deepest Secret
Invisible
The Things That Keep Us Here

The
DEEPEST
SECRET

A NOVEL

CARLA BUCKLEY

BANTAM BOOKS TRADE PAPERBACKS
NEW YORK

The Deepest Secret is a work of fiction. Names, characters, places, and incidents are the products of the author's imagination or are used fictitiously. Any resemblance to actual events, locales, or persons, living or dead, is entirely coincidental.

2014 Bantam Books Trade Paperback Edition

Published in the United States by Bantam Books, an imprint of Random House, a division of Random House LLC, a Penguin Random House Company, New York.

BANTAM BOOKS and the HOUSE colophon are registered trademarks of Random House LLC. RANDOM HOUSE READER'S CIRCLE & Design is a registered trademark of Random House LLC.

Originally published in hardcover in the United States by Bantam Books, an imprint of Random House, a division of Random House LLC, in 2014.

Grateful acknowledgment is given for permission to reprint the lines from "i carry your heart with me (i carry it in". Copyright 1952, © 1980, 1991 by the Trustees for the E. E. Cummings Trust, from COMPLETE POEMS: 1904–1962 by E. E. Cummings, edited by George J. Firmage. Used by permission of Liveright Publishing Corporation.

This book contains an excerpt from the forthcoming book *The Good Goodbye* by Carla Buckley. This excerpt has been set for this edition only and may not reflect the final content of the forthcoming edition.

Buckley, Carla (Carla S.)
The deepest secret : a novel / Carla Buckley.
pages cm
ISBN 978-0-553-39373-6
ebook ISBN 978-0-345-53966-3
1. Secrets—Fiction. I. Title.
PS3602.U2645D33 2013
813'.6—dc23   2013020477

Printed in the United States of America on acid-free paper

www.randomhousereaderscircle.com

2 4 6 8 9 7 5 3 1

Book design by Diane Hobbing

For Jillian, Jonathon, and Jocelyn,
whose hearts I hold (within my heart)

here is the deepest secret nobody knows
(here is the root of the root and the bud of the bud
and the sky of the sky of a tree called life; which grows
higher than soul can hope or mind can hide)
and this is the wonder that's keeping the stars apart
i carry your heart (i carry it in my heart)

—e. e. cummings

The
DEEPEST
SECRET

By the window, she sits in her favorite chair, jumping a doll up and down in her lap. A shadow flickers in the doorway behind her. Someone else is watching her, too.

THURSDAY, AUGUST 28

SUNRISE 6:56 AM

SUNSET 8:11 PM

EVE

Birthdays are supposed to be happy occasions, so Eve plans a party. There are the usual anxieties. Who would come? Would Tyler like his presents? Then there are the special worries, the ones other people didn't have to think about. She won't focus on those.

She makes a cake, a bigger-than-life-size iPad that takes a day and a half to decorate instead of the six hours the Internet site promised. The problem is getting the paint the right consistency so the lake doesn't bleed into the shoreline. And all those tiny icons. She's tossed dozens in the trash, false starts where the Facebook *f* was too wobbly and the camera came out looking as though a giant thumb had pressed down hard. She hesitates over balloons. Do they even matter at night? In the end, she decides, *why not,* and drives home from the party store with so many fat balloons crammed into her backseat that she can't see out her rearview mirror. She imagines being pulled over by the police for driving under the influence of helium.

Melissa's in the kitchen when Eve arrives home, and helps carry in the bags. She reaches for the balloons and frowns at the rainbow of colors. "Pink, Mom, *really*?"

Melissa's long black hair is pulled back in an untidy topknot Eve knows her daughter has worked for hours to achieve. One of her tank top straps is twisted, revealing the pale strip of skin beneath where the sun hasn't lingered. Eve wants to tug it straight and warn her daughter to be careful, but Melissa has heard it all before. "Pink looks good in moonlight," Eve says.

A knock on the kitchen door. It's Charlotte and Amy, arriving early to help. Dear Charlotte. What would Eve do without her kindness, her humor? Charlotte has pulled her through the dark days. She has kept Eve sane.

"One spicy chili dip, extra sour cream by request," Charlotte says, setting down the dish on the counter. She's wearing a determined smile on her face. Amy looks mutinous. Eve guesses they've been having another mother-daughter battle all the way down the street.

Charlotte's hair is short and dyed dark red. It cups her head and suits her high cheekbones and long neck. The day after Owen served her with divorce papers, Charlotte went out and had her long blond hair chopped off. *What do you think?* she'd demanded as she stepped into Eve's kitchen. She'd run her fingers through the short wisps, making them stand up. *Do I look like someone who knows how to have a good time?*

Amy's carrying a package, the electric blue wrapping paper crumpled at the corners and the white ribbon twisted into a crooked bow. "It's Force Field Three," she confides in a whisper, as if Tyler could hear her all the way from his room upstairs. "Do you think he'll like it?" Her brown eyes are wide and her lashes pale gold, a smatter of freckles across the tops of her cheeks. She's a sprite, a funny little elf always dressed in shades of pink, much to Charlotte's private dismay. She thinks it shows no imagination.

"He'll love it," Eve promises, putting a hand on the child's small shoulder. Is it okay that Tyler spends so much time staring at a computer screen?

They go out onto the patio, the air heavy with heat. Amy skips off to help Melissa tie the balloons to the trampoline. The sun's holding itself just above the horizon, sending out greedy shoots of orange light that carves shadows across the patio and grass. Eve used to love the sun, would lounge outside for hours, letting it toast her skin, her face tilted to the warmth. But this is as close as she comes to the sun now.

"Any word from David?" Charlotte asks, and Eve shakes her head. There weren't that many flights between Columbus and Washington, DC. It could be that David had raced to make the last one and hadn't had a chance to call beforehand. *I'll try and be there,* he'd said. *If* he could wrap up the project he's working on. *If* he could catch an earlier flight. She could drown in *ifs.* "He's bringing Tyler's present. He would have let me know if he wasn't going to be here." She says this, wanting reassurance. She says this, wanting to make it true.

"Maybe he wants to surprise you."

Wouldn't that be wonderful? The gate would creak open and David would step into the yard, his brown hair rumpled over his high forehead, that knowing smile that reached up to his blue eyes. David used to love to surprise her with a note taped to the bathroom mirror, a single flower sent special delivery.

Her parents haven't called, either. But at least they'd sent a card, a blue envelope propped on the kitchen table where Tyler would find it when he came downstairs. Inside would be the usual check, which Tyler would pretend to be thrilled about. Money meant nothing to him. How could it?

At 8:11, the bolt shoots back and Tyler shuffles out of his room, his camera in his hand. "Happy birthday," she says, throwing her arms around him. He ducks his head in embarrassment, lamplight winking across the lenses of his sunglasses.

"Happy birthday, dweeb," Melissa says, lightly cuffing him on the shoulder.

His friends are on the patio, elbowing and jostling. Four of them, when there should be seven, but at least his best friend's there. The boys are all different heights and sizes, caught at that awkward stage where they don't even look like they belong to the same species. They cheer when Tyler steps out to join them. He fits right among them, not too tall, not too short. He smiles when he sees the glowing paper lanterns. "Cool," he says, and holds up his camera.

The pizza arrives and Charlotte helps her set out the food. Amy flits around, snatching up a piece of fruit, chasing fireflies blinking in the distance. A few neighbors have shown up. It's painful to see Albert without Rosemary. He's aged, moving slowly, holding onto the back of a chair for support. Sophie makes a brief appearance, and so does Neil Cipriano, who stands a careful distance away from everyone. No sign of the new neighbors, the Rylands, but that's no surprise. Charlotte had been the one to sell them the house, and she'd raved about how wonderful they were. *You'll love them,* she'd assured Eve. *They're the sweetest family.* But Charlotte knew her reassurances meant nothing until Eve had a chance to talk to them about Tyler. Eve had stopped on her way to the party store to greet them as they stood in their driveway watching the movers unload their furniture. Holly had listened to Eve's request, but it had been Mark who'd reached out to accept the basket of incandescent light bulbs. *Sure,* he'd said. *No problem.*

What would she have done, otherwise? Tyler would never have been able to walk out his front door, let alone go into his own backyard. She'd called David to share the news and gotten his voicemail. *Guess what,* she'd said, leaving her message, not knowing when he'd pick it up.

Tyler seems to be having a good time. He's jumping on the trampoline with his friends, the fabric sagging alarmingly low, burdened as it is by the weight of five adolescent boys. They've rigged the sprinkler to rotate beneath them, and they're howling with laughter as the water sprays back and forth. Eve had offered to rent out a movie theater, or drive everyone to a nearby cave to spelunk, but Tyler had shaken his head at every suggestion. *Nothing,* he'd told her. *I don't want anything.*

He's growing up, David said when she worried Tyler might be depressed. It would be reassuring if that was true, but what if it wasn't? Tyler hadn't liked the therapist she'd found. *I'll find someone else,* she'd offered, but Tyler had scowled. *Just stop, Mom,* he'd said, and so she has. But she and the other XP moms talk. Fourteen's a dangerous age, old enough to understand, but too young to accept. Fourteen-year-olds chafe against restrictions, defy the rules that have kept them safe. She's heard about the terrible battles the other mothers have waged. *Doesn't he know that he has to wear his sunglasses? I caught her sneaking outside!* She's listened and commiserated. Tyler's already started to take risks. He won't wear his mask when she takes him to his medical appointments. He hates it, keeps it on the shelf of his closet. It's not like she can force him to put it on. The other mothers listen, murmur reassurances. *Even the best kids rebel.*

She brings out the cake, candles flickering in the darkness, and they sing happy birthday. She sees her husband's features reflected in their candlelit son, the fullness of his lower lip, the roundness of his eyes. Tyler makes a wish and blows. Charlotte glances at her and immediately picks up the knife and begins serving cake, so that Eve can step back into the shadows and compose herself.

Fourteen birthdays so far. She remembers them all: His fourth, when all the kids ran around barking, wearing floppy Dalmatian ears she'd hot-glued out of black and white felt, and ate birthday cake baked in a big steel bowl like dog food. His fifth, where they fished for prizes with magnets tied to strings. His seventh, when they wore cowboy hats and roasted hot dogs over a bonfire. His ninth, when she wrote *HAPPY BIRTHDAY!!!* in phosphorescent chalk on the sidewalk all the way down to the park where his friends waited to jump out and surprise him. His eleventh, when she converted the backyard into a moonscape, and everyone ate astronaut ice cream and flung glow-in-the-dark Frisbees that trailed white blurs of false light.

They'd all been wonderful, in that imperfect way birthdays are, but the best had been his very first, before they knew. She'd set up a wading pool and Tyler had splashed in and out all afternoon, clapping his hands, his dimpled knees churning. Her parents and David's father had been there, laden down with presents, so many that she had to set a few aside to open later. Three-year-old Melissa had run around singing her favorite Barney song and fallen asleep in David's lap. It had been the happiest birthday by far. There would never be another like it.

TYLER IN THE NIGHT

The balloons tied to the trampoline hover above the grass like small animals on leashes, restless. Their smooth sides are shades of gray. The kitchen light behind him falls on the patio stones, bleaching them pale yellow. Everything else is shadowed. Tyler doesn't remember what it's like to see the world in full color.

It's cooled off. Earlier, it had been steamy, but his mom wouldn't even think about moving the party inside. The earth would have had to roll off its axis for her to do that. The radio's playing and she's humming along. It's that stupid song about walking like Egyptians. *What does that even mean?* he'd asked her once, and she'd laughed. *Who knows? We were starved for music in the eighties.*

He shakes open the plastic trash bag and his mom drops in forks and crumpled napkins, paper plates smeared with frosting. "I think everyone had a nice time," she says.

It had been weird when Dr. Cipriano showed up that evening, stepping through the gate holding a gift. How many kids had their dentist come to their birthday party? Zach hadn't kidded Tyler about it, but he could've.

"I can't believe how tall Mitch has gotten. I almost didn't recognize him." She crouches to retrieve a cup lying on its side beneath the table.

The sharp peak of the house next door cuts into the night sky. All day he'd heard the shouts of the men coming up through the air vents in the floor of his bedroom. His mom texted him to say she'd gone over to talk to them and the new neighbors had agreed to use regular light bulbs. She'd typed five smiley faces, one after another. The lights are on upstairs, and shadows move across the windows. A ceiling fan rotates in the blue-painted room. A tall bookcase stands against the wall, empty. "Where do you want this?" a man says, startling Tyler, he sounds so close.

A woman's voice answers him.

They could have come to his party, but they hadn't. They *had* just moved in, his mom said. She'd invited them, along with almost everyone else on the street, as though they were One Big Happy, which was lame. The people he'd wished had come, hadn't. His dad had gotten stuck in DC; Rosemary was gone, and of course Yoshi couldn't make it all the way from Japan. Yoshi's not his best friend, but she's *something*. She told him she was planning a special surprise for his birthday, and he'd waited all day but he never heard from her.

"Zach says he's playing football this year." His mom plucks a long curl of ribbon tangled among the rosebushes.

Zach's been freaking out about high school starting. He and Tyler had downloaded the school map from the website and plotted out Zach's schedule, tracing the route he has to take from building to building. Turns out Zach only has five minutes to get from one end of the school to the other in order to make it to gym on time.

Don't worry, Tyler had said. *You can do it.* And Zach had answered, *Dude. It's not like middle school.*

For Tyler, high school will be *exactly* like middle school. He'll turn on his computer, click the mouse, and nod to the teacher standing in front of the classroom. His mom's told him that there will be a lot more kids in his classes, which is supposed to be a good thing. *You'll have the chance to make new friends.* But her voice had that forced cheer to it that tells him she's worried, too. And all he can think about is that he won't be in any of the same classes as his friends.

"What about you, sweetheart?" She picks up a ball of wrapping paper. He and the guys had taken turns kicking it across the grass. "Did you have fun?"

"Sure." He knows how much she wants to hear it. She'd spent ages planning, making the food, decorating. But how could he have had fun? It's not like when he was little and thought birthday parties were cool. *Yay,* birthday cake. *Yay,* presents. But now he gets it. *Yay,* fucking nothing. He twists the top of the bag closed, carries it over to the garbage can. He looks down into the deep darkness. He wishes he could crawl inside, too, and pull the lid on over him.

Something zaps him on his cheek. Surprised, he touches his face and finds it's wet. Is it raining? Puzzled, he looks up to the sky, sees the stars there, twinkling. Another splash, this time on his hand, and he looks across the yard to where his mom stands, holding the Super Soaker Mitch had given him.

The only thing that can beat that is the garden hose, turned on full blast, and he's aiming it across the lawn as his mom ducks behind the fort when the French door opens.

"What are you two doing?" Melissa demands.

He turns and the spray of water dashes across his sister. She squeals and jumps back. "Seriously?"

"Oh, honey. We're sorry." But his mom's laughing, and he can't help it. He starts laughing, too.

"I hate you both." Melissa tosses her hair and goes inside.

His mom puts her arm around him. They're both wet, and the smell of grass is all around them. The small, tight things inside him loosen. "It's late," she says against his hair. "You go to bed. I'll clean the rest of this up tomorrow."

He pauses in the doorway. "Thanks," he says. "You know. For everything."

"Happy birthday, sweetheart."

He taps his nose with his forefinger, then his cheeks—first the right one, then the left. His forehead, chin, and the nape of his neck. His hair gets in the way, so he starts over. Nose, cheeks, forehead, chin, neck. This time it feels right. He tugs his earlobes, right, then left. He takes a deep breath. Okay. He's ready.

He pulls on his gloves and takes a flashlight from the junk drawer. His mom keeps flashlights in every room. His dad jokes they're the only family in the neighborhood prepared for the apocalypse.

Unlocking the door's the tricky part. His mom has superpowers when it comes to hearing the latch click. One, two, *three*. The snick of metal is a whisper, barely audible. Still, he waits to make sure his mom doesn't appear behind him, yawning and tying her bathrobe around her. *You okay, Ty?* He doesn't have to worry about Melissa. She always sleeps with her iPod playing.

The backyard's dark except for where the moon shines down and picks out the stones of the patio, the metal arms of the chairs. He inhales, filling his lungs. What is it about the air that's so much cleaner when no one else is breathing it?

He lets himself out the back gate and onto the dark street. There aren't any streetlights. Back when he was little, his mom went to court and asked that the lights be turned off just on their cul-de-sac. There's a newspaper article with a photograph of her, leaning against a streetlamp with her arms crossed. They'd wanted to take a photograph of him, too, but his mom had said no.

It's almost midnight—is he too late?

Sophie's porch light is on, lighting up an apron of front lawn. Her VW bug sits in her driveway. Melissa's told him it's pale blue, a pretty color, but beneath the white-yellow glow of the porch light, it just looks dirty. Sophie uses a regular light bulb, not halogen, so it's safe. He could dance in front of her porch and it wouldn't hurt him a bit. All her other windows are dark, which makes it seem like she's upstairs asleep, but Tyler knows better.

He hurries around the corner, but just as he reaches the edge of her deck, the downstairs light flares on. He fumbles with his camera, opening the lens, and glances up to see her coming forward to the glass and reaching up for the blinds pull. Tonight she's in that black leather dress again, the one that bares her shoulders and laces tightly up the front. It's nothing like what she'd worn to his party earlier, long pants and a loose top buttoned all the way to her chin. He presses the shutter just in time to capture her before the blinds tilt shut, the light shining behind her and showing every curve of her body. Then the bright light goes dim, and he knows she's turned on her computer. He wonders what video game she's playing, and whether he's ever played against her online, but he doesn't know her gamer tag.

Narrow cypress trees stand all around Dr. Cipriano's house. Tyler pushes his way through the stiff branches and crouches to peer through the ground-level windows that look down into the basement. He's gotten some interesting shots of Dr. Cipriano working away at that thing he's building, his shadow leaping against the far wall as he hammers. But tonight the windows are all dark.

A yellow glow shines out Albert's window, falling on the grass and lighting up the piles of oak leaves, making them look pointy and sharp. Soon all the leaves will be dropping. Deciduous trees produce an enzyme that cuts off food to the leaves, so they die. He's never heard of one that didn't, but maybe there's a tree somewhere that doesn't have that enzyme—a tree that stays green all year long. There are almost sixty thousand different enzymes in people, and he's missing only one.

He crunches across Albert's yard and looks into the kitchen, which is exactly the way Rosemary kept it when she was alive—the framed pictures of cartoon chefs wearing funny hats hanging at a diagonal across one wall, the four blue-and-white canisters on the kitchen counter, the rooster-shaped salt and pepper shakers sitting beak to beak, like they're talking to each other. *What do you think they're saying?* he'd asked Rosemary, and she had looked thoughtful. *Talk is cheep?* Albert's nowhere in sight, but a flame flickers beneath a pot on the stove.

Albert used to be a pilot. His basement had maps taped to the wall, with long red lines showing the routes he flew. Bangkok, Paris, Sydney. Albert's been everywhere. *But I always came home,* he used to say with a smile. After Rosemary died, Tyler had helped Albert take down the maps. *Can I have them?* he'd asked, and Albert had set one surprisingly light hand on his shoulder. *Sure,* he'd said. *They're all yours.*

Next door is the Farnhams' brick house with its big patio and bay windows covered by drapes. It's the one place he can't go anywhere near. He holds up his middle finger as he turns onto the bike path.

The playground's empty, the swings hanging straight, the slide looming dark and silent. It was right there, by the basketball court, where he and Rosemary saw The Beast. Actually, Rosemary's the one who saw it. He turned his head too late to see anything but a distant pale smudge disappearing into the woods. Rosemary told him it might have been a wolf or even a mountain lion. He's been looking for The Beast ever since, but so far, he hasn't even come across a paw print.

He steps off the path and into the woods. He moves carefully, not wanting to startle anything. He stops to check the nest where baby bunnies had curled up, nose to tail, but it's still empty. The babies must be big enough to be on their own now. Voices sound nearby and he freezes, craning his neck to see where they're coming from. A few more yards and the trees part to reveal the small bridge that spans the creek. Two people are there, their heads and shoulders just visible in the dim moonlight.

He sets his camera on a low-hanging branch and fits the remote to it. He bends to peer through the viewfinder. The rest of the world disappears and it's just these two people looking at each other, a man and a woman. He can see the bumps on their noses, the curves of their chins. They're holding hands, their fingers twined on the wooden railing. He presses the button and captures this moment, fixes it forever. These two people will never stand exactly this way again, with the exact same leaves hanging overhead, the exact same starlight gleaming all around.

He's tried to explain to Zach why this is so cool. *It's like running a touchdown,* he'd said, and Zach had nodded. *I get it,* he'd said, though Tyler's not sure he does.

He takes another picture. At the soft *click,* the woman looks around. He holds his breath, heart pounding. But she doesn't spot him standing there motionless in his dark clothes and she turns her attention back to the man, and after a few minutes, they walk away, still talking softly.

He goes over to the bridge and shines his flashlight down into the water. Minnows dart in every direction, shivery brown shapes. Rosemary had once told him that fish stayed awake all night, just like him. That had comforted him, knowing that someone else was awake besides him and the crickets.

Rosemary had liked crawling around in the mucky creek with him, never freaking if something crawly touched her or plopped into the water beside them. His mom worried because Rosemary was old, and might fall and hurt herself, but Rosemary had laughed and said she'd lose it if she didn't use it. So his mom had stopped telling him he couldn't go and instead had gotten him his first cell phone. *If anything happens,* she told him, *push this button and I'll come right away.* But Rosemary never did fall. She fell asleep one day and never woke up.

He reaches the stand of red cedars, their long gnarled branches poking up and their wrinkly mess of leaves hanging low. Squeezing between them, he shrugs down his hood and yanks off his gloves. The air is cool against his palms and he flexes his fingers, scooping up the freshness. He sets his tripod on the dirt and screws on his camera. He plugs in the remote switch and checks the f-stop and shutter speed. Pulling out his cell phone, he sits down to wait.

Facebook's quiet. Everyone's asleep, probably. They have to get up early for Orientation. It's all Zach talked about at the party, him and the other guys. Everyone's meeting at Timmy Ho's beforehand for doughnuts. They've got one mom driving them to school, and another one picking them up. Then everyone's going to the North Pool for one last swim before the season's over. Tyler's studied pictures online of the North Pool, the sparkling water and bright red tubes curving up to the sky. It seems like a pretty good place to have a party.

Leaves rustle. He sucks in his breath, leans forward to peer through the branches.

Something tall and ghostlike drifts into the clearing. It's that doe. He's glimpsed her before, nibbling on Charlotte's tomato plants. Two smaller shapes meander after her. A one-year-old and the brand-new one, speckled and small. They float across the ground, pausing to eat the plants growing here and there. His blog followers will love this. They're always complaining that his images are too far away. So he waits, finger hovering above the button, then presses down. The shutter clicks as loud as a firecracker. The three deer crash away through the trees, and a moment later, it's as if they were never there. He feels bad that he interrupted their meal and hopes he got a picture to show for it. He stands, stretches. He's got twenty more minutes until his sunscreen starts to wear off. He's already had three lesions carved out of him. The scars form a triangle on his right calf. No recurrence yet, but he's seen the tightness on his mom's face when her gaze rests on it. She hasn't noticed the burn on his arm. He wishes it would hurry up and go away before she does.

Across the street, light flickers in the living room window at Amy's house. Someone's watching TV. Curious, he crosses the street and goes up to the window. An opened bag of chips sits on the coffee table, and a can of soda sits tilted on the arm of the couch. Charlotte would be really pissed if she saw that, but she's not there. No one is.

The stove light's on, a comforting circle of light in the darkness. His mom leaves theirs on when he's feverish and sleeping on the living room couch. He'll lift his head from the cushions, see the glow tunneling out from the kitchen beyond, and know his mom's nearby. He goes closer to the glass and there's Amy, hauling a kitchen chair across the floor. She rocks it into place in front of the pantry and climbs up. Reaching high to the top shelf, she brings down a package of cookies. When she jumps to the floor, her short nightgown flies up.

Amy had insisted he open her present first and she'd pushed in to stand beside him when he blew out the candles. When Charlotte told her it was time to go, Amy had climbed onto the trampoline instead. Everyone's jumping had bounced her against him. *I hate Robbie,* she'd said, and when Tyler said Robbie wasn't so bad, she'd narrowed her eyes and leaned closer with chocolate cake breath. *He just pretends to be nice,* she'd hissed. *He calls me a little bitch and he calls you vampire boy.*

It's time to go home. Dante may be online and wanting to game. Too bad Tyler caught Alex cheating. It used to be fun to play with him, too.

The houses all around him are dark. There's only the quiet tapping of his shoes on the sidewalk. The wind shivers through the cul-de-sac, loosing a blizzard of small leaves that rain down on him. He stops, delighted, and holds out his hands, lifts up his face to let the leaves gently pelt him. They swirl around him like he imagines butterflies might. They tickle his skin. They dance along the ground.

This is me, he thinks. *I am here, a part of all of this.*

FRIDAY, AUGUST 29

SUNRISE 6:56 AM

SUNSET 8:10 PM

EVE

Where was he? Pressing her cell phone to her ear, Eve looks through the window as though she could conjure the sight of David, arriving home in a taxi or maybe in a rental car. Up the street, Charlotte's porch light shines through the gloom. She wonders how Charlotte's date with Robbie went. There's an urgency to her friend's relationship with her boyfriend that makes Eve uneasy. Robbie's asked Charlotte to move in with him. *You caught him reading your email,* Eve had protested. *Going through your texts. You can't live with someone like that!* And what about Amy, who's already suffered through her parents' divorce and clearly dislikes Robbie? But Charlotte won't listen. *I'll make sure Amy's okay with it. Children are more resilient than we give them credit for,* she'd said, and Eve had thought sadly, *Not all of them.*

Three rings, four. She hangs up before his voicemail picks up.

The blinds rap against the glass; a cool breeze gusts in. A storm's on its way.

Tyler's on the floor behind her, game controller in hand. This is their time together. This has always been the best time, her favorite part of the day, when it's just the two of them. They can talk about anything and everything, and for these few minutes, life feels limitless with possibility. Her beautiful boy, with his creamy skin and piercing blue eyes. His eyelashes are long and dark, his hair black like hers but curly like David's. It falls over his forehead and hides his eyes; it protects the nape of his neck. He's been begging for a haircut, arguing that he'd put on extra sunscreen, wear a ball cap even indoors. How terrible to deny him such a small request.

Down the hall, Melissa's alarm clocks blare like deranged donkeys. She has three of them set around her room. In order to silence them, she has to get up and turn each one off.

"Breakfast is ready," she says, and Tyler pushes himself up from the floor to follow her into the kitchen. He's tall and gangly, awkward with his new growth and height. He's lost his sweet baby profile—his jaw is firm now instead of curved; there's a small bump on the bridge of his nose, the cartilage growing in. Just the other day, she spotted golden fuzz beneath his lower lip. It's impossible to think he'd be shaving soon. The doctor predicts Tyler will be six feet tall when he's done growing, maybe six feet two inches. The doctor gives this information to Eve as though this is a gift, and all Eve can think is how utterly normal her son is in every way, how utterly healthy in every way but one.

She glances at the chart taped by the door, then at the clock. They've got forty-three minutes. Tyler's classmates are probably just waking up, getting ready for Orientation. Tyler hasn't said a word about starting high school. Eve had tried to arrange it so that he'd be in at least one class with his friends, but there'd been too many obstacles. David had told her that this wasn't too surprising, given how many kids were in the freshman class, but Eve couldn't help but wonder. Zach may have wanted separation, and his mother had put in a request.

She forks a steaming waffle onto his plate. "Guess what? I got another client. You'll never guess what she writes. Werewolf mysteries."

"Cool." He sits with his arm curved around his plate as though afraid someone will snatch it from him. He eats in big bites, barely chewing, the way he always does. He's impatient to get through life. She's the one who wants to slow it down.

"I was thinking you could animate the werewolf's eyes and make them look as if they're glowing."

He raises his head, and she feels hopeful. But all he says is, "Yeah, maybe."

As he reaches for the syrup, she sees it—the red mark on the inside of his elbow. "What's that?" she says. She can barely hear her own voice.

He shrugs, goes to pour the syrup, but she's grabbed his wrist, taken the bottle from his hand. "Mom," he protests, but she's turning his arm over to peer at the skin. Maybe just an indentation from lying on something, maybe a simple scratch? She runs the side of her thumb gently across the area. It's flat, warm to the touch. *Please, God. Let this be a normal, ordinary adolescent pimple.* But it's not. She'd known it the moment she'd spotted it. It's too big, maybe an inch long, and it has a definite boundary where a sleeve rode up, exposing the tender flesh. A sunburn. "When did this happen?"

"I don't know, Mom. Come on."

But he does know. Of course he does. Why won't he admit it? She scans the kitchen for her cell phone, spots it lying on the counter beside the waffle maker, and goes to fetch it. "Hold out your arm, honey."

Obediently, he stretches out his arm and she aims her phone, taps the button. The shutter clicks. She brings the phone closer and takes another picture, turns his wrist to let the light fall differently.

A third picture, a fourth. She'll send the images to the doctor's office right away, then wait the interminable hours until the office opens and the dermatologist can review them and get back to her.

"Can I eat now?" Tyler says and she nods, her mind elsewhere.

When was the last time her son wore short sleeves outside? When was the last time he was even out of her sight? Then she knows: Saturday evening. She'd run to the store, a quick trip, and returned to find David and Tyler collapsed on the couch, panting. They'd just come in from playing basketball, and as she unloaded the groceries, she'd been happy to know they'd spent that time together. "Dad let you take off your hoodie, didn't he?"

"It was hot," Tyler mumbles.

And then a car must have driven past, flashing its headlights across her son, trapping him. Fear sweeps over her, anger, and at the heart of it all, helplessness. She can't even leave her son alone with her husband for thirty minutes.

"It's okay, Mom," Tyler says. "Dad covered me."

But not quickly enough. Tyler's watching her, his fork halfway to his mouth. He's protecting his father, when it should be the other way around.

"Absolutely," she says, but of course it's not. It's been almost a week; the burn should have faded by now. What does that mean? Not every exposure is equal. Some inflict damage; some can be benign. The terrible thing is not knowing which is which. She forces a reassuring smile on her face, and after a moment, Tyler forks off another bite of food.

She pours more batter and lowers the lid on the waffle maker. All's quiet from Melissa's room. Suspiciously quiet. "I'll go get your sister," she says.

Melissa lies tangled in her sheets, breathing through her mouth, the way she did as a baby, with her hand curled tight beneath her chin. When Melissa was tiny, she would rub her right foot back and forth to soothe herself to sleep, and Eve would later find the sock wedged between the mattress and the crib. *Why the right foot?* Eve had mused, and David had replied, *I don't know,* and they'd laughed.

Eve flips on the overhead light. Melissa groans and rolls over. "You don't want to miss your ride," Eve warns.

"I *know.*"

Back in the kitchen, she uncaps the bottle of vitamin D pills and shakes one into her palm. Tyler takes it and swallows it down with a big gulp of milk. "Want me to make you another waffle?" she asks.

"I'm okay," he says.

Dr. Brien might ask her to take some more pictures, or he might tell her to bring Tyler in right away. She glances to the dark window. They were predicting rain, a blessing.

Melissa shuffles in. Her face is puffy, her hair hanging loose. This is her purest self, the one that's just for family. She's already in her jodhpurs and wearing the T-shirt with the name of the stable stitched across the front. It looks a little tight. She's growing so fast. Eve's always running her old clothes to the donation center, or passing them on to Charlotte for Amy.

Melissa slumps into her seat. "The Internet's down again."

"I'll fix it," Tyler says.

Eve slides a waffle onto Melissa's plate. "Your last day of camp," she says to her daughter. "Looking forward to it?"

Melissa breaks off a corner of waffle and nibbles it. "I'm looking forward to getting paid."

Melissa and Brittany have taken it upon themselves, as senior counselors, to provide prizes for their small band of campers. They're going early today to hide them all around the stable, having spent the evening before writing clever horse-themed clues and filling the house with their giggles.

"What did you get?" Tyler asks. In another life, he would have been a pirate, lured by the sparkle of jewels, the shine of precious metals. For years, he'd lugged around a metal detector everywhere on their walks. Eve would find it lying on the bathroom floor or leaning against a kitchen chair. He'd unearthed all sorts of intriguing things from the woods around their house, and they'd carry them home to clean and examine: the bone-shaped dog tag; brass and aluminum keys; a real silver spoon, bent and battered; a man's watch, the links crusted with dirt, the glass face cracked and cloudy.

"Stuff," Melissa mumbles.

"Things from the dollar store," Eve says, wanting to fan this spark of interest in her son. He should have mentioned the sunburn. He should have told her. "Nail polish, bead necklaces, things like that."

"Seriously?" he says.

"They're not for you, obviously," Melissa says, irritated. "Do we have any milk?"

Eve shakes her head. "Someone left it out." The second time this week, and this time the milk had turned.

"Thanks a lot, Tyler," Melissa snipes.

Tyler looks up. "It wasn't me."

"Sure," Melissa says.

Her dreamer, always staring into space. *What are you thinking about?* she'd ask him, and he'd say something like, *Did you know that two people who live together for a really long time can make their hearts beat at the same time?* "Well," Eve says, patting his hand. "Whoever it was, please don't do it again."

He frowns at his plate.

"Mom?" Melissa says. "Everyone's getting together later at Sherry's. So can I go?"

Eve's heard things from the other mothers about Sherry. *She's fast. She drinks.* It's hard to reconcile these rumors with the sweet blond kindergartner Eve remembers from Melissa's Brownie troop. "Who's everyone?" she asks, stalling. Melissa's circle of friends has grown so small these past few years. Eve hates to say no.

"Brittany, Adrian." Melissa shrugs. "People you don't know."

"Will Sherry's parents be home?"

"I guess."

Which means *no*. "I'll give them a call."

"No one else's parents are calling."

As if this is the least bit persuasive. "I promise not to say anything to embarrass you."

"Just forget it." Melissa shoves back her chair. "Brittany's here."

Melissa's departures are always so swift. Eve misses the days when she was allowed to be part of the process, entreated to find shoes, select barrettes. Now Melissa leaves in a surly whirlwind, out the door in seconds. Eve follows her daughter into the garage and punches the button on the wall. The garage door rumbles up to reveal a little blue car waiting on the driveway with its headlights off, pulsing with hip-hop music. Brittany sits behind the wheel, round-faced, with dark eyes and a careless smile. She's had her license for four months, which makes her the most popular girl among her friends. Melissa's counting the days until she takes her driver's test, crossing off the squares on the kitchen calendar one by one. She's already campaigning hard to use David's car when he's out of town.

Eve waves to Brittany, who waves back and turns down the radio. "Hi, Mrs. Lattimore."

"Hi, honey. You know the rules, right?"

"No texting. No speeding. No one but Melissa in the car." She says it in a chant.

Melissa's finished putting on her boots. She climbs in the passenger seat, frowning. She doesn't like it when Eve quizzes her friends. *Don't you trust me, Mom?*

Eve does trust Melissa. It's the world she doesn't trust.

Brittany backs the VW down the driveway, and Eve reaches up to press the button. The garage door lowers, sealing the space in darkness. When she hears it bump the ground, she opens the kitchen door and goes back inside.

Tyler's up in his bedroom, sitting in front of his monitors with his back to her. The minty smell of toothpaste lingers in the air. He has never once tried to fool her into thinking he's brushed his teeth when he really hasn't, unlike Melissa, who'd been quite the con artist when she was little.

"Who's online?" Eve asks. He's got his hand on the computer mouse, and if she were to take a step to the right, she'd see his forearm and then the tender crook of his elbow. She can't. She can't look at it, knowing. Tyler must sense it, the way she stands so strangely behind him and out of sight.

"Joaquin. Alan P."

"Yoshi?" she asks, but he shakes his head. He gnaws his thumbnail as he stares at the screen. He's worried and trying not to show it. He's not that innocent and trusting little boy anymore. He understands what even a small sunburn means, or what could be going on when he doesn't hear from his XP friends. It had taken her ages to get him to agree to talk to the psychologist she'd found. The man had come highly recommended. They'd waited two months to see him, and he'd even agreed to come and meet with Tyler here, in their house. But he'd come downstairs after an hour behind Tyler's closed bedroom door and shaken his head. *Let me know if he changes his mind,* he'd said. *He was stupid,* Tyler told her later. *And he smelled like cheese.*

But Eve knows the real problem was that he'd asked Tyler questions her son didn't want to answer. *Are you afraid? Are you unhappy? How has this life been for you?*

She breaks a rule with herself. "I heard from that doctor at Johns Hopkins, the one who's working on a cream. Remember?" She doesn't like to tell him about possible cures. She doesn't like raising his hopes only to watch him suffer when they're not realized. "He says he's made a small breakthrough." There are so few people with XP that doctors haven't searched for a cure. But sometimes a potential cure arises from other research. She's begged the scientists to forgo human trial and just give Tyler the new medicine. She's told them she'll sign any legal papers, argued that he doesn't have the time to go through the normal process. Over and over, her pleas have fallen on deaf ears.

"Great." He doesn't look up with that eager, wide-eyed grin. He doesn't even glance up with skepticism. He's seeing beyond the edges of her assurances, just as she's growing more emphatic in making them.

"What's wrong, honey?" she says, and he spins his chair around to face her. He glowers at her, his lower lip pushed out. He looks just like the small boy she remembers. "I *told* you," he says. "It wasn't me."

She's confused. So he's not thinking about his sunburn. "Are we talking about the milk?"

"She lies right to your face."

"Melissa? Come on, Ty."

"You always believe her. She doesn't even have to say a word."

Where is this coming from? Maybe Melissa had been the one to leave the milk out this time. "I'm sorry. I'll try to pay more attention."

"You don't even know," he mutters.

"Know what?"

He stares at the floor, still pouting, then pushes back his chair. "It's time."

She glances at the clock and sees that he's right. Every morning, the sun rises two minutes later. Every morning, she gains this tiny fraction of time with him. Until the vernal equinox, when it all snaps back.

"Have a good day." She hates to leave. "I'll see you at eight-ten."

She stands in the hallway, as Tyler closes the door and turns the latch. That small, hard click. It's the most ruthless sound in the world.

Dr. Brien calls at 8:32. "Eve," he says, "it's okay. Put aloe on it and watch for any changes."

"Okay," she says. "Thank you." Another dodged bullet. She picks up her cell phone to text Tyler the news.

DAVID

The Metro station's crowded, even for a Friday. Men and women in suits carry briefcases, their faces set in impassive, don't-talk-to-me ways. Laborers, tourists, kids in private school uniforms, the cords of their iPods dangling from their ears. They speak to one another in code, bursts of words that send them smirking or laughing. He pictures Melissa among them. She'd like the Metro. It's clean, fast.

The lights along the track blink, and the crowd shuffles forward. Down the dark tunnel, glowing headlights appear. The ground trembles and the train emerges, whooshing to a stop. He lines up and, as the doors slide open, pushes his way inside. There's a pregnant woman behind him, and he moves aside to let her take the last remaining seat. She smiles at him in gratitude.

The escalator carries him up to the busy sidewalk. Tall buildings line the street. Traffic's bumper-to-bumper. The sun has come up while he was underground. The pale blue sky is flat and hard with heat. His phone pings, and he checks the display. Eve's called twice, he sees. He'll listen to her messages when he gets to his office.

He signs in at the lobby, slides his pass through the reader, nods to the security guard, and heads for the elevator. At the sixteenth floor, he gets out into that familiar canned air smell. Beige hallways stretch away in two directions. Gold letters hang on the facing wall, spelling out the firm's name. In three months, no more than six, his name will be added to the list of partners.

The musical *ping* of the elevator and Renée steps out, balancing a cardboard tray of paper cups, her lips pursed in concentration. She's wearing her navy suit, her blond hair pulled back in a ponytail. "Surprise." She pulls a cup free and extends it. "Double shot, one sugar."

"You're a mind-reader." The brand the office uses barely qualifies as coffee, and the little coffee shop in his apartment building has been closed for months. He takes a welcome sip.

"No, I just know your office light was still on when I left last night." She falls into step beside him. "Did Tyler have a nice party?"

"I assume so." *No big deal,* Tyler had mumbled on Skype last night. He'd seemed to mean it. David couldn't recall his own fourteenth birthday. He probably hadn't even had a party, and if he had, he wouldn't have cared whether or not his father had attended. Sometimes David feels as though he's looking down a long tunnel at his son and catching only glimpses.

"It must be hard, living so far away from your family. I don't know how you do it."

At first, there had been an exhilaration to his homecomings, every weekend like a honeymoon. Covering Eve's mouth so the kids couldn't hear her moan, her hands gripping his shoulders so hard, she left marks. They'd promised each other they'd make it work, but now he sees all the ways in which they've failed. She calls and leaves terse voice messages, and he takes his time getting around to listening to them. "How's your ankle?" Usually, they run together after work, but last night she'd had to go alone.

Renée makes a face. She's not traditionally pretty. Her teeth are a little too big, and her chin a shade too narrow. But David's noticed how all the guys in the office can't take their eyes off her. "I iced it when I got home," she says. "Getting old sucks."

She's thirty-three, which hardly qualifies as old. But he knows what she means. He's forty-two and can remember when he used to run six miles and barely break a sweat. They've reached his office and he hands her his coffee so he can fish out his key. "What's your weekend look like?" he asks.

"Filled with the usual wedding craziness. Dress shopping with Jeffery's mom, reception hall hunting. It's ridiculous how far in advance you have to book these places." She rolls her eyes. She's from North Dakota, where there are no waiting lines for anything.

He opens the door and she leans against the doorjamb. "What kind of wedding did you have?" she asks. "No, wait. Let me guess." She gazes around the room, at the framed photographs, the fake fern on the credenza that his secretary insisted livened up the place, the rows of books slotted into the bookcase. "Something very simple and grand. Eve wore satin and carried gardenias. Am I right?"

Miles and miles of lace, pink lilies and yellow daisies clasped in front of Eve as she walked toward him, her eyes steady on his, his heart bumping against his ribs. He'd looked around, grinning at his good fortune, only to see Eve's father glowering from the pew. The old man had hated David from the get-go. "Something like that," he says.

"I knew it." She hands him back his coffee. "Well, I guess I'd better get cracking on the Compton file."

"Let me know if you need any help."

"You wouldn't have a magic wand, would you? I'd love to make it disappear."

A magic wand would be something. Eve's been searching for one for years.

The request comes through around nine. Preston, the fellow just down the hall, has called out sick. Can David get the spreadsheets ready for Tuesday's meeting with the client?

"Sure," he says, his mind scrambling over his work plan for the day. He'll skip lunch, that's a given, and if he leaves by five-thirty, he should still be able to make it to National in time to catch his flight.

Preston's secretary emails him the files and he clicks them open. Pages filled with numbers, tidy columns that show the ebb and flow of their client's accounts.

Renée stops by. She's removed her jacket and opened the collar of her white blouse. A necklace glints gold against her throat. "Don't tell me you're working through lunch again."

He glances at the clock and is surprised to see it's almost noon. Clocks are everywhere at home, mounted beside each door, above the charts Eve prints out of each month's sunrise and sunset schedule. Everywhere he turns, it seems, he encounters the motion of a minute hand. "Preston's sick."

"More likely his wife didn't show up to take their kid for the day." She tilts her head. "Why don't I bring you back something? Which do you want, turkey or roast beef?"

These are his usual orders. She'll even know to tell them to hold the mayo, add an extra dill pickle. "Surprise me."

"Sure."

He returns his attention to the spreadsheet opened before him. He checks Preston's algorithms for the third time, and they seem tight. So it's something else, something that he's not seeing.

It's the deposits that don't match. He flips back a few screens, studies the numbers there, then carries them forward. There it is.

The decimal's in the wrong place. A small error, and he can understand Preston having made it.

He moves the decimal, but now the numbers go off-kilter in a different way. He has a sense of foreboding. Page by page, he begins to study the second and fifth columns.

"Here you go," Renée says. She's standing there, hip cocked, holding a Styrofoam container. "I got you chips, too." The smile on her face dims. "What?" She comes around the desk to study the laptop screen. He points to the column of numbers. "Seven thousand dollars. Gone."

"But how?"

"Preston stole it."

"No." Her breath stirs the hairs at the back of his neck. "No way."

"I know, but there it is." He's always liked Preston. The man shows a rare sense of humor in those interminable monthly budget meetings. They've gone out for the occasional beer and talked about the Skins' chances. "It goes back eight months."

"What!" She straightens. "Fifty-six *thousand* dollars?"

"Somehow he thought he could get away with it."

"This is awful." She leans back against the desk and looks at him, her arms crossed. "What are you going to do?"

"I don't have a choice."

"Maybe you should talk to him, give him a chance to come clean."

"That won't change anything. The client's coming in Tuesday. He's going to expect a report."

"Right." She frowns. "What if they're not the only ones he's targeted?"

"That's what I'm worried about."

She gives him a rueful look. "Good luck."

Stan's office is down the hall, the door standing wide open. He looks up when David knocks on the doorframe. "Don't tell me you're done already."

"There's something I need to show you." David holds open his laptop, scrolls through the screens. He highlights a column of numbers. "And this is only one client. We could be talking hundreds of thousands of dollars."

Stan takes the laptop. "I'm not sure what I'm looking at."

"See here? These columns should be the same."

"Okay."

"So if you do this . . ." He taps a key.

Stan frowns. "This is really serious."

"I know."

"Maybe it's a mistake."

"No. He's done the same thing to a different account each month so that he spreads the monies out. He was trying to avoid triggering an audit."

"Damn." Stan shakes his head. "Well, it's a good thing you caught this."

Back in his office, setting his laptop on his desk, David feels a twinge of guilt. Which is ridiculous. Preston's the one who should feel guilty. He opens his bottom desk drawer and pulls out the 35 mm single-lens reflex camera he'd picked up for Tyler's birthday. Eve had done the research and given David very specific directions. He hadn't even known they still made film cameras, but she'd insisted. If Tyler was serious about photography, and Eve believed he was, then he'd want to learn how to develop and print film. There were differences, apparently, between digital and film, important differences, and Eve wanted to give Tyler the opportunity to understand them. She makes all her decisions regarding Tyler with great care, even the small ones, as though by choosing the right path, she can forestall the inevitable.

I'm sorry, the specialist had said. They'd waited months to see him. Their regular doctor couldn't explain the blisters that bloomed across their infant son's face and belly, or why he suffered strange fevers that could only be relieved by cool baths and Eve rocking him in a darkened room. The man had sat down facing them, his hands loosely clasped in front of him, as if he were saying, *We're all in this together.* But David had immediately sensed that whatever the man was about to tell him would draw a dark thick line, and only he and Eve would be standing on one side of it, and this man would be on the other, the safe side, peering over.

David had leaned forward, desperate to understand what the doctor was saying. The words made no sense. Tyler was perfect. Anyone could see it. He was sweet-natured and sturdy. He held tight to your hand when you walked to the park. He chortled when you played peek-a-boo, and blew spit bubbles, and curled up in your lap to read a story. He was perfect, and no one could say otherwise. But this doctor was shaking his head with a terrible finality, and David finally understood. Horror swept through him and left him shaking. Eve was weeping and, blindly, he turned to her and pulled her into his arms. She pressed her head against his shoulder and he held onto her tightly. They were together. They had each other. They would get through this.

David looks around at his office, the bleak walls. He thinks of his apartment, echoing and cheaply furnished. If he could, he'd take every single day of his own future and hand them to his son, three dozen years, four dozen. If only it were possible. But the specialist had been clear. There was nothing anyone could do to save Tyler, not even conjuring magic tricks out of thin air.

EVE

Late that afternoon the heavy gray sky bursts open to release slanting washes of rain that bash the pavement and shake the trees. Thunder booms and lightning flares, crisp and startling against the dark clouds. The weather forecasters are delirious with delight. It's been a dry summer and the farmers have been suffering. *Watch out for local flooding,* the fellow on Channel Six warns at noon. He's practically bouncing, he's so happy at having something to report.

Eve works in the dining room, encircled by lamplight. Three clients have emailed with website event updates. They need them posted immediately. The werewolf author's eager to see a preliminary design, and Izzie's asked about revamping her site to reflect her recent foray into adult fiction. *Can two sites be linked to one?* Izzie wants to know. She's been a good friend. She's believed in Eve from the very beginning. Eve checks into the forum, sees with relief that

Nori's online. She messages her. *How's Yoshi doing?* Nori writes back: *It's taking a lot out of her, but the doctors think it might work.*

Maybe. There's only a ten percent chance a second round of chemo will work. The cancer cells usually adapt during the first round. But Nori and Eve tell themselves that ten percent is so much better than zero. They have learned to live within those narrow gaps of possibility.

Eve turns off Skype and her screensaver image blooms across the screen: Tyler and Melissa, arms wrapped tight around each other, cheeks pressed close. Melissa had been eleven and Tyler nine, both of them in that pre-adolescent stage where Eve could still kiss them good night and hold their hands when they walked to the park. She has hundreds of pictures of her children—no, thousands—but this is her favorite: Melissa with those bangs that refused to lie flat and a blueberry stain on her blouse, and Tyler with a gap-toothed grin and crooked collar. Melissa hates this picture. She complains that she looks fat and stupid, which is, of course, untrue. She looks joyful, and so does Tyler, their bond so pure and strong. Every time Eve looks at this ordinary photograph taken on an ordinary day, she feels peaceful. She feels whole.

Eve shuts her laptop and rises to unhook the UV meter from where it hangs beside the door. The dining room is walled in glass. This house has more windows than any of the other houses on their cul-de-sac. In a fit of whimsy one day, David had walked around and counted. She's attached special films to the glass that are guaranteed to keep out ninety-nine percent of UV radiation, but there's always that remaining one percent. All it would take is one particle of UV to kill her son.

She holds up the meter. The arrow wobbles but holds steady at zero. Maybe she can let Tyler out a little early tonight. It's a tricky call, and one she needs to consider. Heavy cloud coverage is the good thing about bad weather. The bad thing is that it could change in an instant. Here in central Ohio, clouds sweep across the sky with gusto. In five minutes, it could be a clear sunny day and the only sign that it had just been storming would be the puddles shimmering on the ground. That burn on his arm—is it any paler?

David answers the phone on the third ring.

"I called you earlier," she says. A pause that tells her David is collecting his thoughts, distancing himself. She tries to picture him, standing in his office—or is he sitting? He's Skyped, held up the laptop so she can see his surroundings for herself, but it's a hollow substitute. It's impossible to render three dimensions satisfyingly into two. She doesn't know the space her husband occupies, how it feels, smells, encloses him or expands around him. Sometimes she missed him so much she felt dizzy with desire. "Tyler got burned."

"What? How? Is he okay?"

David sounds confused. So he hadn't known. He hadn't been keeping it a secret from her, which means he hadn't even thought to check their son. "When you went to the park last Saturday," she says, "you let him take off his sweatshirt, didn't you? I was only gone thirty minutes, David."

"How bad is it?"

No apology, no promise to do better in the future. Nothing. "Dr. Brien said to keep an eye on it."

"It happened in a second, Eve. We were talking, laughing. We turned onto our street. I didn't even hear the car approach."

"That's supposed to make me feel better?" Dimly, she hears the back door open and her daughter stomp into the kitchen. Eve moves into the living room and lets herself outside to stand on the porch. The air is wet. Everything around her is black and gray, and lashing. Water rushes down the curb and pours into the storm drain. "You should have been here last night."

"I know. I wanted to be there, but I couldn't. Tyler understood."

That's just like Tyler not to reveal hurt feelings or disappointment. Tyler's always been stoic. He's never been one to feel sorry for himself. "What he understood was that your job is more important to you than he is."

"Don't be dramatic. He knows I have responsibilities."

"To your family."

"Yes! To provide for them."

Eve leans against the railing, listening to the rain, welcoming the cold dampness. Her cheeks are burning with fury. "One day, David. What difference does taking off one day make?"

"Stan's already asked me if I want to take on a less challenging workload. I told him no. But I can't keep taking off weekends like this."

"You don't take off weekends. You work from home." He sits on the couch, laptop opened before him, for hours each day and long into the evening.

"It's not the same. I'm never going to make partner at this rate."

They need that extra income. They need that job security. "Of course you will," she says uncertainly.

"It's been two years," he says, and now she understands he's moving the conversation in another direction, a place she literally doesn't want to go. "We can't move to DC." This is what he wants, what he's been hinting at for months. But she's made a safe haven for Tyler here, in this house, in this neighborhood. She won't uproot him. "It's too dangerous." David knows this. He knows this just as well as she does, but he no longer seems to care.

"We can make it work. We can drive in tandem, at night. I'll find a house ahead of time and make sure it's safe."

"Like you did last Saturday?" she snaps before she can stop herself. A strained pause that writhes with recrimination, with blame. She doesn't want this. She loves him. She needs him. They all do. "It's just that . . . Tyler's doctors are here."

"We can find new doctors, Eve. There's no shortage of them here."

New doctors won't be as familiar with Tyler; they might miss a crucial early warning sign—the slightest pigmentation change, the smallest freckle. David doesn't understand how hard she's worked to forge these relationships. He's not the one who takes Tyler to his appointments, talks to the doctors and the nurses in an effort to unite them in the unrelenting effort to save her son. He's uncomfortable around doctors and in medical settings. "We can't pull him out of school. Not just as high school's starting."

"He sits in his room and watches a computer screen. He can do that anywhere."

"No," she says between her teeth. "He can't." It had taken her months to set everything up, meet with the teachers, pave the way for them to adapt to her son's unique needs. *He won't want to be singled out,* she's told them. *Kids can always meet here for projects, as long as it's after dark.* Tyler doesn't build rapport with his teachers. He doesn't have impromptu opportunities to ask questions in the hall, to work with his classmates on projects. They'd tried, the kids in his group taking the computer and sitting with it, but it had been a failure from the start. Something always went wrong. The kids didn't listen when Tyler volunteered something. Someone knocked the computer askew and he couldn't see everyone. Someone in another part of the room said something that he didn't catch. Group projects had had to be conducted with kids who were willing to go out of their way to come to their house. Often it was Eve herself who *was* the group.

"You're underestimating him."

But she's not. "What about his friends? It's so hard for him." It's not enough for Tyler to have friends he only knows online. Zach's important. He helps normalize Tyler's life. She loves hearing them debate at the dinner table and roughhouse on the trampoline. She loves hearing Tyler laugh.

"He'll be all right. What's important is that we're a family."

What was important was keeping Tyler safe. "Other families live apart." Military families, for instance.

"We're not like other families."

No, we're not.

The front door opens behind Eve. Melissa's standing there. "What are you doing?" she demands.

"Talking to Dad. Go inside. I'll be in in a minute."

"I'm taking a shower." Melissa slams the door.

Eve looks down the street to Charlotte's house, the lights there shining through the murk. Brave Charlotte, always smiling, picking through the debris of her broken marriage. "I wish I could do it, take a deep breath and risk it, but I just can't."

She misses the carefree person she used to be, that joyful girl. Being Tyler's mother has turned her into someone who's endlessly vigilant. She tortures herself with horrifying scenarios just so she can come up with a plan. What if there was a fire and they had to evacuate the house? What if she had an accident taking Tyler to one of his doctor's appointments? What if a tornado touched down and tore off the roof? The sun's a powerful enemy. It's much stronger than she is.

"I know," David says, and she hears the misery in his voice. Who else knows their suffering but the two of them?

He had stood in the doorway of her dorm room, grinning down at her as she sat cross-legged on the floor, and the rest of the world had fallen away. She remembers everything: how he'd clasped the doorknob, easy, his untucked blue shirt and sockless sneakers, the light behind him so that, for a moment, until he moved, she couldn't see his face. His voice, the way he'd looked at her—she'd known in that instant. He'd never actually proposed marriage. He'd never had to.

"I miss you," she says simply.

"I'll be home soon."

"Don't forget Tyler's camera."

"I've got it right here."

And on this uneasy truce, they hang up.

The shower's going in the hall bathroom, the water splashing against the tiles. Eve remembers when she had to fight to get Melissa into the bathtub; now she has to fight with her not to use up all the hot water. She takes the chicken out of the refrigerator, the sprigs of fresh rosemary, the round yellow onion. The rain intensifies, the wind hurling it against the windowpanes and making them tremble. She assembles everything in a glass baking dish, then presses a sheet of aluminum foil on top. She'll ask Melissa to pop the casserole into the oven while she's gone, and it'll be ready by the time she and David return.

She goes upstairs and knocks on Tyler's door. "I'm leaving." She waits, knowing he has to go through his tapping ritual first. A minute later the door swings open and her son stands there, the hood of his sweatshirt pulled over his black curls, his sunglasses shielding his eyes from view. His sleeves fall to his wrists, hiding the sunburn, but it's there. So close. They'd come so close.

"You can come out if you want," she says. "But keep an eye on things, okay? If the rain looks like it's letting up, run another UV check." What sort of treat is it for him to be allowed a little extra freedom if he spends the whole time safeguarding it?

He follows her down the stairs and stops in the kitchen. "Wow," he says, looking through the rain sheeting the windows. "It's really coming down."

She glances around for her car keys. She usually hangs them on the hook, but there they are, tossed on the counter beneath a dishtowel. "Traffic might be slow," she says, pulling her raincoat from the closet. "And I have to get gas, so don't worry if it takes a little extra time."

Tyler stands in the kitchen doorway, watching her. She feels all the threads connecting them. She could go a hundred miles, a thousand, and those threads would never snap.

"Love you," she calls, as she slides behind the steering wheel. She waits for him to step back and close the door after him before she presses the garage door opener to raise the door. The wind and rain rush in.

Does she dare leave him? He's safe, isn't he? But she'd thought he was safe last Saturday night. Thirty minutes. That's all she'd been gone, just long enough to pick up milk and bread. And then the car had appeared and David hadn't even thought to mention it. Tyler had kept it from her despite knowing that it might have needed emergency care. She grips the steering wheel. Her life is a carefully constructed house of cards, every piece precisely balanced. All it would take is one gentle nudge for everything to come tumbling down.

GONE

A red patch, two inches square. Small enough that Tyler had been able to hide it from his mom all week. Small enough that he'd pulled on a short-sleeved shirt that morning, unthinking. How stupid that something so freaking small could loom so large. Still, when his mom had texted him to say that Dr. B had cleared him, Tyler had felt sick with relief.

He scrolls through his camera for something to put on Facebook. The one of Zach jumping on the tramp is a good one, with his eyes squeezed tight and his mouth stretched in a crazy grin. Not this one of Mitch, smacking at a balloon that bounces away from him and looking bored. Tyler deletes it.

He'd forgotten he'd taken this one of Robbie and Charlotte. Charlotte's talking, her hand in motion, her rings sparkling in the flash. Robbie's watching her with a squinty look. He'd really fooled

Tyler. He'd seemed so friendly, even though he was old, like maybe thirty-five, showing him how to grip a baseball bat and giving him cool things from his restaurant—colored plastic stirrers and cork coasters. He could game for hours, swearing and pounding his knee when he's losing, leaning back and throwing up his arms when he wins. He has a tattoo of a sad-faced angel on his shoulder and another one of barbed wire twisted around his calf. He'd once showed Tyler how to mix gin and tonics. Fill the glass with ice, pour in a third of gin, two thirds of tonic, cut and squeeze a slice of lime and drop it in. Stir with a forefinger and suck. Robbie had winked at this step. Then he'd laughed when Tyler took a nervous sip before running to the sink to gulp water and wash the nastiness down his throat.

Delete.

Next is the picture of Melissa leaning against the patio table and texting, her head bent. She looks nice. This is the Melissa he used to know.

Tyler had been hoping for a film camera for his birthday, but he knows they can be expensive. His mom's explained that he can borrow one from school while he's taking Photography 101. She's met the teacher and come home to tell Tyler how much she liked him. But sometimes his mom likes people who turn out to be lame, or doesn't like people who Tyler thinks are hilarious. So he'll wait until school starts before he decides whether she's right this time.

He doesn't know why he took these pictures of Amy. It wasn't like she'd been doing anything interesting. Her Hello Kitty nightgown's too tight around her baby boobs and so short that he can clearly see her bright pink underpants. Gross. He wishes he could scrub his eyeballs. He holds his thumb over the delete icon and hesitates.

His laptop sounds, letting him know he's gotten another hit on his blog. He'd posted the deer photograph and gotten a bunch of comments right away. *Sweet! How did you do that?* Then, *Your stuff is shit.* He traces the IP address, hunts down the poster. *Fuck you, Jersey boy,* he thinks, and bans him from the site.

His dad's plane should be in the air now. His mom took Tyler to an airport once, parking the car outside the metal fence. He remained huddled beneath the sleeping bag while his mom ran the UV meter. Then she came back to the car and opened the door. *Come on out, you two,* she said. She spread a blanket on the grass and he and Melissa and their mom sat there, sunglasses on, arms wrapped around their knees, watching the planes roll down the runways and glide skyward. They looked like fat-bellied lizards, blindly nosing up to the stars. *Where do you think that one's going?* his mom asked, and it was a race between him and Melissa to come up with some crazy place name. Twitty. Bugwash. Middle Wallop. Beziers, which was especially hilarious because it sounded so much like *brassieres.*

He gazed up at the red and white blinking dots, all those planes filled with people, heading to another city, or coming home after being away. *I wish I were going somewhere,* he said, and Melissa reached over to tickle him and he laughed so hard, he rolled off into the grass.

Zach chats him on Facebook:
Hey dude you get your schedule
yeah did you
I got jenkins for math she's so hot
I got drago
that sucks brian says she's a real bitch
Oh dang why
Brian failed her class she's really unfair
Why is she unfair
Tons of homework and she doesn't grade on a curve
Brb
Tyler shuts his laptop and goes down the hall. Melissa's in the

bathroom, leaning close to the mirror, holding a tiny brush against her lashes, and scrolling it up. He watches, hypnotized by her deft motions, until she snarls, "What, perv?"

This is prickly Melissa. This is cactus Melissa and if he gets too close, he'll get stabbed. "Zach says I got the crappy math teacher." He's not really worried about the teacher. It's the kids he's thinking about. Some of them may not like having him in their class. He wants to tell Melissa this. He used to be able to tell her everything.

"Like he'd know." She tilts her face and flutters her lashes experimentally, then leans back in with the brush to apply another coat. She's wearing her red shirt that hangs off one shoulder, her black bra strap showing, and her jeans with the big holes cut across the thighs and knees. She's drawn eyeliner all the way around her eyes. It makes her look mean.

"His brother told him. He says she doesn't curve."

"What do *you* care about grades?" She doesn't even look at him.

Her phone buzzes, jiggling across the counter, and she snatches it up to read the incoming text. She frowns, bites her lower lip. "Shit." She drops the tube of mascara into her cosmetics bag and pushes past him.

He steps back to let her go. "What's the matter?"

"Nothing."

That's a lie. She's in her room, pawing through the clothes heaped on the floor of her closet. She yanks her purse free. Turning, she sees him standing there in the doorway. "Look," she says. "I have to go out. Don't set the house on fire."

He's not the one who set the dishtowel on fire making popcorn while their mom was at the store. "Did Mom say you could?"

"Sure."

Another lie. He tries again. "Is Brittany taking you?"

Brittany's always over. She's only interested in horses because Melissa is. His mom says some people are leaders and some are followers. *What am I?* he'd asked, and his mom had looked thoughtful.

You're an independent thinker. Which means he's neither. Once again he slips through the thin crack where no one else goes.

Melissa doesn't answer. She reaches for the car keys hanging from the hook beside the back door. He's shocked.

"Melissa, you *can't.*"

She slides on a jacket and flips her hair out, over the collar. "Make good choices," she says.

This is what their mom says when she leaves them to run to the store or the library. When his mom says it, it feels good. But here Melissa is, making bad choices. She's going to that party even though their mom said *no.* She's taking the car even though she doesn't have her driver's license. "I'm going to tell," he says, and at this she stops and glares at him. She's taller than he is and he feels small.

"Go ahead." Her eyes are narrowed. Then she smiles. "Who do you think Mom's going to believe?"

She climbs into their dad's car. The garage door shudders up. Wind gusts in, rustling the newspapers stacked in the corner. Rain falls in heavy gray sheets he can't even see through.

There's a bright fork of lightning over the houses and, without thinking, he steps back, behind the door. One of the XP moms told his mom that lightning has UV in it, and so he's never been allowed out in a rainstorm. *Big deal,* Melissa said when he complained about having to stay inside. *No one's allowed to go out in lightning storms.*

He risks another look. Tiny red taillights shine up at the top of the street, then wink out, swallowed by the storm.

The phone rings in the kitchen behind him.

EVE

She screws the gas cap on tight and climbs back into the car to start the engine. Which way should she go? Right is the shortest route, but the highway will be jammed. Left, then, along the less-traveled roads. She waits for a lone car to pass before pulling out behind it onto the road. It's the same model as David's. What was it he'd said? *We can drive in tandem at night.* As though that could create a protective bubble around them. One of the XP moms had been driving her daughter somewhere and her tire blew. She'd awakened in the hospital, with her little girl in the bed next to her, shrieking in pain as the doctors tried to figure out what was wrong.

The rain's falling harder now, hammering the car roof, smearing the windshield. The wipers can't keep up. She switches on the defogger. In the distance ahead, twin taillights glow red. Damn. She forgot to ask Melissa to take care of the chicken. She reaches into her pocket for her cell phone.

Put chicken in oven at 350

She presses the arrow to send the message and looks back up.

There's something right in front of her, growing larger.

She clutches the steering wheel, mashes her foot against the brake pedal. A sudden bump sends the car spinning. Her headlights pick out tree trunks, pavement, something pale, tree trunks. She jolts to a stop. She's gripping the steering wheel, breathing hard.

What was that she had glimpsed as she spun around—an animal? It had been larger than a dog, maybe one of those baby deer she's spotted at dusk. How awful. She fumbles for the door handle, gets out of the car. She's facing the wrong way. She turns, puts her hand up to cover her eyes, squints through the lashing rain. There's nothing in the road. Maybe the poor thing limped off into the woods, wounded. She needs to call animal control. Automatically, she reaches into her pocket for her phone, but of course it's not there. She'd been holding it.

She scans the seats and the floor. There it is, in the passenger foot well. She looks back through the windshield at the rain. She'll just take a quick look. Reaching into her glove compartment, she pulls out her flashlight.

She climbs out into the storm. She's soaked in an instant, the rain pummeling her, cold and blowing. She snatches at the hood of her raincoat and sloshes along the side of the road toward the trees. Water washes across the road in tides of motion. She crosses to where the ground falls steeply away to the river below and peers through the darkness. It's impossible to make out anything. She's absolutely drenched, the wind buffeting her. She glances behind her to the waiting car. She can barely see it from where she stands. Then she turns back, presses the button on her flashlight and directs the fragile beam of light at her shoes to guide herself as she climbs down the embankment, skidding in the mud. The wind blowing rain into her face. It's so dark. The trees cluster close. She grabs at branches to keep herself from falling, and when she reaches a level place, she looks around.

Down at the river's edge, a blotch of . . . pink? She moves more quickly, her heart racing, stumbling the last few yards.

A punch of lightning that bleaches everything.

It can't be.

Not a deer, not an animal at all. A small figure in a pink rain-coat. Little pink boots, lying at an angle. The wide forehead and narrow chin, the long blond hair. *Amy.*

She falls to her knees, panting, grabs Amy's wrist, presses her thumb against the skin, feeling for a pulse. There's nothing, not the tiniest flutter. *Come on come on.* She moves her thumb around, searching. She has to be wrong. Amy's skin is so cold. *Oh God.*

She remembers CPR. She's practiced it a million times.

She pushes the sides of the pink raincoat away, presses down hard on Amy's chest with the heels of her hands five times. When she takes Amy's head between her hands, it lolls alarmingly. *No.*

She leans over. Two breaths. Back to chest compressions. Two breaths again. The world squeezes down to silence.

Come on come on come on. It's going to be okay. Amy's going to be okay. *Focus focus don't give up.*

Rain falls on the back of her head, slides down her neck. Thunder crackles. The woods flash white. Amy doesn't blink when the lightning flares. She's staring up. There's nothing in her eyes.

Eve can't stop. She won't stop.

Two breaths. Five compressions. Two breaths. Five compressions.

Her breath is ragged. Her arms ache and her eyes burn with tears. "Please." She says this out loud, over and over, stopping only to breathe into Amy's mouth. Trees shake. Water runs into her clothes, finds her skin. Amy is limp, utterly and completely limp.

She stops. She just stops. She pulls Amy into her arms. This small girl, whom she's known and loved all these years. It can't be. It can't.

She sobs, rasps out words that make no sense, pulls Amy's soaked hair from her cold forehead. Help. She needs to get help, tell someone what's happened. She lays Amy's limp body down, water running in rivulets all around them, and pulls her cell phone from her raincoat pocket. "It's okay," she tells Amy. She can barely hear herself in the downpour. "It's okay. Mommy will be here soon." Oh God. How will she tell Charlotte?

She swipes droplets from her shaking fingers, taps the tiny phone icon. The phone lights up. She presses 9-1 . . .

A text message scrolls across the top of her phone. David! He's wondering where she is. He's wondering why she's taking so long. But no. This isn't the message he leaves.

Sorry forgot the camera

She stares, bewildered. What camera? Then it all rolls back. Tyler's camera, the one he's been longing for. The one Eve researched and ordered; the one David picked up in Washington and was supposed to bring home yesterday. Yet here he is, telling her he's left it behind.

The screen of her phone's gone black, waiting for her to finish dialing. All she has to do is press the button on the side of the phone and tap the final digit.

The operator will answer. Eve will describe her location. Emergency personnel will swarm down the side of the ravine. The police will take her away, just like they had that boy last year who'd plowed into a taxicab, killing the driver. He'd been texting, too, and now he was in prison, serving four years.

Her phone slides from her fingers. She scrabbles in the leaves for it, stares at the screen.

Sorry forgot the camera

What will happen to Tyler?

David forgets to make doctor appointments. He opens doors

that should be kept closed. He wants to drive her son across the country to a strange house. He tells their son it's okay to take off his sweatshirt. He doesn't even think to check him over later.

The rain slashes through the trees, unforgiving. It courses down the embankment; it turns everything black and gray and lashing. Fog rises up. She is kneeling in muck. She is soaked to the bone.

Her parents can't help. They won't. Melissa's too young. David's sister lives in Arizona. There's only David, and all he had to do was remember to bring home Tyler's fucking camera.

Amy lies beside her, leaves blown all around. She's gone. She's past saving. But Tyler's still here. He's waiting at home. He needs her. He has no one else. God help them both, he has no one else.

Sorry

Eve staggers to her feet. The ground sways. She can't look behind her, at Amy. The slope stretches before her, a thousand miles to the dark sky. Her feet slide beneath her. She grabs at trees to haul herself up. The road seems so far away. She puts one foot in front of the other, sinking each one into the sodden earth and then pulling it back up with effort. She breaks free of the woods, stumbles out onto pavement, where the rain comes harder, scouring, punishing. She wraps her arms around herself, though it's no use. Where's her car? She can't remember which direction she'd come from. There it is, hulking on the side of the road a distance away.

Three tries before she fits the key into the ignition. The engine catches and the road is illuminated. The world is drowning in rain. She's drenched to the marrow, her teeth chattering. She's never been so cold in her life. Her hair snakes wetly down the back of her neck. It wraps around her throat, and she drags it free. She presses the pedal and the car lurches forward.

She can't think about Amy. She can't think about Charlotte. She won't think about David. Tyler's the one who matters. She says this over and over to herself as she drives on through the darkness, the storm gathering around her and pressing down.

COME OUT, COME OUT
WHEREVER YOU ARE

The house phone never rings. Tyler shuts the kitchen door and goes over to the phone hanging on the wall. He scans the display. It's Amy's cell phone number. At least it's not his mom or dad, asking to talk to Melissa. He picks up the receiver. "What?" he says, irritated.

But it's Charlotte. "Tyler, let me speak to your mom."

"She's not here. She's picking my dad up at the airport."

"Damn, that's right. Listen, have you seen Amy?"

"No."

"Are you sure?"

It's a demand, and stern. Charlotte's never mean.

"Yes." And now he's curious. Why would she think Amy was over here? He's just told her she's not.

"Could you check, please?"

Amy couldn't have come in without his knowing, but maybe she's coming down the sidewalk. "Hold on."

There are two locks on the door, one a deadbolt and one a chain up high from when he was little and his mom was afraid he'd sneak out during the day when she wasn't looking. He undoes the locks and swings open the door. Rain pounds the porch roof, streams down in curtains. He squints into the darkness beyond. Up the street, red taillights bounce as a car backs out of the Farnhams' driveway. No sign of Amy. No sign of Melissa returning. "I don't see her."

"Check the patio."

"But it's raining."

"Tyler, please."

Charlotte sounds really worried. "Okay," he says, puzzled. He twists the lock and opens the French door to peer into the black of the patio. No pale face turns to him. No flash of pink in the dark. It's raining really hard. No way would Amy be out in it. "Sorry," he tells Charlotte. "She's not here."

"Let me know if she shows up, okay?" Without waiting for a reply, Charlotte hangs up.

DAVID

The Columbus airport's noisy and crowded. Several flights had arrived simultaneously. David walks past security, the pretzel place, the gift shop. Eve hasn't responded to his text message. He hadn't even realized he'd left the camera on his desk until he'd arrived at airport security and looked around for the bag to set it on the conveyor belt. Tyler will be disappointed, but it's not the end of the world. Eve will be annoyed. No doubt she's still upset about the sunburn. David had had no idea. Tyler had never said a word about it. Well, thank God it turned out to be nothing.

He's looking forward to this three-day weekend. He and Tyler can grill out every night. Tyler loves to adjust the flame, stab food with long-handled forks. This is as close as David can get him to the hunting trips his own father used to take him on, across the Nebraska prairies.

Melissa will probably be busy with her friends. She used to Skype with him for hours while he was holed up in some hotel in San Francisco or Raleigh, gabbing away in front of the laptop screen, twining hair around her forefinger. She'd carry the computer around the house and give David tours. Here's the water stain on the ceiling that Mommy just noticed. Here are the new pillows she helped Mommy pick out for the couch. She'd even take him outside, the screen going black while they waited in the garage for the door to lift, then the light would burst in and she'd walk with him outside to show him the withered brown stalks by the deck. *Ty and I planted lilies,* she'd announce. *There was a big jumping spider!*

Now she gives David clipped two-minute segments over the phone. Just the highlights, and lately, even those have been winnowed down to monosyllabic responses to his questions. He's running out of things to ask her.

He looks up, and at first he doesn't recognize Eve. Not because he doesn't expect to see her here—they had stopped meeting outside security a year ago—and not because she's dripping wet, but how could he have forgotten how beautiful she is? He walks toward her and sees other men are looking at her, too. He can't help it. He feels a swell of pride.

She's searching the crowd, half-turned away, and when he calls her name, she whirls around. Her eyes are blank. She looks . . . lost.

"What's the matter?" he asks, reaching for her, their earlier argument dissolved. She's shivering. When he kisses her, her lips are cold beneath his.

"I'm glad you're home."

This touches him. She'd been worried about the delay, anxious about him flying through rough weather. She doesn't like how much flying he has to do. "I'll drive," he says, and she nods.

They begin walking to the exit. She's caught his hand between hers and is leaning against him. He squeezes her hand. Is that Melissa's shirt she's wearing? It's amazing that she and their daughter are now the same size. "I got your message about our new neighbors," he says. "That's good news."

The instant the previous owners listed their house for sale, Eve had wanted to march over there and make sure they told the new owners that they couldn't use halogen light bulbs in their outdoor fixtures. David had had to dissuade her. *People are reasonable,* he'd said. *Like the Farnhams?* she'd retorted. Which was true. Eve had lost her battle with Joan and Larry.

"What did you think of them?" he asks. "Our new neighbors?" She looks at him with some confusion. He repeats the question and her expression clears. "Fine," she says.

He frowns. Normally, Eve would give a complete rundown of all the facts she's gathered, from what kinds of cars they drive to whether they bring their trash to the curb in a timely manner. She'd add her impressions of how they interact with the other neighbors, and whether or not they'll be a pleasant addition to the cul-de-sac. But she's silent, staring straight ahead. He can only see her profile.

"I'm sorry I forgot Tyler's camera," he says. "I had it right there on my desk. I'll talk to Tyler, explain that I left it at work. He'll understand."

She doesn't answer.

They step outside. The rain is noisy here, rapping hard on the metal roof of the parking garage. Cars gleam; dark puddles lie everywhere. There's the car, skewed at an angle beneath the security light. "Keys?" he asks, and she drops them in his outstretched hand. He presses the button and the car doors unlock. It's good to slide in behind the steering wheel. The car smells clean and faintly of Eve's perfume. He buckles up. They both begin to speak at the same time.

"David," she says, just as he says, "You'll never guess what happened today."

They both stop. "Sorry," he says. "I interrupted you."

She's huddled in her seat, with her knees drawn up and her arms wrapped tight around them. She's clearly freezing. He switches on the heat. "It's okay," she says.

"Remember Preston Berry? The guy who works down the hall from me? He was out sick today and I ended up covering for him." He switches the wipers on high and accelerates onto the swooping highway. Passing cars send up rooster tails of water, their brake lights sparking. "I wish Stan had asked someone else. Turned out to be a god-awful mess."

He tells her about poring over the numbers, about how they looked fine at first, but when he went to plug them into his own spreadsheet, they fell apart and that's when he discovered the deception. As he talks, he hears himself sorting things through. *Eve's listening intently,* he thinks, not interrupting or asking questions, but letting him pour the whole story out. It always helps to talk to her. "I'd never have thought Preston would do something like that, you know? I guess it just goes to show you can't really know what someone's capable of." They've reached their exit, and he turns off the highway. They're almost home.

"Did you have to tell?" she says.

He glances at her. Her features are hidden by darkness, her hair drying into loose curls that hang about her face. "Of course I did. We have to make things right. Our clients count on us. They trust us. I'd be just as guilty as Preston if I didn't say anything."

"But what if he goes to prison? He has a family."

"People with families go to prison all the time."

"I didn't realize you were so unforgiving." Her voice is like a stranger's.

"It's not a matter of forgiveness, Eve. It's a matter of right and wrong. I can't believe you don't understand that."

In the wash of headlights, a distant figure is running along the sidewalk just ahead. Lightning flares, and he glimpses bare legs, short hair. What lunatic is out jogging in a storm? The figure turns and raises a hand. Charlotte? He brakes and she runs over. She's wearing Crocs, her pale ankles flashing, and her face is contorted with fear.

Eve opens her car door.

"I can't find Amy," Charlotte says, breathless. "I've looked everywhere—"

Eve's out of the car, her arm around her friend, leading her through the rain to where Charlotte's house waits in darkness.

LITTLE RED RIDING HOOD

The back door bangs open, and Tyler pushes himself up from the floor where he's been gaming. It's got to be Melissa, finally home. He hurries into the kitchen and stops at the sight of her. Her hair hangs in messy clumps; mascara smudges the tops of her cheeks. "What took you so long?"

She sways, staring at him with big eyes. It's like she doesn't even see him there. It's freaky. "Melissa?" he says uncertainly.

She shoves past him to the kitchen sink. Grabbing the faucet, she leans over and throws up right into the sink. He stands back in horror as she heaves. What should he do? His mom always gets a damp washcloth, but he doesn't want to get near Melissa. At last, she turns on the faucet, splashes handfuls of water in her face. He doesn't dare look at what's swirling around in the basin. She pats around the counter, finds the dishtowel lying there, and presses it to her white face.

"Are you sick?" he asks. His mom would want to separate them. Taking him in to the doctor is a big deal.

She switches off the water and swipes a hand across her mouth. "What a crappy night."

He eyes the dishtowel, now lying balled up on the counter. He'll use tongs to carry it into the laundry room. "Maybe you should go lie down."

"Coffee," she says, which is weird. She never drinks it, except during exam week. She lurches to the pantry, her arms held out for balance, looking just like a zombie.

Wait a minute. He's seen this kind of thing on TV shows. She's not sick. "Are you *drunk?*"

They both hear it at the same time, the rumbling of the garage door. "Fuck," she says. But before she can move, the back door opens and their dad comes in, wearing his long beige coat speckled with raindrops.

"Hey, you two." His dad sweeps them into a damp hug. He smells of cold air and, very faintly, the cologne Tyler gave him for Father's Day. It makes his dad seem both familiar and foreign at the same time.

Now Tyler smells the liquor rolling off Melissa, a thick sweet smell that makes his nose wrinkle. His dad has to smell it, too, but when he pulls back and looks at them both, ruffling Tyler's hair and clasping Melissa's shoulder, his face doesn't show any reaction at all. His eyes look tired, the skin tight at the temples. "I've missed you guys."

"Where's Mom?" Tyler asks.

"Out looking for Amy. Charlotte can't find her."

Still?

"You guys hungry?"

"Yeah," Tyler says, but Melissa shakes her head. "I have to take a shower," she mumbles.

His dad glances at the raw pieces of chicken resting in the dish on the counter, then dumps it into the garbage. They can have ravioli instead, a loaf of French bread smeared with butter and garlic. His dad opens the drapes and pulls up the shades as if to release something trapped inside. Normally, Tyler likes the view of the night sky framed by the windowpanes, but tonight he feels exposed, skinned down to his nerve endings. They're waiting for the phone to ring, to tell them the good news. But all they hear is the steady drumming of the rain on the roof. All they see is rain washing down the glass.

When Melissa comes back in, she sets the table. Is she still drunk? His dad doesn't seem to notice how slowly she's moving, how she's gripping the backs of chairs. They all sit and his dad holds out the container of Parmesan, but Melissa shakes her head and pushes away her plate. She puts her elbows on the table and rests her head in her hands. She's not even pretending to eat. If their mom was home, she'd ask Melissa what the matter was, but she's not, and so it's just him and his dad, chewing and swallowing.

"Hey, listen, buddy," his dad says. "Your mom and I got you that camera you wanted for your birthday."

"A 35 mm SLR?" He'd been studying them for months online. This explains why his mom had been vague about going to school and borrowing one from his photography teacher. She'd known all along that they were getting one for him.

"I meant to bring it home with me, but wouldn't you know it? It's sitting in my office. I'll bring it with me next time, okay?"

"Okay."

His dad's watching him. "So how did your party go? You have a nice time?"

What's he supposed to say, that he invited seven guys and only four showed? That his mom filled in the empty places with grown-ups? That other kids have parties at laser tag galleries and amusement parks, and the best he can do is a trampoline and balloons in his backyard? No wonder his dad hadn't wanted to come. "Okay, I guess."

"Anything new with Zach?"

Zach's got a girlfriend. He's on the football team. His mom's offered to videotape the games so that Tyler could watch them later, but he'd said no. What was the point of watching them on a little screen? "He got a job."

"No kidding. Doing what?"

"Bagging groceries." Tyler's Googled *bagging groceries.* A whole bunch of videos had popped up, and he'd paged to the images of ordinary people wearing uniform vests. That was what Zach was being paid nine bucks an hour to do. It didn't look hard. He couldn't understand why a store would pay Zach to do something people could do for themselves.

"Good for him," his dad says.

Zach's saving up to buy a car. He's only nine weeks older than Tyler. When he gets his license, what will Tyler be doing?

After dinner, Melissa goes into her room. His dad works in the living room, his laptop balanced on his knees. He glances up as Tyler passes. "You okay, buddy?"

"I'm going to watch the storm," he says.

"Just make sure you stay on the porch. And keep your sweatshirt on."

He should have guessed his mom would have told his dad. They'd probably argued about it, too. The air is fresh and cool, salty with the smell of earthworms, and fragrant with flowers. *This is lavender,* his mom said, holding a big bunch under his nose, playfully tickling him. *Doesn't it smell great?* It feels weird being in the house without her.

The windows of Amy's house glow yellow through the rain, light touching the police cars parked all around. Lightning veins the sky, and he steps back. Amy hates thunderstorms. He can't believe she'd be out in one. What made her leave her house, warm and dry?

He tugs his cell phone from the pocket of his jeans, peers at the screen, but it's impossible to make out anything through his sunglasses, so he pushes them up to sit on his forehead. He thumbs through his texts, finds Amy's avatar, Little Red Riding Hood. *Why her?* he had asked. *Because she wasn't afraid of the wolf,* she had replied.

There are three texts from her, all in a row. *my mom sux. i hate robbie. can i come over?*

He'd ignored them all.

He looks up and sees a policeman walking through the rain and down the sidewalk toward him.

EVE

What's wrong with her? Why isn't she talking? She should say something, anything, but Charlotte's holding her hand so tightly between hers; she's clinging to Eve and it's all Eve can do to stand beside her best friend as the police thunder up and down the stairs, tromp through all the rooms. The words are there, bundled up on her tongue, pressing against the roof of her mouth and demanding to be released, but she's clenching her teeth and clamping her lips together. She's trembling with the struggle to keep them inside. *I know where she is. I know what happened.* And then the sharpest ones of all: *I did it.*

"Does your daughter have any emotional problems?"

"No."

"Has she talked about hurting herself?"

Charlotte's fingers crush Eve's hand. "No!"

"Is she on any medication?"

"None."

"Does she use drugs?"

"She's *eleven*."

"Do you think someone took her from her room?"

"No, I heard her go out. We had a stupid fight and she was supposed to be in her room, but I heard the front door close and when I went to call her for dinner, she wasn't there."

Eve's already waited too long. She'll be charged with hit and run, with leaving the scene. They'll know she was texting. How many years will she get? What would Tyler do without her? She can't think about Amy. She can't. She can't look at Charlotte, whose fear is filling up this room.

"Have you notified the father?"

"We're divorced."

"Was it amicable?"

"No, but Owen wouldn't take Amy, not without letting me know."

"Where does he live?"

"Grandview."

"How can we get ahold of him?"

"I'll give you his phone number."

Now she's in the kitchen, turning on the water and making coffee. The cups rattle in her hands. Charlotte's other daughter, Nikki, bursts through the back door and throws her arms around Charlotte. She comes over to hug Eve, too. The room feels hot and cramped, distorted by lamplight. Eve's wearing Melissa's old clothes, pulled from the bag in the trunk, stuff that she'd been intending to take to Goodwill. She'd grabbed the first things at hand and gone into the bathroom at the airport to change. She'd rubbed the mud from her face and hands, balled up the clothes she'd been wearing and pushed them deep into the trash receptacle hanging on the tiled

wall. She'd covered them with handfuls of paper towels. She'd refused to look at herself in the mirror.

"I don't want to be here," Charlotte pleads. "I need to be out
looking."

"Let us do that. The best thing you can do for your daughter is
to tell me about her."

"I've *told* you about her."

"Do you mind telling me again?"

It won't be long now. Police are everywhere, stomping around in
their boots, flashing the beams of their heavy-duty flashlights into
every corner. They'll comb the ravine and spot her, bring her home
to Charlotte. This will all be over soon.

Eve opens her mouth and a few words slip out, but they're the
safe ones. "Sugar? Milk?" She closes her mouth again and feels the
bile clawing at the back of her throat.

Owen's here. He's yelling, pacing. He turns to the police officer.
"What about an Amber Alert?" he demands.

"We only issue one if your daughter was seen getting into a car."

Owen stops. He shakes his head. "She must have! Where the hell
else would she be?"

A policeman strides into the room, holding something in a large
plastic zippered bag. It's Amy's backpack, a pink camouflage print.
Charlotte had bought it just the day before, when she'd taken Amy
shopping for Tyler's present. Amy had pleaded for this particular backpack and Charlotte had finally acquiesced. A teddy bear keychain
dangles from the zipper, its black eyes staring sightlessly. Is it Charlotte
who reaches again for Eve's hand, or the other way around?

Everything's quiet when Eve lets herself into her own house. She
longs for a shower, hot water and steam. Her leg throbs from a long
scrape and she needs to soap it clean. God knows what other bruises

are hidden beneath her clothes. She had plunged through those trees, heedless. David's asleep on the couch. She stands there and looks down at him. All the words have left her. Still, she scrapes up a few and finds a piece of paper to write them down:

Gone to the store. Home soon.

She folds the note and props it up where David can see it when he wakes.

In the garage, she goes around the front of her car and shines the beam of her flashlight along the fender. The yellow circle of light plays along smooth metal and then stops on the dented right corner. So she hasn't imagined this. She forces herself to her knees to study the damage. The dent is deep, maybe a foot long. She doesn't see any blood. Thank God, there's no blood. She presses the flat of her hand against the metal, as if she can feel Amy's heartbeat. She squeezes her eyes shut, then opens them and pushes herself up. She climbs behind the steering wheel. She's shivering again.

The streets are empty, just a few cars passing her in the rain that falls quietly now. The pavement shines with reflected light from the grocery store on the right, the drugstore on the corner, the Italian restaurant closed for the night, its neon still glowing red and green. Every wink of light makes her wince. A car shoots past and she turns her head away. Did the driver see her?

At last, the gas station appears up ahead. No one waits at the pump. She doesn't know where the camera's posted and she drives slowly, scanning the roof of the convenience store. Yes, there it is. She's too far away for the camera to pick out her face or her license plate.

She makes a wide circle, far from its blank eye, and pulls up to the air pump, a metal box standing at the back of the building, the long black air hose curled and hooked into place. Eve stops five yards away and eyes the distance. Then she presses the accelerator. The car lurches forward, into the sharp corner of the pump, scraping the metal hard. The car shudders at the impact. She looks around, heart thudding. No one's there. No one's walking over to investigate.

She drives around the side of the building to the automated machine. She lines up the front right tire onto the metal track and rolls down her window to feed a twenty-dollar bill into the slot. She has four choices, and she picks the most expensive option, the Deluxe Showroom Wash. She presses the button and turns off the engine. The conveyor belt catches the wheels of her car and she bumps slowly forward. Soap squirts out in foamy silly string, neon green, lemon yellow, pink. Amy loved pink. Tyler used to sit in his car seat and kick his legs, laughing as long felt ribbons slapped the glass, waving and dancing as if they were underwater sea creatures.

Had Amy glanced toward her at that last moment and recognized her sitting behind the steering wheel? *Please. Let it have happened too quickly.* She pounds the steering wheel. This is not how things were supposed to go. This is not the life she wants. Hot tears stream down her cheeks. She bashes the steering wheel with her fists. *How could this have happened?*

Her car sways and is pulled along, emerging onto the pavement beneath the glare of a streetlight. She stumbles out, unhooks the long tube from the wall, and turns it on, rasps the mouth of the vacuum against the carpet, drawing up every crumb of mud, every crushed blade of grass. The fender is crushed. White paint mars the metal.

She climbs back into the car, switches on the engine, and drives back around to feed in another bill. She scoops her change from the tray and lets the conveyor belt drag her through again. She weeps for Amy, for Charlotte, for her own children.

She goes through the carwash six more times, using up every bill in her purse, emptying her wallet of change, and scraping loose coins from the ashtray. The sun is lifting itself over the horizon by the time she finally heads home. There is no clerk standing behind the register watching her pull out. There's only one car at the pump, the driver crouched beside a tire. He doesn't even glance over as she accelerates away.

SATURDAY, AUGUST 30

SUNRISE 6:57 AM

SUNSET 8:08 PM

DAVID

The searchers are divided into groups. They will proceed on foot, methodically, covering every inch of soggy terrain, the nearby park and playground, the riverfront, all the places Amy could have wandered to and gotten lost. If they find anything, they are not to touch it but to call the police immediately. They have the hotline number. They have a photo of Amy and a description of what she'd last been seen wearing. David's assigned a partner, the woman who works at the bank and who's been involved in searches before, for a missing college student who turned up in another state. She tells him she called off work for this one. He tells her Amy's like a daughter to him and his wife. Until he says this, he doesn't realize it's true.

Damn Charlotte, anyway. He hates himself for thinking it, but if she'd been a better mother, hadn't been so obsessed with her new boyfriend, had kept a better eye on her daughter, his whole weekend wouldn't be fucked up. Then he thinks of his own daughter. What if it were Melissa everyone was looking for? He feels slightly sick, shuffles through every sodden pile of leaves, turns aside every stone to study the mud beneath, toes through the flattened clumps of grass uprooted by the rainstorm, looking for any trace that Amy had been there. A pink plastic barrette, a sequin from her T-shirt. But he finds nothing. Nothing at all.

The new neighbors are coming out of their house as David arrives home. Puddles gleam here and there. Branches hang low with wet leaves. The wife has her head down, the skirt of her dress weaving in and out through the motion of her legs; a little boy trudges behind her. The husband carries a red-and-blue-plaid infant's car seat. He opens the back door of the car in their driveway, motions to his older kid to climb inside. Those early, sleep-deprived months with a newborn. Eve had called it sleep-depravity.

David gets out of the car and crosses toward them. "Hi," he says, extending his hand. "David Lattimore."

"Mark Ryland." The man's got a military look about him, his blond hair cropped close, his features chiseled, his brown eyes guarded. "This is my wife, Holly."

They're both so young, maybe in their early twenties. Had David ever been so youthful? It seems so far away to him now. "I understand my wife told you about our son," he says. "I wanted to thank you for your understanding."

"Sure. No problem."

"Let us know if you need anything," he says, glancing inside the car at the baby. Another boy, if the blue hat on the baby's head is any indication. So Mark has two boys to go camping with and to take to ballgames. "Our daughter's sixteen, if you're looking for a babysitter."

Mark Ryland nods. "Good to know."

"We'd better go," Holly says, and David nods, steps back.

There's a weird vibe between the two. Well, it can't be easy, moving into a new place with two young children, just before another child goes missing.

As David walks back to his waiting car, his garage door rolls up with a groaning protest. Melissa ducks beneath the rubber lip. "Finally," she says. She climbs into the passenger seat, holding her riding boots. Her face is pale, her eyes shadowed. She'd probably stayed up late and only just now woken up. "Hurry," she tells him. "Or I'll get stuck with Sammy." Sammy's the horse she doesn't like, the one that throws his head and refuses the bit.

Not a word about Amy. She bends forward, lacing her boots. All he sees is the back of her head, the line of her shoulders as she jerks the laces. Had he been so self-absorbed as a teenager? Probably. His entire junior year had been consumed by thoughts of a certain sophomore with a slight overbite and a dimple that appeared when she squinted. It's a miracle he passed any of his classes.

Eve's reassured David about Melissa. *All the kids wear those kind of shorts,* she tells him when he reacts with horror at how skimpy his daughter's clothing is. She shakes her head and smiles when he worries about how low-cut her shirts are. *You just don't want your little girl to grow up,* she teases. But he doesn't think that's entirely it. Last weekend he found a couple of tens missing from his wallet. Melissa had been wide-eyed with innocence when David asked her about it. It had made him wonder if he'd been mistaken. Eve had brushed off his concern. *Really, David,* she'd said. *Melissa would ask if she needed to borrow some money.* Which was true. Melissa has always been a good kid. She's been a rock.

Tyler, on the other hand, had asked a million questions, drifting from window to window to stare out into the rain. Look how he'd followed the policeman around the night before, as the man searched the house. *Did you look in the park?* he'd wanted to know. *She likes the swings.*

Melissa's two years older than Tyler. She understands Amy's disappearance differently and there's nothing David can do to shield her from it.

"Melissa," he says to her now. She's got her hand to her forehead, shielding her eyes. "I don't want you hanging out at the gas station anymore with Brittany." The two girls like to do that, walk up to the UDF and peruse the candy shelves, stocking up for a sugar-loaded sleepover. Even after Brittany got her license, this is a favorite pastime. Don't they realize the world is full of predators? "Not until we know what happened to Amy." And maybe not even then, though he doesn't add this part.

"Seriously, Dad? I'm *sixteen*."

Light-years away from Amy's eleven years, she means. He knows better.

"Seriously," he says firmly, and she slumps against her seat, her chin lowered. He has lost some ground with her, and he searches for a way to regain it. "Looking forward to school starting?"

"Can't wait." Her sarcasm is heavy. She tugs back her hair and snaps an elastic band around it. Her helmet lies by her feet, her thick padded vest rests on the seat behind them.

Still, he persists. "Taking any interesting classes?" This is Eve's domain. She's the one who goes over the curriculum with the children, meets with the guidance counselors to discuss test scores and aptitude tests. Tyler's scored off the charts in math. Eve had been delighted and wanted David to be delighted, too, but the news only sharpened his own pain. It's not as if it could go anywhere. How could it?

"Dad."

"What about Brittany? You guys in any of the same classes?"

"I wish."

"She's not taking choir with you this year?"

"*I'm* not taking choir."

"But you love singing."

"I suck at singing."

"No, you don't." He's amazed to hear this. Hasn't the house always been filled with her lilting voice, practicing all sorts of songs?

"Yes, I do. You're only saying that because you're my dad."

"But it's true."

She doesn't reply, just stares out the window. When she was little, she wanted to be a rock star. He wonders what she wants to be now. "Are you still seeing that boy . . ." What is his name? "Adrian?" He doesn't get what Melissa sees in the kid. It's not as if he isn't polite, always saying *Hi, Mr. Lattimore* and *Thank you, Mr. Lattimore*. He even makes eye contact. But ever since his arrival on the scene two months before, Melissa's grown so sullen.

"People don't see people, Dad. They date." Her voice is lost, aimed at the window.

"Wow, am I out of touch." His words mock him. He's more than out of touch with a younger generation. He's out of touch with this girl, the magical child who always ran to greet him at the end of the day, who always kissed him on both cheeks before she went to bed. She no longer runs to him. He can't remember the last time she even *told* him good night.

The barn sits at the end of a narrow gravel road, carved into runnels by last night's storm. The creek beside the road is higher than he's ever seen it, swirling over the smooth stones that fill its bed and lapping at the grassy banks. Melissa opens the car door before he's even put on the parking brake. She trudges away, moving slowly, as if her entire body aches. Maybe Amy's disappearance has taken a toll after all.

When she was first learning to ride, he was the one who had to saddle the horse for her, heaving the heavy saddle onto the horse's back and fastening the big straps under the animal's belly. But now she does this on her own, so he walks in the opposite direction and finds a place at the fence that circles the riding ring. They're in the indoor ring while the outdoor ring dries out. There are a few other parents there, two mothers and a father who stands with his back to the ring, his cell phone to his ear. There used to be a dozen of them collected around the fence, but now they're down to four. Most of the girls in Melissa's class are driving themselves to their lessons. Next week Melissa will take her driving test and join their ranks, and he won't be responsible anymore for ferrying her around. For eight years, he's looked forward to reclaiming his Saturday afternoons, and now that it's almost upon him, he feels the clanging echo of loss.

Melissa appears, leading a big black horse. So she got Sammy after all. She pointedly doesn't look at him as she walks into the ring where the other girls are waiting. Their horses jerk their heads, high step away. They don't like Sammy, either.

Tyler's told him that Zach's got a job bagging groceries. David remembers his first job, at a gas station, the feeling of satisfaction of earning that paycheck. Eve's mentioned that Zach has a girlfriend, too. All the doors flying open in his world that are nailed shut in Tyler's.

His phone buzzes. Eve, with news? But no, it's a text from Renée. *Help! I'm being held captive. Send chocolate!*

He smiles. *Dress shopping?*

We've moved on to hats. It's torture.

Where's Jeffery?

Playing golf, the coward.

Haha. This is good bonding time. Jeffery's one of four boys, and the first to get married. Renée's doing double duty as bride-to-be and future daughter-in-law.

I'm going to elope. I swear it.

There's a shout and he glances up at the ring. Melissa sits tall in the saddle, her shoulders straight and her eyes narrowed with focus. She's so small and that horse is so huge. She doesn't look the least bit nervous or afraid. His phone buzzes and he looks back down.

How's your weekend going?

Not so good, he texts. *A neighbor girl's missing.*

That's terrible!!! Do the police know what happened?

Not yet.

How sad. I'm so sorry. I shouldn't have bothered you.

No problem.

The mother next to him gasps. He looks over just in time to see Melissa slide right off Sammy and land in a tangle on the ground. He grabs the fence, about to vault into the ring, when the mother beside him says, "It's okay. She's okay."

He sees that she's right. Melissa has rolled to her feet and is brushing the dust from her legs. She has her face turned down. She's trying not to cry. When she raises her chin, though, her jaw is set, her mouth in a determined line. She looks just like Eve. She grabs the reins from where they're hanging and yanks Sammy around so she can climb back up into the saddle.

They're in the car headed home when his phone buzzes. "You have to tell Cheryl not to give me Sammy anymore," Melissa's saying.

"She's just trying to build your confidence." He pats around the central console to switch the phone off when Melissa snatches it from his grasp.

"No texting and driving," she says, mimicking the stern voice he uses when he goes over the driving rules with her. "Keep your phone in the glove box whenever you're behind the wheel."

"I wasn't," he says. "Give me the phone."

"Ooh, this must be an important message"—she glances at the display—"from Renée?"

"She's someone I work with." He holds out his hand, but she leans away.

"She teach you how to text?"

"Melissa," he says, warning, and his daughter gives him a side-long glance before dropping his phone into his palm.

"Gee, Dad," she says. "Chill."

He should shut off the phone or set it down. But when he brakes at the stoplight, he can't resist glancing down to see Renée's message.

I'm going to kill Jeffery.

"Dad," Melissa says impatiently.

"Want to stop for ice cream?" he suggests. "Our last lesson to-gether. We should mark the occasion." He texts back, *Hang in there,* then slides his phone into his pocket.

EVE

She's bone and sinew and flesh, empty and adrift. There's nothing warm or good or whole about her. Whoever she once was, whatever she once was, is gone, scraped away and vanished. This is her true selfish and misguided self finally being revealed to her. This is what evil looks like. She stares at her hand as it turns the page in the binder. How can it look so ordinary?

The April day Charlotte moved into the neighborhood, Eve had been at her computer, reading an online article about an XP documentary someone was filming about a child in Arizona. She had been studying the photographs of the toddler, who had freckles and a vacant gaze, trying to figure out whether the boy had been blinded by the sun, when a sharp rat-a-tat on the window glass startled her. It had been Charlotte, asking if she had any bottled water for the movers—she couldn't find her cups on the truck. Charlotte thought

EVE

She's bone and sinew and flesh, empty and adrift. There's nothing warm or good or whole about her. Whoever she once was, whatever she once was, is gone, scraped away and vanished. This is her true selfish and misguided self finally being revealed to her. This is what evil looks like. She stares at her hand as it turns the page in the binder. How can it look so ordinary?

The April day Charlotte moved into the neighborhood, Eve had been at her computer, reading an online article about an XP documentary someone was filming about a child in Arizona. She had been studying the photographs of the toddler, who had freckles and a vacant gaze, trying to figure out whether the boy had been blinded by the sun, when a sharp rat-a-tat on the window glass startled her. It had been Charlotte, asking if she had any bottled water for the movers—she couldn't find her cups on the truck. Charlotte thought she wasn't very friendly because she didn't invite her in, and so she kept her distance for a few weeks, before showing up one evening bearing a plate of brownies, having learned about Tyler from Rosemary Griggs.

I didn't know, Charlotte had begun apologetically, and now, sitting beside Eve in the police station, she says, "I don't know."

The two of them are flipping through the huge binders, staring at photographs of men and some women. How can there *be* so many sexual predators? How could Eve have lived in this area for thirteen years and not known that these monsters lived so close? They probably got their gas at the same station, shopped at the same stores. She could have passed them on the sidewalk, smiled at them in the library. They shouldn't look so damned average. Their faces should be disfigured, scarred in some way. They should look guilty, but most of them wear a smug expression, even cocky. This one resembles Melissa's riding instructor. This one looks the spitting image of the man who takes their monthly electrical readings. Every time she pauses to consider a particular image, Detective Watkins asks her if it's someone she's noticed in the neighborhood. Over and over, she has replied *no.* She doesn't know any of these people. She's never seen any of them before.

Amy lies a mile away. The police have searched the ravine, fanned out in all directions from where they'd found Amy's backpack, lying beside that little wooden bridge near the playground. Why hasn't one of them radioed in? Robbie's at work, clearing his schedule. *I'll meet you back at the house,* he'd promised Charlotte, holding her for a moment before letting her go. He'd nodded to Eve and then climbed into his car.

Charlotte pushes away the final binder. Her dark red hair stands out starkly against the pallor of her skin. Bits of mascara cling to her eyelashes. They collect in the hollows beneath her eyes. "I don't know what to feel anymore."

All morning Eve's watched her friend ricochet between different versions of hope: that there's a face she recognizes, that there isn't. Only Eve knows that there's no hope anywhere at all in this room, that Charlotte could sit here a thousand hours, study the faces of a thousand monsters, and it wouldn't make any difference.

"I need you to think about that list you gave me," Detective Watkins says. "Is there anyone else you can think of to add to it?"

"I can't . . . I don't know."

"Think. Is there someone who worked on your house?"

"Just the painters. The maid service, the guy who drops off my dry-cleaning."

"What about a friend of your son's?"

Scott's twenty. He's never going to get over this. And then Charlotte will have lost two children.

"Is there, Eve?" Charlotte asks. "Is there someone I've forgotten?"

All these innocent people who are going to be getting a knock on the door. Innocent. The word is so lovely and round. "I don't think so," Eve says.

"I need you to keep thinking," Detective Watkins says. "The fact is, most child abductions are committed by people the child knows."

"I don't know anyone who would steal my daughter!"

An accident. It had all been an accident and now she's sitting here, in this airless room beside her friend whose agony is so raw that it's reeling Eve back to that time when she had been filled with an endless dark despair. She had clawed her way out of it. She thought she'd been successful.

"Someone will have seen something," Detective Watkins says. "It's just a matter of time before someone comes forward."

That car in front of her, had there been a brief red flare of brake lights? If the driver had seen something, they would have turned around. They would have called the police.

"Do you really think so?" Charlotte asks. Her hope is so raw, so vulnerable. Detective Watkins gathers the binders toward her. "I do. That's how most of these cases are solved."

Eve focuses on the dingy beige wall with a crack running through it. Her secret stretches out like a fissure. When Tyler doesn't need her anymore, she'll tell Charlotte. Three years, maybe longer if he's sick. The crack on the wall wavers.

"You haven't heard anything from the search teams?" Charlotte asks, and the detective shakes her head.

"Nothing yet."

Owen's out there, organizing people. They're meeting in front of his store. He swears he's going to find his daughter, and Eve knows that if anyone could, it would be him. But he hasn't called, either.

How can Amy have vanished so completely? Is it possible that Eve's imagined the entire thing? Just as soon as these questions flicker through her mind, she pushes them away. She'd been wrong. There had been some hope left in this room after all.

They find a deli a few blocks away. Charlotte would have kept on walking if Eve hadn't taken her elbow and steered her toward the open door. The place is quieting down after the lunch rush, and only a few of the tables are occupied. They sit by the window, and Eve orders matzo ball soup for both of them. Charlotte sets her cell phone on the table in front of her, and so does Eve. David's with the search teams. He'll call to let her know if they find Amy.

"That little girl in California," Charlotte says. "They found her two years later. I mean, she went through hell, but she's okay now. And what about that girl who wrote a book? It's hideous what happened to her, but she's alive. She's back with her family."

"That's true." The words are broken pieces of glass in her mouth.

"And what about the baby who was taken out of her crib? They got her back almost right away. They got it on the news and the babysitter confessed."

Yes, Eve remembers that case, too.

Charlotte sets down her glass. Her nails are bitten to the quick, the red polish worn to smears like drops of blood. "Don't look at me like that."

"Like what?" Eve says, startled. Her guilt must be plain.

"Like it's the end of the world. It's not. It's *not*. We're going to find Amy. Tell me that. Say it right now."

"Yes," Eve says. She forces herself to smile. The muscles in her face ache. "We'll find Amy." They will find Amy, but Charlotte will never get her back. Eve's falling from a great height. The air whizzes past her ears. Her stomach's cramping. It's a second before Charlotte's face comes back into focus. Her friend is staring around the restaurant. Thank God she's not looking at Eve.

"We have to get the flyers up," Charlotte says. "We can start here. I'll put one in the window."

"We'll ask."

"It's a good picture. Tyler always takes great pictures of Amy."

Tyler had held up his camera as Amy grinned wide, her bangs crooked across her forehead. She'd followed Tyler around like a puppy and Charlotte and Eve had joked how Amy would eventually wear Tyler down. They never took the joke too far. There was that line that stopped everything.

"I just don't understand why she went out," Charlotte says. "She's so scared of storms."

The pieces of last night don't fit together. Nothing makes sense. Amy's backpack had been found in the park, but she had dashed across the road in front of Eve a full mile away. There's that hope again, lifting its coy little head, murmuring that maybe none of this has happened the way she remembers. Hope is a liar.

"The police won't let me have her teddy bear," Charlotte continues. "It was in her backpack and they say it's evidence."

Eve had cradled Amy, kissed her cheeks. She'd cried, her tears dripping into Amy's hair. She'd left behind plenty of evidence. But it had been raining so hard. Water had poured from the sky, washed across the landscape, drained into the rivers and creeks. It could have swept everything away, even fingerprints.

Their soup arrives. Eve craves a glass of white wine, something crisp and clean to drink. It would taste good going down and she would order another one, just keep drinking until either her phone or Charlotte's rings and someone tells them something has happened, that Amy has been found. But by the time they finish their meal, neither phone has sounded.

DAVID

"There's more to life than chocolate," he tells Melissa, who's holding her cone carefully over a paper napkin. She never eats any other flavor, no matter how long and tempting the list is. Raspberry swirl, apple pie, mocha hazelnut fudge. She doesn't so much as glance at the selections. She just steps up to the counter and places her order.

"Chocolate's good," she replies, though she hasn't taken a single lick.

He turns onto their street.

"Who's that, Dad?" she says, squinting.

A woman stands at their front door, her black sedan parked at their curb. She turns to look at them as he steers the car into the driveway. She's wearing a navy pantsuit and her expression is grim.

"I don't know." He parks the car, gets out to greet the woman walking down the path toward them.

"Mr. Lattimore?" She holds up a badge. Now he sees the gun holstered at her hip. "I'm Detective Watkins. I'm looking into Amy Nolan's disappearance. I understand you spoke with an officer last night, and I wanted to ask you a few follow-up questions, if you don't mind."

They haven't found Amy yet. Dread settles in his gut. Charlotte and Owen must be going through hell. "Of course."

She's looking at his daughter. "You must be Melissa."

Melissa frowns. "Yes."

"I'd like to talk to you, too. Is that all right?"

"If I have to." Melissa drops her uneaten cone into the trashcan.

David would never have spoken to an adult that way, especially not a police officer. Melissa's just frightened, he reminds himself. "Hold on," he tells the detective. "I need to close the garage door."

Gone from home so much of the time and yet this is his conditioned response, to make sure the exterior door is closed before opening an interior one. He finds himself doing the same thing hundreds of miles away, puzzling his coworkers as he scans the room before standing to open a door.

Detective Watkins makes no comment as the door thuds all the way to the pavement, sealing them in darkness. He opens the kitchen door, and she precedes him into the house, her gaze skimming the dishes in the sink, the sun chart pinned to the doorway. Melissa's taken off her boots and is standing there in her tank top and jodhpurs.

"I have to take a shower," she says, and he puts his arm around her slim shoulders. Can't she understand the urgency? "Let's talk to the detective first," he tells her. "Okay?"

"Whatever," she mutters, scowling. She won't look at Detective Watkins. She stares at the ground, recalcitrant as the police officer guides her through the events of the previous evening. *I don't know. I guess. No.* It's a relief when Watkins finally says, "All right. I guess that's it."

"So can I shower *now*?"

David's embarrassed. He looks at Watkins, as if to say *teenagers,* but the woman's not looking at him. She's looking around the dark room, the lamps on in various corners. "Go ahead," he tells Melissa, and Watkins turns to him. "Is your son home?" she asks.

Of course she'd know he had a son. The uniformed officer who'd been by the night before had made a note of all their names, but this sudden request of hers sets him on edge. She knows more than she's saying. "I don't know if anyone's mentioned this to you, but my son's got xeroderma pigmentosum. He can't be exposed to ultraviolet light. It will kill him." Blind him, deafen him, take away the use of his arms and legs, eat into his brain and make him a vegetable. A rare disease, and only a few thousand in the world had it. *Even with the best of care,* the specialist had said, *Tyler most likely won't live past twenty.*

"Is there somewhere we can talk?" Detective Watkins asks.

"This way."

They go up the narrow flight of stairs. This was one of the first things he and Eve did when they learned of Tyler's disease—install a lightproof door here and give up the second floor of their house to their son.

"Tyler," he calls through the closed door. "A police detective's here to talk to us about Amy."

"Okay. Hold on."

No doubt his son's lounging in his desk chair, feet up on the desk, or feeding photo paper through the printer and waiting impatiently for the results. The multicolored lamp will be throwing out its crazy colors. The overhead light will be shining, and the desk lamp, and the bathroom light. Even the nightlight on the floor will be switched on. *Why does he do that?* he'd once complained to Eve, and she'd answered, *Because he can.*

"He's putting on sunscreen," he tells the detective, and she nods. But it's more than that. Tyler's going through that strange ritual of patting his face in a certain order. He won't open a door until he does it. *He's just checking to make sure his sunscreen's on,* Eve said when David brought it up in therapy. *It's more than that,* David argued, and Eve had snapped, *What are you trying to say, that our child's not normal?*

The snick of metal on metal. Watkins looks at him with surprise. "Your son locks himself in?"

"Yes," he says shortly. Ever since that friend of Melissa's had inadvertently opened Tyler's door while he sat at his desk doing homework. Eve had heard the shrieking and come running. He thinks this is why Melissa has so few friends—she's careful about who she brings into the house.

These are the rules: during the day, they go through the garage door and then through the kitchen door, which, positioned as it is behind the wall, doesn't let in the light. Just after sunset to just before sunrise, when the air is completely drained of UV, they can go through the front door or the French doors that lead out onto the patio. At all other times, the drapes are to be kept drawn tightly, and every week, the UV-filtering films they've adhered to the windows are to be checked for peeling, cracking, or scratches. They track the passage of the sun closely. Its movement across the sky has made this house a prison.

"Okay," Tyler calls, and David turns the knob.

"Move quickly, please," he tells the detective.

Ahead is Tyler's small bathroom, then a room on either side. David turns right. Tyler sits at his desk, in front of his two computer monitors and television, looking like an air traffic controller, with all those screens arrayed in front of him.

The walls are covered by scraps of paper that flutter as the door opens. David used to think there was no order to what's essentially a massive collage, until Eve pointed out how Tyler had arranged his kindergarten drawings on one row, then his crayoned attempts at forming letters, his first story written on huge lined sheets of paper.

Tyler went through a self-portrait phase, the earliest ones at the bottom, in colored pencil and marker, graduating up to art pencil and charcoal, each tooth drawn with accuracy, each hair in his eyebrows waved more or less the way his eyebrows really grow. Weaved throughout are his brief foray into Cub Scouts, his early interest in dinosaurs, the map that Eve made of the neighborhood for one of his birthday parties, and Tyler's later, and more comprehensive, focus in photography, evidenced in the plethora of photographs Tyler has taken, of his friends, Melissa, Amy. Receipts from the purchase of his laptop, binoculars, skateboard, and tennis shoes—everything has its place somewhere on Tyler's walls.

"Hi, Tyler," Detective Watkins says, looking around with curiosity. David wishes he could stop her. "I'm Detective Watkins. I'm trying to find Amy so that I can bring her back home. She's not in any trouble, but if there's something either of you know that could help us, that would be really great." Is it his imagination or is she studying Tyler with particular curiosity? David moves toward his son, stepping into her line of vision.

"Okay," Tyler says. "But I don't know what." He's studying her in his usual focused way, with his eyebrows drawn and his chin lowered, and David realizes that maybe letting the detective get a good look at his son is worth it if his son is getting a good, long look at a police officer, a rare up-close-and-personal examination of something he's heretofore witnessed only on a television screen.

"I hear Amy's a friend of yours." Watkins steps sideways, her angle now oblique.

"I guess."

"When was the last time you talked to her?"

"At my birthday party."

"When was that?"

"Thursday night."

"What about last night?" Watkins asks. "I understand she texted you."

"She wanted to come over. But I didn't *talk* to her," Tyler says, emphasizing this, letting the detective know that's not the question she'd asked. Good for Tyler.

"Did she say anything to indicate that she wanted to run away?"

"No." Tyler shrugs. "But she's always running away."

"Why is that?"

"Because of the divorce?" Tyler says this as though it had been a trick question.

"Do you have any idea where she might have gone?"

"No," Tyler answers. "I mean, usually she came here."

"But she didn't this time?"

"No."

"She didn't knock on the door or ring the bell?"

"We don't have a doorbell," David interposes. He'd disconnected it when Tyler was little and sleeping through the days. Even now that Tyler's on the same schedule as the rest of them, David hasn't gotten around to reconnecting it. But this is a small detail and he has no idea why he's volunteered it. Maybe it's because of the intent way this woman's looking at his son. David had wanted to jump in and disrupt the flow.

"Did she ever mention anyone she was afraid of?"

Tyler hesitates. "Not really."

"Not really?"

"I mean, not anyone real. She didn't like it when I played war games; she hated the vampire stuff on TV."

"Did she ever talk about a special relationship with an adult?"

David's dismayed at the angle her questions are taking, but of course this has to be the natural progression. Amy's gone. The world's an ugly place. You have to be suspicious.

Tyler makes a face. "Gross."

"A teacher? A neighbor, maybe someone from church?"

Tyler shakes his head.

"Okay, well, do you think she's the type of girl who might get into a stranger's car?"

David leans forward. "Is that what they think happened?"

"We're considering all possibilities. So, is Amy that kind of girl?"

"No way. Not Amy," Tyler insists. "She wouldn't get into anyone's car, not even if they had a kitten or something like that."

"A kitten?" David asks, and his son nods.

"Creepers use kittens and puppies to lure kids, stuff like that."

David hadn't known that. What kind of world is it that his children are growing up in? He looks at the detective. "Is that what you're thinking now, that someone took Amy?"

She closes her notebook and nods at Tyler's computer screens. "That's a pretty cool setup. You like to play video games?"

"Yeah."

She nods again. "What else do you do?"

What does she expect to hear, about Tyler's soccer team and his plans for Homecoming?

"I don't know. Ride my bike, maybe."

"And photography, right?" Her voice is pleasant, her gaze serenely intent on Tyler. "You sure took a lot of pictures of Amy. Was there something particularly interesting about her?"

"They're friends," David says. Where the hell is she going with this? More than that. "She's like a sister to Tyler."

"She was always over here, wasn't she?" She's not answering him. She's looking at Tyler. "Hanging out with you when she could have been playing with kids her own age."

The inference hangs poisonous in the air. Is she crazy? "My son takes a lot of pictures of everyone." He yanks open a desk drawer, pulls out a thick handful of photographs.

"Dad," Tyler says, reaching for them. "Stop. They're in order."

David ignores him. "See?" He fans them out. His hands are shaking. "Nikki, Scott, Charlotte. Melissa, her friends. My wife."

"Sir . . ."

"This interview is over," David says. "Stay here," he tells Tyler. "I'll be right back."

Outside, he draws the front door closed behind them. "Look," he says. Watkins stands on the lower step, squinting up at David in the early afternoon sun. "My son just has a disease. That's all. He's not some kind of *freak*."

"I understand that, but a little girl is missing."

"There's no way my son had anything to do with that."

"We all think we know our kids."

What the hell does that mean? "It's not a matter of knowing what our kids are capable of. It's a physical fact that my son was here when Amy went missing."

"We'd do anything to protect them. I know I would."

"Are you insinuating I'm hiding anything? I was flying home from DC last night. If you check . . ."

"We already have, sir." She closes her notebook. "Keep an eye on your daughter."

She turns and walks to her waiting car. The bright sun strikes the chrome of her car and makes him see spots.

Tyler's sitting on his bed, his photographs scattered across his navy blue comforter. He looks up as David enters the room, and David can see the confusion and fear in his child's eyes.

"I don't get it, Dad. What's wrong with taking pictures?"

"Nothing, Ty. Nothing at all. They'll find her." David sits beside his son and looks at the images of smiling faces arranged there, photographs of everyone in Tyler's small world, everyone Tyler knows. The only one missing is David.

EVE

Eve suggests taking Charlotte's SUV. *I'll drive,* she says. Charlotte doesn't reply. She's focused on the tasks at hand—printing and distributing flyers. They will paper this town with Amy's smiling image. Everywhere, there will be reminders to the public to keep an eye out for this little girl. Everywhere Eve turns, she'll be branded anew, her evil heart punished and punished and punished again.

Charlotte's car is filled with reminders of Amy—the hardened drips of milk staining the cup holder, the silver CD sticking out from the CD player. *I could marry Harry Styles!* The rainbow sticker pressed to the dashboard, and the faint scent of chlorine that rises from the pink-and-purple beach towel lying on the floor behind their seats. Eve cracks a window, but it doesn't help. Charlotte gazes out the window, leaning forward, as if she was willing Eve to go faster.

They reach the school parking lot, and Charlotte climbs out. Eve takes the box of flyers from the backseat. They will tape some here, on the front door that Amy had walked in and out of for six years. An American flag snaps in the hot wind. In the field beyond, children dash around kicking a soccer ball.

"She loves this place," Charlotte says. "I don't understand it. It's so dumpy. The hallways reek of food."

Minivans line the curb, parents waiting impatiently behind their steering wheels, focused on errands they have to run, chores they need to do. They don't know how wonderful their lives are.

"She knows I'm looking for her, right?" Charlotte asks. "No matter what, she knows how much I love her."

"Yes she does. She knows that."

If Eve could, she'd climb into one of those minivans and drive away. She'd let the babble of children's voices rise and fall around her. She'd drive past the park and the library and the grocery store, and pretend she was someone else, anyone else. For a while, surely that would work.

"Who would do something like this? Who would take a little girl away from her family?"

"I don't know." *I do. I do know.*

"Those sick women who cut babies out of pregnant women. What if someone like that has Amy? What if it's a predator? Oh my God. She won't understand."

"Stop, Charlotte. You have to stop." For Charlotte's sake. And yes—a whisper—for her sake, too.

"I can't. I can't. How can I? What if I never know what happened to her? How can I live, not knowing? But I know they'll find her. She's okay. I know she is."

Eve keeps a calendar, not the monthly ones of sunrises and sunsets that she tacks up by every door, but a secret one, in her heart. On it she tracks the time she has left with her son. It's a rough guess, one that gains days every time he has a good medical checkup and loses weeks when he has a bad one. The ending point floats in the air, and for the first dozen years, she couldn't see it. But now that dark dot is coming into view, and if she squints, she can almost see it. And beyond it, there's nothing, absolutely nothing.

Why haven't they found Amy? A small voice inside Eve pipes up hopefully. *Maybe they never will.*

This isn't her quiet cul-de-sac. It can't be.

Vehicles are parked bumper-to-bumper along the curb. There are news vans from other cities—Cleveland, Chicago. People throng the street, reporters, neighbors, strangers, all of them taking up space as if they have every right to be there. They don't. They have to leave, go and take their hateful curiosity somewhere else.

Charlotte and Owen stand outside their house, microphones bunched in front of them. Their children are off to one side. Nikki wears a bright yellow sundress, defiant. Scott has his hands in his pockets and his chin lowered. He is aware of every camera pointed his way. He's terrified and angry, both.

"Amy's allergic to peanuts," Charlotte says. "Even touching one can cause her to break out in hives. If you have her . . . if she's with you, you need to know."

Remember to focus on your daughter, Detective Watkins had told Charlotte and Owen. *Talk about what she's like, what her special interests are. Use her name frequently. We want to humanize her. We don't want to talk about repercussions or punishment.*

"Amy's eleven years old, four feet ten inches tall. She has brown eyes and long blond hair. I wouldn't let her get her ears pierced so she drew on her earlobes with a blue Sharpie. She . . . Amy . . . saw pictures on TV of the children without clean water and she decided to start saving her allowance to help build a well."

A woman nods, taking notes.

"Amy loves the color pink." Owen speaks clearly into the microphone. "She'd eat Brussels sprouts if they were pink."

Amy's bedroom is painted a throbbing bubblegum color, her bedspread and curtains deeper shades of rose. There's a fat fuchsia beanbag chair, and neon pink shades on the lamps. She'd begged for a bright pink carpet, but Charlotte had drawn the line.

Eve stands with Albert in his driveway. Next door, Joan and Larry Farnham stand in their own driveway, holding hands, the way they always do. Nearby, a man says to his cameraman, "Make sure you're focusing on the mother, get it if she breaks down. People love that."

He glances at Eve, through her, and then back to Charlotte and Owen.

"A terrible business." Albert's white hair stands in tufts all over his head, and despite the warmth of the day, he's wearing a long-sleeved button-down shirt and corduroys. He's gotten so small since Rosemary's death three months before, shrunken inside his clothes. He used to figure so large in Eve's life, a reassuring ballast. He had helped David nail boards over Tyler's bedroom windows. Rosemary had searched for cotton gloves in Tyler's size; she had glued tiny pictures of salamanders and creepy-crawly bugs onto sunglass frames so that he begged to wear them. And now Rosemary's gone, and it's just Albert, shambling alone through the rooms of his house.

Neil Cipriano walks over. "Any news?" he asks, and Eve shakes her head.

Sophie Wu pushes her way through the crowd, young and slim, her long black hair gleaming, every strand in place. When Sophie moved in, Eve had gone over with her basket of light bulbs and an offer to replace any that burned out. Sophie had shaken her head. *No, no,* she'd said with sympathy. *Don't even worry about it.*

"This is crazy," Sophie says. "I had to park at the top of the street."

"It'll be over soon," Albert says, and Eve looks at him. Does he know something? But no, he means the press conference.

Charlotte and Owen have stopped talking and now the FBI agent is saying something in response to a reporter's questions.

"We'd have noticed a stranger hanging around," Sophie says. "Wouldn't we? I mean, this is a dead-end street. It's not like people can just drive through. But I'm not home much. You're home, Eve. Did you see anyone?"

"I'd have to think about it." How can she be intentionally dangling the thread of suspicion? Keeping silent was one thing, but when did she decide to start lying? She doesn't want to be this person. She wants this person to stop talking.

"You ask me, it had to be someone who knew Amy's comings and goings." Neil's got his hands shoved into the pockets of his pressed khakis, his blue button-down shirt open at the collar and the cuffs neatly rolled up. His cheeks gleam, closely shaven.

He can't mean it. He can't know what he's saying.

"The police warned me to be alert for people who've suddenly changed their appearance or their routine," Albert says. "Maybe gone missing for a period of time."

"Like who?" Sophie wants to know.

"Like one of us," Neil replies baldly.

Eve had driven right past their houses at four in the morning, a time she never left her home. She'd been intent on getting to the carwash, and she'd been paralyzed with fear driving past the police cars parked in front of Charlotte's house. She hadn't looked to see if any of her neighbors was watching. Had one of them seen her return an hour later, tires splashing through the puddles, her bumper hanging low as rain clouds roiled overhead?

"Really," Sophie says, but she's not looking at Eve. She's eyeing the Farnhams, standing just a few yards away. She lowers her voice. "Don't you think it's strange that no one's ever seen inside their house? They never leave even their garage door open."

It was true. Larry and Joan parked their cars in their driveway, and Larry wheeled his lawn mower out the side entrance. They kept their drapes closed and slipped in and out of their front door, barely opening it wide enough to let themselves inside. Eve couldn't wait for the sun to go down so she could pull open the drapes. She kept the windows opened at night, whenever the weather allowed. She chafed at being closed up indoors, but the Farnhams seemed to welcome it. Sophie's right: it is strange.

"The police searched their place," Albert says mildly, and Sophie testily replies, "Not until today. They weren't home last night. The police asked if I knew where Larry and Joan were, and I told them I didn't know."

"Well, it is the weekend," Neil volunteers. "People do go out."

"Not them," Sophie says. "I don't think they have any friends. It's just the two of them."

Albert looks thoughtful. "Amy *was* over there a lot."

Not Albert, too. "Only because Larry was building a goldfish pond," Eve says.

"Wow, Eve," Sophie says. "I never imagined you'd be sticking up for him."

"I'm not," Eve protests, but no one's listening. Charlotte's talking into the microphones and cameras again, and everyone has turned to watch her. Eve risks a glance down the street toward her garage. The door's closed, hiding her car. She'd pulled the car in so far that the fender had bumped the wall. She imagines she can hear it ticking.

HOLLY

"My mom's freaking out," Zach says. "She says there's a predator loose. I can't even bike to work. She has to drive me."

Tyler leans back in his desk chair. He's been going through his photographs, the ones he keeps in his bottom drawer—Sophie tipping a bottle over a glass; Charlotte sitting in her armchair with her zebra-print reading glasses perched on her nose; Amy crouched by her old dollhouse, reaching in; Dr. Cipriano holding up a measuring tape to his basement wall. Tyler taps them together and slides them back into their hiding place behind the box of printer paper. "Sucks," he says with feeling. He can't remember the last time Zach called him on the phone. They usually text or message each other on Facebook.

"She's calling people to form a watch group. She call your mom yet?"

"I don't know."

"She will."

Zach's mom and Tyler's mom weren't friends, though. They pretended to get along, but Tyler and Zach both know it's not real. Their moms smile and say polite things, but they don't hang out, not like Tyler's mom and Charlotte always do. But when Zach's family moved to a bigger house a few miles away, Tyler's mom had seemed sad.

"You see anything?" Zach says. "You were right there, man. Like *CSI.*"

But Tyler hadn't been looking out the windows the whole time. He'd been gaming; he'd gone into the kitchen for a snack. If only he'd been paying attention. He could have saved Amy. "Want to come over?"

"No way my mom will let me. You come over here."

"I'll ask."

They hang up. In sixteen minutes, Tyler can leave his room. Though it won't really be sixteen minutes. It'll be seventeen minutes, maybe even eighteen, before his mom knocks. She always makes him wait an extra minute or two, just to be sure. Clocks have a way of slowing down or speeding up, she says. He used to fight with her about it when he was little. It wasn't just about that minute; it was everything else, too. He wanted to go to McDonald's, ride a roller coaster, visit the ocean. He blamed his mom for making him stay inside, but she never budged. She only shook her head and looked sadly at him. *I'm sorry,* she'd say, and he'd retorted, *If you were really sorry, you'd say yes.*

Then one night Melissa came into his room and stood there, arms crossed, glaring at him as he lay sprawled in his bed. *You don't remember what it was like,* she'd said. *But I do. So cut it out.*

He puts his head back against the wall. The poster across from him reads *Play the Lottery. Win.*

Amy was always crawling into places she didn't belong: in Tyler's fort, up that tall tree in the Farnhams' backyard. Once, she'd climbed into the backseat of Dr. Cipriano's sweet Chevy Impala and lain down where she'd been completely hidden. Tyler had searched everywhere and had been about to give up when Dr. Cipriano came out and found her there. Tyler had been humiliated being caught playing hide-and-seek with a little kid. Amy had begged and begged after that, but that was the last time they ever played together.

He hadn't told Detective Watkins any of that. He didn't like the way she'd looked at him, as if she didn't want him to see how curious she was about him. Sometimes people had a hard time being around him. Melissa's friends were usually nervous the first time they met him. Tyler's teachers could be extra smiley on Skype or have faces as flat as stone. Not all the kids Tyler hung out with could deal with it. Once, when he was five, a kid in his Cub Scout den jerked away when Tyler accidentally bumped into him. His mom had invited him to Tyler's birthday party that year. But of all the kids, he was the only one who didn't come.

Pizza's a welcome treat, but Tyler's the only one eating. His dad hasn't touched his food, and his mom's just pleating a paper napkin between her fingers. Even Melissa isn't fighting him for the last slice. She's picking off circles of pepperoni to stand in a greasy stack on the side of her plate.

"I saw Owen today, out with the search teams." His dad's red across his forehead and nose and down his arms. Normally, this is the kind of thing his mom would be all over, but she hasn't said a word about it. It's Amy. Her disappearance has shocked the normal right out of his mom. She just sits there, looking at him, looking at all of them, but not like she's really seeing them. "I would've expected Scott to be there, too, but I must have missed him."

Melissa looks up at the mention of Scott's name. She used to have a major thing for Amy's brother, back when everyone called him Scotty. Melissa used to sit on the front porch and watch Amy's house, waiting for a Scotty sighting.

"The police went all over the area," his dad tells them. "Searching yards, knocking on doors. They're going to bring out sniffer dogs and search helicopters."

Wait until he tells Zach. "What kind?"

"AW139s."

Monster aircraft, the newest breed. They don't bring those out for nothing. If they couldn't find Amy, nothing could. "Can anybody help search? Can I?" He'd like that. He'd look places no one else would think of.

"Oh, honey," his mom says, and he knows there's no point in asking again.

"Can we talk about something *else*?" Melissa says.

Why shouldn't they talk about it? Doesn't Melissa want to know where Amy is? Then he gets it: the way Melissa's picking at her food, her face so white. She's hungover. Her Facebook status has changed. She's no longer in a relationship. Tyler's never really liked Adrian, who always stared when he didn't think Tyler would notice. Melissa's called him on it more than once. *Dude,* she'd said. *Cut that out.* He remembers how worried Melissa had been about getting a boyfriend, about how she asked their mom why boys didn't like her. He'd have thought that finally having a boyfriend would make Melissa happier and less worried, but in fact, the exact opposite has happened.

"Can I go to Zach's?" Tyler asks.

"Why don't you see if he can come over here?" his mom answers.

"He always comes over here. Why can't I go over there for once?"

"Are you sure Mrs. McHugh doesn't mind?"

"No." Zach's mom never makes a big deal about having to turn off certain lamps, but his mom always insists on coming in and making sure before she lets him go inside. *People change light bulbs when they burn out,* she told him when he protested, embarrassed at the big production she was making. *They don't think about it, so we have to.*

"Let's give it a break, buddy," his dad says, reaching for his beer. "This is a bad time for everybody. You boys can hang out later this weekend, okay?"

Later, his parents come and sit with him in the living room as he watches TV. His mom's got a package wrapped in striped paper. Her face is puffy like she's been crying. "Your dad tell you about your birthday present?" she asks, and when he nods, she hands him the package. "This was supposed to go with it."

It's flexible, and light. He shakes it, just to make her smile. His dad says, "What do you think it is?" and he answers, "A football." This is from when he was little and thought every present was a football. His mom's smile deepens to her eyes, and now it looks a little more real.

He tears the paper and pulls out a folded piece of dark fabric, with zippers and long sleeves. "A shirt?" he guesses, but it's not. It's shaped like a sausage. He turns it all around in his hands, then looks at his parents.

"It's a film-loading bag," his dad explains.

His mom leans over. "See, you put the canister of film in here and zip it closed, to keep out the light. You stick your arms through these sleeves so you can unwind the film onto a reel. What do you think? You won't have to send in your film to your teacher. You can develop it at home."

"That's cool." He'd never seen anything like this online. But that's the way his mom is. She's always coming up with ideas.

His dad stands. "Guess I'll turn in. Been a long day. Happy belated birthday, Tyler."

"Thanks."

His dad goes down the hall.

Charlotte's on TV, and so is Owen. Their house is behind them, with its black front door and that wicker rocker on the porch that

Charlotte and his mom sanded one year and painted red flowers all over. The television camera pans over the crowd of reporters shouting questions. Detective Watkins is there, her mouth in a line.

Charlotte wears her hair short and red like fire. Tyler remembers when it was a plain yellow caught back in a barrette. Her mouth tilts up on one side when she smiles, though she's not smiling now; her brown eyes have a downward slant. Her nose is narrow and long. If Tyler looks at each feature separately, they look ordinary, plain. But put together on Charlotte's face, they all work together. She wears lots of gold jewelry, black mascara, and has her toenails painted purple even during the winter when most people wear socks. There are lots of ways in which Charlotte and his mom are different, but that doesn't seem to matter to them. This version of Charlotte doesn't have on any jewelry. Her lashes are pale and her eyes wide, and it's weird how much she looks like Amy.

Now there's the picture Tyler took of Amy, the night she graduated from elementary school and got some attendance medal, right there on the TV screen. His mom and Charlotte put copies up everywhere, he knows, in hopes a passerby might see one and say, *Wait, I know that kid—she's playing in my backyard right now!*

"Where do you think she is, Mom?"

"I don't know." Her voice is a little wobbly. "I wish I did."

"Do you think she ran away?"

His mom hesitates. "Maybe."

Which means *no*. Which means she thinks somebody took Amy, and that something horrible was going to happen to her. Maybe it already has.

The news ends and then a rerun of *The Big Bang Theory* comes on. The guys are looking for dates and end up in a comic-book store. They're talking about coitus, which Tyler knows means sex. He blushes, glances to his mom to see why she hasn't turned the channel, and sees that she's fallen asleep, her head tilted toward her shoulder. Her hand is curled in her lap as if she's holding onto something small and precious.

He reaches for the remote and switches off the television. The whole house is quiet, everyone sleeping but him.

A tube of sunscreen sits on the table beside the door. His mom keeps sunscreen by every door. He squeezes some out and rubs it across his face, the back of his neck, and all over his hands. He slides his socked feet into his sneakers, fits sunglasses to his face, and tugs down the hood of his sweatshirt. He takes his digital camera.

It's a carnival out there, his dad had said, which was supposed to mean something fun, but his voice had been grim. His mom had kept the drapes closed and told Tyler and Melissa they couldn't answer the door, no matter how many times someone knocked. But now the street is empty, all the cars and people gone.

Tyler taps his nose, his right cheek, his left. He can feel the sticky sunscreen beneath his fingers. He has nightmares where he's forgotten a patch, a small square of skin that turns brilliant red and then bursts into flames. His forehead, his chin, and the back of his neck. All systems go.

He's hunkered down in his usual spot when Sophie's downstairs light flashes on. She appears in the window, her hair scraped back and her shoulders gleaming. Her tight black dress makes her waist look tiny, and her neckline is so low that her breasts look as though they could spill right out of her top. He raises his camera and takes a picture, quick, before the blinds snap shut. But they don't close. He takes a second picture, not believing his luck. Still, the blinds remain wide open. She's standing there and she's not moving, not at all. Can she see him, crouched among the bushes at the back of her yard? Is that what has her frozen in place?

No, she's looking *down* at something, not out at him. Crouching, he creeps out from the bushes, goes slow. Still her gaze doesn't lift. Now he can see the silver ridge of a computer monitor over the windowsill. She's staring at the screen, a crease between her eyes. He's so close he could reach out and touch her face, which is smooth and milky white. Her lips are painted shiny red. They look soft and pretty.

She lifts her chin and looks straight at Tyler, sending him stumbling back into the bushes beneath her window. His heart's pounding. She's going to yell. She's going to come right outside and haul him up the street to his house. But her expression doesn't change as she reaches up. An instant later, the blinds shut. She hadn't seen him standing there. He'd gotten lucky.

Dr. Cipriano's house sits in shadow. No lights on in the basement. No lights on in the little shed out back. The lid is lowered on the hot tub by the back door. Dr. Cipriano used to have a friend who lived with him, and he and Dr. Cipriano used to sit in there and talk quietly, so quietly that Tyler never could hear what they were saying. But then Bob moved out.

The woods are alive with rustling noises, the air filled with that wet vegetable smell that's always there after a storm. A bunch of kids are hanging around the swings, talking and laughing. Tyler removes his sunglasses, tugs down his hood. Still, they all stop to stare. Like *he's* the intruder? These are *his* woods, *his* neighborhood. Then he realizes they're thinking of Amy, too.

He follows the path through the woods. Ahead is the little bridge.

This is where the police found Amy's backpack. Amy had been so excited when Charlotte had brought it home for her. *It has a keychain with a little pink teddy bear.* Tyler had thought it sounded lame. *You're going to get beat up,* he'd warned her, but she'd shrugged. *What do you know?* Which is true. What does he know?

He knows it's stupid, people have been searching everywhere, but he turns in a circle, his flashlight beam skittering along the grass and dirt, jumping into the dark spaces between the trees. If the police had been here, they'd left no sign of it. He bends to shine the light up along the curved wooden beams. There's no face looking down at him. What did he expect, that she'd be hanging upside down for a whole day, knowing her mom and everyone else are freaking out?

Crickets chirp all around him. Tyler's never caught one. They always go silent as he sneaks toward them, only to resume the minute he gives up and turns around. It's like they're taunting him, which of course they aren't. Crickets aren't the highest on the insect totem pole, brains-wise. There's a parasite that crawls into a cricket, eats all the food the cricket takes in, and then when it's grown into a worm, releases chemicals that make the cricket jump into a pool of water so the worm can wriggle out and swim away while the cricket drowns.

He follows the path that winds back to his street, past the playground, now empty and silent, and up to his own cul-de-sac, the houses standing around like soldiers. Amy's house is bright, every window shining. He's walking by the new neighbors' house when a woman hisses through the hushed darkness. "Wait!"

He doesn't know that voice, has no idea where it's come from. He stops and looks around.

"Don't move," she warns. He sees her now, sitting on her porch, a pale face and bare arms floating in the darkness. "There's a skunk, right in front of you."

He looks down into the dark shape of the bushes beside him. It's probably the same one he's spotted creeping around the playground. "Man. I almost kicked it."

"We must have grubs. Damn it." Is she upset about the grubs? Or the skunk? "It's the second one I've seen. There must be a family somewhere."

"Yeah. They live in the storm drain."

"No kidding."

She sounds young. He can barely see her, sitting there, just the shadows of her eyes, her mouth, hair that curves to her shoulders. "Are you the babysitter?"

"Hardly."

Does that mean she's the mom? "I'm Tyler. I live next door."

"I know."

Of course she does. His cheeks burn with embarrassment.

"I'm Holly." A baby's wail splits the air. "And there's Christopher, right on cue. It's like he's got a clock inside him."

Tyler knows all about clocks. He feels like he has one inside him, too, booming in his ears. "Shouldn't you get him?"

"He'll stop." She waves a hand. "So I guess you know that little girl, don't you? She's your friend."

No, Amy's just that bratty little kid who follows him everywhere. But how can he tell her that? Holly doesn't say anything about his sunglasses. She doesn't ask why he's wearing jeans and a hooded sweatshirt. "I guess."

"Mark says she's probably a thousand miles away by now."

Then they'd never find her. This isn't something his mom would have told him, or anyone else. No one ever talks to him like this. "Who's Mark?" Mark's wrong. He has to be wrong.

"My husband. He's a cop. Just joined the force, which is why he works the third shift. He has to pay his dues. Which means I have to, too."

"Oh." There's a silence. Is she waiting for him to say something? "Where did you come from?" His mom and Melissa sat in his kitchen and talked, after everyone learned the house next door was going to have a new family living in it. They'd wondered what kinds of jobs they had, whether there would be kids. *They can't be any worse,* Melissa had said, meaning than the old family that had moved out, and he'd agreed. The old family had had two big slobbery dogs they let wander all around the neighborhood.

"Toledo."

He knows kids from Japan, Pakistan, New Mexico, Alaska, but he's never met anyone from Toledo. "That's cool," he says, and she smiles.

"Mommy?" It's a little boy's voice, coming from right on the other side of the screen door.

"Go back to bed, Connor."

"But there's too much noise."

"Sleep in my room."

"I don't know which one it *is*."

"Of course. Of course you don't." She stands, sighs. "I hope they find your friend."

"Thanks."

"Skunk's gone," and then so is she, the door closing softly behind her.

Sure enough, way over in Amy's yard, there's a small white flash of fur.

His mom's still asleep on the couch, but she's moved to stretch out fully on the cushions, her hand beneath her cheek.

"Hi, Mom," he whispers, but she doesn't wake up.

In his room, he turns on his computers. His gamer tag is xpkid1000, which is supposed to be funny. As if there are a thousand XP kids gaming. In the whole world, there's maybe a thousand, total. Dylan's online, and Mustafa. They want to try out Tyler's new game. He picks up his controller. He won't mention his strange new neighbor.

Holly's his discovery.

SUNDAY, AUGUST 31

SUNRISE 6:58 AM

SUNSET 8:07 PM

EVE

At first she doesn't know where she is, then the room swims into focus. She pushes herself up from the sofa cushions. Her neck hurts and her cheek from where it had pressed into rough tweed. The room's dark but has the feel of daytime, that perceptible energy that comes and goes with the sun's arc—the increase of traffic outside, birdsong, the thump of the newspaper landing on the stoop. How long has she lain here, five hours? Six? Tyler had been beside her while they watched TV the evening before, but she's alone now, the television staring blankly at her. The clock below it reads 7:01. Three minutes past the safe zone.

She scrambles to her feet. "Tyler?"

She taps on his door, and when there's no answer, reaches for the key lying above the jamb. When she cracks open the door, she sees him asleep in his own bed, his laptop open beside him. She sighs. Of course he's here. He knows the rules as well as she does. She stands over him and looks down, seeing with relief that the mark on his arm has entirely disappeared. Just like that—a miracle.

She scoops up his jeans and shirts from where they lie in a pile on the floor. David told her what Detective Watkins had said, that the woman had actually treated Tyler like a suspect. They'd been in the kitchen and she'd turned to him in horror. *It doesn't mean anything, Eve,* David had said. *She looks at Tyler and all she sees is a teenage boy who has to stay locked up in his room.* Eve had dropped the soapy sponge in the sink. *Meaning what?* she'd demanded. *That Tyler's not normal?* How could he talk about Tyler like that? How could he be so sanguine? *Calm down,* he'd said. *It doesn't matter what she thinks. Tyler was home with Melissa all night.*

The basement is cool and smells of earth.

She lifts the washing machine lid and drops in the laundry. Here is the water heater, the dehumidifier, the radon system, all thirteen years old. She'd rubbed cotton pads across the baseboards and walls, and sent them in for analysis, also thirteen years ago. She'd sealed and repainted every surface with eco-friendly paint, ordered drapes made of organic fabrics, and thrown away all the detergents and toxic cleaning products. She'd ripped up all the carpets to expose the hardwood floors and polished them by hand to a soft sheen. She'd made this house as safe as she could, when she'd learned how unsafe the rest of the world would be for her child.

Along the far wall stands the bench press they'd gotten Tyler last year, the air hockey table, the pinball machine. Shelves filled with games, including the blocks and magnet toys that Tyler played with when he was little and that Eve can't bring herself to give away. A large workbench with various tools hanging from hooks, a model rocket in various pieces in disarray on the floor. Tyler hasn't been down here in weeks.

And in the corner on the floor, almost finished, is the dollhouse she'd been making for Amy—Amy, who had loved playing with dolls even though she was about to start middle school. Amy, who had wanted to be a mom when she grew up. Eve looks down at the dollhouse, with its cheerful colors and lovely symmetry.

No house is safe.

Charlotte's house stands open, every window bare, just the fragile screen of the storm door between the front hall and the world. The garage door gapes wide, revealing the chaotic interior. Owen was the one who maintained the garage, but since the divorce, the sports equipment and lawn implements have taken over, dropped wherever, leaning in piles. Charlotte said she didn't care. Charlotte said she had enough on her hands raising three kids in a single-parent household.

Eve raps on the doorframe and opens the door. The foyer is warm with early morning sun, the wood golden, dust motes dancing in the air. "Hello?" she calls out, and Charlotte's mother, Gloria, appears around the corner.

"I'm so glad you're here," Gloria says, hugging her. "That detective's on her way over. She might have some news."

Gloria sounds strangely hopeful. "What kind of news?"

"They've gotten a call of suspicious activity in Metro-Dade Park."

Metro-Dade is miles away, north of Columbus. Why would Amy be there? "What does that mean?" Eve asks, following Gloria down the hall to the kitchen.

"Well, I don't know. It could be anything, I suppose. A homeless guy sleeping it off, teenagers building a bonfire."

Charlotte looks up from where she sits at the kitchen table, writing on a pad of paper. "Or Amy. They could have found Amy." Her hair is damp, combed back from her face, her lips chapped. Shadows circle her eyes and Eve realizes this is the very first time she's ever seen her friend without a touch of makeup. It makes Charlotte look vulnerable, and old.

Eve feels old, too. She feels slow-moving and numb.

Robbie's beside Charlotte, leaning back in his chair. He's in jeans and a wrinkled gray T-shirt, a red OSU ball cap slanted on his head. She's never seen him without one, a holdover from when he used to play semi-pro ball. A yellow SpongeBob Band-Aid is wrapped around his thumb. Eve guesses he had opened Charlotte's medicine cabinet and helped himself—this is how comfortably he's shoehorned himself into Charlotte's life. He straightens and gives her a sober nod. "Hey."

It's so easy being with him, Charlotte had confessed when she told Eve she was falling for him. *What you see is what you get.* But was that ever true of anyone?

Charlotte's sister, Felicia, is at the kitchen sink. She comes over to hug Eve. She and Charlotte look alike, the same narrow faces and wide-set eyes, but Felicia's the cooler-headed sister, the one who thinks first, who doesn't give her heart so carelessly away. "Did the reporters give you any trouble?"

Eve shakes her head. "There's no one out there."

"They'll be back," Felicia predicts grimly. She pours a glass of orange juice and sets it before Charlotte. "Drink."

Eve glances at the paper Charlotte has been writing on. *The guy at the bank who gives out lollipops. Hank. The purple-haired woman at Starbucks. Daisy???*

"Remember when Detective Watkins told us that most abductions are by people the child knows?" Charlotte says. "I looked it up, Eve. It's worse than most. It's *ninety-nine* percent. So I figure that if I make a list of every single person that Amy knows, the person who took her has to be on it. Right? I mean, what do we really know about those people who have the haunted house every Halloween?

Or that crossing guard who knows every single kid's name? Is that normal?"

Eve would be on that list. She would be at the very top.

"The police want Charlotte to take a lie detector test," Felicia says.

"What?" They can't suspect Charlotte.

"They say it's standard procedure," Felicia answers.

"They aren't asking Owen to take one," Robbie says.

"You should do it, honey," Gloria says. "Prove that you have nothing to do with this."

"What if she gets a false positive?" Robbie says.

"She won't," Felicia says. "Eve, could you help me bring in my suitcase?"

Eve follows Felicia out to the garage. As soon as the door shuts behind them, Felicia whirls around. Her eyes are narrowed. "Robbie says he was at work, but the bartenders can't swear he was there the whole time," Felicia says. "So where was he?"

"His place is a zoo on Fridays." Charlotte's told her this. *Do you know how much money Robbie makes in a single night?* "They were probably too busy to notice."

"She tell you he wants to move in together? Did she tell you he hacked into her email account, stole her Facebook password?"

Charlotte had been so excited getting ready for her first date with Robbie. She'd bought her first thong, a lacy lavender wisp that she'd pulled with a flourish out of the shiny pink bag. *I'm already dealing with stretch marks. I can't throw panty lines at him, too.*

"He's completely snowed her. He wants to open a joint account, the works. He got here last night and hasn't left, not for one minute. He's not worried about Amy. He's watching Charlotte like a hawk. Why? What's he afraid she's going to do—or say?"

The back door opens. "The police are here," Gloria says, and for a moment Eve's frozen in place. But the police aren't here for her. So she follows Felicia and Gloria back into the house, where Detective Watkins is standing with Charlotte. The detective looks at Eve, unsmiling, her brown eyes flat.

"Was it Amy?" Felicia's voice wobbles, and Charlotte shakes her head. "It was another little girl on a school field trip." She speaks in a monotone. Robbie pulls her toward him, and Charlotte rests her head on his shoulder. It's disconcerting. Owen should be here. Charlotte and Owen, together.

"We're fielding dozens of false alarms," Detective Watkins tells them. "I told your husband that's what would happen if he offered a reward."

"I don't care," Charlotte says. "Whatever it takes. I'm with Owen on this."

"What do we do now?" Gloria asks.

"Now we go over that last day again, minute by minute," Detective Watkins says. "There's got to be something we overlooked, or someone who's not telling us everything they know."

Minute by minute. It doesn't take even that long, Eve knows, for someone's life to change forever.

DAVID

The way he remembers it, Eve had always just sort of been there, part of the larger group he hung out with at college. The six or sometimes seven of them would head downtown and eat Chinese, or at least what passed for Chinese in small-town northern Ohio. They'd bike to the reservoir and stretch out on the grass, fall asleep with the sun full on their faces; spread their books across the library tables and take turns fetching cups of coffee; stay up late and debate things that seemed essential at the time: Did altruism exist? Were people born evil or did circumstance make them that way?

Occasionally, he and Eve would find themselves alone together. They'd start out in a group, but then people would separate and she'd be walking beside him, her elbow bumping his. Or the group would make plans and some would show up late or leave early, and it would be just the two of them at the table. He's not sure when things changed, when he began to look forward to seeing her, when his heart beat a little faster when he did. This has always frustrated Eve, who could recite every detail of their first meeting—what she was wearing, what he was wearing, who else was there, what he said, what she said—but it was all just a blank for him. Eve couldn't understand. *How can you forget the first time you met your wife?* she'd demand, and David would reply, *I would've paid more attention if I'd known we were going to get married.*

David knocks on Tyler's bedroom door. "Hey, buddy," he calls. "You up?"

"Uh huh," comes Tyler's muffled reply.

"I'm headed out to join the search teams. Your mom's at Charlotte's. She'll probably be there all afternoon. Your sister's still asleep."

". . . 'kay."

"The reporters are back, so don't worry if you hear a commotion outside." Tyler can't look out a window to see. David had hated boarding up his son's bedroom windows. It had felt like a punishment, denying his son the simple joy of watching the world. The only alternative would have been to fix up the basement, and Tyler would still have been without windows. "Need anything before I leave?"

"Could you pick me up some photo paper?"

"No problem." As a boy, David had accompanied his father everywhere—to the post office, hardware store, barber, bank. *Shake a person's hand,* his father had instructed. *Look them straight in the eye.* All the small ways his father had shaped and guided him. But David has never had these moments with Tyler. How will his son learn to be a man? Not that that was likely, anyway.

Today's search group includes a number of college students. They call to one another as they straggle along the grassy verge lining the highway. Deeper in the woods are other teams, armed with sticks to push things aside, cell phones, water bottles. The community's rallying around. Surely with all this help someone will turn up some small clue that will lead to Amy.

There's a flurry of excitement when word filters through that Amy's been found in Metro-Dade Park. David finds himself grinning at the man working beside him, a stranger. But on the heels of that good news rushes the bad: it wasn't Amy, but another child who'd strayed away from her mother. Amy's still gone.

It's mid-afternoon before he climbs back into the car. He's tired, and yesterday's sunburn prickles. He starts up the car and pulls out of the parking lot. The streets look normal, just as they always do on sunny weekend afternoons: sprinklers lazily rotating, the air filled with the buzz of lawn mowers and the distant sounds of children playing in the park. It's a disjointed feeling, seeing how normal everything can appear. He pulls off the road and into the small parking lot outside Owen's hardware store.

Paper garlands of American flags droop overhead; the sale tags are bold red stars. Old yellowed linoleum, long rows of shelving. The smell of metal is heavy in the air. There are maybe a couple dozen shoppers, more than David's ever seen before in the place at one time. It's the drama of fear, of the terrible unknown, luring them in.

"Howdy," the man in the front of the store says. His name tag hangs from his smock. *Bud.* "You looking for a grill? We got a great deal going."

"No, but maybe you can help me. My yard's covered with holes." David had noticed them that morning—small depressions dug into the grass too irregularly placed to be from tent poles or soccer cleats. An infestation of some sort.

"Shallow, big as a half-dollar?"

"Exactly."

The man nods. "You got grubs. Those holes are where the skunk's digging them up."

"So we have skunks, too?"

"They'll be gone the first hard frost. What you want is grub bait. Aisle five."

There's someone stocking the shelves in aisle five, a lanky kid in a polyester smock who moves aside to let him pass, and David realizes he knows this particular boy. He's Charlotte and Owen's son, Amy's older brother. "Scott?"

Scott looks up, and recognition dawns. "Oh, hey."

Scott had been the kind of teenager who got into stuff, who skated on the edge. He ran around with a pack of boys armed with air guns, covering the neighborhood with tiny plastic pellets and scaring the crap out of Rosemary when one of them shot her wind chimes into a frenzy. Then it had been potato guns, which packed a hell of a wallop, and then it had been Melissa discovering him smoking weed at the playground. "How are you doing?" David asks.

Scott shrugs. He stares down at the box in his hand. "Do people even use moth balls?"

"Probably not many."

"I didn't think so. I don't know why we have half this stuff in here, anyway." Scott drops the package into the carton at his feet. "I don't even know why we're open today, but Dad says people are counting on us." He looks around. "What people?"

True, the customers don't look like they're buying anything. They're standing around in small groups, eyeing one another and whispering.

"They bothering you?" David asks, and Scott shrugs.

"They don't know who I am. They're not regulars. They're just creepers. There was a reporter here earlier, but Bud wouldn't let him in."

"It's good to have some media attention."

"I guess. My mom posted Amy's picture on some websites. The foundation people told her it was a good idea, but I think it's stupid. I mean, who looks at those things?"

Did putting faces on milk cartons work, or printing them on

those cheap, flimsy postcards that occasionally came in the mail? Every one of those represented someone's heartbreak, someone's terrible desperation, but David can't recall ever once actually focusing on the childish features looking out at him. Eve would have. She would have looked long and hard and committed those faces to memory.

"You never know," David says. "It can't hurt, right? Anything to get the word out. Someone will have seen something."

"Then how come they haven't reported it?"

"The police are getting lots of calls."

"You always hear when kids go missing. But you never hear about them coming home."

Two women are looking over at them curiously. David meets their gaze, and they move on.

"Why Amy?" Scott says. "She's just a little kid."

David knows about terrible odds, about random bolts of lightning that skewer a person in place. "Sometimes things happen for no reason."

"Sure." Scott's twenty, barely a man himself. Amy's only eleven. It feels like a particularly vulnerable age, old enough to comprehend but too young to withstand.

"It's going to be all right." David reaches out to pat Scott on the shoulder, but the boy lurches away. Too late, he remembers Scott doesn't like to be touched. It's one of his many phobias. Eve had tried to persuade Charlotte to get her son some help, but Charlotte hadn't wanted to force Scott to do anything.

"So, you looking for something?"

"Apparently we have grubs." David can't believe he's dealing with holes in his yard when a child is missing. But things still needed to be taken care of. Bills had to be paid, home repairs made. The whole world couldn't just roll to a stop. "I need something organic."

"I don't know if this is organic, but it's what people are using." Scott pulls down a box. As he hands it over, his sleeve rides up, exposing a line of oozing red bumps along the boy's forearm. "Whoa," David says. "That looks painful."

Scott yanks down his sleeve. "Poison ivy. It's everywhere."

David turns onto his street and brakes at the unexpected sight of dozens of vehicles choking the narrow cul-de-sac. Reporters' vans, call letters emblazoned on their sides and antennas protruding from their roofs. The reporters themselves stand in the street, turning in a wave as he edges his own car past. Their shouts punch through the glass.

"Are you a neighbor?"

"How's Charlotte?"

"How does it feel, knowing a kid's gone missing?"

How does it feel? David has watched the news and seen questions like this hurled at survivors and victims. How does it *feel*?

There's a sharp tap on the window, a woman peering in. He knows her. She has looked out from the television screen, reporting on local events at six pm and again at eleven. She's plain-faced, with strong features. He has always liked her serious demeanor, her sincerity, and so he powers down the window. "What's going on?"

"I'm Grace Sheridan, reporting for WCMU. Are you a neighbor, sir?"

He knows who she is. Of course he does. Is there anyone in Columbus who doesn't? "Has something happened?"

"Did you know the missing girl?"

This feels arrow-sharp, her use of *did*, not *do*.

For years, David has been waiting for melanoma to rise up and claim his son. Eve takes Tyler to the dermatologist every three months, the ophthalmologist every six months. She combs through Tyler's hair and shines a flashlight onto his scalp. She has him open wide to check his gums and tongue, searching.

Now, however, evil *has* materialized, slithered out of Friday night's storm to snatch an eleven-year-old girl off her own street. All the terrible things that gnaw at David and Eve since Tyler's diagnosis, that drive them into long, weighted silences and cling to them at night, have been revealed to be illusory. Here, at last, is a real demon with teeth and claws that stalks quiet suburban streets and uses kittens and puppies to prey on the innocence of children. "I have to get home."

"Call me if you'd like to talk." Grace Sheridan holds out a business card. He politely takes it but he longs to shove her back. He presses the button and the glass rolls up, separating the two of them. He's surprised by how fiercely he despises her.

In the gloom of his garage, he drops the business card into the trash can before opening the kitchen door and calling into the house: "Melissa?" *Keep an eye on your daughter,* Detective Watkins had said.

EVE

She walks along the shoulder of the road. She swings her arms and keeps her face relaxed, as if she's simply out for an afternoon stroll. The earth is rutted by Friday's storm; broken branches lie everywhere. The sparse grass is battered and defeated. Cars shoot past, making the skirt of her dress billow and whipping her hair across her mouth. The sun bakes the tops of her shoulders, shines into her eyes, and sends a drop of sweat rolling down her spine. It's a long walk, but she can't take the car. Not yet.

She reaches the bend in the road and slows. Is this where it happened? There aren't any telltale tire marks where she'd slewed her car around. The trees look untouched, no bright scrapes of bark rubbed bare, no flattened sections of muddy berm. There's nothing at all to tell her where to stop, and she keeps her gaze trained on the woods, long shadows stretching across the pavement and into the trees, studying how two birches arch together in a certain way, how the pines sit stolidly in an undulating line. None of it sparks a memory. She's gone almost a mile and is about to give up and turn around, when she sees a branch snapped at knee-level. It matches the cut on her leg. There aren't any threads caught in the splintered wood. There seems to be nothing at all to link her to it, but still. She grips it and twists it free.

The slope is much steeper than she remembers. The darkness had camouflaged its danger. How had she managed to make it all the way down intact? Amy hadn't.

Amy had appeared in front of Eve's car and Eve hadn't had time to stop. She'd struck Amy hard enough to dent her fender and send Amy crashing down through the trees to arrive at the very bottom. Amy was dead by the time Eve reached her. These are the facts. And also this: Eve had left Amy, abandoned her to the dark and pouring rain, and driven away.

Had Amy been conscious as she hurtled down the steep incline to her death? Had she suffered? Children's bodies were so fragile, everything soft and unformed. Little Amy, whom Eve had loved. *Please let it have been quick.*

She concentrates on putting one foot after the other, making sure to step on soggy layers of leaves and tufted grass, places that won't reveal her trespass. Others have been here before her: it's shocking to see the curved ridge of a boot print pressed hard into the muck, another one by some low bushes. But mostly the surface shows the path of Friday night's downpour, the dirt carved deep into rivulets, water standing in pools among tufts of grass and stands of weeds. The air is heavy with moisture. It clogs Eve's throat. It coats her skin.

It's slow going. Her breath rasps in her ears. She startles when a bird shrieks and flies up suddenly a few yards away. How can she explain her presence here? This is not a destination; this is not a place people choose to go. This is a place where they somehow end up.

Trees reach tall into the sky, green, scarlet, orange, bright yellow. Sunlight flashes on the water below. She and the children have explored these woods in the nighttime. Tyler's voice calling, *Here I come, ready or not!*

At last, she reaches the bottom. The sandy ground levels out, the water begins. She picks her way toward the shore. Amy should be right here . . . and yet she's not. The pebbled silt of the riverbank is pocked by soaked leaves and strands of rooted grass. There is no small girl. There is no pink raincoat. Was Eve psychotic? No. An animal must have dragged Amy away. Bile rises up her throat and she clamps her lips tight. She walks all the way to the water's edge and stares down at the placid brown river, at the distant motorboat and the private docks across the way reaching into the water. It all looks so peaceful.

Around the bend lies that old boathouse. Melissa had insisted the place was haunted, so Tyler hid one night, jumped out, and yelled, *Boo!* Melissa had pretended to be surprised, squealing, then chased Tyler around and around. Their laughter comes to her now, in and out through the trees, skipping across the air like a ghostly stone.

Her eyes fill. How is she going to get through this? How can she still be standing, breathing? How can she be thinking of what to make for dinner, whether she's remembered to wash Tyler's jeans? How can she be filling her head with such ordinary things? This is her lot. She has to get through it somehow. She has to.

She will go home and start dinner. She will do another load of laundry. She will hook herself to the things she can do without thinking. She must let the perfect normalcy of them carry her along until she can stand on her own. It's everything else that will be so hard.

She's still holding the broken branch. She throws it high, into the river. It lands a distance away and floats, jagged ends stabbing the air. She watches, willing it to sink into the brown water and disappear, but it sits there, out of reach and resolute.

DAVID

Robbie shows up late that afternoon, the rat-a-tat on the front door summoning David from where he sits on the couch, working at his laptop. He peels back the strip of duct tape covering the peephole, expecting to see another reporter's bland face looking back at him, and instead sees Robbie's dark features. David opens the door. "Hey," he says, shaking Robbie's hand and holding the door wider. Eve's asked David to give the man a chance, so David had nodded at the guy's jokes, listened to his stories about the customers at the bar he owns, but that's as far as it's gotten. They'll never be friendly, not the way it was with Owen. He closes the door behind them and locks it. A conditioned response from when Tyler was young and loved latching and unlatching the front door. "Any news?"

"No, but you'd never know it, the way those reporters are after us. They're calling, looking in the windows, swarming around the car when we pull out. I had to go the back way just to get here. But Charlotte won't let me tell them to buzz off. She says it's a small price to pay to keep Amy in the news."

They're standing awkwardly in the front hall. What does Robbie want? "Offer you a beer?"

"Wish I could, but I told Charlotte I wouldn't be gone long. I just came by to see if Tyler could take a look at my cell phone. The mike's not working."

His son, the neighborhood tech genius. David glances at his watch. "It's almost time for him to come out. Come on in."

They sit in the living room. "How's Charlotte doing?"

"Oh, you know. She's trying to be strong, but the whole thing's so fucked up. I don't know about that police detective who's running the case. Detective Watkins. She's giving Charlotte a real hard time. I don't think she has a clue. What did you think of her?"

Who is Robbie, anyway, but the guy Charlotte's dating? "She seems to know what she's doing. I don't think the fact that we haven't found Amy is a reflection of her inability to do her job."

"She keeps asking Charlotte the same questions over and over. When did she last see Amy? What did they argue about? Like it's going to do any good."

This is the real question, isn't it—does Charlotte know more than she's saying? The mother's always the first suspect. But Charlotte had seemed genuinely worried when David saw her Friday night. She'd been out in the pouring rain, running heedlessly along the side of the road. Unless she'd been running away from something.

"What was Amy doing outside?" David asks.

"Charlotte says she went out to cool off."

"Why leave the porch?"

"Who knows? Probably trying to scare Charlotte."

Who hadn't known her daughter had gone off into the storm. "You ask me, she was lured away." Kittens and puppies.

"Huh." Robbie hunches forward, elbows on his knees, hands knotted together.

"Too bad no one saw anything."

David and Tyler lay the pieces of the grill across the stone pavers. Tyler's wearing his sweatshirt, jeans, socks and shoes. His hands are covered with cotton gloves. It's a beautiful evening and here his son is, hiding from it.

The French door opens behind them, and Eve comes out to join them. She'd dressed quickly that morning, moving from the bed to the closet. How many times has he watched her draw up a zipper, fasten a button? It's been six weeks since they've had sex, and even then it had been quick and passionless. Eve has made no gesture, no comment at all to show she's aware. Does she even miss him? He had thought they'd gained some ground at the airport, the way she had clung to him, but that moment had fizzled into nothingness. Look at the night before, when he'd told her about Detective Watkins's insinuations about Tyler. She wanted him to be upset, too, but what did she think he could do about it, sue the police force? He's been home two days and Eve won't even look at him. It's Amy's disappearance; it's Tyler's birthday. It's everything, balled up into sadness and anxiety and fear.

"Are the reporters still out there?" he asks, and she nods.

"You don't think they'll be there much longer, do you?"

"I hope not." He snaps a burner into the control valve.

"Is Melissa home?"

"She's in her room. She's been there all day."

"Oh." Dark shadows ring her eyes. She sinks into a chair and puts her elbows on the glass table. "What are you two up to?"

"I got us a new grill." Tyler loves grilling, and their old grill was well past its prime. David had imagined that Tyler would enjoy assembling it with him. What kid doesn't like wielding tools and making things work? But Tyler's listless in his help. David's asked him for the wrench and his son only looked at him blankly.

"Wow."

"Yeah, it's got six burners and a warming rack."

"Double wow. I guess we're cooking out tonight?"

"How do hamburgers sound?"

"Great. Burgers sound great. What do you think, Ty?"

"Sure," Tyler says. He's got the instruction sheet spread out and is studying the small print.

"Any news?" David asks, though he already knows the answer. Eve would have said something right away. The energy around her would have been different.

"No." It's clear she doesn't want to talk about Amy. She watches Tyler, her eyes soft with hope. He wishes he could see what she sees. *I don't know how to be the mother of a boy,* she'd confided when they learned she was pregnant with Tyler. It bothered her those last few months. She wandered the aisles of the baby boy clothes in the department stores; she'd pick up a toy truck and put it down again. Then came that early morning when he returned to the maternity ward after phoning his father with the news, to find her propped up in bed, gazing down at their newborn son in her arms. It had been a full minute before she'd even realized he was in the room.

"I see you mowed the lawn," she says.

"Half of it, anyway." He'd gotten lucky. The police detective had emerged from Charlotte's house to issue a statement, and all the reporters had flocked to her. He'd never mowed a lawn so quickly in his life. He'd left swaths of grass untouched. "I'll tackle the backyard tomorrow." This is what they talk about lately, the lawn, the bills, what kind of floral arrangement to send his sister on her birthday. "Did you know we have grubs?"

"No. Is that bad?"

"The skunks will eat them," Tyler says.

"How do you know that?" David asks. Tyler possesses such a

wide and strange assortment of trivia. It saddens him, thinking of what could have been.

Tyler just shrugs.

"There are holes all over the yard." David has spent this day searching the ground in one way or another. "I've looked into it. There's some poison I can spread around, but nothing natural."

Eve never allows weed killers or fertilizers in their yard. She scrubs the counters with baking soda and cleans the toilets with vinegar. She buys organic food. They don't know what could harm Tyler. They don't dare find out.

"We could always tear it up and put in a rock garden," Eve says. "Then Tyler could pretend he's an astronaut landing on the moon."

"I'd rather go to Mars." Tyler pushes himself up. "We need flashlight batteries."

Eve watches him go. "He'd be such a great astronaut," she says dreamily.

David grits his teeth. Tyler isn't going to grow up to be anything at all. "I hate it when you do that."

"Why? It's not as if I say it to him."

"You live in a fantasy world. Tyler's melanoma is going to reappear. It may already have."

"The doctors will treat it."

"What if they don't catch it in time?" And even if they do, there's no guarantee.

"David, why are you doing this?"

Her stubbornness is astounding. "You're the one who talks to the doctors. You're the one who does the research. You know the facts better than I do, so why do you ignore them?"

"What do you want me to do—give up?"

"Of course not. I just want you to be realistic."

"Why is that so important to you? What does it matter what I think?"

"Because all you think about is him."

"Someone has to!"

"Meaning I don't?"

"You couldn't even remember to bring home his birthday present."

"It's just a camera, Eve. Get some fucking perspective."

"You didn't even check him over. He could have been seriously hurt."

So that's what this was about. "But he wasn't."

"But he could have been."

She can never leave anything alone. It always has to be her way. There's never room for anyone else's opinion. "It's always what Tyler wants, what Tyler needs. What about what I want? We don't go to movies. We don't eat in restaurants. We've never gone on a vacation. What about Melissa? Do you think of her at all? Something's wrong with our daughter. Something's really wrong, but you don't have a clue."

"You want me to face the facts?" she hisses. "Well, how about this one? What if that was Tyler's *last* birthday?" Her eyes are blazing, her fists clenched. She looks so self-righteous.

"Did it ever occur to you that work isn't the only reason I stay away?"

Her face goes blank. Then she stands so abruptly her chair topples backward with a crash. The patio's quiet after she leaves, reproachful. He grinds a bolt securely into place.

In two months, they will have their first hard frost. The days will grow shorter, the sun weaker in the sky. Tyler can be up and among them for longer and longer stretches of time. They've grown to love the long dark nights, trudging through the snow, all of them equally covered head-to-toe in wool and fleece. For those few months, they could almost imagine what it feels like to be a normal family. It used to be enough.

MISTER

Got a second? Robbie had said, coming in and sitting down in Tyler's desk chair. He'd spotted the photographs spread across the desk at the same time that Tyler had, picking them up and shuffling through them as he talked. *The mike on my cell keeps cutting off. Can you take a look?* Tyler had watched nervously, his heart pounding. At any second, Robbie was going to stop and stare with a frown. *Dude, were you taking pictures of me?* But then Robbie dropped the photos and leaned back to pull his phone from his pocket. It was an easy fix, just resetting preferences. Robbie would know that. He knew all about phones, so why was he really there? But Robbie left without saying, rapping his knuckles on the desk before standing. *Thanks, dude.* He'd left behind the heavy stink of cologne. Tyler turned the fan on in the bathroom to make it go away.

He raises the cover on the grill. Smoke churns up, blinding him.

He steps back, coughing. It had been torture, trying to put the stupid thing together. His dad had watched every move he made, waiting for him to screw up.

"This lady came into Kroger's today." Zach's voice is tinny, coming over the speaker on Tyler's cell phone. Tyler's got it lying on the metal tray attached to the grill. This thing is monstrous. It could grill a dozen burgers and a dozen pieces of chicken all at the same time, easy. But all it has on it are four small patties. Cheese drips onto the flames, making them sputter. "She said she was a psychic and that she dreamed she saw Amy someplace dark and cold."

"Like where?" Tyler asks. From where he stands on the patio, he can see Holly's house. Lights are on over there. He hears Holly's voice, the slam of a door.

"I don't know. She was talking to the other people in line. What do you think? Do you think she could be right?"

They've watched those shows where psychics talked to people in the audience and made them cry. It seemed pretty real. "Maybe. Like a cave."

"That would suck, man."

Amy's scared of spiders. They used to torture her by dangling plastic spiders from tree branches so she'd run away and leave them alone. It makes Tyler feel bad, remembering this.

"They're putting together special patrols to walk kids to school," Zach says. "They're even going to have parents standing on the street corners."

Tyler hadn't heard anything about that. Why would he have? He wasn't walking to school. He's never walked to school a day in his life. "You scared?"

"No way." But Zach doesn't sound like he means it. "What about you?"

"No." He is, though, a little.

"You want to head over to Alan's later? We're having a brawl."

Alan has every gaming platform they make. There'll be kids sprawled across the floor and couches, drinking pop and wearing headsets. But Tyler knows how it will play out. Everything will be cool until just before dawn, and then the quiet knock on the door. His mom, come to pick him up. The other mom will stand there in her bathrobe and talk as he gets his things together. The whole point of a sleepover is to be awake when everyone else is asleep. With him around, that never happens. Someone's mom always has to stay up.

"Maybe another time," Tyler says, and they hang up.

"Good job," his mom tells him as he comes in with the platter of food.

They eat on the patio, the way they always do when the weather's okay. His mom worries about him getting fresh air. Melissa says there's nothing fresh about the air in Columbus, but his mom tells her it's the principle of the thing.

"How was the mall?" his mom asks Melissa.

"Didn't go."

"I thought you wanted to find something to wear for school."

Melissa's been on the phone with Brittany for weeks, talking about dresses, jeans, shoes. She's like this every year before school starts. "I don't care anymore."

"Oh, honey," his mom says. "Why don't I take you to the mall tomorrow?"

"No." Melissa jabs at her food with a fork, but she doesn't bring it to her mouth. His mom's not eating, either. It's only Tyler and his dad, reaching for the ketchup, spooning beans onto their plates. "Brittany's coming over later."

"It might be tricky." His dad looks up. "With all those reporters out there. Tell her to drive slowly. Or, if you want, I can drop you off at her house."

"Like I'm *three*?"

"You could climb over the fence and go the back way," Tyler suggests, and Melissa looks at him. For a moment, he sees the spark of approval in her eyes.

"You can't go through our neighbors' yard," his mom says.

"They won't mind," Melissa says.

"What about their dog?"

"It's just a stupid little dog. It won't hurt me."

"I'm sure it'll be okay, Eve," his dad says. "They'll understand, given the circumstances."

His mom's face goes still. His dad isn't looking at her, though. They've had another fight, Tyler guesses, probably about him. Their fights usually are. He's heard their voices through his bedroom vent. It's always his name that catches his attention and makes him stop to listen. He's never heard their actual words.

Circumstances is just another word for *Amy, missing*. "What if they never find her?" Tyler asks.

"They will," his dad says.

"But what if they don't?"

"They'll never stop looking," his mom insists.

Yes, but Tyler knows there's a difference between looking and finding.

So that's what Dr. Cipriano's been doing—he's been building a cage.

Tyler crouches by the narrow basement window, peering in around the cobwebs littered with dead leaves and twigs at the room below. Cement floor, beige painted wall, and something new: a box, made of wooden two-by-fours and chicken wire. It's huge, big enough that Tyler could crawl in and stretch out if he wanted to.

Dr. Cipriano comes into view, dragging a big paper bag behind him across the cement floor. He ducks into the cage and shakes out the bag's contents. Tyler squints to see. It looks similar to the straw his dad spreads out to protect new grass.

Dr. Cipriano rolls the empty bag into a tight cylinder. He's talking to someone. Who? Tyler leans close to the glass to see, but whoever it is is around the corner and out of sight.

Holding his camera against his chest, Tyler crabwalks past the stiff branches of the cypress tree that reach out to snag his sweatshirt and yank down his hood, over to the next window. Now he can see the shadow of someone lying there and just the very tip of something pale and narrow—a finger, waving this way and that. The only person Tyler's ever seen in Dr. Cipriano's house was Bob. He doesn't think this is Bob's finger. It's too strangely shaped, for one thing. It's the wrong color, for another. Tyler raises his camera to his eye, but everything goes black. Dr. Cipriano's turned off the light.

Tyler pushes himself up. Next time, he won't stop at Sophie's house first. He'll come directly to Dr. Cipriano's. Sophie's house had been a bust, anyway. Her window was dark and stayed dark the whole time Tyler crouched outside, waiting.

Something's moving over in Albert's yard, something small and determined. It's Albert's cat, Sugar, creeping through the tall grass, the pale tip of her long tail barely visible. She's after something. That would be good—an action shot. Tyler follows her across Albert's yard and stops as she crosses into the Farnhams' yard.

He eyes the small white box perched above the Farnhams' back door. It just sits there, pushing him away. Tyler's old enough now to push back.

The Farnhams' grass is cut short and even, springy beneath his shoes. There are lots of interesting things all around him: a gazebo, a water fountain, a wishing well, a pond with a little statue of a boy with a watering can. Wind chimes dangle from the branches. He ducks to avoid hitting them. Something sparkles in the distance and he fumbles for his flashlight. Then the world around him bursts into brightness.

"Get out of here!"

Tyler drops like a stone. Light's swarming all over him. He shoves his face against wet blades of grass, slides his hands beneath his body. He can't breathe.

"Shoo!" It's Mr. Farnham.

That halogen bulb blasts UV into the air like a laser.

"Leave it alone, Larry," Mrs. Farnham says. "It's not hurting anything."

"There are leash laws, Joan," Mr. Farnham says, and Mrs. Farnham says, "You can't put a cat on a leash."

Light travels 186,282 miles per second. Even The Flash can't outrace it. It's hot on his clothes, swarming through the fibers and down to his skin. Denim's safe, his mom's told him. But there's a hole that he hasn't shown his mom, behind his knee. UV particles are diving into his leg, digging deep. No. He'd feel it. His skin would burn like fire. His skin would bubble into blisters and burst, exposing his insides. He has nightmares about this, his skin peeling away and leaving only blood and muscle and bone behind. He's fooling himself. That's not what happened last Saturday night. He'd been utterly and completely surprised to pull off his shirt that night and find the redness blazing his arm.

"Sir, ma'am!" A new voice, a stranger. "Jason Freed, Seven TV. Do you have a few minutes?"

Go away! Tyler doesn't dare open his mouth. He's hot, steaming hot, sweat prickling his skin.

"This isn't a good time," Mrs. Farnham says. "It's late. We're all upset."

"I understand," Jason Freed says. He sounds closer. "It's a terrible thing when a child goes missing. It impacts the entire community. That's why I'd like to talk with you, get your perspective. It's Larry and Joan Farnham, is that right?"

"How do you know that?" Mrs. Farnham demands.

"It's all right, Joan," Mr. Farnham says. "What do you mean, our perspective?"

"Well, you live right across the street," Jason Freed answers. "You probably know Amy very well."

"We've watched her grow up," Mr. Farnham says.

"From all accounts, she seems like a nice little girl."

"Mischievous, I'd say," Mr. Farnham corrects. "And curious. Always wandering over here, looking for coins in our wishing well, wanting to help me build a goldfish pond. She's very outgoing."

"The police think she was abducted."

"Well, that's the natural conclusion, isn't it?"

"They're looking into the similar disappearance of another little girl in Lancaster. Do you think you could have a serial predator in your neighborhood?"

"What do you mean, a serial predator?" Mrs. Farnham says shrilly. "What little girl?"

Tyler's hood's still up, isn't it, keeping UV particles from sliding down each strand of hair all the way to his scalp?

"She disappeared eighteen months ago."

"I never heard a thing about it!"

"She was initially thought to be a runaway, but now the police are taking a closer look." Jason Freed's nearer now, his voice rolling over Tyler. "There are reports of a red car driving past that little girl's house several times before she disappeared. The police chalked it up to a coincidence, but now they're not so sure."

"A lot of people drive red cars," Mr. Farnham says.

Mr. Farnham has a red car. It sits right in his driveway.

"Sure," Jason Freed agrees. "You say Amy's outgoing?"

"Oh yes. That kid'll talk to anyone and everyone."

"Anyone in particular?"

"Well, she's good friends with the boy who lives at the end of the street."

"Larry, no—"

Tyler doesn't lift his head. He doesn't dare breathe.

"That right? Which house is that?"

He can feel the three of them staring down the street to his house, the slanted roof, the windows hidden behind the bushes his mom insists add one more layer of protection. They can't see inside. They can't *know.*

"How old is he?"

All he'd have to do is look down. Tyler's right there, inches away.

"I know what you're thinking," Mrs. Farnham says. "But it's not that. That boy is sick. He almost never comes out of the house."

"Don't even try to talk to him," Mr. Farnham warns. "His mother's a piranha."

Tyler clutches the grass. He has to clench his jaw from blurting out something.

"She's just trying to protect her son," Mrs. Farnham says.

"It's more than that, and you know it," Mr. Farnham snaps.

"You're right. I wouldn't have any idea what it's like to be a mother."

The screen door slams.

"I guess I'd better go talk to her," Mr. Farnham says. "Good luck with your story."

The screen door bangs shut again.

"Got that?" Jason Freed says, and another voice answers, "Yep." They walk away, their footsteps crunching on gravel.

Will he hear it when the light goes off? He doesn't dare open his eyes to see. He forces himself to lie still. He counts down from thirty. Thirty's a safe number, isn't it? Tyler counts, thirty, twenty-nine, twenty-eight . . . At one, he raises his head.

Everything's dark. It feels so good. He rolls over and over, to the bottom of the Farnhams' yard. He tugs off a glove and yanks up his pants leg, pats his calf. It doesn't feel hot. He presses harder, digging the hard curve of his fingernail into his skin. There's no tingling. He touches his nose, his cheeks.

It's a few seconds before he can stand. By the time he makes it to his own backyard, his legs have stopped shaking. He twists the door handle and hears a little kid yell, "No, no, no!"

Holly's voice comes over the fence. "Don't brush your teeth. See if I care."

Tyler should go inside. He should turn on the bathroom light and check his arms and legs, but he walks over to the fence and peers through the slats. A little boy's crouching on the other side, pushing a toy truck on the wooden planks of the deck. Holly stands over him, her hands on her hips. She's looking right at Tyler.

"You can come over if you want."

His face goes hot, but he undoes the latch of his gate. "Hi."

"What a horrible day. Every time I got the baby down, that damned doorbell rang." Her hair's loose, curly about her face, light-colored, probably blond. He can't tell what color her eyes are. The collar of her dress lies open, revealing smooth skin and the bones of her clavicle. She pulls something from her pocket. A pack of cigarettes? Tyler's never seen a cigarette in real life. No one's allowed to smoke around him, but Holly goes ahead and lights it with a lighter, its tip flaring bright red. She tilts back her head and exhales smoke into the air. It smells, he realizes, but not in a bad way. He takes a tentative sniff, but carefully, so she doesn't notice.

"Excuse me, do you have a minute?" she says, making her voice eager. It's exactly what Jason Freed had said. *"Do you know what happened to little Amy? Aren't you afraid for your own children's safety?"*

Holly doesn't sound afraid. She sounds annoyed, but still he offers her reassurance, telling her what his dad said. "The police will find her."

She looks at him, and he feels a flicker of uncertainty.

"Why don't you tell me the last time you saw Amy Nolan?" she says, her voice slow and firm.

"You sound just like her." If he had his eyes closed, he'd swear it was Detective Watkins standing there instead of Holly.

"I was going to be an actress. I did a couple of commercials, auditioned for some shows."

He can believe it. He can see her fitting right in on TV. His mom says people on TV wear lots of makeup and have people do their hair all the time, even stopping the video camera to make adjustments. People aren't as perfect as they appear in movies, she's told him, or as they do in magazines. But he thinks Holly looks pretty enough. He sneaks a peek at her full mouth. He can't imagine her needing anyone to fix her hair or put makeup on her face. As soon as he has the thought, he blushes, and is glad it's too dark for her to see.

Connor says, "What's that?" He's rocked back on his heels, staring at Tyler.

It comes out *dat.* "A camera."

"Why?"

Why is it a camera? It's not a question that makes sense. Holly's watching him. "It takes pictures." Why is he talking so strangely? It's like he has a washcloth stuffed in his mouth, so that his tongue can't shape the sounds right. "Want to see?"

A nod.

"Want me to take a picture of you?"

Another nod.

Tyler holds up the camera. As the flash goes off, he automatically closes his eyes. Camera bulbs use xenon gas, so he's safe, but he can't help it. When he opens them, Connor's still kneeling, and Holly's blinking.

"See?" He holds out the camera to show them the image in the tiny window.

"He looks like his dad," Holly says. "They both do."

Connor studies the picture for a long moment. "Again, mister."

Tyler's never been called a mister before. It makes him grin.

"Do you mind, Tyler?"

The sound of Holly saying his name gives him a little thrill.

"Sure." She seems to be in no hurry to hustle her kid to bed. Maybe their schedule's turned around, too. At last a family's moved into the neighborhood that's on the same schedule he is.

In his bathroom, he studies his calf, and then his face in the mirror, searching for redness, a soft white blister. But there's nothing. There's just his brown eyes staring back. *His mother's a piranha,* Mr. Farnham had said.

MONDAY, SEPTEMBER 1

SUNRISE 6:59 AM

SUNSET 8:05 PM

EVE

Tyler's dead, gone from her and lying hidden inside the dark wood coffin. Eve can't see him. She can't touch him. She scrabbles at the wood, trying to pry the lid open, but David won't let her. He's grabbing her arms and holding her back, saying, *It's time to let go, Eve.*

She wakes with a start, her heart pounding. That awful dream. She can still feel the hardness of the wood against her fingertips.

David speaks into the predawn stillness. "Can't sleep?"

Sleep is for the righteous. It hangs just out of reach, unattainable. "I had that nightmare again."

"About Tyler?"

She doesn't answer.

"Eve, I'm sorry. I really am. You're a great mother."

"No. You're right. I need to pay more attention to Melissa."

"She understands." He reaches over to pull back a strand of her hair, tucking it behind her ear and baring her face. She wants it hidden. She closes her eyes.

Melissa's always had to understand. *Why can't you come to my play at school? Why can't we visit Grandma and Grandpa?* "I ask so much of her. I always have."

"She's resilient. She's stronger than either of us realizes."

"She lost her childhood, too."

"You've given her a great childhood."

His voice is full of kindness. Hearing it, tears well up in her eyes, slide down her cheeks. She'll never have goodness with him again.

"Shh," he says, moving closer. She lets her head fall against his warm shoulder.

"I'm sorry, too. I know it's hard on you, being away."

He rubs a thumb across her cheek, tilts up her chin. "We'll figure it out."

He is so familiar to her. So dear. He is perfectly replicated in their son. They are joined in this precious way. Together, they have made life, and a family.

"David." She has to know.

"Hmm?" He presses his lips to her temple, lowers his mouth to hers. She kisses him back, wanting him to make her whole again. Human. But she has to know. She has to see where this could all end.

She pulls back half an inch. "What if I die?" *What if I go to jail?*

"You're not going to die." He slides down the strap of her nightgown with gentle fingers, tracing circles across her skin, gooseflesh popping up. He bends closer, cups her breast.

She covers his hand with hers. "Tell me. What would happen?"

"You're just upset. Stop being morbid. You're fine."

She's not fine. She's the furthest thing from fine. How can he look at her and not see that? "How would you manage? Who would take care of Tyler?"

He pulls back and looks down at her. She can't see his face in the darkness. "Jesus. Can't you let it go, just for once?"

She falls silent. They both know the answer.

He rolls away.

The television's on in Charlotte's kitchen, its volume muted. The smell of burned coffee hangs in the air. Charlotte's been up all night again. Her friend hugs her close, smelling of stale air. She's thin and brittle, but her grip is strong. She whispers into Eve's hair, "I'm so glad you're here." A final squeeze and then Charlotte releases her.

Eve turns to the coffeemaker so that Charlotte can't see her face. She rinses out the glass carafe, fills the reservoir with fresh cold water, spoons out the grounds, depresses the START button. Her eyes are dry by the time she pours two cups and brings them to where Charlotte sits, her cell phone on the table in front of her. "Detective Watkins promised she'd call."

"It's still early."

"If I don't hear from her by nine, I'm going down to the station."

They keep their voices low. Gloria and Felicia are asleep upstairs in Scott's old room, while Scott's on the couch in the den. Nikki's in her own bedroom, but she should have been in her dorm room. Robbie's in Charlotte's room, sleeping in her bed, just a few feet above their heads. Everything's unmoored.

"They've stopped monitoring the phone lines," Charlotte says. "Detective Watkins said if there was going to be a ransom demand, we would have heard already. What do you think? Should I insist she set the tap back up?"

Charlotte's skidding down that other path, that terrible one that ends in despair. This is her dear and true friend, and Eve can't—she won't—say one word to spare her. Sorrow fills her, curls sour in her stomach and pushes up her throat. How can she just sit here and do nothing? "She's probably right."

"I don't know. Something's changed. She won't tell me if they've gotten any more tips. She won't even be specific about where they're searching. What does she think I'm going to do, follow them?" Charlotte's eyes are red-rimmed, her nose pink. She snatches a tissue from the box on the table. "It's that damned polygraph. They're trying to pressure me into taking it. They say I'm being uncooperative."

Among all this grit lies a cinder of hope. The police aren't looking at her. Eve despises herself for thinking this. "Maybe Owen knows where they're searching today."

"If he does, he won't tell me. I can't believe the way he's acting, like *I'm* the bad guy. Our daughter's missing and, damn it, I *need* him."

"He's upset. He's afraid. He'll come around. He needs you, too."

"And the kids need us. Nikki can't stop crying and Scott's not taking his medication. He says he is, but . . ." They both know how obvious it is when Scott is off his medication, how frightening and worrisome. "Owen has to talk to him. Owen's the only one Scott will listen to."

"What can I do?"

"Ask David to call him. Would you do that?"

"Of course." Eve clutches at this small thing. She'll ask David to talk to Owen, and in this infinitesimal way, she will have done something good. If she leaned close and spoke softly, described the way the rain had blown across the road in sheets, how she'd only glanced down for an instant, would Charlotte understand? Would she agree to keep it a secret, just between the two of them?

Of course she wouldn't.

Charlotte sucks in a breath. "At least Scott's here, instead of that crummy place of his. Maybe after this he'll move home."

After this. There will never be an *after this.* What does Charlotte think that place looks like? Eve herself can't picture it. She can't look beyond the next hour, as it ticks inexorably past.

A floorboard creaks overhead—someone shifting in bed.

"I can't decide whether or not Nikki should start school." Charlotte rotates her mug between her hands. Her fingernails are bitten down to the quick. Charlotte, who gets a manicure twice a month. "We don't know how long . . . I don't want her to put her plans on hold. She can always come home if I need her. Right?"

This is the pattern, asking each other these questions they can't ask anyone else. They have been each other's safe refuge. "What does Nikki want?"

"To stay home. She says she doesn't even want to talk about college."

Nikki had been so giddy when she got her acceptance letter. She'd run straight to Eve's house with the news.

"I don't want her to leave. I know it's selfish."

"She can defer a semester." As if everything will be better by then. A lie, one of many. They come easier now. They gather velocity and strength.

Footsteps on the stairs and Felicia's there. "I thought I heard voices."

"Did we wake you?" Eve says.

"No. Kyle called. He wanted to know where I'd put Harrison's birth certificate."

"You should go," Charlotte says. "You shouldn't miss Harrison's first day of kindergarten."

"I want to be here. Kyle will take pictures."

Nothing about how tomorrow would have been Amy's first day of middle school. They're all thinking it.

Tyler hasn't said a word about starting high school. He'd been so excited, though, when Melissa started kindergarten. He'd touched all her school supplies, opening and closing the box of colored pencils, twisting the caps off the Magic Markers, sliding his hand into the flaps of the shiny folders. Little did he realize that Melissa starting school would mean the end of their precious routines, all of them synchronized and strong. Little did he understand that watching his big sister go off to school would be the first crack between him and the rest of the world, one that would only widen over time.

Eve holds up the coffee carafe and Felicia nods. Then her gaze shifts.

"Not again," Felicia says, and Eve sees that she's looking at the television. It's a reporter standing in front of Charlotte's house, a man whom Eve had driven past just minutes before.

"Turn it up," Charlotte says, but Felicia shakes her head. "It's more of the same, honey. You don't need to torture yourself by watching it." She extends the remote and switches the television off.

"But there might be news," Charlotte says.

"Then you'll hear it directly from the police." Felicia's voice is firm, and Charlotte sits back. She takes the cup of coffee Eve's poured for her. "I should go out and talk to them. I need to keep Amy in the news."

"You need to be careful," Felicia cautions. "They don't care about you or Amy. They just want the ratings."

"How about Trish Armstrong?" Eve finds herself saying. "She has that noon radio program. She's always been so great about promoting the walkathon. I'm sure she'd be happy to help." Eve's sweating again, hot and cold with it. She wants to go home and be with her family. She wants to sweep the floor and think about what to make for dinner, hear her children call to her from another room.

"Fifty-seven hours," Charlotte says. "Two and a half *days*."

"It's still early," Felicia says.

It's not early. It's been an eternity. They've been trudging through each hour, one by one, the minutes grinding past, piling up at their feet. When will they say that it's too late?

"I can't stand this." Charlotte shoves back her chair and paces. She rakes her hands through her hair. "What the hell is going on? Where is she? Why doesn't she come home? I didn't mean to make her run off. I can't do this. I *can't*."

"You can, and you will," Felicia says. "Eve and I and Mom are here. We'll do this together."

Charlotte stands by the window, her arms crossed. The dawn paints her face in shades of pink and orange. "It's not knowing that's the worst."

"I know."

But sometimes the worst part *is* knowing—having all the ugly, undeniable facts spread out in clear view and not being able to do a damned thing to change any of them.

"Fifty-seven *hours*." Charlotte leans her forehead against the glass. "My God."

"We'll never stop looking," Eve says. At last, a blinding truth.

DAVID

It's a miracle Eve hasn't been pulled over. David's been meaning to attach the registration sticker to her license plate, but one thing or another had kept him from remembering. It's been a month now, and maybe it's the regular sight of the police cars on his street that nudges the item to the top of his to-do list. He crouches by the back of her car and presses the decal into place, rolls up the scrap paper and stands. Eve's parked the car so far in that the fender's touching the wall. The rakes in the corner have fallen and are leaning across the hood. He climbs in and starts the engine, backs the car up a few feet. The rakes slide with a clatter to the floor, and he gets back out to stand them up again. He goes around the car and stops in astonishment. When did *that* happen?

He finds Eve in the laundry room. She holds up a pair of Tyler's jeans to the overhead light, checking for holes. She buys Tyler so much denim clothing that he's told her they should invest in Levi's stock. She slides her hand up through the leg and spreads apart her fingers.

"Look at this." She's found something, a hole, a place where the fabric's worn. He knows she's picturing Tyler suffering a burn, igniting skin cells below the surface that mutate and spread to other organs. "I can't believe Tyler didn't say anything."

She'll patch the fabric on both sides. She'll iron them hard, then pull the material between her hands to make sure they stay put. She'll enjoin Tyler to check his clothes for holes or tears before he puts them on, but it doesn't matter what they do. They could move to Alaska, where the sun barely shines, and live in a cave in the middle of a forest, but eventually the disease would win. It always does. Every time Eve tells David about another XP child whose condition has worsened, a buzzing starts in his ears, blocking her out. He doesn't know how she can do this, stand in front of the inferno and let it scorch her skin.

"I just saw your front bumper," he says. "What on earth did you hit?"

She stiffens, the denim stretched tight, her hand a claw. Then she's rolling up the jeans and setting them aside. "It's the stupidest thing." Is her voice trembling? "I was pulling out of the Giant Eagle gas station and I bumped into the air pump."

"Doesn't look like you bumped it. Looks like you ran into it."

A pause. "Why would I do that?" She reaches for another pair of jeans.

Obviously, that's not what he meant, but what she's saying makes no sense. "The air pump's nowhere near the gas pumps. What happened? Did you swerve to avoid something? Was the ground wet?"

"I don't know. I guess I wasn't paying attention."

But Eve always pays attention. She never exceeds the speed limit. She always comes to a full stop. "How can you not know? The fender's barely hanging on."

"I've had a lot on my mind."

"I know, but you should have told me. I might have been able to take it to the body shop before I left town. When did this happen?" He'd have noticed it when she picked him up at the airport. So sometime afterward?

"Last night."

He thinks. When had she been out?

"I'll take it in." She's pushing laundry into the machine and slamming the door shut.

"Try the place on Sawmill. They'll have to replace the entire fender. See if they can jury-rig something in the meantime."

She stops, her hand on the bottle of detergent. There's a line between her eyes. Her lips are pale, her warm beauty drained away. "They can't fix it right away?"

"They'll have to order parts. Could be a while. Ask if they can give you a loaner car."

"I can't do that."

That's Eve. She wouldn't dream of driving a car without UV films on the glass, but she wouldn't hesitate to drag a fender along the pavement.

"This is going to cost us a fortune. I don't know where we're going to find the money."

"I'm sorry."

"Well, it's not like you did it on purpose. You almost ready? I'll go say good-bye to the kids."

Melissa's in the bathroom, the door closed. The clack of bottles being set on the counter, the muffled whir of a hair dryer. He raps and the dryer silences. "What?"

"I'm heading out," he says. "I'll see you Friday night."

The bathroom door cracks open to reveal his daughter, her face flushed and her wet hair waved back from her forehead, a towel wrapped around her. "Swear?" she says. "Because I have my driver's test Saturday morning."

"Swear."

She pushes past him, traipses down the hall. Just six months before, she'd have thrown her arms around him and held tight. She goes into her room and slams the door.

David knocks on Tyler's door. "I'm heading out. Good luck tomorrow."

"Okay." Tyler's voice comes muffled through the thick wood. "See you."

Tomorrow his son starts high school. Melissa starts her junior year. In two short years, she'll be going off to college. David has to leave for the airport, but how can he? Eve's waiting in the kitchen, and they go out, closing the door behind them.

He's backing the car out of the garage when a man appears by the window and bangs on the glass. Another reporter. "Great," he mutters, braking and rolling down the window. "Sorry, but we're not going to answer any questions about Amy."

"I get that. I was hoping to talk to you about your son."

Tyler?

The guy sticks out his hand. "I'm Jason Freed, with Seven TV. And you're Mr. Lattimore? Mrs. Lattimore?" Another man stands on the steps behind Freed, a heavy camera balanced on his shoulder. He's bald and perspiring. He doesn't look pleased to be out in this heat. Freed's got an insincere smile on his face that makes David wary. "I understand Tyler's fourteen now. How's he doing?"

How does this stranger know anything about his son? David glances at Eve, who's leaning against the door, her face shadowed. Then he remembers the interview Eve had done years before when Tyler was just a toddler. He turns back to Jason Freed. "Why?"

"I'd like to do a profile piece on him, maybe get people interested in his case. You and your wife have a foundation, right? These kinds of stories can really generate a lot of community support."

It's true. That first piece had brought in eleven thousand dollars, money that went directly to helping uninsured XP kids pay for treatment. It had been a drop in the bucket.

"How's Tyler's prognosis now?"

"The same. It's an incurable disease."

"But if you keep Tyler out of the sun . . . ?"

"By the time he was diagnosed, the damage had already been done. It's true for all XP kids."

"I'm sorry. So what's a typical day like for Tyler?"

"David." Eve speaks quietly, her hand on his arm. "We need to go."

David looks at her. "You want to schedule something later?"

"No."

He's surprised. Eve's always willing to talk to anyone in an effort to raise charitable interest in their cause.

Freed leans closer, raises his voice. "Let me talk to Tyler, Mrs. Lattimore. The camera's safe. We won't use a flash."

Eve's fingers dig into David's arm. "Please," she whispers.

"Sorry," David says, and Freed steps back.

Traffic's heavy on the highway, families returning from a long weekend or going home from one. He flips on the turn signal and glances over at Eve. She's looking out the window. This is the way she is, physically present but mentally lost in her own musings. He'd be telling her about something or other, and she'd turn to him and say, *I read an interesting article about vitamin D,* or, *What if we wrote our congressman again?* and he'd realize that she hadn't been listening at all, had been wandering down the twisted, turning paths of saving Tyler.

He wants to reach across this yawning space between them and pull her back. "How does your week look?"

"Charlotte's taking a polygraph tomorrow."

"You're going with her?"

"I would, but it's Tyler's first day."

"He'll be all right." Safe in his room, door locked. "Charlotte needs you, you know. She must be going out of her mind."

A pause, and then she says, "I meant to ask, could you talk to Owen about Scott? Charlotte thinks he's stopped taking his medication."

"Why doesn't she talk to him?"

"She's tried, but he won't talk to her. He says this is all her fault."

"Can you really blame him?" She looks at him, and he lifts his hands from the wheel. "I know that's not fair. Sorry. But I don't want to get in the middle of this." He'd made that mistake before after Owen initiated divorce proceedings. David had met the man for a drink, broached the subject of not abandoning his marriage, and Owen had shaken his head and pushed himself away from the bar. *Thought you'd see my side of things*, he'd said before walking away. At the time, David had. Things had been very clear to him. Charlotte had broken the rules. Owen was the victim. Now he sees the grays, the blurry lines. He understands how loneliness might drive a person to make terrible choices.

Eve looks away.

Another mile passes. They'll reach the airport within minutes. He feels desperate, caught in this hopeless cycle. He doesn't know his wife. He doesn't know his children. "Eve," he says, and she glances at him. "We need to talk about this."

She frowns. "About what?"

"This." He lifts his hands from the wheel, drops them back down. "Us. It's like we're not even married. It's like we're business partners."

"That's horrible! How can you say that?"

She has to feel it, too. "Look, I know you're upset about Amy. We both are. But we need to fix this."

"*You're* the one who took the job in DC."

"I had no choice and you know it. It was either that or go on unemployment. Is that what you want me to do, quit?"

"Of course not."

She saves everything he makes. She wants to be able to afford the latest experimental treatment, to be able to fly Tyler to wherever a possible cure might arise, no matter what corner of the world it's in. Every penny has to be stored away in case a miracle happens. And miracles cost money.

"Something has to give, Eve. I can't do this anymore, live hundreds of miles away. Melissa will be leaving for college soon. And Tyler—"

"Don't."

He feels a rising tide of frustration, and, yes, anger. "Don't what, Eve? Throw your own words back at you?" *What if that was Tyler's last birthday?* "You're letting fear paralyze you. It's destroying our marriage." It's made her shrill. It's made her impossible to be with.

"I don't want to fight, David. We have to work this out. The kids need us."

That's what it always comes down to: what's best for Tyler, what's best for Melissa. Nothing about how she wants this for herself, too. He understands now that that dark thick line that once encircled them has wavered, repositioned itself, and left him standing on one side and Eve on the other.

He looks straight ahead. "You have to stop blaming yourself." This silences her. And into that silence he says, "We both made Tyler. It's on both of us."

They hadn't known they were carriers. They hadn't had any symptoms; they'd never even heard of XP. So they let sunlight filter into the nursery; they took Tyler for walks in his stroller; they played with him on the playground. They did all the normal things parents did with their children, and in that innocent first year, they signed their son's death warrant. Both of them—equally. Together, they've created a doomed child. Together, they've created this unhappy life.

THE BOATHOUSE

The sky's bright pink behind the houses. There's enough light left to see that the grass really is green, the flowers really are pink. It's been a nice day. Tyler feels the truth of that against his face, the backs of his hands, the air there soft and warm. Everything looks relaxed, the leaves hanging from the branches. Sliding the spatula beneath the foil packets of fish, he lifts them up and sets them on the platter. They smell good, buttery and garlicky. He wishes salmon tasted as good as it smelled. His mom makes him eat salmon every week. *It's packed with antioxidants,* she tells him, which is supposed to be a good thing.

The door opens behind him, and he hastily tilts the telescope up. His mom comes out, bringing a basket of bread. "Remember when you had an imaginary friend, and I had to set a place for him every night?"

She's been doing that a lot lately, talking about stuff from when Tyler was a kid. He wishes she would stop. "No." He's not lying. He really doesn't remember.

They sit around the glass table. Fat candles flicker between them, making them look like spooks. His dad's gone, so it's just the three of them. "Hey," his mom says to Melissa. "I see you've gone through your clothes. You sure you want to get rid of so many?"

Melissa doesn't even look up. "Yes."

"But you just bought a lot of them."

"Exactly. So it's my money and I get to decide."

"All right," his mom says slowly. "I'll drop them off the next time I go."

"Good."

His mom sighs and looks at him. "I wanted to tell you that I'm going with Charlotte to the police station tomorrow morning. I won't be long."

Which means he'll be home alone. He knows the rules. No opening his door to anyone. Keep his phone charged and beside him if he needs her. Call 911 if he smells smoke. Make sure his mask is on his nightstand. She always gives him a heads-up before she leaves, and she always answers him the second he texts her, even when he's saying things like, *We need chocolate milk* and *Can I rent a movie?*

He likes the idea of being old enough to be trusted with such a big responsibility, but he worries. What if there is a fire? What if a stranger forces his way inside and surprises him alone in his room? The lock on his door isn't that strong. It's not meant to keep out burglars. But Zach's been allowed to stay home by himself ever since he was eight. "Why do you have to go to the police station?" He wonders which one it is. He's been on Google Earth, zeroed in on a few buildings, but there's nothing to see. Just rooftops and parking lots.

"Oh, it's nothing. Charlotte's taking a polygraph."

He knows what a polygraph is. People are always getting into trouble when they take one on TV. "How come?"

His mom hesitates, which tells him he should pay attention to what she's *not* saying. "They always have to rule out the parents in cases like this."

They think Charlotte did something to Amy? "That's stupid. Moms don't hurt their kids."

Melissa snorts. "Oh, that *never* happens."

"Melissa," his mom warns, but Tyler doesn't want her to make Melissa stop. "On purpose or by accident?" he demands, and his mother looks sad.

"It depends," she says, which is really no answer at all.

For as long as he can remember, his mom's warned him about the path that leads down to the river. She always makes sure to walk between him and where the ground falls off steeply on one side. What if he falls and breaks a bone? Emergency rooms have lots of lights. He'd had to go to one once when he was little and had a high fever. He'd had to wear his facemask and long sleeves and jeans, and he kept trying to rip them off, he was so hot. It had taken two nurses and his mom to hold him down. The doctor had sent him home with a tube in his arm and a nurse had to come to remove it the next day.

On moonlit nights, the stars shine like coins on the surface of the water. During the winter, the water turns white as it freezes. Snow piles up along the banks, and the course of the river is revealed, a crisp, irregular path that cuts between the rocky hillsides. People in Minnesota wait for their lakes to freeze so they can drag little cabins out into the middle where they huddle inside and fish through holes they chop in the ice. Sometimes they miscalculate the depth of the ice and plunge through.

Farther east, the gradient grows shallower, and there's a path that leads between people's houses and down to the water. The river's wider there, and calmer. His mom's figured out a way of taking sidewalks and trails that lead from their house through other neighborhoods—the house covered in ivy they nicknamed the Bush House, the house with stumpy slabs of limestone ranged across the yard like gravestones—and then through the woods to the water. They were both pretty excited the first time they did that and found the old boathouse standing there.

Pine needles slither beneath the soles of his shoes. Crickets chirp all around him; mosquitoes rise up and buzz in his ear. He walks down to the water that sometimes looks gray, sometimes sparkles, but tonight looks flat and dead.

The boathouse squats on the corner, weathered walls and a crumbling roof. But it had been a good hiding place when he was a kid. His mom made him and Melissa wear glow sticks snapped into circles around their necks so she could keep track of them, which defeated the purpose of hide-and-seek. He'd been nine when he'd figured out Melissa was humoring him when she claimed she couldn't find him.

The boathouse has no doors, just doorways and squares cut out as windows. The last time he was here was on the Fourth of July, when he persuaded his mom to let them watch the fireworks across the river from here. They stared up at the dark sky exploding into streamers of light and smoke. Firecrackers are safe. He can watch a million of them, just like everybody else.

His shoes squeak across the damp wooden floor. Cobwebs glimmer in the glow of his flashlight. He takes a photograph of them strung across the rafters, adjusts the shutter and f-stop and takes another. Some of these pictures will be better than others. He leans out through the windows to take shots of the river below. That might be cool, to do a sequence of the water, varied only by the fish swimming past.

The wind shifts and he inhales a rich, acrid odor that scrapes against the roof of his mouth and hollows out his throat. Skunk. He gags.

Where? He looks all around the small space, but it's not in the building with him. It must be somewhere outside. The click of his shutter must have startled it.

He tiptoes to the doorway and searches the shore for the bright white tail, listens for the scratching of its claws on the ground. Leaves rustle in the breeze. It's gone, disappearing into the brush as silently as it had appeared. He takes a few pictures of the shore before heading back home.

A car's turning out of his cul-de-sac and onto the road, the light from its headlights racing across the trees in front of him. He jumps back just in time. Some headlights are safe and others aren't. There's no way to tell which are which. Yoshi's told him that being blind is no big deal. *You get used to it,* she's said, but what good is a photographer who can't see? He waits for the growl of the engine to fade into the distance before stepping out of hiding.

The reporters' vans are still there, so he takes the back way, walking behind Amy's house, stepping over the crumbling logs that line her yard from where the old neighbors kept their firewood.

"Well, hello," someone says, and he freezes, his face red. It's Holly and she's sitting right there on her deck in a folding lawn chair.

"Hi," he says. "Sorry," he adds.

Light shines down from an upstairs window, shining on her head and shoulders, the tops of her legs. He averts his gaze.

"Don't your parents mind you wandering around late at night?" she says.

Is she threatening to tell them? But no, her voice holds no challenge, just mild curiosity. "I can take care of myself," he says.

"I suppose it's different when you're a guy."

Guy, she said. Not *boy.* Is this how she sees him? The thought warms him. What's she doing, sitting out here in the dark by herself? He goes closer, walking across the grass. He thinks she's smiling, but he's not sure.

"So what do you do?" she says. "When you walk around?"

He can't tell her he looks in people's windows. He knows how creepy that sounds. "Take pictures," he says, which is something even Zach doesn't know. *Cool*, Zach would say, but then he'd talk about football practice or the car show or the trip to New Orleans his parents dragged him on.

"Of what?" she says, and she sounds interested.

"Animals, mostly."

"And little boys who don't brush their teeth?"

She's making a joke, wrapping it around the two of them. "Yeah."

"You can pull over a chair, you know. I don't bite."

There are more chairs leaning against the wall. The old neighbors used to have a big glass table with rocking chairs all around it, but it went with them when they moved. He unfolds a chair and sets it up beside Holly, but not too close.

"Want some lemonade?" she says.

"I'm okay." That's the thing about Holly, maybe the thing he likes best. She's never asked him what it felt like to have to hide from the sun, whether he thought about dying, or if he was afraid. She never goes to that place that matters so much to everyone else.

There's a tiny spurt of fire, and he sees she's lit a cigarette. He doesn't mind. He kind of likes the smell of it. "So what do you think?" she says in a voice that tells him she's letting him in on something. "Do you think it's better to have dreams and lose them, or not to have dreams at all?"

He's not sure what kind of dreams she's talking about. He's never heard of anyone losing a dream. Forgetting one, maybe. "I don't know," he says, hearing how lame that sounds, feeling very much like a *boy* and not like a *guy*.

"What about you?" She blows out some smoke that curls around in the air and disappears. "What do you want to do with your life?"

Oh. Those kinds of dreams. His mom's told him that he can grow up to be whatever he wants, but they both know that's impossible. He can never be a lifeguard, never work in an office building. There are so many things he can never be. "A photographer. Or an astronaut." Why not?

"That's a good dream. Maybe I could be an astronaut, too."

Sure. They could both grow up and fly in spaceships.

"I don't know anything about the stars, though," she says. "I don't even know where the Big Dipper is."

"Really?" As soon as he says that, he wishes he could take the word back. It makes it sound like he thinks she's stupid. But she doesn't seem to notice. "I have a telescope. I can show you sometime."

He knows all about stars. He's spent hours studying them through his telescope. At one point he even thought he'd be an astronomer. Space is constantly expanding, stretching galaxies farther and farther apart. And maybe somewhere there's a space for someone like him. "Why would somebody have a cage in their house?"

"Like what kind of cage?"

"A big one."

"A dog, maybe?"

Not a dog.

She sighs. "How did I end up married with two kids?"

His mom gave up her career when he was diagnosed. When Zach's mom went back to work, because she was *going nuts staying at home* and her *brain was rotting,* Tyler asked his mom if she wanted to go back, too, and she gave him a funny look and said, *No way, Jose.* "You must have been a great actress."

She looks at him. Has he said the wrong thing? But her mouth curves into a smile. She taps the ash from the end of her cigarette. "What a sweetie you are."

But Tyler hears her real words. *I see you.*

TUESDAY, SEPTEMBER 2

SUNRISE 7:00 AM

SUNSET 8:03 PM

QUARTER MOON

EVE

Someone's shaking her awake. She opens her eyes and sees a blurry figure bending over her. It's Tyler. She sits up, suddenly alert, heart pounding. "What is it? Are you okay?"

"Owen's here. He wants to talk to you."

"Tell him I'll be right there." The world is fuzzy, black around the edges. She's only slept a few hours, a flimsy sleep, plagued with broken images. She kept jerking awake to the realization that she was forgetting something important, something that required her to sit up and take stock of her surroundings, and it made her tick down the usual list: Tyler, Melissa, David. Each time her mind had stalled with terrible certainty on *Amy*. Amy, who's alone out there somewhere. Amy, who would have returned home if she could.

Owen's in the living room, looking out the window. The drapes are pulled open, and moonshine gleams on the wood, the glass. "Owen?"

He turns. He's haggard, his face sunk in deep folds. He's short and powerfully built, but he's collapsed in on himself. He seems smaller somehow, and the magnetism that radiates from him is gone. He's just a man, not the guy with the booming voice and quick temper. "Sorry to wake you."

"What is it? Have they found her?"

He shakes his head, and she feels the corrosive rush of relief. Every hour that passes pulls the events of that night farther away. With every minute that goes by, people's memories are blurring and evidence is wearing away. But she's not free yet.

"I need to talk to you," he says.

Tyler's hovering in the dining room. He's been gaming, his controller lying on the coffee table, the TV screen frozen on the scene of a soldier running across a burned-out courtyard. "Go to bed, Ty," she tells him gently. "Classes start in a few hours." It used to be when he couldn't sleep, he'd wake her and she'd keep him company. To Owen, she says, "Let's go into the kitchen. I'll put on some coffee."

Coffee would be good. It would clear the fog in her head.

They sit across from each other at the kitchen table. The blinds are open in here, the way they keep them at night. Through the window, she can see the trees in the backyard, the corner of the new neighbors' house. A light burns in an upstairs window. She guesses someone's up with the baby.

"Tell me," he says. "You're Charlotte's best friend. Tell me she isn't mixed up in this."

"No! Of course she's not."

"I want to believe her, but she's lied to me before."

"I know."

"It was going on right under my nose, and I never had a clue."

Charlotte had kept it from Eve, too. But Eve had noticed how

Charlotte and Robbie had angled themselves away from each other at that Christmas party, and she'd known instantly. Until then, Robbie had been just another one of Charlotte's clients, a name Charlotte had mentioned from time to time. Eve had urged Charlotte to talk to Owen. God help her, she'd told Charlotte to confess. Eve had believed there was room in their marriage for honesty, and she'd been wrong. David had been annoyed. He'd warned her to stay out of it. And now . . . he's retreated.

It's like we're not even married, he'd said, and her heart had plummeted down a thousand flights. *Maybe no one's safe. Maybe there's no such thing as a true love that lasts a lifetime.*

Eve finds her voice, reaches for his hand. "She would never hurt Amy. You know that."

"They'd been fighting so much lately. Every day I got inundated with texts and phone calls from Amy, wanting to come live with me."

But Owen wouldn't take her in. "Nikki and Charlotte argued, too. Remember?"

"Little stuff, not like this. This was on a whole new level. Charlotte even locked her out of the house one night. Amy called, crying. She was only outside for a few minutes, but still. You don't do that to a kid."

Eve hadn't known about that.

"It's Robbie," Owen says. "How could she fall for a jerk like that? What does she see in him?"

"Maybe she sees the person she wants to be."

"I don't know her. I have no idea who she is anymore."

She's still holding his hand. They've never touched before other than the brief hugs at the occasional dinner. "She's still the same Charlotte." It's Eve who's changed. Or maybe this is who she is, who she's been all along.

"You make sure she tells the truth today," Owen says. "You hold her to it."

Tyler sits, spooning cereal into his mouth. Melissa sits across from him, holding a glass of juice and texting, her thumbs moving rapidly over the face of her phone. They don't look at each other. They're not talking at all. It's as if they're strangers. This shared grief, never brought out into the open but always lying just beneath the surface.

"You look nice," Eve tells Melissa. She didn't even know her daughter owned a pair of jeans that weren't ripped or a shirt with actual sleeves instead of straps or that hung off the shoulder. Maybe this is a sign her daughter's growing up.

Tyler pushes back his chair and carries his bowl to the sink. He'd been full of the usual questions. *What if the teacher asks a question I don't know the answer to? What if I look like a dork on camera?* This is why she needed to be home. *You couldn't possibly look like a dork,* she'd told him. *And no one knows the answers on the first day of school.*

"I'll be up in a sec," she tells him.

The school bus is due any minute. Eve peels back an inch of drapery fabric, pushes aside the blinds. They're under siege, imprisoned within their own house. But for this brief slice of time, the street is blessedly empty of strange cars. It's a gift, this peace. Jason Freed had stopped them in the driveway, a cameraman right behind him, aiming his camera into their car. Eve huddled against the door and averted her face, but the man had stood only a few feet away. He could have captured her image. Somewhere it could be playing, and someone could be watching. Maybe someone who'd been on the road that stormy night.

"Mom?" Melissa says, impatient.

"All right, you can take the bus. But if the reporters are back this afternoon, I'll come get you."

They go into the garage and close the kitchen door behind them, even though Tyler's in his room.

The garage is cool and dark. Melissa punches the button on the wall. The garage door slowly rolls up, creaking along its tracks. For years, Melissa's left this house—to catch the school bus, climb into a friend's car. Eve feels the weight of all those departures, all those minutes and hours her daughter has been gone from her. *Don't go,* she longs to beg. *Stay with me.*

Pale yellow sun washes across the pavement. Melissa ducks beneath the garage door and straightens her shoulders. She is preparing herself, and Eve loves this small, simple act of courage.

"Have a good day," Eve calls. *Be safe.*

Melissa trudges up the street to the ravine road. She won't tell Eve who sits next to her at lunch. She won't explain why she won't wear braids anymore or whether she's finished her summer reading book. This is normal, right? Melissa's just trying to sort herself out, establish herself apart from her parents. But Tyler had said, *She lies right to your face.* David had said, *Something's wrong with our daughter.* It's Eve who hasn't seen it.

It would be easy to go into Melissa's room and search for clues. Eve's mother would have done it. She believed that a teenager should have no expectation of privacy. Her mother had been disappointed when Eve didn't tell her about David until they were engaged. Eve had been determined to be a different kind of mother. She had told David this when they were expecting Melissa. He had smiled and shaken his head. *We'll still make mistakes,* he'd told her. *They'll just be different ones.*

How is a parent supposed to balance the needs of a healthy child against a fragile one? It can't ever be equal—not the time, nor the resources, nor the hours lying awake in the dark consumed by tangled thoughts—but the love can be exactly the same. The love has always been split precisely down the middle, an effortless divide. Melissa knows this. She must know this.

There are other kids waiting at the corner. They turn as Melissa approaches, and she steps among them.

———

The police station echoes with brightness, doors leading off everywhere, people coming and going. Phones ring. Conversations are cut off in midstream as doors open and close. This could be any office building, anywhere, except for the uniformed officers with their heavy gun belts. They wear their guns so easily. At any moment, they could pull them out and point them at her. *We know what you did.*

She's pinned to her chair. Why had she agreed to this? Charlotte doesn't need her. She's got Gloria and Felicia, Nikki and Scott. But Charlotte had asked, and David had made Eve feel ashamed for hesitating. But she feels her heart banging against her ribs. Charlotte could say something that might unravel everything. She might say something that would make the police stop and take another, harder look at Eve.

"What's taking so long?" Scott says.

"It's only been an hour," Gloria says. "These things take time."

No one asks her how she knows this. It's a platitude, and they all recognize it.

"This is so stupid," Nikki says. She's small and sturdy. She's done gymnastics for years; she wears her makeup like armor. Even the black lines around her eyes are firm and straight. "Why are they wasting their time? Why aren't they looking for Amy?"

"They are," Gloria says. "Everyone's looking for her."

Charlotte's behind a door fifteen feet away. She'd had to go alone. She couldn't take anyone in with her, not even a lawyer. All she had was herself and her version of events.

"What do you think they're talking about?" Nikki asks.

"What do you think?" Scott says.

"This is all my fault," Nikki says. "If I'd been home, I could have caught Amy sneaking out. I would have stopped her."

"News flash," Scott says. "The world doesn't revolve around you."

"I never said it did," Nikki says, tearful.

"Scott, please," Felicia says.

Nikki slumps onto the bench beside Eve, and Eve puts her arm around the girl's shoulders and draws her close. This is the way it's always been: Charlotte's children going in and out of her house, her children going in and out of Charlotte's. She thinks about Tyler, locked alone in his room. So many things could go wrong. During tornado season, when the sky looks the least bit threatening, she never leaves the house.

The door down the corridor opens, and Charlotte emerges. She looks grim but composed. "Least that's over." She ignores the man coming out behind her, with a big black case and a sheaf of papers. Eve doesn't like the watchful look on his face.

"How did it go?" Felicia asks.

"It went," Charlotte says. Her face is shockingly pale. "Come on. I have to get out of here."

Outside, the sun makes Eve squint. Charlotte and her children walk ahead, Felicia with her arm around her sister. Gloria puts her hand on Eve's arm, draws her to walk more slowly beside her. She's in her seventies. She's had a hip replaced. Eve slows down. Charlotte moves farther and farther ahead.

"The police are convinced that Charlotte's covering something up," Gloria says suddenly.

Eve looks at her. Gloria's face is set in weary lines. Her hair is white, softly curled. "It's all those terrible cases you hear about that's making them think that way."

"Yes, and just like all those terrible cases you hear about, Charlotte's the one without an alibi."

"She called the police as soon as she realized Amy was missing."

"No, she didn't. You know as well as I do that she looked around the neighborhood for her first."

"But Amy was always running away."

"It still looks bad."

Surely it was pure disbelief that kept Charlotte from immediately picking up the phone. Any mother would have done the same thing, checked all the usual places first before succumbing to the horror that her child was gone.

"Children don't change much," Gloria says. "I could always tell when Charlotte was hiding something."

"You can't mean . . ." Eve says, horrified.

"I don't know what it is. I just know there's something she's not telling us."

Everyone else is waiting for them by the car. Eve unlocks the doors and they climb in. She drives them home.

The rainbow sticker's been scraped away. The beach towel's gone. Felicia maybe, or Gloria, has done her best. But the CD still protrudes from the player.

Gloria keeps up a determined monologue about all the things they need to do that afternoon: print up more flyers and pass them out, search the online list of predators once again, call the national foundations for missing children. Charlotte sits in the passenger seat, her face turned to watch the buildings roll past, and makes no reply.

The highway's clear, the usual jockeying among drivers for position at the merges. They pass the grocery store and Gloria asks Charlotte if she needs anything, and Charlotte just shakes her head.

Eve struggles to focus on the road. The lanes merge into one another. She has to blink hard to straighten them out again.

There's a teenager out walking a black-and-white dog. A man bikes past, and a mail truck is stopped at a mailbox, the postal carrier reaching into the wooden box. The school playground is noisy with children; the shouts and whoops reach the car as they bump over the speed humps. Felicia rolls up the window to let the car fill with silence again. Eve holds onto the steering wheel, lets it guide her into their cul-de-sac. The reporters are back. Their cars fill this street. Car doors fling open, and the reporters step out, their faces turned toward them. They recognize Charlotte's car. Eve feels a surge of pity and shame, the two waves cresting and dragging her under.

"It's her!"

"Look this way, Charlotte!"

"Can you give us a statement?"

"Faster," Scott urges, low in Eve's ear.

She's drifted to a stop, men and women all around the car, banging on the windows, waving their hands, their mouths moving like hungry fish. "Mrs. Nolan! Charlotte!" Their voices come through the glass. Charlotte stares ahead, her profile carved and still. But her hands clench and unclench the purse straps in her lap.

Eve fumbles for the garage door opener and pushes down hard on the accelerator. The car shoots forward.

Nikki gasps and Scott laughs in Eve's ear. "Good," he hisses.

"You can't come in!" Gloria calls out. She sounds weak, uncertain, every minute of her seventy years. "Go away!"

The car slides beneath the garage door. The antenna twangs against the lip of the door. As soon as they're safely inside, Eve presses the button again and the door descends, inch by inch. She waits for a reporter to scuttle beneath it like a cockroach. But no one does. She switches off the engine, and they all sit, motionless, exhausted.

You live in a fantasy world, David had accused, but he's wrong. She's in hell.

DAVID

The partners call a meeting to announce that Preston's no longer with the firm. Everyone stands around in the conference room, talking in low voices, uneasy. *What happened? Was he sick? Worse—was he fired?*

"That was quick," Renée murmurs to David. He can't help feeling responsible, which is ridiculous. Preston's brought this on himself. The ego of the man, thinking he wouldn't get discovered.

Stan pulls him aside afterward. "Got a minute?"

"Sure."

They go down the hall and Stan closes the door to his office. "So listen," he says. "Preston left behind a real mess. We're trying to unravel just how deep this thing ran, without alarming our clients. We've got a forensic accountant coming in to help, but I wonder if you'd shoulder some of Preston's workload, at least until we can find someone to replace him."

This is exactly the kind of high-profile work that the partners will want to see from someone they're considering having join their ranks. Still, David hesitates. He's already putting in thirteen-hour days. "All right," he says slowly. "Where do you want me to start?"

"The most pressing thing is the cost-benefit analysis Preston was doing of that hospital purchase."

"The one in Connecticut?" David's ambivalent about acquiring a hospital. Their bread-and-butter is hotel management. He knows nothing about the health-care industry.

"We have to act fast. There are a number of other parties sniffing around. Before we get into any sort of bidding war, I need to know where we stand." The phone on Stan's desk rings. Stan reaches for it and pauses. "Tell you what. Why don't you ask Renée to help you?"

"Jeffery's mom is driving me crazy." Renée slides papers into a folder. "She doesn't like the reception hall we picked. She says it's too far for her relatives to drive."

They're in the conference room, surrounded by papers and empty coffee cups. It's late and most people have gone for the day. It's surprising to see how organized and tidy Renée is. He'd never have guessed it from the way she keeps her car. Every time he gets into it, he has to watch where he places his feet. A tube of lip gloss, a magazine or a book, a bundle of flowers wrapped in stiff cellophane and tied with ribbon.

"What does your mom say?" In his experience, it was the mother of the bride who called the shots. Eve's mom had decided everything, from the color of the cummerbund David wore to the wording on the invitations. He'd been happy to hand it all over to her. Eve had been so close to her mother. They were always talking on the phone. They laughed at the same things; they talked in short-hand. But those phone calls have dropped away, like so many other things.

"My mom's terrified of Jeffery's mom." She taps together some papers and extends them. "Did you want to read this?"

"Sure." He's got some business school contacts he's reached out to who have given him some names. It's important to talk to people in the health industry to get their perspective. He's made a few calls and they have appointments for the next day.

"It's not just the reception hall," Renée says. "She doesn't like the menu or the color of my bridesmaids' dresses. They're *my* brides-maids. I can't wait for this whole thing to be over."

It won't end there, though. "When you marry someone, you marry their whole family," he says.

"That's a disturbing thought. Jeffery's brother is a pothead."

He laughs. He glances at the clock. It's after eight o'clock. His family's eating dinner. Eve will have lit the candles on the patio table and be leaning forward in the orange glow to talk with Melissa and Tyler, wanting to know how their first day of school has gone.

There are footsteps outside in the corridor. It's one of the part-ners, his hand lifted in greeting as he strides past. A moment later there's the click of the front door closing. Silence echoes all around them. Still, Renée lowers her voice as she leans forward. "So what do you think? Do you think they're going to press charges against Pres-ton?"

"Probably."

She makes a face. "Poor guy. His wife's a psycho."

"How do you know that?"

"People let all sorts of things drop at happy hour."

David's never around for the office get-togethers. He's always leaving for the airport just as people are congregating by the eleva-tors. They'll wave to him. *C'mon,* they'll call. *One drink.* He always turns them down. "Like what?" he asks.

"Let's see. The guy who fixes the copier has a black belt. Hard to believe, right? Hal's color-blind, which is why he wears such awful ties. Rosalie's pregnant with twins, but that's a secret. She doesn't want her boss to know. Oh, and Stan cheats at golf."

"Stan cheats?"

"Jeffery says so. Of course, Stan would have to cheat, Jeffery's so good at golf. Did you know he always gets a hole in one?"

David's never liked golf, chasing a small white ball around manicured grass. The really hard game is tennis. "Golf's a lot of walking."

"Yeah, well, Jeffery's obsessed."

Figures Jeffery would enjoy something he wouldn't break a sweat doing.

"I wish Jeffery would talk to his mom," Renée says. "I tried giving him the silent treatment, but honestly? I think he enjoyed it."

He and Eve hadn't argued in the days leading up to their wedding. The early years of their marriage had been joyful.

"Do you get along with your mother-in-law?" Renée asks.

"More or less."

She's waiting for more.

"We don't see Eve's parents much," he admits. "They're nervous around Tyler. They're terrified they'll hurt him."

"So your kids don't know their grandparents?"

"They visit on Skype, send cards." Why should he feel guilty divulging this? Women talk about this stuff all the time. He's been horrified by the things Eve's told Charlotte.

"That's too bad. What does Eve do?"

"She's a website designer." She had wanted to go to New York and work for an advertising agency. But, of course, that had never happened.

"That's cool."

"You'd like her." Eve has a way of listening that draws people out. Strangers were always giving her their life stories. He would come home and find the mail truck parked at the curb and the postal carrier in heavy conversation with her. She'd be late returning from running errands because another shopper had sought out her advice or the checkout clerk had had a bad day and wanted to tell her all about it. He was always rescuing her at parties from people who'd buttonholed her in a corner, back when they went to parties.

"Would she like me?"

"Sure," he says, but is it true? Eve might think Renée's too shallow, too easily swayed by what other people think of her. Eve wouldn't appreciate Renée's other qualities, her willingness to laugh at herself or to take risks.

"Maybe I'll meet her someday."

"Next time you're in Columbus." Which is the only way it would work. No one from the office knows Eve or any part of that side of his life. He's standing in two separate worlds, one foot in each city. Just as soon as he arrives in one place, he's getting ready to leave for the other.

"I've never been to Columbus. There are a lot of places I've never been."

"Maybe you'll get the London office." This is something he's yearned for, even while knowing it's impossible, but she shakes her head.

"Jeffery would never go."

"He might change his mind."

"I doubt it."

David understands wanting something and being constrained from getting it. Even if Tyler were perfectly healthy, David doubts Eve would want to transplant the family overseas. She would find it daunting, having to figure out a new culture. Driving on the left side of the road would make her timid. Her courage comes in other ways, other places. Look how she is with the children. She's never flinched once. "Ready to call it a day?" he asks.

Renée begins turning things off, the copier, the coffeemaker David's secretary had set up on the credenza. "How early do you want to start tomorrow?" she asks.

"Want to say seven?" This is how they'll manage, by extending the day on both ends. As soon as David gets home, he'll fire up his laptop and try to catch up on his own workload.

"Deal."

Outside in the hall, waiting for the elevator, she asks, "How long have you been married, David?"

"Almost eighteen years." How is that possible? Almost half his lifetime.

"Wow. What's the secret?"

It's okay for him to share this. He's not violating a confidence. "Sometimes I think it's just inertia."

She gives him a curious look. "It must be hard, living apart."

The elevator arrives and they step inside. He jabs the button for the lobby and the doors close. "We try to make it work."

"But it hasn't?"

Renée's a friend. She's concerned. "It's been tough." He knows that somehow he's crossed a line.

"I'm sorry."

They ride the rest of the way in silence. The doors open to the brightly lit lobby, shining expanses of marble and smoky glass. They step out onto the pavement, into the warmth of the night. Buildings stand tall around them. Restaurants glow with fairy lights. A nearby door opens, releasing a swell of laughter. A bald man stands on the far corner, playing a saxophone that sends liquid notes skyward.

"There's Jeffery," she says, waving to a tall man standing in the doorway of the restaurant across the street. "Want to join us?"

He's not in the mood for Jeffery's company tonight, his politicking and grandstanding. "Maybe another time."

"See you tomorrow."

He watches her dart across the street. The saxophone player salutes her with an appreciative cascade of notes, and she laughs and waves. Renée steps into Jeffery's arms, and they kiss.

He remembers the first time he kissed Eve. They'd been walking back from a movie one night, the green smell of growing things in the air, the moon sitting fat and full in the sky. They'd been talking about the film, trying to decide whether they'd liked it, when suddenly he didn't want to talk about it anymore. He wanted to feel her in his arms, feel the texture of her skin against his, taste her mouth. This girl, nothing else mattered. He'd pulled her toward him and she had come. Her lips had been soft, and they'd kissed for a long time, standing there on that sidewalk as cars drove past and honked, and the trees waved all around them. Until then, he hadn't had any idea how lost he'd been.

Where does that leave him now?

He turns and heads down the street to the Metro.

THE WOLF

"Put it on." Yoshi looks like crap, her face thin and her hands lying still. She looks like Kevin did, when he was so sick. She's not even wearing a hat to cover her bald head. But her smile's the same. "I want to see how it looks."

This is a joke. Yoshi's blind. She always ends their conversations with *See you later!* Which is another joke. "It's on." The mask is on his nightstand in the other room. The mailman had delivered it and his mom had brought it up and watched while he opened it. She'd laughed at the sight: Yoshi had cut the plastic in swirls to look like The Flash.

"Liar."

How can she tell? She's magic, this way. "I will."

She pouts. "You don't like it."

"No, I do." They'd argued about his old mask. He'd told her he never wanted to wear one again and she had told him he had to. *Not if I don't want to,* he'd answered, even though he'd felt like a baby saying it.

When Tyler was seven, Yoshi was ten. She told him XP kids only lived to be twenty. *You're lying,* he'd said, knowing she wasn't. XP kids didn't lie. They were all in the same boat, so they never used fake words to talk about what was going on. *I thought you should know,* she'd said. Anger had boiled over. He'd found his mom in the laundry room. She'd barely had a chance to turn around when he punched her, made his hand a tight, hard ball and smacked her right in the arm. She'd grabbed him, wrapped her arms around him, and held on, rocking him. *Why didn't you tell me?* He was crying so hard he was hiccupping. *It's just a number,* she'd said. *Scientists are finding cures all the time.* All they had to do was wait.

"Yoshi," he says, and scoots closer to the screen and lowers his voice. His mom and sister are downstairs, but he knows how sound travels in this house. "I met a girl."

"Sure you did."

"No, really. I did."

She rolls her eyes, but she's interested. She's always asking if he has a girlfriend. She tells him that he's a real catch and that he shouldn't settle for just anyone. "How?" she asks. "Online dating?"

"Her name is Holly. She just moved in next door."

"Yeah? What's she like?"

It's hard to describe her. "She wants to be an actress."

"She must be pretty."

"She's got blond hair and blue eyes." He's found her on Facebook and studied her profile pic. She has 487 friends, which is more than he has. She's liked a bunch of movies he'd never heard of, and he'd written down the titles. Before he knew it, he'd pressed the ADD FRIEND button.

"What grade is she in?"

"Ninth," he lies. "Same as me."

"Wow. So what makes her so special?"

Another hard question. "She's funny. We can talk about everything."

"Have you kissed her?"

He blushes, hot. "Not yet."

"You better hurry. Girls like boys to make the first move."

"Okay."

"But no tongue. That's gross." She sighs and lies back against her pillows. "I have to go. I'm tired."

"I really like my mask," he says, but she's already turned off her computer. She didn't even sign off in her usual way.

Below, he hears the knocking on the front door and, a moment later, his mom's pleased voice. Then someone's pounding up the stairs to his room. "Dude! Let me in!"

"Hold on." Tyler unlatches his bedroom door and goes into his bathroom. Zach's the only friend who's allowed to come into Tyler's room when it's still daylight. Tyler had had to beg his mom, and the first few times she'd stood outside the door and watched to make sure.

"Okay," Tyler calls out, and he hears his bedroom door open and close. Then Zach raps sharply on the bathroom door and Tyler comes out.

Zach's wandering around, looking at Tyler's pictures. "Did you know Grace Sheridan's outside your house?"

Tyler shrugs. Grace Sheridan had to be somewhere, didn't she? "You got your hair cut," he says. Shaved short so that it's only bristles. It looks cool. When they were kids, Zach brought over his brother's clippers and cut Tyler's hair for him. Tyler's mom had come into the bathroom and stared at Tyler's hair lying all over the floor. She'd looked like she was going to cry, but all she said was *Here, Zach. Why don't you let me even it out?* But that was the last time Tyler had short hair.

"Football," Zach says with a shrug.

Zach's mom is downstairs, talking to Tyler's mom, their polite voices drifting up, the clip-clop of their shoes going down the hall and into the kitchen.

"You figure out your locker okay?" This had been a big deal to Zach. He'd freaked about it all summer.

"Yeah, no problem." Zach reaches for Tyler's guitar, tightens the strings. "What about you? How was Drago?"

"We have to do all the practice problems at the end of the chapter."

"Told you she was lame." Zach plays a few chords. He's really good at guitar. He can play bass, too, and he's written songs. When they were in middle school, they thought they'd be in a band together.

"Who's in your homeroom?"

"Brian, Alan P. That dick, Gary."

"Sucks." Tyler's homeroom teacher never turned on Skype, so he doesn't know who's in his homeroom. Maybe it's not important.

"I almost missed the bus this morning. It came early. My mom was so pissed. She had to run after it." Zach laughs. "You should have seen her, waving her arms like a total dweeb."

That's another thing Zach's been worried about, where to sit on the school bus. Only the dumbasses sit in the front rows and Zach had been worried that by the time he boarded, all the good seats would have been claimed. But Zach sounds okay. In fact, Zach sounds pretty happy.

Zach strums a few notes, playing a song Tyler doesn't recognize. "We had a special assembly today about stranger danger."

"No one told me about it."

"Oh. Probably because you don't need to know that stuff." Zach holds out the guitar. "Hey, man, you mind if I borrow this for a little while? Savannah wants to learn to play."

"Sure."

"That's cool. Thanks."

"Zach?" It's Mrs. McHugh, calling up the stairs. "You ready, honey?"

"Dang," Zach says. "I got to go. I got a ton of homework."

Which they used to do together but can't anymore because they're in different classes.

After Zach leaves, Tyler lies down on his bed. The tiny red light glows from his laptop, swelling and shrinking, swelling and shrinking, like it's sucking on a straw. One day it will burp right in his face. He rolls onto his back.

Melissa's not home yet. He wonders what she's doing.

She could come into a room behind Tyler, and he'd know she was there, just by the change in the air. He could be in his room and hear the garage door go up and know she was home by the footsteps going to the refrigerator, to the kitchen table, down the hall to her room. They used to play a game: she'd take a picture with her cell phone, way up close, so that he'd have to work to figure it out. *Brittany's nose?* he'd guess. *A jar of marshmallow creme?* It always made her laugh. She used to laugh all the time.

But something's happened to her. She no longer charges into a room. She shields her laptop from him, holds her cell phone close so he can't read her texts, keeps her bedroom door closed.

Everyone's changing but him.

Tuesday is Albert and Rosemary's anniversary, his mom had explained, *and Albert shouldn't be alone. So I've invited him for dinner.* That had been last week, but Tyler can tell by the blank look on his mom's face when Albert knocks on the door that evening that she'd forgotten all about it. "Oh, Albert," she says. "I'm so glad you're here. You can help me interrogate the kids about their first day of school." She smiles at him, and while he's opening the bottle of wine he brought, she quickly sets another place mat on the table outside.

"So," his mom says, when they're all seated. "How was your day? Tell us everything."

"Fan*tas*tic," Melissa says.

"No, no," his mom says. She's holding the glass of wine that Albert poured for her. It glows ruby red in the candlelight. "We want specifics, don't we, Albert? Did you like your teachers? Do you like your classes? What are the other kids like?"

She's always careful to ask questions like these, the general ones that he can answer, too. But he's heard her talk to Melissa differently, when it's just the two of them and she doesn't know he can hear. *Who did you have lunch with?* she'd ask. Or, *Do you want to try out for band?*

"What do you want me to say?" Melissa says. "That I had a great day? That I learned a lot? Well, I didn't, okay? My day sucked." She shoves back her chair so hard she bumps the table and makes the milk in Tyler's glass slosh. After she's gone, there's a small silence.

"I'm sorry, Albert," his mom says.

"Ah, Eve. Don't you worry about me. I remember what teenagers are like."

His mom seems so sad. "My day was okay," Tyler says, to distract her. Though it took a while for his math teacher to get the visual going. His American history teacher talked to the board as she wrote, and Tyler knows he missed a bunch of things. There had been a sickening moment when his LA teacher called his name during roll and couldn't hear his response, so Tyler had to shout *Here,* just as the classroom fell silent. There had been a few giggles.

"Oh, honey, I'm so glad. What about your photography teacher? Did you like him?"

"I guess." The dude didn't look at Tyler once. Everything jiggled as he carried the laptop around to show everyone the studio and film-developing closet. The darkroom was the worst. All Tyler could see in there was a weird red glow, and people kept turning the water on and off.

"Rosemary would be happy to know you're taking photography." Albert's smiling. "She always said you had real talent."

Rosemary had given Tyler his first camera, an old Polaroid she'd discovered in a drawer. *Let's see if it works,* and they'd walked all around her house, taking pictures of the most ordinary things—the flowers standing in a glass vase, the cookies laid out to cool on the baking rack. Tyler had watched the white film darken and take on colors and shapes, and he had felt something change inside him.

His mom's looking at him. "So everything worked out?"

What does she want him to say, that this was a big day, a day like no other? It hadn't been that way. It had been an average day, filled with average things. It had, in fact, been less than that. "He said he'll show me how to use my film-developing bag," he offers, and this seems to be the right thing to say. She sits up a little straighter. She turns to Albert.

"How's Sugar doing?" she asks, and Albert brightens. "Oh, she's become a real hunter. You should see what she brings home."

Later, Tyler's on the patio looking through his telescope. His mom and Albert sit in the kitchen behind him. They can't see him, so he tilts the telescope down. The first time Tyler used his telescope, his dad warned him to keep it focused on the sky. It only made Tyler wonder what would happen if he didn't. So when his dad went inside, Tyler lowered the telescope and the house all the way behind theirs had leaped into view. There had been a family there eating dinner. Nothing interesting until the mom and dad got up and left the table and the older brother had punched the little brother in the arm. That was the first time that Tyler had realized there were things to see in people's windows, but only when they didn't know someone was looking.

Holly's house is dark, everything impenetrable, gray on gray. Is she even home? "I miss Rosemary," Albert says softly.

"Oh, Albert. I know you do. She was a wonderful person."

"I loved her. I loved her so much."

"I know you did."

"You think I made the wrong choice?"

"I think you made the brave choice."

"I couldn't say no to her. I'd have done anything for her."

"I know."

"She was in so much pain."

"It was terrible. She wasn't herself."

"I just miss her."

"We all do."

Is Albert *crying*? He risks a glance behind him, but Albert has his back to him. All Tyler can see is the wavering line of Albert's shoulders and the thin hair combed across his head. His mom sees him and her expression changes. He puts a blank look on his face, letting her know that he didn't hear anything. Her face clears and she stands to put the kettle on.

He's up in his room, printing out his pictures, the stiff piece of paper slowly scrolling up, revealing Holly's face inch by inch, when his mom raps on the doorframe. "Hey, Ty. You brushed up?"

He yanks the photograph from the printer and slides it into his desk drawer. "Uh huh."

"It was nice to see Albert, wasn't it?"

The next photographs are sliding up, the ones he took the night before. He can't stop them now. The paper will get jammed and then his mom will want to help unstick it. She'll see all his pictures and look at him with a puzzled frown. *When did you take these?* she'll say.

"Maybe we should ask him to come every Tuesday night. What do you think?" She's looking through his old pictures, the ones he took over the summer. He keeps the secret ones in his bottom desk drawer. "These are wonderful, honey. You should show these to your teacher. I'm sure he'd love to see them."

He doesn't answer. He's staring at the picture that's rolling up from the printer.

"Your dad told me that Detective Watkins talked to you the

other day. I don't want you to worry about anything she said. It doesn't mean anything, okay? You know your dad and I will protect you."

It's the shot he took leaning out the window of the boathouse, the one aimed down into the water. There's something there, something that doesn't belong.

"Ty?"

His mom's right behind him, looking over his shoulder. He moves in front of the printer. He can't tell her. It would be the end of Holly. "I'm out of sunscreen." This will make her leave fast.

"Oh no. Are you sure?" She goes right to the bathroom and he hears the cabinet open. "You've got one tube left," she says, coming back into his room. "I don't know how I lost track. I'll order some more right away."

"Okay."

She reaches up to brush back his hair. "Love you."

Go, go, go. "Love you, too." He shuts his bedroom door behind her, trying not to slam it. She's standing on the other side, waiting to hear the lock click, and so he does this, grabbing the metal latch and twisting it hard.

It's after midnight before he hears the television go silent downstairs.

A quarter moon hangs above the treetops, precisely cut and glowing, looking like a decal someone had flung up there that had stuck. He pedals hard down the path.

The headlamp on his handlebars lights up a branch lying across the path, and he swerves to avoid it. His tires hiss against the asphalt. The trees stand tall all around him. The sound of his own hard breathing is the only thing he hears. The trees break apart and there's the big flat river. The path ends in pebbles.

Now that he's here, he's scared. One o'clock in the morning. The dead of night. The expression had confused him the first time he read it. He'd corrected it aloud to his mother: The alive of night. She had looked at him with such love that he'd felt it shine all the way through his skin and into his bones.

He leans his bike against a tree and crunches across the shore toward the boathouse. The boards creak beneath his shoes. He won't think about what's waiting for him. He'll just do it. He switches on the flashlight. Cobwebs leap out at him, the brown-gray planks. An insect swoops out of nowhere and he rears back. Then it's gone. He leans out the window to aim the flashlight beam into the yellow-brown water. The light jitters over a cloud of small insects hovering above the water, shines on the dark shape of a moving fish. So it had been a shadowy trick, the light slanting in a certain way and making things seem real that aren't.

Then something thin and pale drifts out into the water below, curls a little, then retracts, vanishing from view.

He stares, not wanting to see it, but seeing it nonetheless. He waits, and it reappears. Strands of long golden hair, Amy's hair, sweeping back and forth with the rolling current of the river.

Miles away, but really only two, there's a gas station. He knows what these are. He's seen them on TV. He's been in the car when his mom's refueled, huddled under his blanket, heard the clatter of the gas cap being twisted off, smelled the pungent reek of gas. He tells himself he'll recognize the line of pumps and the building standing behind them. It will all feel familiar. He follows the pulsing dot on Google Maps that represents his halting progress as he pedals to the second dot. When the two dots merge, he looks up.

It's a big building, all glass and light. Structures arch beside it, underneath a bright blue roof. Cars whiz past. This is a big road. He's never crossed a road this big before.

He stands back among the trees, well back. He's clammy with sweat. Nothing about this feels familiar. Nothing about this is right.

So many cars, their headlights carving out tunnels of light. He wants to turn around and go home, wake his mom up and tell her everything. But he's not a little kid anymore.

The phone booth is tucked along the side of the building. But there are cars everywhere. The building has big windows. It glows with light. It throbs with it. He doesn't have his meter with him. He can't get near it. This is what happened to Yoshi. She knocked her mask aside as she reached up for something and now she's sick.

Everything has a rhythm, a rise and fall. The sun, the moon, the tides, the school bus, even the reporters on his street. So he counts, cars coming from one direction, cars coming from the other. He loses track and counts again, sticking out his fingers one by one. All he needs is one Tyler-size space.

He finds one and marks it. He tells himself to be patient, that it will come again. The second time it shows up, he's across the street, running hard and not stopping to look. He's on the grassy stretch and around the side of the building when headlights bounce on the wall in front of him. He feels the heat sweep across his shoulder blades. The door opens, releasing a blast of music. The door slams. Will the driver come over to investigate? No, the footsteps crunch away.

He fumbles the receiver off the hook and presses 911 with his gloved fingers.

"Nine-one-one. Please state your emergency."

Maybe he's wrong about what he'd seen. Maybe it had been pale grass growing in the mud.

"Please speak up, sir."

"Amy." He mumbles, pitches his voice low. He'll growl the words to this stranger on the other end. "That girl who's missing? She's in the Scioto. She's trapped under the boathouse."

He bangs the receiver onto the hook. His heart is an animal.

Amy hadn't been afraid of the wolf, but the wolf had gotten her anyway.

WEDNESDAY, SEPTEMBER 3

SUNRISE 7:01 AM

SUNSET 8:02 PM

EVE

Tyler's quiet, his head bowed as he stares at the laptop opened in front of him on the cool, dark patio. *No,* he mumbles when she asks if he needs her to pick anything up for his photography class. *No,* when she offers to stop by the library and pick him up some more books. *I don't care,* when she suggests switching sunscreen brands to one that Dante's mom recommended. He just shakes his head when she suggests taking a walk. His toast sits untouched on the plate, his hot chocolate cooling in the mug. Her misery seeps through this house, infecting everyone in its path.

The chairs are damp with dew. Mosquitoes hover. "We should get a screened tent." Eve swats away an insect, searching for a bright jewel, something to make her son smile or look intrigued.

Melissa's not talking, either. She'd closeted herself in her room with Brittany the afternoon before, where they'd talked in low voices and stopped when Eve rapped on the door to offer them a snack. *No, thanks, Mrs. Lattimore,* Brittany had called out, leaving Eve to wonder what was keeping her own daughter from replying.

"Did you do your homework?" Eve asks.

"Yeah." He doesn't look at her.

Her children are unhappy, and Eve needs to reassure them. She's always found the words before and been rewarded with a hug or a quick smile, but now she falters. She doesn't trust herself to say the right thing. She glances at her watch and sees with cowardly relief that dawn's twelve brief minutes away. "It's time."

Without a word, he scrapes back his chair.

"I'll be up in a minute," she tells him.

Melissa's in the kitchen, her long hair falling forward as she bends to fit things in her backpack.

"What do you want for breakfast, sweetheart?" Eve asks, going to the pantry.

"I'm not hungry." Melissa taps papers together on the kitchen counter. "Did you sign these?"

"You have to eat something." Eve scans the bare shelves. When was the last time she went shopping?

"I'll get a demerit if you don't sign."

She takes the pen her daughter proffers. "Where?" she asks, and Melissa stabs the bottom of the topmost sheet. She skims the contents—all the rules about using the Internet at school—and Melissa groans. "Mom."

So Eve signs her name, over and over, while Melissa waits impatiently. Her daughter hasn't said a word about Amy, not a single word. "Is there anything you want to talk about?"

"I'm fine."

Of course she's not fine. "Let me find someone you can talk to. I'll call around, find someone who's cool—"

Melissa takes the papers. "Like you did for Tyler? No, thanks."

"Well, what about your guidance counselor? I'm sure she'd have some good advice."

"Mom, really? All she'd want to talk about is Tyler. What does it feel like for *me*? Do I feel *cheated*? Have I ever *cut* or used *drugs*? Do I feel pressure to be *perfect*, to make up for everything?"

The XP moms all talk about this. Their warnings go round and round. "Honey—" Eve begins.

"You want to know what I really feel? Do you?" Melissa zips her backpack and stands. "I wish it was *me* who was sick."

Where is this coming from? "Melissa," Eve says, horrified. "Don't say that."

"Why? Because if it was true, you wouldn't have had Tyler?"

This is true. This is absolutely, devastatingly true.

Melissa has a look of twisted triumph on her face. "I have to go. Perfect children aren't late for school." She wrenches herself from Eve's grasp and stumbles away, slamming the kitchen door behind her.

The mechanic hadn't even looked at her as he tapped computer keys. *Saturday,* he'd pronounced, scribbling the date on a piece of paper and pushing it across the counter toward her, *and that's rushing it.* Something had broken in her. She'd just stood there, not moving. *Lady, are you all right?* he'd asked, and she couldn't even answer. If she opened her mouth, she'd start telling him everything. It would burst out of her and she'd never see Tyler again. *Tell you what,* he'd said. *Have a seat. I'll see what I can do.*

What he'd done was perform magic, in six hours. Eve had sat in the waiting room, thick with the smell of rubber and oil, watching without seeing the small television set in the corner. The mechanic had kept coming out to check on her. *Go get something to eat,* he'd said. *I'll call you when it's ready.* But she knew that if she moved a muscle, the magic would stop, so she sat there, as the phone rang and the TV played on, and finally, the car was ready.

Even before she turns onto her cul-de-sac, she knows something's happened. There are media vans parked along the shoulder, still more thronging her street. She drives slowly, her fender new and shining. No one looks at it. They're all staring at Charlotte's house. She pulls her car all the way into the garage and goes back out again, into the crush of reporters. She pushes her way through them. Felicia opens the door the instant Eve knocks. "I'm so glad you're here."

"What is it?" Eve steps into the foyer, and Felicia slams the door. Charlotte and Gloria stand by the window, looking out. "What happened?"

"The police called. Someone reported finding a body."

Eve feels the wall bump her back. She doesn't want to know. Once the words are said, they can't be unsaid. "Amy?" she manages. The word slips out, oily.

"They won't tell us," Gloria says.

"It isn't," Charlotte says. "I'd know it. I'd feel it somehow."

"Of course you would," Gloria says.

"Come away from the window, Charlotte." Felicia says it softly. "You don't want your picture showing up on the news."

"I don't care." Charlotte's gripping the window frame, staring out at the reporters who aim their cameras and wave their arms.

"Eve, take Charlotte outside," Gloria says. "Felicia and I will answer the phone if it rings."

Charlotte shakes her head, but Felicia looks pleadingly at Eve.

"Come on," Eve cajoles. "Keep me company." And Charlotte allows herself to be led across the kitchen and out the back door.

It's hot outside, unyielding. The chairs stand around the glass-topped table as if they'd been pushed out in haste. The broad umbrella stands furled. There is no refuge.

Eve has spent hours here, days, weeks. She knows the seasons of this yard, how fog collects in winter, and every spring one azalea bush blooms a discordant red among the pink. The only constant is Amy's old baby swing hanging straight from the tall oak, its blue plastic seat like a cup, grayed with age, the safety bar dangling askew from the rope.

Charlotte paces barefoot. "Why haven't they called?"

"They will. They know you're waiting."

"How hard can it be to confirm? They should know right away." It's impossible to think about the reasons why. "It's not Amy. It can't be. It's just another false alarm." Charlotte steps off the patio and onto the grass.

This is a mistake, being here instead of home with Tyler. The police will be showing up. They will have news. They might know something. Eve could be trapped here. She might not be able to get home.

Charlotte wanders among her flowers, orange helenium, purple verbena, pink resurrection lilies, white phlox, yellow roses. She grows sturdy, colorful varieties, cuts them and arranges them in glass vases, and takes them to the open houses she holds. *Flowers can make a sale,* she says. As long as Eve's known her, Charlotte has brought by flowers. In winter, it's pine and holly twined around white candles.

Eve joins Charlotte at the back gate. They look out at the yards of people they don't know. Meandering between these yards is their walking path. This is where Charlotte told Eve about the terrible night that Owen moved out. This is where Eve told Charlotte about her miscarriage, the baby conceived before they knew. This path crosses the road and leads down to the river, steep in places. They have always been careful following this path.

"I keep thinking of the last thing I told her," Charlotte says in a low voice.

"Don't," Eve says, but Charlotte goes on.

"'Go to your room,' I said. 'I don't want to see you right now.' That's what I told her. I told her to get out of my sight."

"Everyone loses their temper."

"Not you. I've never once heard you raise your voice."

"My situation's different."

"Tell me something happy. You must have something."

The truth. Eve has the truth, which is so sad and so terrible that words can't contain it. She looks off into the trees. She makes a decision. "I've heard from Dr. Abernathy."

"From Hopkins?"

This is the sort of friend Charlotte is, that she would remember that. The trees and sky blur, a wash of blue and green and black. "He thinks he might be onto something."

"Really? Like what?"

"A cream containing the enzyme Tyler's missing."

"So he'd use it like sunscreen?"

"Exactly."

"So, wait. Is this a cure?"

"It could be."

Charlotte stares with wide eyes. Pink touches her cheeks. Then she throws her arms around Eve, pulls her close. She is so slight in Eve's arms, skeletal. "Oh, honey, why didn't you tell me? This is wonderful news. What does David say?"

"I haven't told him yet." David's lost hope. Or maybe he never had any to begin with. It only makes Eve more determined to keep it.

"Did you get Tyler's name on the list?"

"It's too early."

"This will be the one! I know it."

"Charlotte?"

They turn at the sound of Gloria's voice. She's standing in the kitchen doorway, her hand on the frame. Detective Watkins stands beside her, sympathy radiating from every inch of her, the softness in her eyes, the way she tilts her head. "Mrs. Nolan," she says, and Charlotte moans and clutches at Eve's arm. "I'm sorry to inform you that we've recovered a body in the river. We need you to come down and make the positive identification."

Amy had been in the river, twisting downstream until she slid beneath that old boathouse, and her hair had snared on the piling. Another storm could have come along and swept her away, but it hadn't. Her hair could have eventually pulled free and let her loose among the river currents. But that hadn't happened, either. Amy had been floating while they all waited, a mere mile away.

Don't leave me, Charlotte begs, and so Eve gets into the back of Detective Watkins's police car. Charlotte leans against her, her face buried in her hands. Her weeping is low and endless. It coils around Eve, who fishes through her pockets for a tissue. At the police station, she goes into the ladies room and unwinds a length of toilet paper, coming out and pressing it into Charlotte's hand.

Charlotte's face is drained of color. She is two-dimensional. Only her green shirt gives her any substance.

Charlotte goes into the room to make the official confirmation that *yes*, this body recovered from the river is her daughter. Eve waits in the corridor. She feels the weight of every stranger's gaze on her. There will be an autopsy and they'll see that Amy fell. An accident. Just a terrible accident. The police will stop treating Charlotte as a suspect, and everything will begin the slow slide to normal.

Owen arrives. He's come from the store, his collar unbuttoned. He's raked his hands through his black hair and it stands up in stiff peaks. He looks around, past Eve. "Where is she?"

Does he mean his wife or his daughter? Eve points, and he goes through the door. Something's buzzing, an irritating sound in this echoing hallway. It's her cell phone. She pulls it free. It's Tyler, wanting to know where she is. She leans against the wall, the firm coolness against her shoulder, and texts back. *Be home soon.*

It feels as though she's been gone for days. The longest she's ever been away from Tyler without any fear had been the four or so hours when she and David had driven to the Amish furniture store to pick up Tyler's big-boy bed. If she'd known it would be their last date together, she would have ordered a bed online and taken David out for dinner instead, somewhere candlelit, with linen tablecloths and real butter in small dishes.

The door opens, and Charlotte steps into the hall. Owen comes after. Charlotte looks around for Eve. Her face crumples when she sees her, and Eve holds out her arms.

"I'll find an officer to drive you home," Detective Watkins says, and Charlotte rests her head against Eve's shoulder.

They wait outside. Clouds have rolled over the sun, erasing all shadow. The world feels free-floating.

"You let this happen," Owen says. "This is your fault."

Charlotte sobs and nods, her head moving against Eve's shoulder. "I know. I know."

"You are the worst thing that's ever happened to me."

"Owen," Eve says, but he steps around her and goes right up to Charlotte. She cringes.

"You're a shitty mother." His lip is curled. He doesn't look like himself. "You've always been a shitty mother."

He wheels away.

It's a long ride home, to where everyone is waiting to hear. How will she tell Melissa and Tyler? They'd loved Amy, too.

DAVID

Tyler had been born on a sultry evening like this. The heat had clung to David's skin as he walked with Eve into the emergency room, the sun casting long shadows into every corner. The woman across the hall had shrieked for hours, but Eve had remained grimly silent during delivery, focused, her hair damp at her temples. Then they'd held their infant son, marveling at his perfection. They didn't notice how ruddy his cheeks were. No one had.

He ties his laces and stands, stretches. Sometimes he feels that the only time he's truly himself is when he's pounding the pavement. He sees things clearer, finds patience, a keener understanding. Eve hadn't wanted to begrudge him this time to himself, he knows, but it had been a source of irritation between them. She'd be waiting for him to come home to hand over the baby or to watch the children so she could run errands. *Can't you run during your lunch hours?*

she'd complain, which of course had been out of the question. Moving to DC had had its costs, but the freedom to run had been an unexpected benefit.

"Ready?" he says to Renée, and she nods.

The C&O Canal is peopled with shoppers and lovers, bikers, and other runners. He and Renée dodge strollers and laughing groups of teenagers. They don't talk until it's all fallen behind them and they're alone. It's a narrow canal, and shallow. Dying sunlight filters in through the branches that arch overhead.

"Guess where we're going for our honeymoon?" she says.

"The Caribbean." She's told him that she loves the idea of motoring from island to island.

"Vegas. Ugh."

"Vegas is nice."

"No, it's not. You know it's not."

"Tell Jeffery."

"I *have*. He got a deal."

"Doesn't really matter where you go." He says this jokingly. He wishes they'd stop talking about it, though.

"Doesn't what I want matter?"

Yes, it does. He and Eve hadn't had much of a honeymoon, just a long weekend on Lake Erie. He'd been in graduate school, and she'd been working small jobs. They planned to do it right, after he graduated, but then Melissa had come along. Still, he hadn't given up. He wanted to take Eve to Greece, to crystal white sand and crisp blue skies. Even after Tyler came along, they'd made their plans, gotten as far as booking the flights when they'd received Tyler's diagnosis. Eve never mentioned Greece again, and he'd quietly contacted the airlines and canceled their trip.

"I wonder if it even matters who he's marrying," Renée says.

They're going up a hill. He tries not to show how breathless he's getting. His calves are beginning to ache, a welcome feeling.

"We can't agree on where to live," she says. "He wants a new build, out in Fairfax." She's getting breathless, too, but she's matching him stride for stride. "You ask me, they all look alike."

"Adams Morgan's nice."

"Exactly. Or Old Town."

They're leveling off now. Old Town Alexandria's right on the river. But Eve wouldn't be happy there. She'd want someplace hidden from streetlights and traffic. Someplace like Fairfax. They haven't spoken since he'd gotten back to DC. He should call her when he gets home this evening, check in with her and the kids, but he has to admit he's welcomed the distraction of work. It's kept him from thinking too deeply about what he knows he has to do. "You could walk for coffee."

"The restaurants. Museums."

A flock of swallows sails past, small black shapes against the orange sky.

"Maybe I'm making a mistake," she says. "Maybe I should've waited."

I want a family, she's told David.

"How did you know Eve was the one?" she asks.

Suddenly, and with great certainty, Halloween their senior year in college. Eve had worn a pink flannel bunny suit, and he'd dressed as a dirty old man. When he went to pick her up, his cheeks peppered with black marker and his bathrobe hanging open, she'd started laughing. She laughed so hard she couldn't stand up. Every time she tried to stop, drawing in her breath and straightening, she'd look at him and collapse into laughter all over again. He began to laugh, too. They finally ended up on the floor, sitting side by side. She wouldn't look at him as she giggled and giggled. He looked at her, those silly floppy pink bunny ears perched on her gleaming black hair, the tip of her nose pink from laughing, and he'd been overcome with a wave of love and desire that left him shaking. All he could think was, *Will she have me?* "I guess I just knew."

"I do love Jeffery. But it's hard."

Love isn't always enough. "Ready to turn around?"

They reverse direction on the gravel path and head back toward Georgetown.

Their footsteps sound on the stones. The path winds beneath stone bridges. Ahead, the brightly lit brick buildings of Georgetown cluster on the banks. Leafy tree branches are black lace against the dark sky. They slow to a walk. He can tell she's still upset. "You'll work it out," he says.

"It'd be easier if he were more like you." She laughs. "Could you tell him that?"

He feels something bloom inside him. It's been a long time since he hadn't felt that everything he did was wrong somehow.

"Have time for a drink?"

He's in no rush to get back to his quiet apartment. "Sure, as long as I'm buying."

"Deal."

They're being seated at a table by the water when his cell phone buzzes. He glances at the caller ID. It's Eve. He accepts the menu the waiter's handing him and sets down his phone. He'll call her back later.

STAR LIGHT, STAR BRIGHT

Zach texts him in the middle of fifth period. Then Tyler gets a bunch of texts, all scrambled. Tyler holds his phone below the computer monitor so the teacher can't see. Every time she turns to face the board, he texts back, trying to sound as surprised as everyone else. What he really wants to know is, do the police know who made the call?

Tyler's seen *CSI*. He knows he left evidence behind. But the police don't have a record of his fingerprints or DNA. They won't ask for a sample, will they?

His mom's been gone all afternoon. She must be with Charlotte. She must know about Amy. She's probably with the police right now, hearing about the kid who phoned it in, who left behind bicycle tracks and curly black hair. He texts her and she texts him back. *Be home soon.* He doesn't even check into his sixth-period class. He keeps his computer turned off, opens his desk drawer, and pulls out his photographs from their hiding spot. This one of Albert stirring something in a pot on the stove, this one of Nikki climbing into her boyfriend's car. Why doesn't he feel sad? He should feel sad, but what he really feels is sick. Then there's Melissa's footsteps on the stairs and she pounds on the door. "Ty? Let me in."

She closes the door quickly behind her. "Did you hear?" She's breathless, her eyes red and her face puffy. "They found Amy. She's *dead*." She looks all around his room like she's never seen it before. "This is so messed up." She slumps down on his bed and puts her face against her folded arms. Only when her shoulders heave does he realize she's crying. He sits down beside her awkwardly, not knowing what to do. "It's okay," he says.

"You don't know *anything*."

Then their mom's there. She comes into the room and he moves so she can sit between him and Melissa. She puts her arms around their shoulders and holds them both close. She murmurs things, soft and steady, that fall like snowflakes all around them.

First, Albert shuffles through the front door, holding onto Sophie's elbow. "How's Charlotte doing?" Albert asks.

He could walk right across the street and see for himself. It's not as if he doesn't like Charlotte, or vice versa, but they're always using his mom to convey a message. *Tell him to help himself to my tomatoes while I'm gone,* Charlotte will say. Or Albert will say, *Give this to Charlotte, will you? The mailman put it in my box by accident.*

"Oh," his mom answers. "You can imagine."

Tyler looks up the street to Amy's house, where all the lights are on. Not Amy's house anymore. Charlotte's house, now.

Then some ladies from Charlotte's church, then one of Robbie's bartenders. Tyler doesn't understand why everyone's here, but they all want to talk to his mom. Zach shows up with his mom, who throws her arms around Tyler's mom and cries in her hair. "I remember when she was born," she says. He's never seen Zach's mom cry. He's never seen her hug his mom, either.

"We had to park on the ravine road," Zach says. "Your street's a mess. That dude from Channel Seven wanted to talk to us, but my mom said no."

Tyler wants to tell Zach how it felt realizing that Amy was lying in the water beneath his feet, how he'd raced through the woods and almost crashed his bike. How scared he is right now, jumping every time there's another knock on the door. But Zach will tell his brother, who will tell his friends, and sooner or later, Tyler's mom will hear about it. And that will be the end of Holly.

A girl with long brown hair and bangs stands close to Zach. Savannah. She looks taller in her Facebook photos. And skinnier. Then Dr. Cipriano, who wanders from room to room. There are strangers, too, people who know his mom and ask, *Is Charlotte all right? What can I do?* Tyler's never seen so many people packed into his house at one time. It looks like a party, but it's not. Everyone's talking in low voices, saying the same things over and over. *I can't believe . . . It's so sad.*

All the kids are in the backyard. Melissa's huddled with her friends on the trampoline.

Some kids look over. Is he supposed to recognize them? Maybe they're waiting for him to wave and say *Hi*. But what if they're not? "They canceled football practice," Zach says, like this is a big deal, like this says everything. "They have the road roped off."

The police are searching the woods. They'll follow his bike tracks back to his house. Any minute, there'll be the *whoop whoop* of the police cars outside and the banging on the door.

"I bet she was shot," Zach says. "Or maybe she was knifed. I bet there was blood."

All Tyler had seen was those floating strands of pale hair.

"She'd be pretty gross, all bloated and stuff."

Tyler imagines Amy swollen up like a big fat balloon, her body pressing against the floor of the boathouse while he stood on top of it, and something roils in his stomach.

"You think she drowned, or did someone put her there, like Refrigerator Guy?" Zach says.

Their name for that old guy who died and left behind a refrigerator filled with the parts of a person. The dude's son had come to clean up and found a head, arms, and legs all wrapped up in aluminum foil and sitting in the freezer. The newspaper said it was probably his ex-girlfriend who'd gone missing thirty years before. The old guy had to have done it. It wasn't like she cut herself up and crawled into the freezer on her own.

"Stop it," Savannah says. "Don't talk like that."

"Sorry," Zach says, sounding like he means it.

After everyone leaves, it's just Tyler and Melissa on the patio. Melissa's quiet, her chin on her bent knees. From here, Tyler can see the sharp corner of Holly's house cutting into the night sky. Clouds move across the stars, blurring them and making them unimportant, but they're still there. Everyone knows that. They can see them for themselves. But no one's seen Heaven.

Their mom comes out and sits with them. She looks tired.

"What happened to her, Mom?" Tyler asks.

"It must have been an accident."

"But she could swim."

"Even strong swimmers can be overcome by the current."

"That river barely moves. A baby could walk into it and be fine."

"Will you just drop it?" Melissa snaps. "Isn't everything terrible enough?"

"Oh, sweetheart." His mom pats Melissa's knee.

His sister jerks away. "Don't *touch* me!"

"Tell me the truth," Tyler says to his mom. "I'm not a little kid anymore."

"No, you're not."

"There are things I want to do."

"Like what?" Her eyes are shadowed.

Like everything. "Drive a car."

"Ty," she starts, and he knows she's going to tell him he can't.

"How could you get your learner's permit?" Melissa demands. "They need to take a photo ID. What if you have an accident and have to go to the hospital? What if you run out of gas? What if . . ." Her voice trails off. Even Melissa doesn't want to list them all.

He knows. There are so many things that it's impossible to get around them.

He can't even go to the funeral.

Rosemary told him funerals were for people who were still living, not for dead people, and she didn't want him to feel bad because he couldn't go to hers. She asked him to think of all the good times they'd had together instead, and so that's what he's been doing. But it's been hard. It makes him wonder if all that's left of people after they're dead are the memories other people carry around. What happens when those people die?

He knows how it'll be. After an XP loss, the forums are busy with virtual hearts and flowers, everyone commenting, their words piling up into thick stacks. But eventually it all stops, and everything goes more or less back to normal.

I'll remember you, Amy. Until I die.

He hopes someone will remember him.

THURSDAY, SEPTEMBER 4

SUNRISE 7:02 AM

SUNSET 8:00 PM

EVE

They're finally gone, the well-meaning neighbors and friends crowding her house, asking the same questions over and over, trying to rattle loose some explanation for what had happened. No one can know. No one can know. And after everyone leaves and the house is quiet again, the truth comes roaring back, shouting at top volume.

She finds herself on her hands and knees, scrubbing the bathroom floor, the toilet, and the shower stall. She takes a toothbrush to the kitchen grout, and scours the baseboards, sponging away the dirt and dust.

She carries the bucket outside to wash the pavers. Dawn's ninety-three minutes away. The air's already thinning, the rounded shapes of the chairs, the trampoline, the hydrangeas along the fence beginning to emerge from the blackness and claim space.

The faintest sheen of pink is in the distance.

There's the fort David built. It's been years since Tyler played in it. Amy had loved it. She had jumped her baby dolls up and down on the windowsills, waving their plastic arms as Eve worked in the garden. Amy had been five or so the day she'd suddenly cried out with pain, and Eve had immediately risen to run over to see what had happened. A spider? Had she twisted her ankle? Amy had held out a grubby finger and wailed, *I got a splinter.*

Eve had pulled Amy into her lap and tilted the finger toward her. Amy had sniffled, collapsed against her, so slight, so small. So trusting. *I killed you.*

Her cell phone's ringing, and she tugs it from her pocket. She flinches when she sees the name on caller ID, but answers it anyway. "Hi, Mom."

"Oh, Evie, I just saw the story on the news. How terrible, how truly terrible. How's Charlotte? I hope she's not alone."

"Her mother's here." Reproach creeps into Eve's voice. She doesn't mean to let it—it's not as if it would do any good—but it's there, anyway. Her mother doesn't demand, *Why haven't you called?* Her mother's accepted this distance between them.

"How are you, sweetheart? I know how important Amy is to you."

This is unexpected, this kindness. It reminds her of how it used to be, when she could tell her mother anything, when they would sit up late into the night, both of them wrapped in their bathrobes, talking. "Oh, Mom." That small thump, her car spinning around and around, everything leaping at her in the bright stab of headlights.

"I bet you're not eating, are you? Or sleeping."

The sympathy in her mother's voice reaches her. Eve presses the heels of her hands to her eyes. How did she get here, in the middle of this twisted nightmare?

"David's not there, is he? You're all alone?"

The truth of this forces her into the chair.

"How about the children? This must be so traumatic for them."

"I'm worried about them."

"Melissa's being quiet, isn't she? You know that's the way she is. She's just like you in that way. No matter what, if you didn't want to talk about something, you wouldn't. I never could pry a word out of you. I had to just wait for you to come to me. She will. You wait and see."

Her mother's right. This makes the world tilt back onto its axis.

"And Tyler." Her mother's voice trails off. She has nothing to offer. She doesn't know Tyler. She's afraid of knowing him. "What can I do?" her mother asks instead. "How can I help?"

"Could you come for a couple of days?" Two days. That's all. She could let her mother take over and she could just put everything down for a while.

"Oh, Evie. I don't know."

No, of course she doesn't. Eve's parents haven't visited in years. *What if we open the wrong door by mistake? What if he gets burned?*

A clatter of the phone, and her father's on the line. "Eve!" he barks. "Did your mother tell you? We've decided to sell the house. Move somewhere where I don't have to take care of a yard. So if there's anything you want, you need to come get it."

She clears her throat. "Like what?"

"Well, I don't know. Your bedroom furniture. You want that?"

The four-poster bed that swayed when she climbed into it? Her nightstand with the chipboard back held on by one precarious screw, the glass lamp that had to have the key turned just so or the light bulb wouldn't go on. Or something that holds no market value but is steeped in family lore and sentimentality: the duck decoy that had been her grandfather's first attempt at carving, the framed sketch of the old family farm? Perhaps this is an invitation to think on a grander scale—the dining room set, her great-aunt's china, her parents' wedding silver. A rug, Crock-Pot, television set?

Maybe this distance is Eve's fault. She could have tried harder to help her mother accept Tyler's illness. Eve had urged them not to worry, that Tyler would stay in his room until it was safe for him to come out, that of course the lamps in the living room wouldn't harm him or the solar ones lining the patio. That even if their schedules didn't mesh, her parents being early risers, there would still be a few hours for them to get to know their grandson before he went into his bedroom for the day or before they went to sleep at night. *He's eightieth percentile,* she'd tell them after a visit to the pediatrician, meaning *he's not fragile.* Meaning *he's normal in every way but one.* But after that disastrous visit when Tyler was five, her parents had refused invitations to spend holidays or birthdays, or attend Melissa's riding competitions. They were okay Skyping, though reluctant, unsure of the technology and always worrying that Eve couldn't hear or see them. And now, listening to her parents' voices on the telephone, Eve realizes she can't hear them at all.

The radio station is in a stolid yellow brick structure across from a strip mall. Inside, it's not much better, plain beige hallways and the glass-walled room of the studio.

Eve and Gloria don't sit in the upholstered chairs but stand by the glass and watch Charlotte on the other side, a microphone in front of her. Trish Armstrong is happy to give Charlotte fifteen minutes. She's a mother herself, she'd said on the phone, and had been following this story with great sympathy. Of course, the police aren't looking for Amy anymore, but Charlotte had insisted on doing the interview anyway, in hopes it jogged loose some clues.

The interview is being piped into the room.

". . . tell us what happened the night your daughter went missing."

Charlotte straightens before replying. She's described those last few minutes a million times in Eve's hearing. Eve could recite them all back, word for word, each one a nail hammered in. Charlotte turns her bracelet around and around. She'd removed her wedding ring the day Owen moved out, months before he filed for divorce. She'd known that their marriage was over right from the start. She'd understood that Owen would never forgive her, and maybe her acceptance of that had hastened her marriage's demise. Charlotte's talking, her mouth forming words, her eyes tracking Trish closely. Her need for Trish's understanding and sympathy is naked on her face. It's painful to see her friend stripped this way.

"What would have possessed your daughter to go down to the river in such a storm?"

They'll never know. It's cruel to wonder. Amy had dashed across the road in front of Eve's car, and Eve had struck her and sent her tumbling down the ravine to her death. Amy had been a pale blur, unrecognizable. But had Amy seen Eve? Had she, at that last terrible moment, turned her head and seen Eve bearing down on her? Eve puts her forehead to the cold glass. *Please let it have been quick. Please let it have been over in an instant, peaceful.*

"We're hoping the autopsy will give us some answers," Charlotte says.

"They're rushing it," Gloria says in a low voice, though Charlotte can't hear her through the thick glass. "That's one good outcome from all this media attention, I guess."

"Yes." Eve focuses on Charlotte's face, the way she holds her chin up, the line between her eyes. But still the thought slides in. Right now, just a few miles away, Amy is lying on a cold steel table, alone, covered with a sheet, waiting for the sharp tip of the scalpel blade.

What will the autopsy reveal? Will they discover some metal shard or paint flake? Eve's hair, her saliva, her tears? It's sickening to be thinking these thoughts. They crowd her brain and throb against her temples. No matter how much aspirin she swallows, pain pounds behind her eyes.

"The medical examiner says Amy's neck was broken," Gloria says. "He said he could tell right away. I hope that means it was fast. I hope she didn't suffer."

The loose feel of Amy's head between her hands. Hot coffee slops over her fingers.

Trish is saying, "What else do you want us to know about your little girl?"

Eve's thinking about this, about how it's impossible to sum a child up in a few phrases, when Trish says, "I understand the police have been called to your house on multiple occasions."

Gloria clutches her arm. "Once. *Once.*"

"That has nothing—" Charlotte begins, but Trish overrides her. "I understand you took a polygraph."

"Yes. I did. So the police could rule me out."

"How did that go?"

"Fine. It went fine."

"I'm so glad to hear that, but I'm a little surprised." Trish adjusts the microphone, brings it closer to her lips. Her voice changes, turns silky. "My sources say it was inconclusive."

A moment of silence. "I don't . . ." Charlotte says.

"You can see how things look, can't you?"

"I . . ."

"Charlotte, did you harm your daughter?"

"Of course not!"

There's something she's not telling us, Gloria had said.

"I've been told the police consider you a suspect."

Charlotte sits back, her face blank. She scrabbles at the microphone clipped to her blouse. She yanks it free and stands. Eve's got the door open for her when Charlotte strides through it. She doesn't look at her. She doesn't seem to see her or Gloria.

It's in the car that Eve says, "Polygraphs aren't reliable. Everyone knows that. They're not even admissible in court."

"It doesn't matter. The police think I'm guilty. You heard that woman. I'm their prime suspect."

"Maybe for now," Eve says, desperate. "But not for much longer." Not after they get back the autopsy results. No one will believe that Charlotte got into her car and ran down her child. *Ran down her child.*

"What makes you say that, Eve?" Gloria asks, and Eve glances in the rearview mirror to see Gloria frowning at her. With the cold suck of fear, she realizes she's made a mistake. How can she explain herself?

It's Charlotte who answers, her thumbnail to her mouth. "Eve's loyal, Mom. She always sees the best in everything."

Loyal. All the good things are draining away, slipping through her grasp and splashing to the ground. She's clutching air.

She looks at Gloria, holds her gaze in the mirror.

Gloria's the first to look away. "Well, let's hope you're right," she says.

DAVID

He can't believe they'd found Amy in the Scioto. He'd searched up and down that river. Lots of people had. But she'd been underwater the whole time. Even the search dogs hadn't been able to find her.

"I tried to call you," Eve says. "I called you four times. Where were you?"

She doesn't say this accusingly, but he feels bad that he hadn't been there for her. He'd intended to phone her the night before, but one drink with Renée had turned into two, and then dinner, and by the time he made it back to his apartment, it had been close to midnight. "How are you doing? You okay?" He's in the office with the door closed.

"It's hard." Her voice breaks.

He wishes he were with her. "I can try to come home early."

"It doesn't matter. Don't bother. I know it's hard."

It's inevitable; Amy's loss reminds them how close they are to losing their own child. It peeled everything back, revealed just how near things lie to the surface. "How are the kids?"

It had been one thing when Rosemary Griggs died. Sad, of course, especially since she'd been like a grandmother to Tyler, but she'd been elderly and so sick. Her death had been expected. The XP kids whose lives had touched theirs all lived so far away. They'd never met. There weren't those constant daily reminders. Their losses could be compartmentalized. Amy's death is different. It breaks all the rules.

"I don't know," Eve says.

"They'll be okay."

"How can you be so sure?" It's Tyler she's particularly worried about. He'd had a hard time after Rosemary died, sitting alone in his room even when he could be allowed out. The therapist she'd found had only made Tyler more upset. *There's nothing wrong with me,* he'd told Eve. *Other than the obvious.* She's done everything she can to give him a normal childhood. She refuses to see that it's impossible.

"They're good kids," he says. "They'll figure it out."

"I hope so. I hope you're right."

"How's Charlotte?"

"David, you'd never believe it. I feel so responsible."

"What happened?"

"She just did a radio interview with Trish Armstrong. Remember her? She's always been so willing to promote our fundraisers, and I thought . . ." He knows she's pacing as she talks, the way she always does when she's deep in thought, wiping a finger along a dusty ledge or picking up a dish and carrying it to the dishwasher. "Somehow she got hold of the polygraph results. It was awful. She *accused* Charlotte."

"Wait . . . it didn't clear her?"

"It was inconclusive. We should have canceled. I led her into a trap."

"It's not your fault," he says. Names rise to the surface, an ugly list. Susan Smith. Andrea Yates. Casey Anthony. He picks his next words carefully. "Do you think Charlotte's been telling the truth?"

"As opposed to what?"

"She *was* the last one to see Amy."

"David, no! Charlotte would never hurt Amy. Never!"

Charlotte's always been more important to Eve than the other way around. Charlotte's the free agent, outspoken and colorful and carefree, the one who can come and go. She has a wide circle of friends and interests that extend into the world. Eve's the one who's had to choose her friends from a very small circle. Not that Charlotte ever abused her unfair advantage, but it's subtly come into play. He remembers that time when the children were small and Charlotte had insisted that Eve get rid of peanut products because of Amy's allergy. Eve pleaded; Tyler loved peanut butter and she didn't want to take one more thing away from him. She'd promised to keep the jar up high, out of Amy's reach, but Charlotte had drawn herself tall and said that in that case, she just couldn't allow Amy to visit anymore. Eve had had to weigh a sandwich versus Tyler having a friend and, by extension, herself. Of course Eve would defend Charlotte.

"Look," he says. "I just want you to prepare yourself."

"How can you even think that?"

"We can't ever know what another person's capable of."

Silence.

This conversation has veered off track. He wants to regain that earlier closeness he'd felt. "I don't mean to keep saying the wrong things. Maybe you're right. You've always had good instincts about people."

"I forgot to ask," she says, "but what happened to that fellow at work?"

"Preston? He's been let go."

"Fired? Just like that? What if he gives the money back?"

"It's not about the money. He stole from our clients. He violated their trust and put us all at risk. Giving the money back doesn't change any of that."

Eve's quiet.

It had once been so simple. He and Eve had fallen in love. They'd had Melissa, who was breathtakingly self-contained, a mystery to him then and a mystery to him now. Then along came Tyler, the eight-pound squalling baby boy, a son completing the perfect family circle. All his choices had been confirmed. He had been cocky with it.

THE NAKED MANNEQUIN

The XP kids are all talking about Yoshi. *We should make a CD of her favorite songs. We should call her, all of us, at the same time. We should send her Oreos. She loves those. Tyler, what do you think?* But he doesn't know.

It's raining again, drops tapping hard on the roof. His mom sits across from him, her laptop balanced on her lap. She's got all the lights shining, but it still feels gloomy. The weather's chased the reporters away, though. Maybe now that Amy's been found, they won't come back.

"Your grandparents called," his mom says. "They're moving into a smaller place and they asked if there's anything we wanted."

He's never been to his grandparents' house. When they Skype, his grandma carries the laptop around to show Tyler what their house looks like, but it's hard to get a fix on it, all the walls zooming in and everything at a wobbly angle. What Tyler really wants to see are his grandparents' faces, but they don't like to look at the camera. At least, they don't like to look at it when he's on the other side of it. They don't seem to have any problem talking to Melissa.

"Like what?" he asks.

"Well, like furniture or dishes. They have some nice paintings."

"I don't know. Do we really need any of that stuff?"

"Well, it might be nice to have something of theirs to remember them by."

"Do they want me to remember them?"

"Of course they do! Your grandparents love you very much." His mom looks upset.

He shrugs. He knows better.

The back door opens.

"Have a good time?" his mom calls, and Melissa pauses in the doorway. "The horses were nervous because of the thunder." She goes into the bathroom to shower.

Tyler tried horseback riding once. His mom had driven him to the barn, where all the lights had been turned off especially for him. She'd taken the back roads, the car bumping over the rough patches and finally crunching onto gravel. Melissa had picked out the gentlest pony. Tyler had held his palm below the horse's lips, felt the tickle of whiskery skin. But then the pony had shifted weight, so big, so heavy, and Tyler had changed his mind. Nothing his mom or Melissa said could change it back.

Melissa's friend Sherry has posted a bunch of pictures from her party. Kids standing around in groups, sitting piled up in chairs. They look like they're having fun. Tyler recognizes some of the kids, Brittany, Adrian, and then there's one of Melissa. He almost goes past it before he realizes it's her in the background. She's talking to someone and she looks mad, the way she's pointing her finger. She's holding a can in her other hand.

Tyler looks closely.

"How's it coming?" His mom's closed her laptop and is coming over.

He changes screens to the werewolf, with eyes that flash red and smoke curling from between its jagged teeth.

"It's perfect." Her hand's on his shoulder, her touch light. "What would I do without you?"

She always makes it sound that way, like she's the one who needs him, when everyone knows. He's the one who needs her.

The stars sparkle like glitter. The woods are alive with tiny sounds, the trees bending over the narrow path that leads down to the water. It seems crazy to think that he and his sister and his mom had ever run along this path, laughing, the lights attached to their caps bouncing and making them look like fireflies. *Be careful of poison ivy,* his mom would call out. Something Melissa had to watch out for, not just him.

The beam of his flashlight silvers clumps of dirt and beaten-down weeds, shows him where to place his feet. He hears the soft hissing as the river below moves against the shore. Beneath him are layers and layers of rock, burrowing all the way down to a hot core of the earth. Ohio's missing a bunch of those layers—two and a half trillion years' worth. No one knows why. He had tiptoed around, imagining the gaping hole these missing layers left behind crashing down and taking him with them if he stomped too hard. Then his mom explained it's like a sandwich missing the cheese. All the other layers still touched. She'd jumped up and down to prove it.

There's the boathouse, rising out of the flat river. Tyler had read and reread the newspaper article. There had been no security cameras at the gas station, and no one remembers seeing anyone using the phone. He'd been lucky—for once.

Things are piled up all around the boathouse, making the walls look fat at the bottom: stuffed animals, bunches of flowers, dolls, all sorts of cards. Crime scene tape sags around the building, tied to small stakes. One torn end lies in the mud.

It's dark inside, darker than he remembers. The water laps outside the windows. The Scioto's a sleepy river, pretty shallow along the banks. His mom had let him wade into the cold swirling water, fully clothed, the way he always had to be. She had held his hand and they'd stepped carefully, things sliding beneath the soles of his shoes. She'd pointed out quick shapes of fish in the water beside them.

He leans out the window, holds the photograph of the fawn, its eyes wide and dark, its ears big and pointed. Amy didn't know about his blog, no one did, but she would have liked this picture. He lets it go and it flutters through the air and lands on the water. It sits there, a pale rectangle floating in the dark.

He pushes his hands in his pockets. He should say something, but what? He clears his throat. He's seen funerals on TV so he knows someone always talks about the dead person, about what made them special and why they'd be missed. But if he were to say anything like that, Amy would start giggling. She'd laugh so hard she'd clutch her sides.

Maybe it's enough that he's here, thinking of her. Maybe Amy can see him; maybe she can't. But if she's there, somewhere, then she'd understand that he didn't mean to ignore her. He didn't mean to let her down.

He feels hollow. Amy had always been a pain, but now that she's gone, she takes everything with her. Who's left to admire him now?

He steps out of the boathouse and a card flutters to the ground. He picks it up from a puddle. It's a nice card, with a picture of a gray kitten on the front. He opens it.

I'M SORRY.

It's Melissa's handwriting. She'd never even said she'd been here. All the things she does in the day that he doesn't know about. He crouches to put the card back and hears rustling behind him. He whirls around.

A dark shape detaches itself from the shadows of the woods and assembles itself into a man. Tyler freezes. Maybe if he doesn't move, the man will go away. Instead, the man calls out, "Who's that? Tyler?"

It's Scott, Amy's brother. "Hi." Tyler doesn't really know Scott that well. *He can't forgive me,* Charlotte had told Tyler's mom. The two of them were sitting on the patio, quietly talking. He'd wondered what Charlotte had done to make Scott not forgive her. Still, the divorce wasn't what had changed Scott. He'd changed before that.

"I thought it would never stop raining." Scott sits down on the grassy bank, and after a second, Tyler sits down beside him. Scott puts something to his mouth and flips a lighter. A tiny spurt of flame wavers in the darkness. Scott tilts back his head and releases a cloud of smoke. "How old are you now, fifteen?"

"Fourteen."

"Old enough." Scott holds out the cigarette.

"I'm not allowed to smoke."

"It's just weed." Scott takes a hit, says in a squeaky voice, "Good stuff, too."

Melissa would do it. She would take a big puff. So Tyler takes the cigarette between his gloved fingers. He's afraid he'll drop it. He puts it to his mouth and sucks in a mouthful. Burning smoke fills his lungs, and he sputters. Scott pounds him on the back. "There you go."

His eyes are watering, but he tries again, sipping on the end of the little cigarette and holding the smoke in his mouth before swallowing it down. He coughs, then hands the cigarette back.

Fog hovers over the river, streamers of pale gray.

"You believe in ghosts?" Scott asks suddenly.

Every hair on Tyler's arms stands up. "No." *Yes.*

"What if people do come back to haunt us? That could really suck."

"You mean Amy?"

"Amy, other people." Scott passes him the thing. Tyler fakes taking another toke. Scott doesn't seem to notice.

"You're too young to get this," Scott says, "but sometimes things you do can't be undone. Sometimes there are things your mom and dad can't help you with. You're lucky, dude. You don't even know yet how fucked up the world can be."

"Well, I have a fatal disease. So I know how fucked up it can be."

Scott rears back. "Yeah, shit. I'm sorry."

"All you do is shine headlights on me and you fucking kill me."

Scott starts to laugh. "Man, that's crazy."

"I live in a box, man."

"Like a vampire." Scott's howling, smacking his knee with his palm. "Like a little vampire dude. What's it like?"

"Sometimes it really sucks. Sometimes it's really lonely."

"I bet. I bet it is." The fog's rolled closer now, hovering between his hand and the ground. "You were friends with Rosemary, weren't you?" Scott asks.

"Yeah. I really miss her."

"She knew she was going to die and she was really brave about it."

"We're all going to die. I guess we're all really brave."

Tyler floats from tree to tree. He's disjointed and slow, like strings are moving him. The thought makes him snort with laughter. Tyler, the vampire marionette.

He wanders past the Farnhams' house and stops. There's something new, a long triangle of light along one windowsill, where the blinds have been pushed against the glass and tilted up. Anyone could walk right over and look in. No one's ever seen inside the Farnhams' house, not even on Halloween, when Mrs. Farnham sits in her driveway with a big bowl of candy on her lap. Tyler stands there, thinking. He shrugs. *What the hell.*

There are a lot of things standing between him and the Farnhams' house. He squints, planning his route. It's like following that treasure map his mom made him, the one he's stuck to his wall, crossing out the old neighbors' name and printing in Holly's instead. He takes an exaggerated step to the right, then to the left, then two steps ahead. He's like fucking James Bond. He tries not to laugh, but it bubbles out of him anyway. He bumps into the wishing well, sending the wooden bucket spinning. He grabs at it, and the world teeters this way and that. He blinks, trying to remember what it was he was doing. Oh yeah.

A few steps later and he's on the broad wood deck. Another couple of steps and he's at the window. He curls his fingers around the windowsill and pulls himself up to stand on his tiptoes. Bricks catch at his clothes. He stares through the glass. *What the hell?*

The room is packed with stuff. He's never seen so much stuff in one place before: towering stacks of newspapers and books. Furniture filled with toys, dishes, vases. Dolls are *everywhere,* their hair curled and tied in big bows, their dresses in bright poufs of color. How do they keep from falling down? A crib's been wedged into the corner, filled with blankets. A mannequin stands beside it, hand pointed up, her features smooth and pretty like she has no idea she's not wearing any clothes. He grins.

"I told you when we got married." It's Mr. Farnham, coming into the room. Tyler ducks down, but he can still hear Mrs. Farnham say in a pleading voice, "I thought you'd change your mind."

"You don't change your mind about something like that."

"Would it have been so bad? Would it really have been so bad? I would have done all the work."

"Joan, honey. You know how I feel. I just didn't want to share you with anyone."

"Not even with our own child?" Mrs. Farnham's crying, her words all choked.

The smack of a screen door. "Who's there?" It's Albert. "Come on out! Show yourself!"

"What's going on?" Mr. Farnham's standing right over him, inches away from where Tyler presses himself beneath the window.

"Someone's sneaking around your house."

"Where?"

Tyler shoves himself away from the wall. The sidewalk sails in front of him, leading him home. Panting, he lets himself in through the French doors. He feels in his pockets for his flashlight, but it's gone.

FRIDAY, SEPTEMBER 5

SUNRISE 7:03 AM

SUNSET 7:59 PM

EVE

It's a horrifying errand. Felicia's the one who insists that Amy not be buried in a dress she'd owned, and so Eve drives them all to Nordstrom, to roam the aisles in search of something sweet and pretty while the piano music from the lobby drifts upward; the cheerful salesclerks, the gleaming marble floors. They spin around Eve. She bumps into a rack of dresses, sending them swinging on their hangers.

Felicia brings dress after dress to Charlotte, who nods woodenly at every suggestion. *Yes,* the pale pink dress with cap sleeves and a big satin bow is darling. *Yes,* the lacy gown in tiered yellows would be just the thing. *Yes,* the sky blue dress with wisps of tulle peeping from beneath the full skirt is special. Charlotte's been receiving emails at her business address, messages that run the gamut from accusation to outright death threats. *You should die you miserable bitch! Someone should KILL you.* The FBI's looking into them all, and Charlotte's been told to close her email account. *But what good's a realtor without a way for clients to contact her?* Felicia's argued. Charlotte herself doesn't say anything.

Eve stares at the skirt of the dress she is clutching, the fabric cool and silky. She's leaving damp fingerprints everywhere. "Why don't we take a break and get something to eat?" Sit in a dark booth somewhere, no one looking at her with any particular interest, and she can hold a bracing glass of ice water to her forehead.

Charlotte doesn't answer, her attention focused on turning over a dress tag to find the size. Over and over, she tries to grasp the small rectangle. Eve takes the tag and holds it so Charlotte can see. Charlotte blinks, looks up. Eve looks into Charlotte's stunned eyes and realizes that there's no chance of taking her friend someplace safer.

Detective Watkins is waiting at the house when they return. Gloria greets them at the door and takes the dress bag from Felicia. "Nikki's upstairs, taking a nap," Gloria says, and Charlotte nods.

They sit in the living room. Eve has no choice but to stay. Charlotte wants her. She's holding onto Eve's arm, so Eve sits beside her on the couch, Gloria on Charlotte's other side. Felicia stands, her arms folded.

"We've gotten the autopsy results," Detective Watkins begins, and Charlotte's fingers dig into Eve's skin. "There were multiple injuries down one side of her body."

"I don't understand," Charlotte says.

"The pattern of her injuries makes it pretty clear she didn't just fall."

"Was she pushed?" Felicia says.

"No. The medical examiner believes her injuries are consistent with her being struck by a car."

Eve's sweating, in her armpits, down her spine. Her skin is covered with goose bumps. Detective Watkins isn't paying her the least bit of attention. She's entirely focused on Charlotte. Still, Eve's clammy, trembling. She feels as though she might be sick. *Shh, quiet.* She remembers cradling Tyler as a newborn, rocking him to sleep in the dim glow of his nightlight. She thinks of his round head, his even breathing, the barely perceptible puffs of air against her skin.

"A car?" Gloria repeats. "Someone hit her with a car. Who?"

It had been dark, rain splashing hard all around. No one could have seen anything. But they had video surveillance at gas stations, didn't they? Had a camera caught her on tape stopping at the exit before turning right? They'd have her license plate number. They'd know she had headed in the opposite direction. Maybe she hadn't escaped the camera at the carwash. What about when she'd driven to the auto body shop?

"So now you know." Felicia's furious, jabbing her finger in the air. "You made Charlotte take that polygraph. You made everyone think she was guilty. You didn't have to put her through any of it."

"She was just doing her job," Charlotte says quietly.

"So you think someone ran her over by mistake?" Felicia demands. "Do you think they knew what they'd done and just left her there?"

"We think it's likely, yes," Detective Watkins says.

So calm, so even, these words of condemnation. *It wasn't like that,* Eve wants to insist.

"I don't understand," Charlotte says. "They hit my child and just left her?"

"How did she end up in the river?" Gloria asks.

"Do you think she was alive?" Charlotte asks. "My God, do you think she could have been saved?"

No! Amy had been gone by the time Eve found her. No one could have saved her. Detective Watkins keeps talking, words landing with terrible accuracy all around her. Amy hadn't drowned. She'd fallen to her death after being struck by a car. Everyone's listening, Gloria with her fingers against her mouth, Charlotte's face drained of color. A word pierces the fog. *Bruises.* Eve sits up. Amy had bruises on her upper arms.

"Maybe the fall—?" Gloria says, but Detective Watkins shakes her head. Amy had sustained those bruises separately.

Eve had grabbed Amy to her. She'd held her tight.

"Detective Irwin will be taking over the case," Detective Watkins tells them. "He'll be in touch with you shortly. You can talk to him about all of this."

"Who's he?" Felicia says.

"He's from Homicide. This isn't a case for Family Services anymore."

Homicide. The word is a knife. It presses against Eve's skin, drawing a precise line of blood. She welcomes the pain.

DAVID

Renée had offered to work through the weekend for him. *Your family needs you.* He'd liked her for that. She's in the conference room when he opens the door to say good-bye. He's leaving early, wanting to be home. She looks at him, and it's clear she's been crying. "You okay?" he asks with surprise. Just thirty minutes before, she'd been intent on her work, her head bent.

"Hold on. I'll walk you out."

She keeps close as they go down the hall. She walks a little unsteadily, but he thinks it's not her ankle that's bothering her. "What's the matter?" he asks as they step into the corridor, and the door wheezes shut behind them.

"That was Jeffery." Her eyes are green, startlingly so. "The wedding's off." She steps forward and his arms go up, automatically, around her. She weeps against his shoulder. He feels her warm breath against his collar, smells the fragrance of her shampoo.

"Everyone gets cold feet."

She shakes her head, rubbing her cheek against his shirt. "He says he doesn't love me. He says he doesn't think he ever loved me."

He pats her shoulder. She'd never forget Jeffery saying that. Even if they reconciled. The words would lie between them and fester. "His loss."

"I'm sorry." She steps back and puts her hands to her face. "I know you have a plane to catch. I shouldn't have said anything."

"No, it's okay."

"My whole life. What am I going to do?"

"Do you have anyone you can stay with tonight?"

"All my friends are Jeffery's. Where am I going to go? I don't have anywhere to go."

"Stay at my place."

"Oh." She sniffs. "Yeah, that could be good."

"He won't have any idea where you are."

"Yeah. Fuck him."

"I can't promise the bathroom will be clean, but you can run on the trail." He fishes in his pocket for his keys, presses them into her palm.

"Yeah. Yeah."

When he steps outside the terminal in Columbus, the air is humid and warm. He can feel the afternoon seep into his clothes, his skin. He walks to the taxi stand at the curb. He's texted Eve to let her know he'll make his own way home. He's glad he doesn't have a talkative cabdriver. He watches the familiar skyline in the distance as they drive down the highway, all the tall buildings poking the sky, beige and brown and black.

"The house with the gray roof." He points, and the cabbie pulls the taxi into the driveway. The man's got a radio program on, but David hasn't been listening. Then Charlotte's voice rings out over the speakers. "That was nothing," she's saying, and he leans forward. "Could you turn that up?" he asks the driver, who obliges, just in time for him to hear, "Charlotte, did you harm your daughter?"

"That woman should be locked up," the driver says.

The garage is cool and dark. Eve's car's there, but she's nowhere to be found. He washes his hands in the small hall bathroom. Melissa's things are all over the counter, her scrunching gel, her pink-handled razor. He remembers when there used to be hair elastics everywhere, on the counter, underfoot, looped over a doorknob, twisted around Melissa's wrist. In the kitchen, he pours himself a glass of water, glances at Eve's color-coded calendar in the kitchen—black marker for Tyler's dental appointments, purple for dermatology, and green for ophthalmology—and there in red, *driver's test!* Tomorrow he takes Melissa in for her driver's test. She's already driving. He can remember her pedaling that little plastic car down the sidewalk with her bare feet. Her Flintstonemobile, Eve called it.

He's pulling the mail out of the box, bill after bill after bill, when music thumps down the street and he turns to see a small white car headed his way. Brittany and Melissa sit turned toward each other, arguing. Brittany should have her eyes on the road, but she's letting the car drive itself. She refocuses just in time to bump the car into the driveway and finally sees him standing there.

She straightens and reaches to turn down the radio, as Melissa climbs out. Brittany's smile is absolutely false, and it disappoints him to realize this. She's always seemed to be a transparent creature, and good-humored. "Hi, Mr. Lattimore."

"Hi, Brittany. How's school going?"

"Fine." Another fake smile and she backs out of the driveway with a squeal, turns around, and heads for the corner. Whatever they'd been talking about hadn't been about something banal like musical groups or smoothie flavors.

"What was that about?" he asks his daughter. She has Eve's shining black hair, her slanted eyes. She's wearing a green T-shirt of some thin silky material and jeans with the denim distressed to white threads. Her fingernails are chewed to the quick and painted metallic blue; long jangling gold wire earrings swing as she trudges up the driveway. He loves her with an intensity that astonishes him.

"Nothing." She stands beside him in the garage and he punches the button. The door slowly starts to lower.

"How are you doing?" She's wearing that adolescent mask, his little girl who used to be so wide open with him, leaning close, confiding. *I want to be famous when I grow up. Cauliflower looks like brains. My teacher wore a purple dress today.* He hates to admit it, but sometimes he tuned her out, focused on whatever he was doing, fixing the lawn mower, replacing a light bulb. Now he's lucky if he gets a couple of syllables out of her, the tiniest glimpses of what was going on in her world, the softest brushstrokes depicting who she was and who she was becoming. He wishes he could reach back in time and shake himself, force himself to stop and actually listen. "I'm sorry I wasn't here."

"It's okay."

She doesn't want to talk about Amy. He understands. He knows how fragile life is. Not everything has to be put into words.

The door slides down, darkness creeping in all around them. He can barely see her in the gloom. Her heart will be broken, too, by some boy, at some time. He wishes he could stop it from happening.

"Those reporters won't be back, will they?" she asks.

"Have they been bothering you?"

She shakes her head. "No, but they just make everything worse."

"Things will settle down."

"When?"

Melissa has such a concrete mind. She believes there are discernible parameters to everything. As a little girl, she wanted to know precisely where the earth's atmosphere ended and outer space began. If he said he loved her, Melissa wanted to know how much, without the least bit of coyness, as if something like that could be contained. So when she asks *when*, what she really wants to know is whether there will come a time when she won't feel sad and confused and lost, and he knows the answer to this is *no*. There are events in everyone's life that mark it and leave a permanent impression that can never be rubbed away. But of course he can't tell her that.

"Soon," he promises her.

The garage door hits the concrete floor with a soft thud. The darkness is complete, making them invisible to each other. His little girl. She could be twenty-one, thirty-one; she could be older than he is now and she'll always be his child. He opens the kitchen door and they step across the threshold into the dim, waiting light.

He's in the kitchen slicing tomatoes when he hears the garage door shudder against its tracks. A moment later Eve comes through the back door. "You're home." She crosses toward him and slides her arms around him, puts her head against his shoulder. He hugs her with his free arm. He can't help thinking of how much slighter Eve is than Renée, the top of her head reaching his chin. It's not fair to compare them, but he finds himself doing it anyway. "I ran into Albert just now," she says, moving away. He feels the loss of it. "He says he caught someone looking into the Farnhams' windows last night."

"He sure about that?" Albert's getting on in years. Ever since Rosemary's death, he'd gotten a little eccentric, letting his yard go, keeping odd hours, and wearing the strangest collection of hats. "Could it have been a reporter?"

"He doesn't think so. The police found a flashlight. Larry swears it's not his, and they fingerprinted it."

"We'd better keep our drapes closed, just in case."

"I hate to do that."

"We could set up motion detectors," he suggests. She likes to keep the drapes open in the evenings, to make up for keeping them closed during the day.

"Aren't they more trouble than they're worth, going off all the time?"

"I don't like the idea of you and the kids home alone while someone's creeping around." Another reason why they need to live in the same city. She hears this, too. She goes to the stove and lifts a pot lid. "Dinner smells good. What are you making?"

"Pasta puttanesca."

They used to laugh at the fancy-sounding name for what is essentially a spaghetti sauce assembled in haste from ingredients they have on hand. It's clear Eve hasn't been shopping in days. He should run to the store, do a load or two of laundry. He'd gone in to dump his dirty clothes and found he could barely push the door open, there were so many clothes on the floor.

"Hey, listen," he says. "You remember Renée?"

"Your running buddy." She's at the counter now, going through the mail.

That, so simple. "She broke up with her boyfriend. I told her she could stay in my place over the weekend."

"That was nice of you," she says, her distraction plain, and just like that, they slip through this thorny discussion unsnagged. She hesitates at the credit card bill and looks over at him.

He nods. "We're going to have to hold off charging anything for a while, at least until we catch up."

"What if we make the minimum payment?"

"It doesn't make sense. Not at those rates. We're going to have to pull money out of Melissa's account."

"Her college fund? David, we *can't*."

Does she think he wants to? "Look, we can't keep falling behind like this. Right now all we're doing is paying off penalties."

"But I'm not spending any money. I don't know what you want me to do."

"We could cut Melissa's riding lessons." Four hundred dollars a month, not including her gear, which she goes through at an alarming pace.

"We can't take that away from her. That's the only thing she does. She loves riding."

"We were two days behind on the mortgage this month. We bounced checks. Maintaining two households is expensive."

She darts a look at him. "Maybe I can get more clients."

"You could work eighty hours a week and it wouldn't be enough."

"It'd be better than nothing." She glances at her watch. "Oh no. I should have texted Tyler to let him know he could come out." She goes out into the hall and calls up the stairs. "Tyler, honey! It's time!" She comes back into the kitchen. "I can't believe I forgot. He was in there for fifteen extra minutes."

She agonizes over every extra minute Tyler spends in his room. It's exhausting. She used to be so lighthearted. She used to make him laugh. "It's fifteen minutes, Eve. That's all."

"How can you say that?"

She's got that self-righteous tone again, as if she's the only one suffering. It sets his teeth on edge. "You're so focused on the minutes that you're not paying any attention to what's really happening here. What kind of life is it if he spends his life watching the clock?"

"It's the most life he has."

"I know how much you've done. I know how hard this is for you. But sometimes I think he'd be better off if he wasn't reminded all the time."

"You're blaming me for being careful?"

"Remember Jamal, Hanna? Their moms were careful, too. Tyler will never be in the clear."

"You don't know that."

But he does know that, and, damn it—so does she. "I can't do it, Eve. Pretend he's normal, pretend everything's fine. Every time I look at him . . . I just see the end." He says this pleadingly, wanting her to understand, but her face is narrow with anger.

"*You're* the one who's taking life away from him."

He takes a ragged breath. "Look. Maybe you're right. Maybe we do need to talk to someone. Let's try that guy, the therapist you found for Tyler. You said he had some experience with this sort of thing."

"I can't," she says. "I just—I can't talk to anyone. I'm going to go check on Tyler. He should be downstairs by now."

Her footsteps sound down the hall. The sauce is burning. He turns off the flame and drops the pot into the sink, where it sizzles and smokes.

David had wanted to try for more children. There was only a twenty-five percent risk they'd have another XP child. And if the worst happened, they'd know ahead of time. They could take precautions from the very start. But Eve had refused, had poured all her attention into taking care of Tyler. She couldn't even fathom having another child. That was the first door she'd shut on David. She'd been shutting doors ever since.

CLAWS

After dinner, his dad hands him a slick yellow bag. "Surprise."

It's heavy, bulky with something that has sharp corners—a book called *Portrait Photography* and a camera, the same 35 mm Tyler's been eyeing online for months. He pulls the camera from the box and turns it over in his hands. His parents are watching him.

"What do you think?" his dad says.

"It's great. Thanks."

"How's your class going?"

"Okay. I have to shoot a roll of film."

"Then we'd better practice loading it." His dad opens a box of film and shows him how to pull out a few inches of the slick stuff and hook it into the back of the camera. By accident Tyler yanks out a long strip. "Happens to everyone," his dad says. "We have more."

His mom's standing over by the window, looking out through

the heavy drapes. "Albert says he saw a Peeping Tom last night." She turns and looks at them. "So let's keep the drapes closed until the police find him, okay?"

"What's a Peeping Tom?" Tyler asks.

"A creeper who looks through people's windows," Melissa answers.

Oh. His cheeks flame and he ducks his head. It's a dirty-sounding word and he hadn't meant to do anything gross. He'd just been curious.

"Don't worry," his mom says. "The police will find him. They got fingerprints off a flashlight they found."

He'd been wearing gloves. But not all the time.

"Tyler?" It's Holly, standing on her porch. Tyler feels warm with the realization that she's been waiting for him. He wasn't even headed her way. He was going to the park to try out his new camera, but now he walks across his yard to hers.

She's standing with her hands on the railing. The light from inside the house behind her outlines her body, shining through the thin material of her dress, revealing the curves of her legs.

"Could you do me a favor?"

She needs a favor from *him*? "Like what?"

"Could you watch the kids for an hour or so? I have to run to the store."

"I've never babysat before." He's always been the one other people babysat.

"There's nothing to it. Christopher is asleep. Connor's watching TV. If he gets thirsty, you can give him some juice."

Doesn't she know any adults who could help her out? "Can't you just take them with you?"

"No, that's impossible. For God's sake. I thought you were one person I could trust."

He's made her mad somehow. "You can," he says hastily.

"It's only for an hour. Come on." She holds the door open. *"Please."*

He's not supposed to walk into a room without his mom checking it with the UV meter first. But Holly's standing there looking at him, so he does it. He steps right over the threshold. Nothing happens. He feels fine. He lets out his breath.

Her eyes are extra bright. "You know to keep the door locked, right?"

Ha. If there's anything he knows, it's that.

Connor sits cross-legged in front of the TV, a fleecy blanket bunched up in his lap. He doesn't look over.

She puts her fingers on his arm. Her touch blazes right through his sleeve to his skin. "I'm sorry about your friend. About Amy."

"Thanks."

She scoops up her purse from a hook on the wall and pulls out a ring of keys. "Mm," she says. "You smell of coconut." She pushes open the door and is gone.

He hasn't been inside many houses. There's Zach's old house that's now Sophie's; Zach's new house; Alan's house; Charlotte's, of course; Rosemary and Albert's; and in first grade, he'd gone to the birthday party of Melissa's friend's younger brother. He's never once been left alone in any house but his. Having two little kids there doesn't count. If something happens, it will be up to him to deal with it.

The curtains hang open in the living room and dining room, revealing big blank panes of glass, and the windows have been pushed up so that the cool night air swims in, making the white drapes billow. The house feels fragile, as though one big gust of wind could blast it to pieces. He takes out his UV meter and presses the button, walking all around. The little black arrow doesn't move. He takes off his gloves and pushes them into his pockets, then unzips his hoodie.

"Are you thirsty?" he asks Connor.

"Juice."

The kitchen's painted brown and has white cabinets. Dishes sit heaped in the sink and plastic bottles stand around the counters, some containing a murky yellowish liquid that looks disgusting. Cardboard boxes are stacked in a corner, marked KITCHEN in heavy black writing on the sides. There are photographs stuck to the front of the refrigerator. Holly in a bathing suit, laughing as sun spills across her face and makes her squint. Connor in a little jacket and pants, his mouth turned down and comb marks in his hair. A puffy-faced baby squints at the camera, just a bit of fluff for hair. A bunch of strangers, all different ages but everyone wearing white shirts and blue jeans, and grinning at the camera. *Hi from the Blakes!* He holds up his camera and presses the button. A photograph of photographs.

The refrigerator's so bare he can see straight to the back. Ketchup, milk, salad dressings, yogurt, a plastic container of something pale green. He takes another picture.

"Where does your mom keep it?" he calls to Connor, but there's no answer.

Maybe the pantry? But no, there's nothing like juice in there, just some boxes of cereal, a couple cans of spaghetti, and a big plastic bag of potato chips closed with a purple clip that says *Neil Cipriano, DDS*—his mom has one, too. But Connor said he wanted juice not chips, so he slowly rotates and scans the kitchen once again. Then he sees it, an opened pack of juice boxes poking out from behind a cloth bag with blue dinosaurs printed on it.

"Here you go," he says.

Connor takes the juice box. "Baby."

That's when Tyler hears the hiccup of sound, like rubber squeaking against glass. Christopher? But he's supposed to be asleep. Holly didn't say anything about what to do if the baby woke up. "What does he want?"

Connor doesn't even look at him.

The crying's coming from upstairs. Tyler tries the first bedroom door, flicking on the light to see an unmade bed and clothes heaped everywhere. A lacy white bra dangles from the back of a chair. He flips off the light and backs away.

The next door's shut and when he cautiously opens it, the cry grows louder, and warmth envelops him, along with a sour smell. There's a small light glowing from the baseboard shaped like an orange lion's head, and he can see the faint outlines of a crib against the corner. He goes over and looks down. There's the baby from the picture on the refrigerator, only this version has a wide-open mouth and tiny clenched fists. He's screaming now, hurting Tyler's ears, turning his head from side to side. He's mad about something.

Melissa's done lots of babysitting. He calls her. It's hot in here and he pushes down his hood. Maybe it's his sunglasses that are creeping the little dude out. He takes them off, but the baby's eyes are squeezed shut. The phone rings, then Melissa's voice. *This is Melissa. You know what to do.*

But that's the problem. Tyler doesn't have a clue what to do. He texts her.

You awake?

Christopher's shrieking. Tyler can see his tiny tongue quivering in his mouth. Without thinking, he stuffs his phone into his pocket and reaches down to pick the baby up.

Christopher stops crying. His head bobs, and his eyes open to look at the floor. Tyler's surprised at how light Christopher is, but he's the source of the sour smell. Tyler wrinkles his nose. It's pee.

There's a dresser with padding on it. He's seen *Three Men and a Baby,* so he knows what it's for. But he really doesn't have any idea how to use it. "Connor? Can you come up here?"

"No, mister."

So Tyler lays the baby down and unzips his little sleeper. He untapes the diaper and drags it off. The little guy's penis stands straight up, making Tyler laugh. He finds a new diaper, one that smells clean and is airy light. There are directions on the back of the package and he studies them. He draws one piece of tape over one hip, then the other. He picks up Christopher and nothing falls off. "We did it," he tells the baby, who's sucking his thumb and watching him.

Tyler had been seventeen months old when they found out he was sick. Until then, his mom's told him, they had no idea. She says he's perfect now, the way he is, but he knows the only time he was ever truly perfect for her and his dad was back then, before they knew otherwise. Christopher looks fine, but what if he isn't? There could be something hiding inside him ready to leap out at any minute, like that creature in *Alien*. He pushes the little guy's fat little legs into the sleeper and zips it back up.

Christopher seems happy now, so Tyler carries him over to the crib. But as he starts to lower him, Christopher jerks out his legs. His tiny chest gets round and hard, and Tyler knows he's going to start screaming again.

So he doesn't want to go to sleep. Tyler slides Christopher into the crook of his arm. The baby's head bobbles and his arm gets squished, but Tyler pulls at the little hand and Christopher rights himself. He peers up through half-opened eyes.

"Hi," Tyler says, and, of course, Christopher doesn't say anything back.

He goes downstairs. Connor hasn't moved. There's a new show on, not a cartoon. "Did you turn the channel?"

Connor drinks his juice and pretends not to hear. Tyler looks around for the remote, spies it peeping out from under Connor's blanket. There's a small skirmish as Tyler grabs for it. He almost drops Christopher. Connor says "No!" but Tyler holds up the remote and changes it back to the Cartoon Network. That's what babysitters do. They make sure little kids aren't watching crap. He sticks the remote in the freezer, on the top shelf.

He carries Christopher around the house, jiggling him, and stops to look at the framed pictures on the wall and on the hutch. Nothing like as many as the Farnhams had standing around. What had he been thinking, going up to their window like that? It was the weed. It had made him crazy.

Here's a photograph of Holly in her wedding dress. She's so pretty, like a film star. This must be her husband, Mark. Tyler studies his face, the way he has his arm around Holly's waist.

Christopher's asleep, his head lolling against Tyler's arm. Tyler takes him upstairs to his room and this time, when he puts him down, the baby doesn't move. Tyler goes out into the hall. It's been more than two hours. Where is she?

He looks at the books on the bookshelf, slides out a yearbook with *Toledo Tigers* printed in bright green across the cover. He turns pages until he finds Holly as a high school senior. Her hair was longer then, but her smile's the same. *Holly Hollywood!* someone had written on the page. *I'll remember you when . . .* Tyler takes a picture.

Connor's watching *SpongeBob*. It's an episode Tyler's seen a bunch of times, but he watches it, too. The clock on the wall ticks. He goes to the window and looks out at his house. He imagines his family inside, sleeping in their various rooms. He yawns, and once he starts, he can't stop.

"I'm hungry," Connor says.

Tyler looks at the clock. It's almost three-thirty. What's Holly doing, taking so long? "Maybe you should go to bed."

"I'm hungry *now*."

So Tyler goes back into the kitchen, stands looking in the pantry. There's a can of soup. There, beneath a limp bag of rice, is a box of raisins. He goes back to Connor. "Soup or raisins?"

"Candy."

"There isn't any candy."

Connor pushes himself up and goes into the kitchen. He opens a drawer and reaches behind the boxes of aluminum foil and plastic wrap to a rolled-up bag of lollipops. Does every family hide food? Connor pulled out a handful of lollipops and left the bag sitting on the counter. Tyler shrugs. If Holly doesn't want Connor to have candy, then she should come home on time to make sure.

Tyler wanders into the bathroom, opens the medicine cabinet. There's a man's razor and a can of shaving cream. He uncaps the bottle of cologne and sniffs. It's strong, pine-scented. That must be what Mark the Cop smells like. He goes upstairs to the bathroom there. The medicine cabinet here has a bottle of contact lens solution, nasal spray, a light blue bottle of makeup remover, a container of Vaseline. He takes a picture, then shakes the small brown prescription bottle. Celexa, the label reads. There's a flat foil package with tiny pills inside. Half of them have been punched out. He finds a pair of glasses and tries them on. Everything blurs and he puts them back.

Colored bottles of perfume sit on the counter, a cup filled with soft brushes. There's a plastic tree that holds long gold and silver chains, and a drawer filled with dangly earrings and bracelets with all sorts of jewels. There's another drawer filled with small brown boxes of makeup. He opens one and rubs his fingertip across the velvet purple surface.

Beneath the sink is a bag of cotton balls, a box of Q-tips, a million cans of hair gunk, a hair dryer, and a box of tampons. He knows what those are. He closes the cabinet.

The crunch of tires outside and he runs to the window to see. Holly? No, it's a strange car, sliding to a stop in front of Sophie's house across the street. He steps back. He wants to look and see, but he has to wait. The minute a car door opens, the dome light flashes on. Until the door creaks shut again, it'll stay lit. His mom's warned him about this. She's removed the bulbs from the dome lights in their cars, but she can't do that to other people's cars. He hears the slam of a car door and peeks out. It's a regular-looking guy, no one

Tyler's ever seen before. A reporter? But the reporters are all gone, and besides, why would a reporter be hanging outside Sophie's house in the middle of the night? As Tyler watches, the stranger reaches into Sophie's mailbox and pulls something out. An envelope that he studies and then replaces. A second later he's walking back to his car. Tyler turns away just in time as headlights sweep through the window and across the far wall. Too late, he remembers his camera.

Holly's closet is stuffed with clothes, all different colors, like a rainbow. Her shoes lie in a tumble on the floor, golden sandals, boots, black strappy things. He's never seen her in anything but sneakers or bare feet. Her husband's closet is filled with jeans and short-sleeved shirts. A dark blue policeman's uniform hangs from the rod, covered with dry-cleaner's plastic. So where's the gun safe?

Down the hall, Christopher starts to cry again. He doesn't sound like he's going to stop. Tyler goes into the baby's bedroom and picks him up. He jiggles him up and down, but this time Christopher doesn't stop. Maybe he's hungry. Holly's been gone forever.

He carries the baby downstairs. Connor's fallen asleep on the floor in front of the TV, curled up like a potato bug. Tyler goes into the kitchen and examines the bottles standing all around. The one by the stove is half-full. Tyler holds it up and squints at the murky liquid inside. It's getting harder to hold Christopher, who's kicking out his legs and clenching his hands. Tyler slides the bottle nipple into Christopher's mouth and wiggles it around. Christopher's mouth shuts and clamps on tight.

Tyler's sweating. He looks at the clock. It's 6:20. His mom's probably looking for him right now. He glances at the window, where the sky is growing lighter. Should he go into the basement? But what if he needs to use the bathroom? He can't stay here all day. His mom would freak out. But how can he leave Connor and Christopher alone? Christopher is finished, his mouth hanging open and his eyes closed. Liquid drips from the corner of his mouth.

Tyler carries Christopher back up to his crib and puts him down. The baby burps, then sighs. Tyler goes into Holly's bedroom and stands there.

Headlights wash across the ceiling. He runs downstairs. The front door opens and Holly's there. "Hi," she says.

"You said an hour. Where were you?" She's not holding any grocery bags, just her purse, which she tosses on the hall table.

"You sound like Mark. I just needed a break, okay?"

"You don't understand. I can't go out."

"It's not that bad."

"Yes, it is." He's frustrated. "Don't you get it? It *is* that bad."

"Let me pay you."

He almost laughs. What's he going to do with money? It's not like he could spend it. His mom would wonder where he'd gotten it.

"Tyler . . ."

He leaves her standing on her porch. He doesn't look back. He runs across the grass to his house, unlatches the gate, and races across the patio to the French doors. He imagines the sun leaping over the horizon and grabbing him in its claws.

SATURDAY, SEPTEMBER 6

SUNRISE 7:04 AM

SUNSET 7:57 PM

EVE

Amy's been found, and the reporters are gone, scattered who knows where. The street echoes, a paper cup lolls on the curb, and the marigolds along Charlotte's driveway have been trampled. Amy had planted them in May, carrying the tiny pots from the back of Charlotte's car. They're annuals. They'll never grow again.

No sooner had Detective Watkins closed the door than Charlotte had twisted the bottle open and shaken two sleeping pills into her palm. She'd gone right upstairs, refusing anyone's company, and left Eve alone with Felicia and Gloria. *We'd better keep an eye on those,* Gloria had said, pushing herself up and taking the bottle from the table where Charlotte had left it.

Eve closes her front door and carries the newspaper into the kitchen.

The French door bangs open and Tyler stumbles into the room

as though he's being chased. "What were you doing outside?" His face is flushed. A fever?

"I just went out for a minute. I was looking through my telescope."

She glances at the clock and puts her palm against his forehead, already thinking. He hasn't had his flu shot yet; can she persuade his doctor to make a house call? But he feels cool. "See anything interesting?"

He ducks away. "No. But I took a picture of the moon."

"You should ask Santa for a stronger telescope."

"I'm asking him for an enlarger, remember?"

"Well, you've been a pretty good boy this year. Maybe you'll get both." David would be annoyed to hear her say this, but how can they deny Tyler such a small request? She might be able to find something used online. What's a few hundred more dollars?

"Can I eat in my room?"

He's got his back to her as he studies the pantry, his shoulders bowed as if he's still figuring out how to manage their new breadth. He spends so much time alone. She almost never sees him. David's right. She does count the minutes. She holds them close, each one. "You just got up. Are you sure you don't want to sit down here with me?"

"Dante's waiting for me online."

Of course he'd want to visit with his friends. This is a good thing. "He's up awfully late. Tell him I say hi."

"Okay." He's got a bowl and spoon in one hand, the box of cereal hooked under a bent arm, his thumb hooked through the handle of the milk container. A second later, he's pounding up the stairs to his room.

She makes peppermint tea and carries it out onto the patio. Tyler's telescope is there, tilted toward the sky. She's glad he's back to watching the heavens. It makes her feel as though his world isn't that small.

The sky's streaked violent orange and purple, as if the sun's being dragged over the horizon. She opens her laptop and checks her email. Clients have been emailing, wondering at the delay in their website updates. Her eyes feel gritty and her throat aches. She'd stared at the ceiling all night while David slept beside her. How could she let Charlotte think that Amy could have been saved, that she'd died in pain, wanting her mother? Eve couldn't. She can't. She's not a monster. Maybe she should turn herself in.

Her computer chimes and she clicks on Skype to see her friend staring at her from half a world away. It's late in Japan, so this timing is unexpected. "Nori, hi. How are you? How's Yoshi?"

Nori reaches forward to adjust the computer screen. "We're at the end now. I wanted you to be the first to know."

She's stunned. "But Yoshi just started treatment."

"She can't take any more chemo."

Loss wells up inside her. "This is so quick."

"I know."

"I had hoped . . ."

"Yes."

She sits helpless. Yoshi's only seventeen. How can Eve leave Tyler now, when he might only have a few more years left? This is what she can't do. She can't abandon her son. She clears her throat and focuses on Nori's face. "What about radiation? Or that clinical trial in Australia?" They've discussed this one, which is geared toward skin cancer. "You could travel at night." Other families have done this. "The airline could have a wheelchair meet you at the gate. You could cover her with blankets. Or what if we try the researcher at Hopkins, see if he has any suggestions?"

"It's too late." Nori's eyes fill with tears. "I know you want to help, but I'm done fighting. This isn't the way I want Yoshi to go, with me frantic and arguing and using up every last second. I want peacefulness. I want calm. Can you understand?"

They're both crying.

"Could you tell Tyler?" Nori whispers.

"Yes, yes. Please tell Yoshi we love her."

Nori swallows. "Eve, it's okay. Tyler will be okay."

But they both know that's not true.

Mark Ryland's pulling into his driveway next door. Eve shrinks back against her chair, not wanting him to see her sitting mere yards away. He's a cop. He's trained to read people's expressions. One look at her and he'll see everything.

David comes out, carrying a paper bag of recycling. "Morning. Who was on Skype?"

"Nori."

He pauses, looks at her. "How's Yoshi?"

It's a simple thing to say, *the chemo didn't work,* but somehow she can't get it out. She can only shake her head.

He sighs. "Yoshi's what, eighteen?"

"Seventeen."

This is where one of them says, *That won't happen to us* or *They'll find a cure soon.* She's usually the one to offer this, the one to keep her gaze firmly forward. This is where she would stand and step into his arms, rest her head on his shoulder.

The door opens. "Ready, Dad?" Melissa's scraped back her long dark hair with an elastic headband. Her hair hangs straight. She's wearing dark jeans and a white top. Her eyes are carefully lined, and she's wearing pale pink lip gloss. She looks older, heartbreakingly so. She looks on the verge of becoming someone else.

Eve says quickly, "Take Daddy's car, honey."

"But I like yours better."

"I might need it later." Eve ignores the quizzical look David throws her. She can't let Melissa drive it. As soon as she can do so without raising suspicion, she'll take it to the dealer and trade it in. She never wants to see it again.

"Whatever," Melissa says, and the door closes behind them.

The patio is quiet. Her tea has gone cold. She should make another cup. The phone shrills inside the house. She lets it go to voice-mail. How many more of these quiet moments will she have?

The sky is pink now, and blue. A bird tweets. It's such a hopeful sound. There's nothing on this earth more hopeful than the sound of birds singing to one another. Tyler's told her that only perching birds sing, those birds with specially adapted feet that allow them to hold onto branches as they call to one another. This is what she feels like—she's gripping a thin branch and the next gust of wind will knock her tumbling right to the ground.

DAVID

Melissa steers the SUV between the rows of parked cars. It's a sprawling lot with plenty of empty spaces, but she grips the steering wheel and keeps her chin lowered, as though she's maneuvering a cruise ship into dock. They've driven down here in silence, not even the radio to accompany them, just David's occasional *Turn here* or *Watch the speed limit.* They wait in line, show their paperwork, and take a seat on the molded plastic chairs. "Remember to come to a full stop at the stop sign," he warns. "Look both ways before proceeding."

She grunts. This is the way she is before horse shows, too, withdrawn and focused.

"So what are your plans for this weekend?" he asks, wanting her to relax. He's worried about her taking this test. He doesn't think she's ready. They've driven the bare minimum of practice hours, and she's still nervous about changing lanes. He worries about her behind the wheel, without him in the passenger seat supervising. Eve disagrees. *Of course she's ready.* But Eve can only see the girl Melissa used to be. "You going out with Adrian?"

"Right."

That's not even an answer. She seems so unhappy. "What would you think about moving to DC? We could find you a new barn. You could break in another Sammy." He shouldn't talk to her about this. It undermines Eve, but he wants to know. Melissa might blossom in another city. They could be a family again.

She flashes an angry look at him. "Since when does what I want matter?"

"Melissa Lattimore?" A police officer is standing there, holding a clipboard.

She can't really believe that her needs don't matter. She's just being a petulant sixteen-year-old. "Good luck," he says. His daughter doesn't even look at him. She pushes herself up and follows the examiner through the sliding glass doors. He hopes the man is kind to her.

She's left her cell phone on the seat beside him. He picks it up. The screen is lit—a text's just come in. It's from Brittany.

dont worry no one saw anything

He scrolls up to see the conversation. Brittany had texted:

did you see sherrys pix from the party

ugh no

theres one of you

tell her to take it down!!!

I did but she wont she says its a pic of her and adrian

shes a bitch like he even likes her

shes just jealous

she called me a whore

she calls everyone that

everyone knows

dont worry no one saw anything

He turns off the phone. He shouldn't have read Melissa's messages. He's sickened to know this girl's calling his daughter names and making her so miserable. Eve's told him teenage girls could be vicious, but he hadn't really understood. He glances to the plate glass window, but Melissa and the examiner have driven off.

No one saw *what*?

"You shouldn't have violated her privacy like that." Eve sets the plates on the patio table. She glances at the clock on the wall. It's three minutes past sunset and Melissa's supposed to be getting Tyler.

"Her phone was sitting right there. Which really isn't justification, I know. But she won't tell us anything."

"She tells us the important things."

"Obviously not. She almost bit my head off when I asked about Adrian."

"I don't think they're dating anymore."

"This isn't just teenage drama." He stops as the patio door opens and Melissa appears.

"Tyler's coming." Melissa pulls out a chair. "You know, Brittany had to try *three* times before she got her license."

She's so pleased with herself. She chattered all the way home from the BMV, actually smiled when he suggested buying a cake to celebrate.

"We're so proud of you," Eve says.

"Can I have the car tonight?"

"And so it begins," he says.

"Does that mean yes?"

"That means where will you be going and when will you be home?" Eve lights the candles and waves away a mosquito.

"Brittany's, and I don't know." She pulls out her cell phone and begins texting.

"Hey," Eve says. "You know the rules. No phones at the dinner table."

"All you have are freaking rules," she says, and Eve shakes her head, holds out her hand. Melissa makes a face and drops her phone into her outstretched palm.

"Unfair. Dad texts in the car."

"I do not."

"That one from Renée. I had to take your phone away from *you*."

This snags Eve's attention. She turns, tilts her head, and then Tyler steps onto the patio and Eve's attention is immediately drawn toward their son. Her entire body changes, relaxes. "Hey, stranger," she says.

"What does *hit-skip* mean?" Tyler says this challengingly.

"Where did you hear that?" David asks.

"It's all over Facebook. People are saying someone hit Amy with a car."

"That's right." Melissa's set down her fork and is listening, too. This is news to her, he sees. He'd been surprised to read about it in the paper that afternoon, then relieved. Things could have been so much worse. "That's what the medical examiner thinks happened."

"Then they skipped away?" Tyler sounds angry and frustrated. "That doesn't make any sense."

David glances at Eve. This is usually her domain, fielding tricky questions from the kids, but her face is still. "It's an expression. It means they didn't tell anyone. They just left."

"Why would anyone do that?"

David holds the serving spoon heaped with food over his son's plate. "They must have been afraid of being caught."

"But why, if it was an accident?"

"Maybe they were driving drunk. That's a crime."

He ladles another spoonful onto his son's plate, waiting for Tyler to indicate that he has enough, but his son's not paying attention. Tyler's frowning at his plate. He's retreated somewhere. Maybe all this talk is bringing home Amy's death in a more real way. Tyler's a sensitive kid. He broods. He holds his worries close and nurses them. This is the result of living in such isolation, of being alone so much of the time.

"Don't worry," David tells him. "The police will find the driver."

"How? Do they know where it happened?"

"I don't know, but I bet they've narrowed it down. There will be some sort of evidence left behind. Or maybe someone saw something." He feels Eve's gaze on him, and he glances at her. "Right? There are all sorts of houses along that road. Someone could have looked out their window and seen something. Or another driver."

"Wouldn't they have come forward by now?" Eve asks, and he finds himself reassuring her, too. "They might not have known what they saw," he says. "But now the police know what they're looking for. Whoever did this won't get away with it."

Melissa sits there, playing with her food. Her earlier happy mood is gone. Inside the house, it's quiet, too. The phone never rings. Kids never come to the door. She lives in isolation, too.

Later, he asks Eve, "Why didn't you tell me about the autopsy findings?"

She turns to slot a plate into the dishwasher. "I guess I didn't want to talk about it."

She's always watched what she said, measuring out her words carefully. It had been intriguing when they were first dating. He'd had to work to get past her cool exterior, and it had been a thrill to discover just how passionate she could be. They've been married for years. They have two children together, and they should be closer than ever. But Eve hadn't wanted to talk about something as important as Amy's death.

All the things they don't tell each other anymore.

SSSSS

His dad keeps eating. His mom pours Tyler's milk. Melissa cups her chin in her hand and scrapes her fork through her food. *Driving drunk,* his dad had said. *It's a crime.* Tyler hadn't even looked at Melissa, and Melissa hadn't looked at him. She'd be different, wouldn't she, if she'd killed someone? She wouldn't just go to school and hang out with her friends. But Melissa was good at lying.

After dinner, while his parents are busy in the kitchen, he goes down the hall and knocks on Melissa's door. He puts his mouth near the wood. "Melissa?"

No answer.

He looks down the hallway to the kitchen, tries again, scratching the wood this time. The door creaks open an inch. It's not locked. He pushes it all the way. Melissa's lying on her stomach, texting.

She's got her earbuds in, so he comes into the room. She looks up with an irritated expression and yanks out her earbuds. "What?"

He closes the door behind him. "I need to talk to you."

"So talk." She's texting, not really listening. He's not sure how to say it. What if he's wrong? She'd be really pissed. But what if he's right?

"You were drinking at Sherry's party."

She doesn't even look up. Her thumbs are moving fast, her hair falling forward and hiding her face. "You don't know that."

"Yes, I do. It's on Facebook. You're holding a can of beer."

Now she looks up, frowning. "Big deal."

So it's true. Fear tingles down his spine, but he pushes on. "And when you came home, you smelled like beer. And you were acting all weird." Stumbling into things, barfing into the sink.

"You're an idiot," she says, but she's sitting up now. She's paying attention, and she looks nervous, which only makes him feel sick.

"You were drunk." He wants her to deny this, tell him he's got it all wrong, but she's biting her lower lip, which she always does when she's hiding something.

"Just shut up," she says, but she doesn't say it like she means it. She says it like she's scared. "You don't know anything."

This is what she always says. *Tyler, you just don't get it. Tyler, you can't understand.* But this time he does know. This time he understands and he wishes he didn't. He's scared, too. His words all come out in a rush. "You were driving drunk." He can't look at her. "You were driving drunk, and then Amy—"

She slides off her bed. She grabs his shoulders, her fingers digging deep. "Then Amy *what*?"

She's taller than him, only an inch, but it feels like miles. He lowers his chin to his chest. He can't say it. No matter what, he just can't. She knows exactly what he's talking about. She can't make him put it into words. "We have to tell Mom." She'd know what to do.

She shakes him hard. "You're not going to tell Mom anything."

"But I have to."

She gives him a vicious shake, so hard this time that his teeth clatter together. "You don't know what you're talking about, so shut up." She lets him go. He stumbles back. He feels the marks of her fingers burning hot all the way through his shirt and sweatshirt. "Stay out of my life, Tyler. All you've done is fuck it up. You fuck up everyone's life."

It's true.

All the times, small and large—they swarm his memory. When Melissa shoved those older boys who were teasing him, when she wore sunglasses trick-or-treating even though they looked stupid with her princess costume, when she stopped being friends with that girl who opened his bedroom door by accident, even though she was the most popular girl in Melissa's class. He can't point to one and say, *There, that's the one.* It's all of them, together. So he has no choice but to stay silent, and he'd known that all along.

Tyler teeters on the doorsill. In or out? It's a warm night, everything soft and gray. The air teases at him. *Olly olly oxen free!* But he doesn't know.

Zach's at the movies with Savannah. His curfew's been lifted now that there's not a monster on the loose. Tyler used to be terrified of monsters. He made his mom keep all the lights on and the closet doors open. He thought all monsters had teeth and long, sharp claws. There are different kinds of monsters now.

Behind him, the air conditioner whooshes on. It's the kind of thing that might wake up his mom or dad.

Out.

He closes the door behind him. He doesn't look over at Holly's house. It could be on fire and he wouldn't know.

A light shines around Sophie's kitchen window. Is she taking a break from gaming to get a snack? He crosses her patio. There's a sliver of space between the windowsill and the edges of the blinds, and that's where he looks, pressing the side of his face against the stone wall and peering in with one eye. At first he doesn't see anything, only the gleaming surfaces of the counter, the refrigerator, the cabinets, and then she moves into range. She's got her back to him. He can see all of her, not just her head and shoulders. Her tight black dress is really short, and her shiny black boots go all the way up her legs. She's holding something down by her side, tapping it against her thigh as she paces. It looks like what Melissa uses for riding, only it's much longer. A whip? Then she turns and goes down the hallway. He waits, wanting her to come back so he can see what she looks like from the front, but minutes go by and she doesn't reappear.

Dr. Cipriano's house is full-on dark, not a glimmer of light anywhere. Tyler walks all around the house to be sure, then pushes himself in between the stiff tree branches that scratch at his sleeves. He kneels by the narrow window and holds up his new flashlight to play the beam of light around the room below. Pale linoleum floor, cement walls, and there—that huge cage. He looks close, but all he can see is gold-colored straw heaped inside the wire cage. There's nothing there. He's disappointed, but relieved, too. What if he'd seen a person in there?

It's weird, though. There's a bright blue plastic kiddie pool in one corner, like the one he used to have when he was little. He holds the beam of light steady, trying to understand what it is he's looking at. Then the straw slides apart, and something pale brown lifts out. Long and tapered, with two diamond eyes. He blinks. It's a snake. It's a *huge* snake. He stands up suddenly, smacks his head against a branch, and nearly cries out.

What's Dr. Cipriano doing with something like that? The dude's always seemed pretty boring before. Tyler's never seen a real snake, not even the little green snakes that his mom says are everywhere. He bets his followers would be interested in seeing this. They're always after him about The Beast. *Is it Bigfoot,* someone from Montana wants to know. *Probably just a cat,* a girl in Utah says. Maybe this will hold them off until he can get a picture of the real Beast.

Rubbing his head, he eyes the shadows around the basement window. He doesn't think snakes can slither up walls and punch through glass, but maybe this one can. He tells himself it's in a cage. He hopes Dr. Cipriano knows how to make cages.

He takes a dozen flash pictures. He's probably pissed the thing off now, so he backs out quickly and brushes the dirt from the knees of his jeans. That's the kind of thing his mom will notice and wonder about.

The bushes grow thick around Albert's house, reaching halfway up the first-floor windows. Rosemary wouldn't have liked that. She told Tyler that burglars could hide there and jump out at a person as they were going inside. Tyler's mom lets the bushes grow high around their house. She says it gives him an extra layer of protection.

Albert's in his La-Z-Boy in the family room, with his white cat, Sugar, in his lap. He's got that big old family photo album opened across his knees, and he's patting his eyes with a white tissue. Tyler's looked through that album plenty of times with Rosemary and laughed at Albert's plaid pants and little vests. Rosemary's pretty in those old photographs, with dark wavy hair. Tyler had only known her when her hair was white. There's one of her holding her baby, a boy named Bruce Wayne. *Don't you know that's Batman?* he'd asked Rosemary, and she'd shaken her head ruefully. Bruce Wayne had grown up to be a man called Wayne.

The Farnhams' brick house has its porch lights on and all the patio lights. It looks like an alien ship about to lift off. All the lights are off at Charlotte's house across the street. It hunkers down in the darkness like it's trying to hide.

There's something lying on the sidewalk, something small. He stops, waits for it to run away, but it doesn't move. He switches on his flashlight and sees the black fur and white splotch. It's a skunk lying on its side. Sleeping? No, this is its feeding time. This skunk is dead.

He walks over and looks down. There's no smell. He nudges it with his toe. There's no blood, either. It looks peaceful, its eyes closed. When squirrels die, their mates hang around nearby and cry. He shines his flashlight around in a big circle. Trees leap out at him, blank-faced. He turns back to the dead skunk. It looks so helpless. He turns off his flashlight and slides it into his pocket.

"Tyler, is that you?"

It's Holly, coming up the sidewalk toward him. She's been waiting for him. He turns and crosses the street. He doesn't want to talk to her.

"Hold on." She's trying to catch up to him.

He just walks faster. She'll see he means it and give up.

"I have something to tell you." Her voice is farther away.

He doesn't care what she has to tell him. He'll never babysit for her again. She can beg him and beg him, and he'll still say no.

"The police have a new suspect. I thought you'd want to know."

He stops and turns around. Holly stands in the middle of the street. Her hair's in a ponytail. She's wearing jeans and a sleeveless shirt. Her bare shoulders gleam in the moonlight, but he can't see her features. "Who?"

She walks toward him, taking her time. And when she gets right up to him, he still can't see her face, only the shadows slanting across her eyes and chin. "I can't tell you anything more."

He clenches his hands into fists. "How come?"

"It's an ongoing police investigation. I shouldn't have said anything, but I know Amy was your friend. All I can tell you is they've got new information."

"I don't believe you." The police must have seen the picture of Melissa on Facebook. But how would they have known to look?

She folds her arms like she's cold. "It's true. They've been working on getting a description of the car. From Amy's injuries, they can tell it was a big car."

"How big?"

"Probably an SUV."

"So? Lots of people have SUVs." There are two of them sitting in his garage right now.

"Yep. But not all of them were on the road that night. They're cross-checking traffic cameras, security tapes. You'd be amazed at how many cameras there are."

He knows this. Melissa will have driven past a traffic camera. She would have sailed down the road and been tagged by a million unseeing eyes. "That still doesn't mean anything."

"Well, of course they're looking for other evidence. Damage to the car, for one thing."

He'd know if his dad's car had been damaged, wouldn't he? "What else?"

"Blood and tissue left behind."

He can't think of Amy this way. "It was raining really hard."

"I know, but stuff can still get trapped in the grille."

"What if they washed the car, used soap?"

"I don't think soap would do it. They'd have to use bleach. But even so, we're talking microscopic particles. They wouldn't be able to get them all."

He breathes deep, thinking about this. "What if they get a new fender?"

"You mean, like take the car to a body shop?" She shrugs. "The police would check repair records; they'd find the original fender and examine it."

He knows this. But it's different when it's a stupid television show. It feels completely different in real life. "But it was an accident."

"Oh, Tyler. That doesn't matter. It's still murder."

He looks at her, light gleaming on her hair like a halo. She's smiling.

In the middle of the night, he pings Yoshi on Skype, but she doesn't answer.

SUNDAY, SEPTEMBER 7

SUNRISE 7:05 AM

SUNSET 7:55 PM

EVE

Charlotte's missing. *She said she just needed some fresh air,* Gloria told Eve, sounding frantic. *But it's been hours.* Everyone's out looking, but it's Eve who turns the corner and spots her friend in the distance. "Charlotte?" she calls out, and Charlotte turns, puts a hand to her eyes. She's gripping a piece of paper in her other hand. The trash bag by her feet flutters in the breeze. She's been taking down the flyers.

"Charlotte, you shouldn't be doing this by yourself."

"It's okay. I just couldn't bear it anymore." Charlotte's head is a skull, her eyes sunken, her skin stretched tight.

Of course not. "Let me help."

Eve reaches for a corner of the paper. It seems important to remove the flyer intact, so she picks at the tape with her fingers. The photograph has faded, but the words are large and bold. *Amy Marie*

Nolan. Missing. Reward. These are the things Charlotte wanted to emphasize. Eve tries to work the paper free from the tape, but it rips, peeling Amy's jaw away and leaving her merry laughing eyes behind.

"Amy's been released," Charlotte says.

Eve has the dizzying notion that Amy's back, that this has all been a freakish nightmare. Of course she's not thinking straight. What Charlotte means is that they can now plan the funeral. They walk to the next telephone pole.

"We've been going through photographs," Charlotte says. "Nikki wants to put together a montage for the funeral."

Only eleven years. There won't be any pictures of Amy in braces, or a prom dress, or self-consciously wearing her first bikini. Amy had always begged for someone to take her picture. *There are so many of Nikki,* she'd wailed. *And practically none of me.*

"Remember our first block party?" Charlotte says.

Eve knows which photograph she's talking about, taken of Charlotte and Owen, Eve and David as they stood in front of the blow-up castle teetering on Rosemary and Albert's front yard, smiling awkwardly. They'd been caught in mid-conversation, Owen turning from whatever he'd been saying to David so that his face was a little blurry. Charlotte had her head tilted toward Eve, and the curve of her pregnant belly is evident. Their friendship had still been new then, and shy.

Eve has studied the space between Owen and Charlotte, as Owen leaned away. Maybe he had been the first to leave their marriage, and Charlotte had been the first to act. Eve and David stand close, David with his arm around her waist. Melissa would have been playing somewhere in the background and Tyler would have been sleeping up in his room, waiting for his turn to join the party. She remembers feeling anxious about that, about being outside enjoying herself while her son was inside, trapped within four walls.

The result had been that she hadn't enjoyed herself at all. She'd kept glancing toward Tyler's bedroom windows and checking her watch.

"Scott fell out of the castle," Eve reminds her, "and broke his leg."

"Larry Farnham kept insisting Scott had fallen on Albert's yard and not his. Just in case we wanted to sue." Charlotte pushes the paper into the trash bag and they set off down the narrow sidewalk to the next streetlight. "Mom wants to use Amy's birth announcement, but I don't know. It's not the most flattering."

Two-day-old Amy with her puffy, squeezed-shut eyes and the red mark on her forehead from the forceps. She'd been dragged into the world, reluctant and blinking, to suit the obstetrician's vacation schedule. Charlotte always said that was why Amy was so stubborn, to punish Charlotte for not letting Amy decide when she was ready to be born.

"We should definitely use the one from her baptism," Charlotte decides.

Amy lying on her back in her long white gown, her arms extended on either side of her as if bracing herself. Those slippery pearl buttons on the back of the dress had drawn the fabric tight, too tight, so Eve and Charlotte decided to leave the top two buttons unfastened. It had been Nikki's baptism dress, but Nikki had been a smaller baby. Amy just barely squeezed in. Her feet peeped out from beneath the hem of the lacy dress, clad in tiny white patent leather booties that kept falling off.

"Remember how we looked everywhere for that shoe?" Eve asks. They'd crawled on their hands and knees and searched beneath every pew.

"Her right shoe, just like Melissa."

They had laughed, saying their daughters were twins separated at birth.

Charlotte had warned that Amy would howl the moment the priest dripped water across her forehead, but Amy had lain peacefully in Eve's arms, her brown eyes calm and thoughtful. Afterward, Eve had kissed her. *Good girl,* she'd murmured. She'd give anything, now, to go back to that perfect moment.

"Remember when Owen hid Amy's Easter basket in the dryer, and I didn't know and turned it on? The jelly beans melted over everything." Amy had gnawed at a sugarcoated towel to try to pry the candy loose. "I don't know why Owen's doing this," Charlotte says, and Eve knows she's not talking about Easter anymore.

"It's okay. The police won't find anything."

Robbie's explained that yes, he took the ravine road from his restaurant to Charlotte's house because there's a good place to pick up Chinese food along the way, and he's explained that he did give Amy the shamrock-embossed shot glass found in her bedroom trashcan because he often gave her small things from his restaurant. The text he'd sent Amy—*shape up or else*—was meant as a joke, not a threat.

What Robbie can't explain is his lack of an alibi. What he can't defend are the two speeding tickets he's gotten. Owen's pressed hard on those two points, and apparently the new detective's listened. He's interrogated Charlotte three times in the past few days. She's afraid he thinks that she and Robbie are mixed up in something bad. *How can he?* Eve asked. *It was an accident.* But Charlotte had not been reassured. *He thinks there's something else going on.* Eve had been confused. *Like what?* But Charlotte didn't know.

First Charlotte, now Robbie. No one was safe.

"It's hard to believe I was ever in love with Owen," Charlotte says. "I really thought we'd be together forever. What a cliché."

"It's not a cliché. It's hard. Marriage is hard," she says, thinking of David's unhappy face.

"My parents made it look easy. They stayed in love until my dad died."

Charlotte knows not to mention Eve's parents, though they, too, are still together. They stuff another flyer into the bag and move on.

"I'm thinking about selling the house," Charlotte says.

Charlotte doesn't think. She does. So what she's really saying is that she's moving. Of course she is. How can she stay in the house where Amy vanished, where her life was cut so abruptly short, where every time she goes out that front door she'll think of the last time Amy had stepped over the threshold? "I'm going to miss you," Eve says. Terribly, desperately.

"I won't move far, just a few miles."

Yes, but it won't be the same, and they both know it.

"I haven't touched a thing in Amy's room," Charlotte says. "I'll have to make decisions."

"I'll help you."

"Okay."

Charlotte squints into the sun. "There's something I haven't told anyone."

Here's a secret, Charlotte's gift for leaving, her compensation, a promise that would keep them friends, no matter what distance separates them. "It's okay," Eve says, not wanting to know.

"It's about the polygraph."

"It doesn't matter."

"It does matter. It matters to me. I lied when I said that I didn't know how long Amy was missing. I knew exactly how long she'd been gone. I heard her sneak out. I heard the door close. I thought, *Good*. I thought she'd sit on the porch and cool off, and then we could have a reasonable conversation about the whole thing."

"You couldn't have known she'd go out in the storm." But Amy was always doing risky things. Climbing that tree in Larry Farnham's yard. Eating a teaspoon of cinnamon on a dare. Sneaking to the park late at night.

"I let her sit out there for thirty minutes. When I went to get her, she was gone."

"Thirty minutes." Half an hour. An eternity.

"I can't stop playing it over and over. If only I'd stopped her when I heard the door open. If only I'd gone out to see if she was on the porch. It was just one of those decisions, you know? I was mad. I was relieved to have the break."

An extra second. That's all Eve would have needed. A single click of the second hand on the clock, and she and Charlotte wouldn't be standing here now, everything shattered, as the heat boils down and strips them bare. Eve sways. She thinks she's going to faint.

Charlotte sits down on the curb, wraps her arms around her bare, bent knees. "I'd do anything to take it back. Anything."

Words. That's all they are. There's no rewinding the clock. Eve sits down, and Charlotte leans into her. Her skin is warm, sticky with sweat.

"Amy died, and I wasn't with her. I was in my safe, dry house, thinking how great it was to have some peace and quiet." Charlotte sighs, a puff of air against Eve's arm. "Did she know she was dying? Did she call out for me?"

Eve could lift this pain from her friend. But Tyler's waiting for her. He needs her. She has to get home to him.

"I can't cry anymore. All I've done is cry. I've used up all my tears."

Eve had wept for months after Tyler's diagnosis, inconsolably, out of nowhere. She'd be standing in the grocery store and reach for his little hand and remember he wasn't there. Everywhere she looked there were small boys out in the daylight, doing ordinary things. She'd emptied herself out, become a shell, and then one day Charlotte had moved in and walked down the street to knock on Eve's front door.

The sun sits hard in the sky, uncompromising. It shoots beams of light through the branches, deflects them off passing chrome bumpers and windows, presses them against the thin cotton of her dress. Sweat trickles down her spine. Insects buzz in the grass. Her temples ache with the effort of keeping silent.

One second, out of trillions and trillions. Just one.

"Go home," Eve says. "I'll finish this."

Charlotte nods and pushes herself up.

A car whizzes past, blowing Eve's hair up in a gust of exhaust. The long ribbon of asphalt stretches out in front of her. Charlotte is a distant figure. Eve scrabbles at the dangling paper, yanks it free, and drops it into the bag at her feet. A hundred down. Hundreds more to go.

DAVID

David stands frowning into the refrigerator, its shelves bare. When was the last time anyone bought milk? Or bread, for that matter? He'd come in from mowing the lawn to make a sandwich and found the dried end of a loaf of bread buried beneath an onion that had sprouted a thick green root. As he backs the car out of the driveway, he sees the new family leaving for church. It's been years since he's attended a church service. Eve refuses. She said she didn't want to communicate with a God who would bless the world with sunshine only to condemn a child from ever seeing it. *What about Melissa's needs?* David had asked, and Eve had answered, *What about Tyler's?*

It's on his way back from the store that he sees someone walking along the side of the road ahead of him. For a brief disorienting moment, he thinks of Charlotte, running along the road that terrible stormy night. He draws closer and sees that it's Eve.

She turns as he pulls up alongside her. She's gripping a bulging trash bag by the neck. He rolls down the window. "What are you doing?"

"Taking down the flyers."

He's gotten used to seeing them on the street signs and telephone posts. He's begun to look through them as though they aren't there. "Good idea. You need any help?"

"No, it's okay. I think I got them all."

"Well, jump in. I'm on my way home."

She opens the door and climbs in, bringing with her the smell of grass and heat. Her shoulders are pink with sun. "Where've you been?"

"Grocery shopping. How's Charlotte? Any news?"

"The funeral's Saturday."

He thinks about that. "Okay. I'll try to make it."

She shakes her head and looks out the window.

"I told you I've had to take on extra work now that Preston's gone. I just don't think I'll make it home this weekend. I know I should have said something, but I thought I'd be further along."

"Okay."

They drive the rest of the way in silence. He pulls the car into the garage and switches off the engine.

"Eve? David?" It's Sophie, on the driveway behind them, peering in. "Can I talk to you for a minute?"

"Sure," he says. "Everything okay?"

Sophie stands there in full sun, as though unwilling to come any farther. She's got that broad-brimmed straw hat perched on her head, shadowing her narrow face. Her white shirt is long-sleeved, hanging loose over her brown slacks. Her gardening gloves are a discordant neon green. He goes out to meet her, with Eve. "You heard about that Peeping Tom, right?" Sophie asks.

"Why? Have you seen him?" Eve asks.

"No. I was going to ask you the same thing."

"I haven't seen anyone."

Sophie gnaws her lower lip. "Not even a car that doesn't belong?"

"I don't think so."

Sophie exhales. "I'm thinking about putting in an alarm system."

"Good idea," he says. After all, Sophie lives alone and her house backs up to the park.

"The company I interviewed suggested changing my outdoor bulbs. They say the ones I have now aren't strong enough."

She sounds defiant, and he wonders why. Then Eve says slowly, "Are you talking about switching to halogen light bulbs?"

"Maybe." Sophie's misery is evident.

He looks at the span of space between his house and hers. How many feet is it—twelve? Fifteen? Not enough.

Eve puts her hand on Sophie's arm. "What about Tyler?"

"I know, but I figure if he goes out your back door and stays across the street—"

"That won't work," Eve says. They don't know how far UV travels. She's consulted scientists about this. No one's been able to give her a definitive answer. They know that UV diminishes as it travels through space, but at what point does it vanish completely? *I wouldn't take any chances,* the dermatologist has warned them.

"What if I only turn them on late at night?" Sophie says.

Eve shakes her head. "You might forget and leave them burning all day. What about during the winter when the sun goes down early? Please, Sophie."

"I live alone. It's different."

"How about installing more lights, then?" Eve looks at David. "We'll pay for it, won't we?"

"Can't Tyler wear that mask he used to wear?" Sophie says.

"Sure." He wants to stop this. Sophie's made up her mind. She's not listening anymore. Can't Eve see that? Eve frowns at him, turns back to Sophie. "He won't wear it. He says it makes him look like a freak."

"Let me think about it." Sophie moves back, pulling away from Eve's grip on her arm. "Okay?"

"How about getting a dog?" Eve says.

Doesn't she see how ridiculous she's being? "Sophie doesn't want a dog," he says, warning. "Come on. Let's put away the groceries."

Eve's not listening. Her attention is focused on Sophie, who's edging away. "Halogen bulbs aren't that much brighter. They really aren't."

She's talking to Sophie's back. She whirls around to look at him, her face twisted with accusation. "Why did you do that? Why did you let her think it was okay?"

"I didn't let her do anything. This is America, Eve. People can choose what light bulbs they want to use." He pulls the plastic grocery sacks from the backseat.

She punches the button and the garage door lowers, squeezing out the light. "Tyler won't be able to leave the house at all."

"Then he'll just have to wear his mask."

"But he *won't*." Her voice sails up.

"He will if he wants to go outside."

They're sealed in darkness. He opens the kitchen door and she pushes past him. "There's got to be a way I can stop her. Maybe I can sue?"

"You sound like a crazy person."

She stops and looks at him, her hands flat on the counter. "How crazy is it to want to save my child?"

All the cures she's chased down over the years, the injections, the gel, some kind of blood treatment. The endless fundraisers. The hours hunched over a computer or staring into space. Everything, everything has revolved around keeping Tyler safe. "You're not the only one, Eve. We're all trying to protect him, but we have to be reasonable." He opens the refrigerator to put the milk away.

"How? How do *you* protect him, David? Tell me exactly what you've done to keep Tyler safe."

"Is that what you think? You think I don't care?"

She pushes the refrigerator door shut, bottles clanking, making him step back with surprise. "You *don't* think. You let things slide. You take the easy way out. You don't make the hard choices."

He throws up his hands. "Where the hell is this coming from? What do you call my decision to live away from this family? You don't call that a hard choice?"

She laughs, a bitter sound.

He stares at her. Her face is contorted, unrecognizable. Unlikeable. "What do you want me for, Eve? You don't let me touch you. You don't talk to me. What am I to you?"

She looks at him. He sees nothing in her eyes, no warmth, no love. She doesn't answer.

Later, they drive to the airport. He can't wait to get back to DC. In all ways, it's the opposite of how it should be. As they drive down the ravine road, they pass a line of police cars parked along the berm, uniformed officers walking up and down the shoulder, studying the ground. He glances at Eve and sees that she's watching them, too.

SECOND BASE

"You know what second base is, right?" Zach spins around in Tyler's computer chair. He's wearing those cool shorts with all the pockets that go down to his knees. His mom's offered to get him some, but Tyler can only wear them at home in his bedroom, so what's the point?

"Sure." Tyler's watched baseball on TV.

"That's how far I got with Savannah."

Oh. He should've guessed. Savannah's all Zach ever talks about, her and Amy. Only now he's not talking about Amy. He hasn't said one word about her since *hit-skip*.

"Cool."

"Yeah. I'm thinking about asking her to Homecoming."

Melissa went to Homecoming when she was a freshman. She'd

worn a shiny red dress with sparkles sewn around the waist. She'd looked like a flower. "Cool," he says again.

"You'd have liked that movie. We got to rent it when it came out."

He and Zach have seen a million movies together. They can recite lines and get each other laughing before they've even said more than a few words. They've debated which are the Top Ten Movies of All Time, and whether *The Mist* sucked or was genius. Zach's a good friend. Maybe he *can* help him figure out what to do. "Listen," he begins, but Zach says, "Savannah's got a friend. Tiffany? You know her."

Tyler shakes his head. He doesn't know Tiffany.

"Sure you do. She came over with everyone else when Amy was found. Hold on." Zach swings around to Tyler's computer. "I'll show you her picture."

"I don't want to see her picture."

"Sure you do. She's super hot." Zach taps keys, and the screen blooms from black to full color. "Dude. How come you're watching this crap?"

It's the driving tutorial Tyler found, showing how to change gears. His parents both drive automatic cars, but Tyler thinks he'd like manual. "Why not?"

"Because . . . you know."

Tyler wants him to say it. "What?"

"Well, it's not like you can drive."

"Who says?"

"I don't know. When can you get out of here? We can jump on the trampoline."

Tyler doesn't want to jump on the trampoline. "Who says?"

Zach frowns. "Jesus. What's the big deal?"

"Tell me."

"My mom, okay? She says not to talk to you about this kind of stuff."

Zach's been watching what he says around him? "Your mom doesn't know anything."

Zach looks mad. He's going to say something mean, and Tyler wants to hear it. But all Zach says is, "Come on, man. Let's do something. Wanna game?"

Zach's being careful. Like Tyler's going to cry or something? "Get out of here."

"Seriously?"

Tyler kicks the chair Zach's sitting in, sending it rolling. Zach pushes himself up. "Whatever."

Tyler listens to the sound of Zach's running footsteps on the stairs, the slam of the front door.

When he goes downstairs, his mom's at the sink, washing lettuce. "Hey, stranger," she says, giving him a smile that doesn't reach all the way across her face. She hasn't really smiled in days. "Why did Zach leave in such a hurry?"

"He had football practice."

"Really? At this time of night?"

"I guess."

"Well, it was nice to see him. I was going to ask him to stay for dinner. I could have given him a ride home."

"Maybe next time," Tyler says, though he knows there won't be a next time.

The evening's purple and filled with the green smell of cut grass and the sweet smoke of barbecuing. Voices come over fences; windows are opened to let out the sound of televisions playing. Holly's standing on her front porch, talking to a man. "Who's that?" Tyler asks.

"Oh, those are our new neighbors, Mark and Holly. I've forgotten you haven't met them yet. Want to say hi?"

Mark the Cop's bigger than he'd expected. His blond hair's

shorter than it was in his wedding picture, and his low voice rumbles all the way across the street to where Tyler and his mom are walking. Holly lifts her hands to her face and pulls back her hair. She looks unhappy. Are they fighting? "That's okay."

Mark turns and goes down the steps. He nods as he crosses to his car. Holly sees Tyler, but she doesn't wave or smile. She leans in the doorway with her arms crossed.

"They seem like a nice couple." His mom's face is puffy, like she's been crying again, but she's smiling, hard. "They have the cutest little boys."

She's already told him this, when she came back from asking them if they'd use regular light bulbs. "Uh huh."

Sophie's in her front yard, crouching by the flowers around her maple tree. She's wearing her floppy-brimmed hat tied beneath her chin and long gardening gloves. Her black hair falls over her shoulders. She looks like an old lady, nothing like what she looks like at night, dressed in black leather. She keeps her head down as she digs in the dirt, even though they're walking right past her. Tyler's mom doesn't say anything to Sophie, either. She just keeps on talking to Tyler about those two little boys, Christopher and Cameron, even though it's not Cameron, it's Connor. Tyler glances behind him and sees Sophie watching them from beneath the brim of her hat. Quickly, she moves around so that her back is to them, and he can't see her face at all.

Dr. Cipriano's unloading a box from the backseat of his car. It's covered with plastic. When he sees them, he sets the box on the ground and flexes his muscles, makes a face for the camera. It's a lame picture, but Tyler takes it anyway. "Nice to have those reporters gone, isn't it?" he says, coming over. He's wearing a short-sleeved green shirt and black jeans that look brand new.

Tyler backs away. That thing in his basement is a *python*. No one's allowed to have them. They swallow things whole—crocodiles, monkeys, deer, even people. He eyes the box on the driveway. He bets anything there's a live, frightened animal inside.

"I keep waiting for them to return," his mom says.

"Let's hope they don't. It'd be nice to have our street back to ourselves. I'm sure Charlotte hated it. How's she doing?"

Pythons can grow to be more than twenty feet long. They kill their prey by wrapping around them and squeezing. He realizes his mom's looking at him. Dr. Cipriano, too.

"Next month, right?" his mom asks.

His dentist keeps an illegal snake. His mom has no idea. "Yeah." She's circled the date on the calendar in black—*dental checkup*.

"See you then."

"Thanks, Neil."

Albert's standing in his front yard, frowning down at the ground.

"Hi, Albert," his mom calls, and Albert looks over.

"Hey. Got a minute? What does this look like to you?"

So Tyler and his mom walk over and look down. It's dark now, and hard to make things out. It looks like Albert's pointing to a heap of small brown pellets. Tyler crouches, and his mom grabs his arm. "Don't," she says, and he looks at her with surprise. "It's just cat food," he says. It's exactly like what Rosemary used to scoop out into Sugar's bowl.

"No, it's not. That's poison."

Tyler's fingers curl to his palms. He'd almost touched it. But he's wearing gloves, the way he always does.

She's looking all around the ground, toeing the leaves with her shoe. "It looks intentional." Her voice is worried.

"Nah," Albert says. "Who would do something like that? Had to be carelessness."

"I don't know, Albert," she says, but Tyler sees her glance to where Mr. Farnham's washing his car, rubbing the sponge down the hood. "But you'd better keep Sugar inside."

"I hate to do it. She loves chasing chipmunks."

"Listen to my mom," Tyler says fiercely, thinking about that huge python curled up in its cage, doing nothing but *watching*. "Rosemary would."

Albert looks at him. "I suppose you have a point. Oh, before I forget, tell Melissa congratulations. I see she got her license."

"I will," his mom promises.

Mr. Farnham is spraying his car with great arcs of water. Suds run down the gutter to the drain. It makes Tyler think of that last stormy night, when Amy died. Mr. Farnham waves, the way he always does, pretending they're friendly. Tyler's mom doesn't wave back.

They turn onto the bike path. "How come the Farnhams don't have any kids?" he asks.

"I don't know. Maybe they didn't want children, or maybe they couldn't have them. Your dad and I were lucky." She puts her arm around his shoulders and squeezes. She's smiling at him, and he pulls away.

"What if one of them wanted children but the other one didn't?"

She sighs. "Well, that would be really sad for the person who wanted children. Why, Tyler? Have they said something to you?"

It's not a lie to tell her. "No."

Kids are playing football in the field. They've got lanterns rigged to light the area and his mom moves over to block him. Tyler and Zach used to throw around a glow-in-the-dark football his mom got him. Once Zach threw the ball too far and it landed in the creek, and they had to run after it, laughing the whole time, as it swept along in the current. Tyler wonders how long it takes to make a memory go away. He wants this memory to disappear and take Zach with it.

They reach the playground. When Tyler was little, he used to think this place was just for him because no one else was ever around. He holds up his camera and focuses on the abandoned plastic bucket sitting on its side.

"You used to love playing in the sandbox," his mom says.

He'd dig in the sand that looked hard in moonlight but wasn't, and turn up the most amazing things. A matchbox car, a yo-yo, rubber balls, and polished pennies that gleamed like gold. It made him think the world was filled with treasure. Now he knows his mom must've done it, pulled the toys out of her pocket when he wasn't looking and dropped them in. What a dumb little kid he'd been.

"Let's sit down for a minute." There's an empty bench facing the basketball court. "I need to talk to you about something."

Melissa? He almost gasps this out loud. Instead, he aims his camera at the kid who's bouncing a ball and jumping high to dump it through the hoop.

"I talked with Nori the other day," his mom says.

He's been focusing on the strings hanging from the basket, trying to trap all of them within his viewfinder, and now he lowers his camera and looks at her.

"Yoshi's pretty sick," his mom says.

He'd been expecting this, but the words crawl through his skin and clutch his insides. He feels a little lightheaded. "How sick?"

"They've stopped the chemo." His mom puts her arm around his shoulders gently. "I'm sorry."

Yoshi's always been different. She knows the deal as much as any of them, but she never let it get to her. She just makes jokes. She's always made him feel better. It's impossible to think of her just . . . stopping. "How long?"

"Maybe a few weeks."

Weeks. It doesn't seem real. "I just talked to her. I never even tried on her stupid mask." They were going to celebrate when she turned twenty-one, that magical, defiant number. They were going to eat cake together on Skype and drink Dr Pepper. But she wasn't going to make it. He knows only two kids who did.

"It's okay."

"No, it's not."

"It won't happen to you."

He pulls away. "You don't know that."

"We're going to find a cure, honey. It's just a matter of time. Until then, we'll stick to the plan, okay?"

Sunscreen applied every two hours. Vitamin D pill taken with every meal. Ibuprofen, too, after his mom found that study that showed it reduced the risk of skin cancer. Stay inside; keep the drapes closed. "You think following the rules will save me. Yoshi followed the rules. She was careful."

"I'm not going to let anything happen to you."

"You can't stop it!"

"I won't give up. I'll never give up." She reaches over and pats his hair the way she always does, combing the curls with her fingers. "I'd do anything for you, honey."

He thinks of Yoshi, how she'd been hoping, too. Melissa has everything, *everything*. But she's the one who goes and does a stupid thing like drive drunk.

Holly's front door hangs open, leaving only the thin screen standing between the inside of her house and the outside. She must be around somewhere close. People just don't leave their doors hanging wide open in the middle of the night. Tyler cups his hands around his mouth and whispers into the darkness. "Holly?"

Silence.

"Holly!"

A sleepy voice drifts down. "Who's there?"

Relief washes over him. He steps off the porch and looks up the blank face of the house. He can't see her anywhere. "It's me. Tyler."

"Just a second."

He paces and she appears, a pale shape coming down the stairs that resolves into Holly, long bare legs flashing beneath the short nightgown she wears. She comes to the door and pushes it open, and he sees it's not a nightgown at all. It's a large T-shirt. She brushes hair out of her eyes. "Hey."

"Sorry," he says. "Your door was open."

"Was it?" She yawns. "You okay? You need to talk?"

He wants to tell her how terrible it's been, how confused and lost he feels, but an ocean of grief suddenly swells inside him. He's going to drown in all the words he wants to say. He will sob right in front of her.

"Hey," she says in a different voice. "Let's sit down."

There's a scratching noise and then a small burst of flame. The rich scent of vanilla rises into the air. She's lit a candle, which she now puts on the windowsill. "That's nice, isn't it? Chases all the scary thoughts away." She sits down on the hanging swing and pats the seat next to her. "I've been feeling blue tonight. I'm glad you're here."

She tilts her head back, closes her eyes. The candlelight robes her in warm, soft colors. She's wearing perfume. Shadow dips into the low neckline of her shirt. He averts his eyes. She pushes her foot along the floor, making the swing sway back and forth. "So tell me," she says. "What's making you so sad?"

Everything. "That suspect you were telling me about," he says, and she opens her eyes, looks at him. "Are they still looking at him?"

"I didn't say it was a him."

He can't swallow.

"I'm sorry, you know," she says, and he blinks. Her words cut through the air and come to him. "About the other night."

It feels like a million years ago.

"I'm so glad you come to visit me. You make me feel better, you know that? You make me feel like I'm not alone." She puts her hand on his thigh. He can't believe it. He doesn't dare move. Her touch is so light, but he can feel the heat from her body. "You know what you are?" He turns to look at her. Her face is close to his. He can see into her eyes, smell her perfume. She leans forward and he holds his breath. She touches her lips to his, and his heart swells. It's beating so hard he thinks it will leap right out of his chest. "My hero," she whispers.

I met a girl, he'd told Yoshi.

MONDAY, SEPTEMBER 8

SUNRISE 7:06 AM

SUNSET 7:54 PM

FULL MOON

EVE

The knock, when it comes, is a sturdy *rat-a-tat* that makes her set down her laptop and go immediately to the front door. She peels back the duct tape covering the peephole and sees a black man in a dark suit holding up a badge. She steps back. An innocent person would want to know what's going on. An innocent person would demand to know. So Eve grasps the doorknob and twists. But she's forgotten to undo the latch first. She fumbles through the motions, her fingers stiff and unwilling. She sucks in a shaky breath and opens the door.

"Mrs. Lattimore?" he asks pleasantly. "I'm Detective Irwin from the Columbus Division of Police. We're investigating the death of Amy Nolan. Would you have a few minutes to answer some questions?"

This is the homicide detective. This is the one she needs to be very careful around. They sit in her living room. He looks around the darkened room, the small globes of light from the lamps, but makes no comment. He opens a notebook and pulls a pen from his pocket. One of those pages will have her name written down on it. There will be comments, maybe questions. This man might have found a loose thread and is here to tug at it and see where it leads. She has to remain calm. If she tells herself she's innocent, then she'll sound like it's true. "Who else lives here with you?" he asks.

"My two children, my husband." He knows this. He must know this. She concentrates on keeping her expression smooth, her hands and feet still. Can he see her pulse jumping in her throat?

"Are they at home?"

Again, this must all be in that notebook he holds, or in a file on his desk. "My husband works in DC. My daughter's at school, and my son's upstairs."

He nods and she has the ridiculous feeling that she's passed some sort of test. This is the first time she's sat down with the police alone. Before, she had been with Charlotte, always with Charlotte. She's known this time was coming, and now that it's here, she's almost relieved. She's rehearsed these words, whispering them to herself as she lay in bed or stood alone in the predawn kitchen, watching steam rise from her cup. *No, I wasn't home. Yes, we're all horrified.* Here's the hard one, the outright lie: *The last time I saw Amy was at my son's birthday party.*

"Why don't we start with where you were Friday night, August 29," he says.

He knows where she was, or, at least, where she says she was. "I was picking up my husband from the airport."

"What time did you leave?"

"Just before seven. My husband's flight arrived at seven-thirty-five, but I wanted to leave a little extra time because of the weather. Oh, and I had to stop for gas." This sounds innocent, doesn't it, volunteering all sorts of details in an offhand way? "I went to the station on Fishinger." If he asks, she'll show him the receipt. She's kept it neatly folded in her wallet, ready to prove she has nothing to hide. *Here's where I was, going about my usual routine. I'm not a killer. I'm not a monster.* She's driven by and glanced at the gas station exit. There had been no cameras posted to make a liar of her.

"What route did you take to the airport?"

He listens as she winds her story, telling him she turned right instead of left out of the gas station, going down the ravine road away from where Amy had come running out of the woods. But he can't know that this detail matters, can he? Every word she says is small and stiff, a soldier of deceit. "Do you know where it happened?" Again, the offbeat casual note. She keeps her face smooth, with just a little normal curiosity on it.

"I'm sorry. I can't talk about an open investigation." She feels rebuked. But it had been a normal thing to ask, hadn't it? "What time did you get home that night?"

Here's where it gets murky. Here's where she has to be careful. "Eight-forty. My husband's flight was delayed." She had to pull over and wipe the mud from her shoes, comb her hair. She had to run into the airport restroom to wash her face and hands, change into the things she'd grabbed from the donation bag of Melissa's old clothes. A shirt and shorts, which she later dropped into a dumpster.

"Did you see anything? Someone driving erratically, maybe going too fast, changing lanes?"

"No." As soon as she says this, she wants to take it back. *Yes.* Yes, there had been a small silver car, appearing and disappearing in the washes of rain in front of her. She'd say she doesn't know why she hadn't remembered it before. But, of course, now she can't.

"Anyone walking along the side of the road?"

"Just Charlotte. We just saw Charlotte." She'd recognized her instantly, the loping form of her friend, and her heart had seized at the sight.

"That's when you learned Amy was missing?"

Hot tears spring to her eyes, even after all these days. Charlotte's frightened face as the rain poured relentlessly all around her.

He looks sympathetic. "So you were gone an hour and forty minutes?"

"Yes." Her voice wavers with emotion, but he can't be surprised by that. There is no flicker of suspicion on his face, and she thinks he believes her. She's tied those loose ends together, kept them from opening and revealing the gap of time where she was alone, down the ravine and crouching by the river.

Her cell phone rings from where it's plugged into the charger in the kitchen, and she says, "Excuse me." She needs this moment. She tells herself she has to see if it's Tyler or Melissa calling. She stands, awkward at leaving a stranger alone in her living room, and when she sees that it's a call from Nancy, Brittany's mother, she doesn't answer. She returns to where Detective Irwin sits, and she has the uncomfortable sensation that he's studied this room thoroughly in her absence, and memorized its contents. Photographs of the children line the walls, pictures of her and David from happier times. "I work from home."

He nods. This is also something he already knows. "Would you mind if I ask your son a few questions?"

"Tyler has a rare condition. He can't be exposed to sunlight."

"He's in his room? Could we talk there?"

She looks at this man, with his even features, his closely cropped hair. He seems relaxed, loosely holding his notebook in which he's been jotting down her responses. He wouldn't consider Tyler a suspect, would he? Detective Watkins had. "I don't know what he can tell you."

"I'd like to go over what he told the other officer, see if he's remembered anything else. We don't know what could be important."

What if she says no? Now that they're looking for a driver, surely they realize Tyler has nothing to do with this. She glances at the clock. It's the end of the school day. Tyler would only miss the last few minutes of math. "All right." This is what innocent people say. Innocent people want to help.

Tyler's quick to answer when she calls through the door. "Okay. Hold on."

"It'll be a few minutes," she tells Detective Irwin. On the other side of the door, Tyler's going through his ritual tapping. It kills her, knowing this.

It's a small landing and she's uncomfortable standing so close to this stranger. She doesn't know where to look, what to do with her hands. It's a relief when Tyler calls and she can open the door and step quickly through and away. She closes the door behind them.

Tyler comes out to sit down in his desk chair. He's in oversize jeans, tightly belted around his hips, the hems tattered. *Mom, this is the way all the guys wear them.* She worries about those frayed threads, but his feet are covered by thick cotton socks. His bony elbows poke out from the short sleeves of his white shirt, the collar rumpled. She wants to pat it into place, run her hand down the smooth muscles of his forearm, grab his hand and intertwine her fingers through his. He's getting so big. She stands close beside him as Detective Irwin pulls over a second chair. "Hi, Tyler," he says. "I'd like to ask you some questions, if you don't mind, about the Friday night Amy went missing."

A quick glance up at Eve. She smiles reassuringly. "Okay," he says.

"You were home that night?"

"Yeah."

"Do you remember what time your mom left?"

This is unexpected and it catches her off-guard, an arrow through her throat. She can't make a sound. Detective Irwin's checking up on her. He must suspect her, after all.

"Sure," Tyler replies easily. "It was six-fifty-nine."

"You're sure of that?"

"Yeah. I got to come out seventy-one minutes early that day because of the storm."

"I see," he says, and for the first time since he entered her house, Detective Irwin seems nonplussed. She keeps her face neutral. She doesn't want to see the sympathy on this man's face.

She waits for Detective Irwin to ask about that—people always want to know how Tyler manages—but instead he asks, "Were you home alone?"

A slight hesitation makes her look at her son more carefully. He's playing with a pencil, scraping his thumbnail against the paint. One of Melissa's pencils, colored with pink and purple psychedelic swirls. He's hiding something, but what?

"No," he says. "My sister was here."

"What did you do after your mom left?"

Tyler shrugs. It's clear he's uncomfortable.

"Why do you need to know this?" she asks.

"I'm wondering if Tyler looked out the window, maybe saw Amy leave her house," he explains, and Tyler says, "I already told that other detective I didn't see her. It was raining too hard to see anything."

"What did your sister do?"

"She was in her room, mostly."

"Who answered the phone when Mrs. Nolan called?"

"I did."

Why is Detective Irwin so interested in this? Charlotte's already told the police she called and spoke with Tyler. There's nothing here, but the man seems to be headed somewhere. She puts her hand on her son's shoulder and he glances up at her, then sets the pencil down and clasps his hands together.

"What did Mrs. Nolan say?"

"She told me she couldn't find Amy, so I looked around for her."

"Did your sister help?"

"No." Tyler's bouncing his knee up and down. He's not a fidgety child. Something's going on here.

"Any of your friends stop by that night?"

"No."

"What about your sister's friends?"

"No," she says, interrupting. "No one came by. My children would have told you if they had."

The garage door rumbles below. Tyler sits back, and she feels a curious sense of relief. Whatever it was—whatever had been about to happen—is gone.

"That your daughter?" Detective Irwin asks. "I'd like to talk to her if I may."

It's all right to let him do that, isn't it?

Melissa's in the kitchen, standing in front of the refrigerator. "Mom," she says, "why's there a strange car parked outside?"

"Honey," she says, and Melissa turns and sees Detective Irwin. Her face closes down. Eve wants to tell her not to worry, not to be afraid. "This is Detective Irwin. He's going around and talking to everyone about Amy."

"Okay." She crosses her arms, leans against the counter.

"Hi, Melissa."

"Hi," she says guardedly.

"School just started?"

"Uh huh."

"What year are you?"

"A junior."

"Looking at colleges yet?"

"Some."

"My son's a senior. Thinking about being a Buckeye."

"That's nice," Melissa says politely.

"So," he says. "I want to talk to you about the Friday night that

Amy went missing. I know you've already gone through this with Detective Watkins, but if you don't mind, I'd like to go over everything again."

"Okay."

"What do you remember about that night?"

"The weather sucked. My mom went to the airport to get my dad."

"And then what?"

She shrugs. "My dad came home and told me about Amy."

"What time was that?"

"I don't remember."

"Okay. So when you went out that night, did you notice Amy on her porch? Did you see her walking?"

"My daughter didn't go out," Eve says. It's troubling that he's gotten things wrong. It suggests that he could make other, worse mistakes. "She was home all night."

Detective Irwin flips back a few pages in his notebook. "Are you sure? Your neighbor reports seeing Melissa drive away about thirty minutes after you left."

"What neighbor?" Eve says, bewildered, then understands. "Albert?" She shakes her head. "He's wrong. Melissa just got her license. She couldn't have been driving that night."

"That true, Melissa?" Detective Irwin asks, and Melissa makes a face. "Albert's ancient. He doesn't know anything," she says.

Unease curls through Eve. This isn't Melissa. She doesn't talk this way about Albert. Eve glances at Detective Irwin. He isn't looking at Melissa. He's looking at her.

DAVID

David had woken up that morning to the strange feeling that someone else was there. He'd pushed himself up from the sofa to see Renée sitting at the kitchen counter in a T-shirt and bright pink sweatpants. She'd looked particularly young with her face scrubbed clean. "Sorry. Did I wake you?"

She'd sprung up from the couch when he came into his apartment the night before. *You should have told me you were here,* she'd exclaimed. *I could have picked you up.* Her happiness upon seeing him had been clear. It had shined into every corner. He'd insisted she keep the bedroom; he'd sleep on the couch. She'd protested, but there was no sense in her finding a hotel at that time of night, was there? They'd ordered pizza and turned on the game. She'd wanted to know about Amy and had listened sympathetically. He asked about Jeffery, and she said he'd been calling, wanting to talk things over. She wasn't ready. She might not ever be ready. Of course she was right. Jeffery had said terrible things to her, things a person couldn't forget. David had pushed away his fight with Eve.

The Steelers rolled over the Eagles. Renée had kicked off her shoes and they'd cracked first one beer, then another. Columbus had felt a million miles away. He'd glanced over at one point and saw tears streaking her cheeks. He'd been moved to say, *Why don't you stay here until you find your own place?* She didn't want to impose, but he gently insisted. He'd like the company, he told her, and she nodded and reached for the tissue box.

The day passes quickly, and just before six, David turns off his office light and heads toward the conference room. Renée's already there. She looks up with a wide smile. "I just put on a fresh pot. The good stuff, not the office dreck. I got it at that little coffee shop in your apartment building. Did you know they reopened under new management? It looks clean. You'll have to check it out."

"I will." He pours them each a cup of coffee and sits across from her. She fits so easily into his life. She knows which elevator in his building jolts at each floor. She knows which news station he prefers, and that he'll eat any topping on pizza except for pineapple. She's no trouble at all, except for the fact that his sofa is rapidly wearing out its welcome on his lower back. He stretches, rubs the spot.

"Thanks," she says, accepting the cup he holds out. "I'm wondering. Do you think we should include the group from Kansas?"

"Geography might bias the results. Let's stick to East Coast examples."

"Got it."

Outside in the hall, doors open and close, footsteps retreat. Everyone's leaving for the day. It's pleasant to be cocooned in this bright, warm space with Renée.

She sips her coffee. "Jeffery called this afternoon. He wants to know when I can come get my things."

"Might be good to get it over with."

"I know. Damn, this sucks."

"Want me to help?"

She looks at him, her face alight. "You wouldn't mind? It's not much, mostly clothes."

"Tell Jeffery you'll stop by later this week."

"Yeah. Make him wait." The smile she gives him seems genuine.

His cell phone chimes. It's Eve. "Hey," he says.

"Can you talk?" She sounds upset.

"Sure. Hold on." He stands up. "Be right back," he tells Renée. In the hallway, he says, "Are the kids okay? Is it Tyler?" This is it. She's found something.

"No, no. Tyler's fine. But he lied to us, David. Melissa, too. Both of them, and now I think she's in trouble."

"Trouble how? What are you talking about?" His little girl.

Melissa had taken the car without permission while Eve was picking him up from the airport. She didn't even have her license. "All right, well, it's not the worst thing that could happen. She's safe, right? We'll take away her phone. We won't let her borrow the car, not until she proves she can be responsible."

"You don't understand. I'm not being clear. The police know. A homicide detective was here. He's the one who told me that Albert saw Melissa drive up the street that night."

"So, what does that mean? Are they going to fine her?" His head pounds. "If the police don't take away her license, I will." He knows better than to suggest punishing Tyler, who had been complicit in this whole coverup. Eve would never hear of it.

"David!" Her voice is shrill. He winces. "Listen! Forget about punishing her. That's not why I called. I think he thinks Melissa did it."

"You just said he knows it."

"No, no, not driving without her license. He thinks she's the . . . driver."

A shiver creeps up his spine. He ticks past the images of that night ten days before. He remembers coming into the kitchen and pulling his children to him. The kitchen had been bright and filled with the aroma of freshly brewed coffee. Melissa's hair had been wet, but she'd just gotten out of the shower. Hadn't she? His head had been busy with a thousand things. Of course he'd never suspected that she'd been out in the storm. Is it possible that Melissa could have hit Amy and managed to keep it hidden from him and Eve? "Do *you*?"

"No!"

Her certainty's reassuring, but Eve could be blind when it came to the children. "What did he say specifically?"

"Nothing, really. It was more the way he looked at her, like he didn't believe a word she was saying."

"Well, she *was* lying, right? But that's no reason for him to suspect her of anything more serious."

"Maybe," she says slowly.

"Melissa knows she's made a mistake. Let's all calm down and see what happens, okay? They're not going to arrest her, not without some sort of proof."

Later, while he's eating sushi from plastic trays with Renée in his living room, their feet up on the coffee table as they watch football, he thinks about this. What sort of proof would the police be looking for? He sets down his chopsticks.

"What is it?" Renée asks, and he shakes his head.

He can't say it. He stands and goes into the bathroom, closes the door. He runs cold water into the sink and splashes it up onto his face, lets it drip down. He grips the sides of the sink and looks down into the basin. The sort of proof the police would be looking for would be a damaged fender.

DO-OVER

Voices crawl through the vent. Tyler sits on the floor, listening hard. Detective Irwin isn't like Detective Watkins. He hadn't spent a second looking around Tyler's room. He'd been focused on Tyler, and he'd listened carefully. Tyler had hurried through his answers, wanting him to leave, and then he did. Only, to his horror, it had been to talk to Melissa.

His mom's waiting for him when he comes out of his room. She's got her arms crossed and she looks upset, like she's thinking a million things all at the same time, all of them bad. His stomach twists. "Come downstairs. I need to talk to both of you."

Melissa's sitting on the couch with her arms wrapped around her bent knees. There's something weird about her and he realizes she's not holding her cell phone or laptop. Tyler sits down beside her, but she refuses to look at him.

"I want you to tell me exactly what happened that Friday night," his mom says.

He glances at Melissa. What has she told their mom so far? His mom would really be hysterical, wouldn't she, if she knew? How much does that detective know?

"Don't look at Melissa," his mom says, and reluctantly, he looks back at her.

"She took the car," he says miserably. Beside him, he feels Melissa stiffen.

"Brat," she mumbles.

"Enough of that," their mom says sharply. "You went to that party, didn't you, Melissa? Why? What was so important that you would do something so risky?"

And now Tyler understands that this is all about Melissa driving the car without her license. The detective must know just this one piece of what happened, which is good news. Which is great news, and he doesn't understand why Melissa doesn't get it, why she's sitting there looking so angry. Unless there's something else he doesn't know about.

"Nothing happened," Melissa says, which is a big fat lie. "I was gone for, like, thirty minutes."

She was gone for more than an hour. She's lying about everything.

A sharp knock on the front door makes them all look toward it. His mom goes over to open the door, and it's Charlotte standing there. But it doesn't look like her, with her hair sticking up every which way, her bathrobe hanging open over shorts and a T-shirt. "Charlotte?" his mom asks. "What is it?"

"Why didn't you tell me?" Charlotte looks around and sees Melissa. Her eyes narrow and she pushes past his mom. Tyler feels Melissa shrink against him.

"Tell you what?" his mom answers, but Charlotte's right there, hauling Melissa up from the couch by her arms and shaking her. "Is it true? Is it?" He's never seen Charlotte like this. She's always been smiley and jokey with them. She's always hugged them and brought them things. "Tell me! Did you hurt Amy?"

His mom's pulling at Charlotte's shoulder. "Stop it, Charlotte. Let her go."

"No! I never saw her! I swear!"

Melissa's so convincing. Tyler wants to believe her. He wants to go along with the urgency in her pleading voice to where everything's okay, but he can't.

"You lied to the police! You lied to me! You lied to everyone!"

Melissa looks scared. "I know. I know, but I didn't *do* anything."

"That's enough!" His mom drags Charlotte, stumbling, away. Melissa rubs her upper arms. Her face is white. She sinks down beside Tyler, her knees knobby and pressed together.

Charlotte whirls on his mom. "I thought you were my friend! I counted on you. I *trusted* you!"

"I am your friend. Of course I am. Charlotte, please." His mom looks so helpless. She and Charlotte have been friends forever. Just like he and Zach had been.

"You never said a word. Not one fucking word!"

"I know you're upset. I'm upset, too, but Melissa did *not* hurt Amy."

"You can't protect her, Eve, not from this. That detective, he's getting to the bottom of this. He's close."

Something rises in Tyler's throat, something hard and round. He can't swallow.

"Really?" his mom says, but her voice trembles. She's terrified and that scares him even more. "That's great news."

"I didn't do it," Melissa says in a small voice. "You have to believe me."

Charlotte stares down at her. Her gray T-shirt has a brown stain on the hem. The pocket of her striped blue-and-white bathrobe sags; the sash drags on the floor. She doesn't even seem to see Tyler. "I don't know what to believe anymore." His mom puts a hand on Charlotte's arm, but Charlotte throws it off. "I can't even believe *you* anymore."

"No, Charlotte," his mom says. "That's not true."

"Stop, just stop. You'd do anything for your kids. Anything. You'd lie right to my face."

His mom lifts her chin. She crosses her arms, and she and Charlotte stand there for a long heavy second, staring at each other. Then Charlotte shakes her head and leaves, leaving the door hanging open behind her, the dark street stretching away. Tyler's mom walks quickly over and shuts it, snapping the latch with a hard *click*.

They sit in their usual spots, his mom on the couch beside him, Melissa curled up in the armchair, but none of them pick up their laptops or their phones. No one reaches for the remote to turn on the television.

"Do you believe me, Mom?" Melissa says.

"Of course I believe you. Of course I do."

But it doesn't matter what his mom believes.

Dawn's close, just a couple of hours away. The night is clear, every star sparkling bright. If he reached up, he could touch them. His mom wouldn't go to bed. Every time Tyler cracked open his bedroom door, he saw the halo of lamplight shining on the living room floor below. He'd actually fallen asleep at his desk, only to wake up with a jerk.

Something's over in Holly's yard, moving low against the grass. The something straightens and becomes Holly. She has a bucket in one hand and a trowel in the other. She's wearing a long silky dress that clings to her back and hips.

He's so surprised to see her, he just stops. "Hi."

Her hair's messy, not as shiny as it appears in candlelight. Things look different in different light. Things that appear soft at night can be hard during the day, just as things that seem hard and crisp in the moonlight can be revealed to be creamy or flexible if you touched them. Grass, for instance.

She doesn't smile back, and he feels embarrassed, like she's not happy about seeing him. Maybe it's because she's in her nightgown. Now that she's turned to face him, he can see the way the cloth molds to her chest. His heart gives a funny leap.

"I couldn't sleep," she says. "I've been thinking about these grubs."

So she's not upset about his being there. She doesn't know that Melissa's in trouble. She's just worried about the skunk. She crouches and stabs at the grass with her trowel. "I've been trying to dig them up. Do you know what they look like?"

"Like white worms."

"That's right."

She's curved up like a *C,* her chin almost touching her knees. The bones of her spine poke up a line of bumps beneath the tautness of her dress. Her feet are bare, blades of grass standing up between her toes.

"Do you want me to help?" He looks around for a fallen tree branch. Grubs don't dig in deep. He can poke them out for her with a sharp stick.

"Can you see with those sunglasses on?"

She's not being mean, just matter-of-fact. "Sure." He can see lots of things with his sunglasses on. He has his eyes checked every six months, even his eyelids are flipped up and examined. His doctor says the reason he has good vision is because he wears shades all the time.

He squats beside her. Her dress is tight around her calves, and there are small irregular patches of polish on her toenails, silver, like moonlight. They work for a while. It's too dark to see much, but she seems intent on the process so he tries to see into the dark earth for the telltale pale gleam of a grub.

"They say the hardest thing in the world is losing a child," she says. "They say you never get over it. Do you think it's true?"

"I guess." His mom gets quiet sometimes, looking at him.

"Do you think it's worse when your kid's little or when they're older?"

"I don't know." He's never once thought about it. Does the age of a person matter?

"It's got to be worse when they're older. I mean, they're lumps when they're babies. It's not like they can talk or anything. They just lie there and cry."

This is a weird way to talk about a baby, especially when you have one. He's splashing around in a big deep pool and can't see the sides.

"Maybe she's relieved," Holly says.

Charlotte's not relieved, though. He knows that for certain. "I think she's just sad."

"Maybe it's for the best. Maybe Amy'll be born to another family and have a different life."

"You mean like reincarnation?" He jokes about this with his XP friends all the time. Although, sometimes, they're not joking.

"What if you could come back as someone different? What if you could have a do-over, not make the same mistakes again?"

What if he could come back as a kid who didn't have XP? "What kind of mistakes?" he asks, feeling brave.

"All of them. What if you could live a perfect life? You wouldn't have to worry about money, or love, or responsibility. You could be happy. You could be free."

"You're not happy?"

"Mark says I should be." She's angry, but what about? Did he say something to upset her? *I was going to be an actress,* she'd said.

Dirt is just the mashed-up pieces of rock. It's soft and yielding, but it once was hard. This dirt is limestone and shale. Way below it, deeper than man has ever gone and probably ever will, lies enormous reservoirs of sandstone, metamorphic and igneous rock. He used to think that he could reach them with his little plastic shovel. He and his mom would carve out holes in their backyard and they wouldn't get too far before he'd give up. Probably, all told, he'd only gone a few inches beneath the surface.

"Holly?" he says, and shivers at the warmth of saying her name. "A new detective came by today."

"Detective Irwin? He talked to me, too." The muscles of her arm are tight as she punches the ground.

"Do you think he'll find out who did it?"

"Probably."

He focuses hard on the hole he's digging, churning up small chunks of dirt. "What if it turns out to be a kid?"

"That won't change anything. Anyone who's old enough to drive is old enough to be tried as an adult."

He bashes the point of his stick into the soil, tearing up pieces of grass, and spies something small, smooth, and light-colored. A grub? He scrabbles at the dirt around the soft gray shape and pulls out a flower bulb. A long scrape marks where the edge of his stick cut into its flesh. "Sorry."

"It's fine."

Still, he pushes the bulb back into the ground and presses the soil all around it. "It'll be okay," he promises.

She doesn't answer. She's stabbing at the ground over and over with her trowel, and if there are any grubs lying there, they're probably being smashed to pulpy pieces. He supposes that's just as good as pulling them up and dropping them into a bucket. "I don't think you have to worry about the skunks anymore," he tells her. "Someone's poisoning them. I saw a dead one the other night."

She nods. "Good."

He doesn't know why this bothers him. Skunks are pests. He jabs the stick into the dirt and sees the telltale pale curve. "Here's one." He pincers the fat creature from its hiding place.

"Kill it."

He looks at the grub coiled in his palm. It had given no resistance to being plucked from its home. It lies there with its shiny little brown head and its miniature antenna, its front legs curled peacefully by its round tail, as though it's sleeping. How can he kill something that has no idea its end is so near? He nudges it with his finger to wake it up and give it fair warning, but it lies perfectly still. Is it feigning death, or is it really and truly dead? Amy had been alive one moment, then dead the next. She would have appeared to be sleeping, too.

He heaves the grub into the air. It lands on the sidewalk, tiny legs churning. The grass is coming alive, every blade defining itself, turning greener right before his eyes.

The rocks that line the flower bed are rosy; birds are singing. Colors begin to emerge from the darkness: the blue of Dr. Cipriano's shutters, the red of the Farnhams' car, the green of Sophie's mailbox. This is the world hidden from him.

The sun's coming up, the earth rolling toward it like a marble across the floor.

TUESDAY, SEPTEMBER 9

SUNRISE 7:07 AM

SUNSET 7:52 PM

EVE

Detective Irwin had been on his way out the door when he stopped and looked as though a thought had just occurred to him. *Mind if I look in your garage?* She had answered right away. *Sure.* Later she wondered if she should have protested out of feigned innocence, but instead she had led the man meekly through the house and out to the garage. He had crouched and studied both cars, shined his flashlight all around. When he stood up his face showed nothing at all. *Just a formality,* he'd said. *We're checking everyone's vehicles.* Thank God she'd been driving her car around. Thank God the fender had some wear on it.

After Charlotte left, Eve had opened a bottle of wine. She never drank when David was out of town—what if there was an emergency?— but she twisted the corkscrew in and pulled the cork out with a resounding pop. She stood at the kitchen counter and drank down half a glass before refilling it, then went back in to sit with the children. They all felt bruised. Charlotte's accusations spun around and around them, the conviction in her voice when she said, *That detective, he's getting to the bottom of this. He's close.* Thinking of it, Eve had gotten up and poured another glass.

After Melissa leaves for school, Eve goes into her daughter's room, breathes in a feral tangle of aromas—the bitter tang of nail polish, sweet floral shampoo, baby powder deodorant. Papers lie in drifts across the floor, covered with her daughter's tiny cramped handwriting. She picks up a sheet, an essay about President Lincoln. Melissa's doodled in the margin, a series of interlocking hearts with her initials, *ML,* and *AB.* Adrian's. Eve glances at the date scrawled at the top right-hand corner, sees this paper's from last spring. Melissa and Adrian had only started dating over the summer, so these hearts were wishful thinking.

Clothes, slippers, the cookie-shaped pillow Melissa sewed in middle school, belts, purses, the rhinestoned shoes she wore to Homecoming freshman year with heels as thin as pencils. Her pony-printed umbrella, the huge floppy cloth doll with long yellow yarn hair that Eve's mother had given her for Christmas ages ago.

Under the bed lie textbooks, more papers, shiny silver CDs.

Her dresser drawers hang open, overflowing with underwear and bras and shirts. She pokes around the back of the sock drawer—not one of them bundled into a matching pair—and feels the smooth surface of glass. It's a bottle of hard lemonade. Four of them, all empty, fitted neatly into the drawer like puzzle pieces and covered up by the mishmash of socks.

She stands there, holding one, and thinks about this. Melissa had somehow gotten hold of alcohol, brought it into the house, and consumed it, all without Eve's knowing. She'd been clever about it. She could have sneaked these bottles into the trash or the recycling, taken them somewhere else entirely, but she'd hidden them here, within easy reach. It's as if she wanted Eve to find them.

Eve drives to school to pick up her daughter. When Melissa comes out of the school building and sees her standing there, her step slows. "What happened? Is it Tyler?"

Eve feels a wash of sorrow. Always this. Look what she's done. "Tyler's fine." She has the impression of something hurtling toward her. Her daughter has needed her, and Eve has been absent. *That detective, he's getting close.* "I thought we could spend some time together." These past days have been a murky blur. She has no memory of them. She feels her grasp on her daughter's life loosening. She wants desperately to pull her child close.

Melissa adjusts her backpack over her shoulder. Her face becomes implacable. "Why, so you can yell at me some more? Dad already did."

"No, not so I can yell at you. Want to go to the barn? It's been years since I've been there." Taking Melissa to her lessons has been David's purview, their special time together.

"You're acting weird. What is it? Is it the police?"

That terrible scene with Charlotte. That terrible, terrible scene. *I thought you were my friend!* "No, I just want to meet that mean horse Sammy you've been talking about."

"I don't want to go to the barn."

Eve holds up the remote and unlocks the door. "Are you sure? Didn't you tell me one of the horses is about to have a foal?" This detail comes to her, bobbing amid a sea of disjointed impressions and conversations.

"You don't even like horses."

"Sure I do." But it made Eve nervous, watching Melissa bounce in the saddle. She was always worried the animals would pick up on that.

"No, you don't." Melissa gets into the car and slams the door.

Eve takes a deep breath. "Melissa," she says. "I talked to Brittany's mom." Nancy had been quick to leave work to meet Eve for coffee. *I promised Brittany I wouldn't say anything, but we mothers have to stick together.*

"So?"

"So I know Brittany's been drinking." *Brittany wouldn't get out of bed. I thought she had the stomach bug. Turns out she was hungover. Can you believe it?* "I know you have, too. I found the empties in your drawer."

Melissa straightens. "You were in my room? You went through my things?"

All those times Melissa kept her bedroom door firmly closed. Eve had had no idea. "How long has this been going on? Have you been drinking at other people's houses?"

"Like it's such a big deal. Everyone drinks in high school."

"I don't care about everyone. I care about you." She reaches out to tuck a dangling strand of hair behind her daughter's ear, but Melissa jerks away.

"I can take care of myself."

"Of course you can't. You're only sixteen. I understand you think that's all grown-up, but it isn't." Melissa scowls and crosses her arms. She looks the very picture of her toddler self. "I love you. I love you so very much. You know that, don't you?"

Some kids clatter by; their laughter reaches them through the closed windows. Melissa scrunches down in her seat. "Mom, stop."

"I know I focus on your brother. I know I don't pay as much attention to you. I'm sorry about that."

"I'm fine!"

But she's not. "You've been so moody lately. Something's bothering you. Tell me. Talk to me."

"If we're not going anywhere, then I'm going back to class." Melissa puts her hand on the door handle, and Eve reaches out without thinking for her daughter's arm. Melissa shakes her free. "Seriously, Mom?"

"Honey, *please*."

"I had sex. S-E-X. Okay? You happy now?"

Eve sits back, stunned. She can't speak. Melissa's face is twisted with triumph.

"Adrian?" Eve manages, but this isn't what she really wants to know. What she wants to know is, *Are you okay? Was he kind?* What she wants to say is, *This can never be undone.*

"I don't want to talk about it."

"We have to talk about it. Are you using birth control? Please tell me you are."

"It's none of your business."

"Of course it's my business."

"Sure it is." Melissa is staring steadfastly out the window. *"God."*

Her mind is spinning. She isn't prepared for this. She hadn't seen it coming. She's never even met Adrian's parents. "Condoms aren't enough. You know that, right? You need to get on birth control." She doesn't want her daughter having sex in the backseat of a car or somewhere where she might not take the time to be careful. "I'll call my doctor and get you in right away. She's very nice. You'll like her." She doesn't want this. She doesn't want to be talking to her little girl about going to the gynecologist. She wants to go back to when it was the pediatrician and stickers if Melissa was good and lollipops when there were shots.

"Just forget it."

"Of course I can't forget it."

"I knew you'd be like this."

"Do his parents know?" What do people do? Do they discuss this; does she tell them their son's been sexually active?

"Oh, my God. You can't call his mom. You can't!" Something small and silvery falls onto Melissa's jeans-clad thigh and darkens the denim.

"Oh, honey. I know you're embarrassed . . ."

Melissa's shaking her head, scrubbing her eyes with her fingers. "I thought he loved me."

Her heart just sinks. "Who? Adrian?"

"He won't even text me. What did I do wrong?" Her voice is so small. She sounds so lost and confused. Her head is bent, her hair falling forward to hide her face.

"Oh, my darling." She takes her daughter's hand in hers, warm and soft. "You didn't do anything wrong."

"He's dating Sherry now. Sherry!"

"I know it hurts. I know." She remembers all those moments that felt like the end of the world, when everything loomed so large.

Melissa looks at her. "I hate him."

Eve nods. "I hate him, too."

"He said I was special."

"You *are* special. He's a jerk."

Melissa's face crumples. "Don't tell Dad."

Eve leans across the console and pulls her daughter into her arms. There had been a time when it would have been unthinkable not to tell something so important to David. "I won't," she promises against the soft silkiness of Melissa's hair. "I won't say anything."

Eve's mother had worried the entire time Eve was pregnant with Melissa. *Are you taking your vitamins? Are you sleeping on your left side? What does the doctor say—is he worried about how little weight you've gained?* When Eve's due date had come and gone, Eve's mother went into a frenzy of phone calls. *Are you having any contractions? Can you feel the baby moving?* And Eve had smiled and reassured her mother. *The baby's fine. I think it's going to be a girl. We heard the heartbeat. She'll come when she's ready.* She'd never felt so at peace. It had been magical, the deep and intimate connection she'd felt to this tiny creature known only by a flurry of kicks and hiccups. And when Melissa finally arrived, eleven days late, Eve had cradled her infant daughter to her—her wide blue eyes and plump rosy cheeks, one hand beneath her chin, her perfect, tiny fingers grasping. *Here you are,* she'd whispered.

Now Melissa's teetering on the verge of becoming a woman. She needs her mother more than ever. Who else can help her navigate these treacherous waters and find her balance through all the emotional upheaval and heartache to come? All those times Eve didn't see. All those moments she let slip by.

Melissa's sobbing, her breath hot against Eve's neck. Eve tightens her hold on her daughter. "I'm here," she says. "I'm not going anywhere."

DAVID

Suspicion is an oily substance. It clings to him at night, soaks into his pores, fills his vision. It trails behind him as he talks to clients. It sloshes in his ears, dulling other noises, making him ask people to repeat things, until Renée looks at him with a worried frown and says, "You okay?"

He should call the police. That detective will tell him what's going on. It wouldn't seem suspicious for David to ask. After all, he has a vested interest. It's his neighborhood, and his wife and Charlotte are best friends. But he doesn't even know the man's name. He tries to convince himself that he's imagining things. Eve's no coward. She would never lie to protect herself. She would never allow their daughter to be suspected for a crime she'd committed. He has no reason to doubt her, but still he finds himself going over and over her description of how she'd damaged the fender, and try as he might, he just can't see it.

He calls her on his cell phone. He's standing in the stairwell. It's a small landing, three paces by three, but it's private.

"David?"

His knees go weak at the perfect ordinariness of her voice. This will be okay. He'd made a mistake. Amy's death has affected him more deeply than he'd realized. It's pushed him into a very dark place. "Hey, I had a few minutes. I thought I'd check in, see if you've heard anything more from the police."

"No, nothing. Charlotte came by last night. It was awful."

"What happened?"

"She'd heard that Melissa lied about going out that night. I tried to talk to her, make her see, but she wouldn't listen. The kids were so upset. And David—Melissa's been drinking. I found empties in her room. Can you believe it? She won't tell me where she got it from, but it must have been someone's older brother or sister. I had no idea. Did you?"

"Well, no, but I'm not that surprised. All teenagers drink."

"You sound like Melissa. But they don't, you know. I didn't. Not at sixteen."

"I only meant it could be worse. You don't think she has a problem, do you? Is that why she's been acting out these past few months?" They haven't talked like this in a long time, close, confiding, united in their concerns and on the same side.

"No, I think she was experimenting. She's not hanging out with that crowd anymore. And now she knows we know. I can't punish her. I've already taken away her phone, the car, Facebook. I hate to make her more miserable. I mean, she's a good kid. She's a really good kid. She's just made a few mistakes."

"Right," he says. "Everyone makes mistakes. Like driving into the air pump." He hears the soft intake of breath, a hiccup of surprise.

Silence. "I said I was sorry about that, David." Her voice is suddenly cool. It helps to hear the change. It braces him to say, "Tell me again. How exactly did you run into it?" He wishes he could see her face.

"I took the turn too quickly. I was upset. I wasn't paying attention."

"Did anyone see?"

"What are you getting at? Why are we talking about this?"

"You had to get the fender fixed."

"Are you *kidding* me?" Her voice is pitched high, breathless. "Are you fucking kidding me?"

He can't tell. He can't tell. She'd embraced him at the airport. God help him, he thought it was because she'd been worried about him. "You were on that road around that time. You were wet." *Tell me. Convince me.* "The police are looking for a hit-and-run driver."

"And you think it's me? Do you really? Do you really think I could do something like that and not tell you? That I could let Charlotte suffer the way she has? Is that what you think of me?"

A long, shocked second that holds everything weightless. He feels ashamed. She'd never allow their daughter to be suspected for something she'd done. What had he been thinking? He hadn't been. All rational thought had left him. What kind of man would suspect his wife of killing a child and covering it up? "I'm sorry, honey." And he is. He's sorry for all the things that have gone wrong between them. Too many to count.

VANISHING POINT

It's not Detective Irwin at the door but Albert, clutching a bunch of black-eyed Susans in a twist of waxed paper. "Hey, Tyler." Tyler looks beyond Albert to the street. There's no car headed toward him; there's no tall man with square shoulders coming up the path in the darkness. Everything looks normal: the cars parked in driveways and the porch lights shining.

"Oh, Albert," his mom says, taking the flowers. "They're lovely. Thank you."

She'd been talking loudly on the phone that afternoon, so loudly that the sound had pulled Tyler over to the vent in the floor of his room, where he'd kneeled and tried to hear what was going on. She wouldn't tell him why when he came out of his room. She just waved a hand and said it was *a difficult time,* but he suspects it's much more than that. *Is it Melissa?* he wanted to know. *Did the police arrest her?*

That would be just like it, for something big like that to happen while he sat around trapped in his room, staring at the clock. His mom's face had changed and she'd stopped and put her hands on his shoulders. *I don't want you to worry about Melissa. Nothing's going to happen to her. I promise.*

That's what she'd said about Yoshi.

They sit around the patio table, the flowers standing stiff in a glass vase his mom pulled out from beneath the sink. Brittany's over, which should make everything feel normal but now it just feels like an echo of how things used to be. No one's laughing or talking, not even Albert, who likes to tell stories about when he was a kid. Tyler's heard the one about how he had to walk three miles to school each day or how he used to deliver both the morning paper *and* the evening one. Brittany keeps sneaking looks at Melissa, who sits there with her chin in her hand.

"How was the barn?" his mom asks.

Melissa doesn't say anything. Brittany glances at her, then answers. "We got to see the new foal. She looks exactly like Vi. She has the same spot on her nose and everything."

"What did they name her?"

"They're having a contest. I put in Polka Dot."

"Oh, how cute."

It's not cute. It's a stupid name.

"How's photography going?" his mom asks him.

"Okay." He'd spent hours trying to make that film-developing bag work. It's not as easy as it had first appeared. He had to stick his hands through two sleeves and fumble around feeding the film onto the wire roll. For some reason, his hands didn't want to do what his brain was telling them, and the film kept sliding out of his fingers. He had to keep putting it down and walking around to cool off. He'd wished he could call his teacher and ask for advice. But what would the dude do, drive over to take a look?

At last, he'd found the courage to pull his arms out of the sleeves and open the bag to examine the closed black reel. He'd followed the directions his teacher had given the class, adding chemicals, agitating, pouring in the cold water rinse. When he unscrewed the top, the film had dropped into his hand, a slick brown coil.

A loud clatter from Holly's house next door makes him jump. Everyone looks over. Holly's bedroom light is on, shining through the window down onto his backyard.

"I ran into our new neighbor at the library yesterday," Albert says in a low voice. "She was walking across the parking lot and her little boy was running after her, crying."

"It's hard when the kids are so young," his mom says.

"You'd know better, of course, but the look on her face worried me. Her husband works all the time. I think she must be lonely."

His mom looks over, but it's quiet now.

"Maybe she needs a babysitter," Albert says. "Why don't you ask her, Melissa?"

Melissa slams her palm on the table, making them all jump. "Why did you have to say anything? You made everything worse!"

"Melissa," his mom says.

"I didn't know," Albert says. "The detective asked me what I'd seen that night. I told him the truth."

"It's okay, Mel," Brittany says. "The police just need to find the real person. Then they'll leave you alone."

Any moment now, the world will break apart, cleanly dividing the now that holds Melissa in it from the time when she'll be gone. She didn't mean to kill Amy, Tyler knows. It had been an accident, but that doesn't matter. It's criminal vehicular homicide. She'll go to prison for years, and when she comes back, she won't be the same. And he won't be around to see it.

The point at which two parallel lines appear to meet at the horizon but don't really is called the vanishing point. Tyler's photography teacher had been surprised none of them had heard the term before. *Imagine that you're walking down a country road,* he'd said. *If you look straight ahead, you'll see the sides of the road come together at a point. But that point doesn't exist. It's an optical illusion.* That's their assignment this week, to take pictures of the impossible: a man holding up a building, fish swimming against the sky. *Have fun with it,* their teacher had said.

Tyler looks up at the velvety black sky, peppered with bright white dots. Stars are optical illusions, too. They all shine bright, but some of them are dead, just their dying light traveling through space to earth and fooling people. No one can tell which ones are still burning and which ones died hundreds of years ago.

Up at the corner, the gray pavement grows brighter. A car's coming. He ducks behind a tree and throws up his arm to cover his face. The car growls to a stop nearby, silences. He hears the engine ticking. The slam of the door and the swift tapping of heels. It's Sophie. He lowers his arm, peers around the tree. She clacks up onto her porch. She'll let herself inside and start turning on her lights, and then Tyler can step out from his hiding place.

But the lights don't come on. Instead, Sophie appears on her porch, holding onto the railing, her face pale in the dim light. Then she runs down the steps and right past Tyler, to Dr. Cipriano's front door. Tyler leans forward and sees her reach for the heavy knocker. Over and over, she bangs it against the metal plate.

Lights flash on at Dr. Cipriano's house. The front door opens, and Tyler ducks back. "Sophie?"

"I'm sorry to wake you, Neil."

"You okay? What's wrong?"

"Did you see anyone hanging around my house earlier tonight?"

"No."

"I just got home . . . I know this sounds silly."

"Go on."

"My welcome mat's turned around. It's facing the wrong way."

Dr. Cipriano steps out to the edge of his porch and looks down the street. Tyler presses himself against the tree. "Want me to take a look around?"

"Yes, thank you, I would. Would you mind checking inside, too?"

"Sure. Let me get a flashlight." A minute later, Dr. Cipriano's back. "Stay here."

"Okay."

Dr. Cipriano crosses the lawn slowly, shining the beam of his flashlight into the bushes in front of Sophie's house. They stand out sharp and black. Then he walks around her house and disappears from view. Tyler jiggles in place, impatient. At last, Dr. Cipriano reappears on the other side. He walks up the steps and into Sophie's house. The light from his flashlight jumps around inside, making ghost circles on the windows. Then Dr. Cipriano jogs down the steps and over to where Sophie's waiting and switches off his flashlight. "Looks clear. But it wouldn't hurt to give the police a call."

"That's all right. I guess I'm just being paranoid. Thanks for checking everything out."

"Are you sure you're okay?"

"It's just all the awful things going on lately. Did you hear Larry Farnham's car was keyed last night?"

"No kidding."

"What's going on around here? This used to be such a nice place to live."

"Want to hang out for a little while? We can watch TV or something."

"I'll be all right."

"You sure?"

"Yes."

"Okay. Let me know if you change your mind."

"I will, thanks. Good night, Neil."

"Night, Sophie."

Charlotte's house has a light burning out front. Charlotte and Robbie sit in the living room. Her face is white as paper, white as cotton. Robbie leans close, says something that makes her frown and shake her head. He grabs her hands, talking faster and faster, until Charlotte suddenly stands up.

She walks away, holding onto the wall for support. Robbie leans forward to look at the photograph albums opened across the coffee table. Then he stands, wanders around the room. He stops in front of Amy's old dollhouse and crouches to pick up a doll with straggly yellow hair. It had been one of Amy's favorites. She had dragged it everywhere, holding onto one plastic hand like it was real. Here it is, dressed in a poufy dress with black shoes, a pink ribbon tied around its head, sitting propped up in that dollhouse that was falling apart. Tyler's mom had been making Amy a new one, with lights that turned on and off. He wonders what she'll do with it now.

Robbie's still holding the doll, staring down into its sleeping face. Amy would hate him touching her things. She would have yelled at him and snatched the doll away. Tyler's hit with a sudden bolt of longing. He misses her, small and fierce, with her messy hair and her freckles, all her stupid questions.

Robbie squeezes the doll's soft body between his hands, then pulls the ribbon free. He rubs the silky length against his cheek, and by the time Charlotte returns, carrying a tray of coffee cups, Robbie's pushed the ribbon into his pocket and set the doll down.

Outside Holly's house, a baby's cry pierces the quiet. Tyler stops on the sidewalk, waits for the flash of a lamp turning on. He searches the windows for the shadow of Holly walking down the hall, going into the baby's room. But the house remains dark. The wail goes on and on, until finally it grows thin and, after another second or two, hiccups itself into silence.

WEDNESDAY, SEPTEMBER 10

SUNRISE 7:08 AM

SUNSET 7:51 PM

EVE

She stares at her laptop screen. The house is quiet. Somehow she'd managed to make breakfast for Tyler and see Melissa off to the school bus, but now she's depleted. She should be working. That's what innocent people do. They stay on track. She opens her email.

Izzie's getting annoyed. She doesn't come out and say so, but the irritation is there, hovering between the sentences and exclamation points. *No,* she's pointed out. Her New York event isn't in December, and what about her book signings in Texas? Eve checks Izzie's original email and, sure enough, she's missed an entire paragraph of content. There's no excuse for the December mistake. Izzie had clearly written July. *If I didn't know you better,* Izzie wrote. *I'd say you were losing your mind, lol!!!*

Eve hears voices outside. She goes to the window and peels the drape back a few inches. Sophie's over on her lawn, talking with the

Farnhams. A flash of white at the top of the street catches Eve's attention. A large van's turning onto the ravine road, large black wording on its side clearly visible. EMERSON SECURITY SYSTEMS.

The garage door moves slowly along its tracks, too slowly. Eve ducks low, the metal edge of the door brushing the hair on the top of her head. Sophie sees her coming. She lifts her chin and braces her body.

"Sophie, please. You said you were going to think about it."

"I did," Sophie says. "And this is what I decided."

"But not *that*." Eve waves her hand at the metal floodlights attached to Sophie's roofline. "*Please.* I can't tell you how dangerous they are."

"I'm sorry, but you can't dictate what I can and what I can't do."

"I'm not dictating. Believe me, I'm not. But don't you understand? Those could *kill* Tyler."

"Sophie has a right to protect herself," Larry says.

"You stay out of this," Eve says.

A front door slams, and Mark Ryland comes jogging down his steps toward them. He looks irritated, his face puffy with sleep. "What's going on? Those things look like they're aimed at my house."

This is good. Someone else is taking up her cause. Sophie will listen and see that her actions affect everyone. Here comes Albert, swinging his arms with determination. "Everything okay?" he calls. His sweater's misbuttoned and there's a curl of shaving cream on his neck.

"I'll only turn them on at night," Sophie insists.

Mark throws up his hands. "While my kids are trying to sleep?"

"Well, you can close your blinds if it's a problem."

"It's already a problem. I don't want those damn things shining at my house."

"It's the only way to cover my front walk."

Albert comes over to stand beside Eve. "What's going on?"

"You're just in time for the Eve Show," Sophie says.

"Why are you acting this way?" Eve says. "We've always gotten along. I thought we were friends."

"Of course you are." Albert pats Eve's arm. "Sophie doesn't mean anything by that."

"Don't tell me what I mean."

Neil's pulled into his driveway and is getting out of his car. "What happened? Did that guy come back?"

"What guy?" Eve asks.

"Sophie has a stalker. The guy's really messing with her."

"It's been horrible," Sophie says. "I came home last night and found he'd turned my welcome mat around. He's left flowers in my mailbox. I've found footprints outside my windows."

"Did you call the cops?" Joan Farnham says.

"And tell them what?"

"Exactly what you told us," Mark says. "We can have a patrol car drive by."

"A patrol every couple of hours? That's not enough," Sophie says. "You can't tell me that's enough. I'm a single woman living alone. I have to protect myself."

"That's true," Neil agrees. "But those lights look pretty powerful."

"She's using halogen bulbs," Eve protests.

Neil turns to Sophie. "Why would you do that? You know we can't use halogen bulbs."

Of course Neil would understand. Of course he'd take her side.

"I'm sorry," Sophie says. "I really am, but I have to think of my own safety."

"Halogen bulbs won't keep you safe," Eve says. "If you don't want someone looking in your windows, keep your curtains closed."

"It's not just that. It's Larry's car being keyed; it's that creeper Albert saw. It's what happened to Amy."

"I didn't know about Larry's car," Eve says. "But what happened to Amy was an *accident*."

"She's still dead," Charlotte says, shockingly there, coming right up beside Mark Ryland. She's wearing an oversize sweater that hangs from her narrow shoulders. Her hair is wet, scraped back to reveal the bones of her gaunt face. Her lashes are pale, her eyes bloodshot.

"Charlotte," Eve says, horrified. "I didn't mean . . ." But Charlotte won't even look at her.

"We all just need to calm down," Albert soothes. "Let's talk about this at the next homeowners' meeting."

"You can discuss it all you want," Sophie snaps. "But it's not going to make me change my mind."

"How can you be so selfish?" Eve says.

"Really, Eve? I already live on a street without streetlights. I already turn off my headlights when I drive home at night."

"Sophie's right," Larry says. "If we had working streetlights, we wouldn't have creeps and vandals roaming around."

"And trying to poison our pets," Sophie adds.

Eve feels a swell of panic. The council voted to allow the bulbs in the streetlights to be removed, but that was because everyone on the cul-de-sac agreed. This was before the Farnhams and Sophie moved in. Eve can't allow the issue to be raised again. "Streetlights don't stop people from committing crimes."

"Sure they do," Larry says.

"Eve has a point," Neil says. "All this stuff that's been happening lately doesn't have anything to do with streetlights. For all we know, it could be one of us who's the rotten apple. We don't really know each other. We don't have a clue what goes on behind closed doors." He turns to Sophie. "You always rush into your house. Why? What's so important you can't stop to chat for a minute?"

Sophie flushes and crosses her arms. "What about that kiddie pool I saw you carry in last weekend? I mean, that's weird. What do you want with a kiddie pool?"

"That strange package I took in for you," Joan says. "The one from Africa?"

"You know," Larry says to Mark, "everything was fine before you moved in."

Charlotte looks at Mark with a frown. "That's true, isn't it?"

"What's that supposed to mean?" Mark swings toward Sophie. "Want to know what I think? I think it's strange that that guy's so interested in you. I think it's even stranger you haven't reported it. Yeah, that's right. I looked into it. If you're so worried about some-one sneaking around your house, why haven't you called the sta-tion?"

"Are you really a cop?" Sophie fires back. "You don't drive a cruiser. You don't wear a uniform. We're supposed to take your word that you're who you say you are?"

"Don't be ridiculous," Eve says.

"Let's not be like this, folks," Albert pleads. "We're all on the same side here."

"Like you're the voice of reason," Larry snarls. "Could you hire a lawn service, for crying out loud? Your yard looks like crap."

Mark snorts. "Says the guy who's building a theme park in his backyard. Isn't there some rule about how much shit we can put in?"

"You should keep your windows closed, Sophie," Neil says. "Un-less you want people to hear you talk about how you like it rough."

"You're one to say anything," Sophie says. "I remember what it was like when Bob was living with you."

Neil's heart had been broken when Bob moved out. "Stop," Eve implores. "Everyone, just stop."

There was a flash of movement behind her. Holly Ryland's com-ing down her front path. She's wearing a peach-colored kimono wrapped around her slim frame.

"I've been seeing Scott around a lot lately," Larry says to Char-lotte. "Has he moved back home?"

"That's none of your business."

"It is if he's planning to take up his old habits. I won't keep quiet this time."

"About what?" Holly stands close to her husband. "What are you talking about?"

"Like strange cars coming and going all the time. Like small packages changing hands. You don't think I know what that means?"

Charlotte stabs a finger at Larry. "Be careful, Larry. You want everyone to know that you're the one who put poison in Albert's yard?"

"I did no such thing."

"Everyone knows you hate animals."

"Maybe it was for the skunks," Holly says. It's a strange thing to say. Her eyes are bright, too bright. Albert's right. There's something wrong with her.

"Why didn't you let the police in when Amy went missing?" Sophie asks Neil. "You made them stand on the porch."

"You did?" Charlotte says.

"All I need is a ladder," Mark says. "And I can take care of those lights right now."

"Don't you dare," Sophie says. "Or I'll call the cops."

"Go ahead. I could use a hand taking those things down."

"Larry's got a ladder," Neil says, and Mark nods. "Sounds good."

"What are you talking about?" Larry says. "You can't take my things."

"No one's talking about taking anything," Neil says. "We just want to borrow a ladder. I know you have one."

"Don't you dare," Joan says.

"Why?" Mark says, and his voice is different now, filled with warning. "What have you got in there that you don't want anyone to see?"

"It's private property," Larry says. "Sophie's right. What kind of cop are you?"

"The kind who wants to take a look," Mark says.

"You have a warrant?" Larry says.

Later, Eve couldn't describe how it happened, they were all

standing so close together, jostling back and forth. She doesn't know who pushed whom first, who threw the first punch, but there were grunts, and then a shout, and she was thinking irritably that it was Sophie screaming, Sophie who'd caused all of this to spin out of control, when someone shoved her from behind. She'd been holding onto Albert, his arm thin beneath the soft cotton of his sweater, and he was dragged from her grasp. The crack was audible. They all stood frozen, looking down at where Albert lay motionless on the pavement.

Of course she was the one to drive Albert to the hospital. He didn't want the fuss of an ambulance, but his arm hung at such an odd angle. His face was white as he climbed carefully into the passenger seat, Mark helping, Joan standing back with her hand pressed against her mouth. Eve couldn't look at any of them. The garage door closed behind her and she drove off, going by all the houses golden with late afternoon sun, holding that hateful steering wheel.

Albert looks so pale.

She pulls into the hospital lot. In front of her is a green minivan, its back window adorned with a row of those white stick-figure stickers of a family. This one has Mom, Dad, two boys, a girl, a cat, a dog. Below, a bumper sticker reads: *Remember who you wanted to be?*

No, she thinks. Not by a long shot.

DAVID

The corridor's dark. Just the corner office has light seeping beneath the door. David lets himself into his own office and sits down at his desk. He opens his laptop and presses a button. He tells himself he's just checking in. But when Tyler's face appears on David's computer screen, David feels a wash of shame.

"Hey, Dad." Tyler sits against his bedroom wall, the mosaic artwork and photographs spread out behind him.

"Hey, buddy. How are you doing?"

"Okay, I guess."

"How's school going? You use your new camera yet?" Why is it so much easier to talk to his kid this way, separated by hundreds of miles, their vision constrained by a computer screen?

"Yeah. It's great."

"I thought everything was moving to digital. I thought no one was using film anymore."

Tyler frowns and David realizes he's taken a misstep. "Lots of professional photographers use film."

David has no doubt he's right. Tyler's spent hours researching online. "So what's the difference? What does film do that digital can't?" It feels important to know, as if by understanding it, he can know his son.

"I can't explain it." Tyler's clearly frustrated. "It's just . . . different. Why? Is it a problem?"

"Not at all. What do you think about building a darkroom in the basement?"

"That'd be cool."

Tell me. Is this what you want? "We could get started on it this weekend." *Would this make you happy? How are you going to manage if your mom and I split? What about if she goes to prison? How are any of us going to manage?*

"You mean do it ourselves?"

"Sure. It wouldn't be that difficult. All we'd need to do is block off a corner, make sure we have a water source and a few electrical outlets. We already know how to make something lightproof." This is meant to be a joke, but Tyler doesn't smile.

"Yeah, okay," Tyler says, but he sounds uncertain. David feels impatient. If his father had suggested building something, David would have leapt at it. He would have been full of questions. He would have wanted to get started right away. But this isn't David and his father. This is David and his son, and everything's different.

"Tyler," David begins.

Tyler hears the change in his voice and sits up a little straighter.

"Your mother told me what happened. That you lied to cover up Melissa's sneaking out."

"I didn't lie!"

"When the police asked you—"

"They never asked me if Melissa was home the whole time. You never asked, either."

Tyler sees everything in black and white. There are no shades of gray for him. "Lying by omission is still a lie. You knew what she'd done was wrong and that you should have told us. Tell me you know that."

Tyler's silent, nibbling his thumbnail.

"I expect an answer."

"Yes." It comes grudgingly.

"I understand wanting to protect your sister." Hadn't David done the same thing when he caught his younger sister smoking or sliding a chocolate bar into her pocket at the convenience store? He'd told her to give him the cigarettes; he'd made her go up to the counter and pay for the candy. "But you're fourteen now. You're old enough to understand consequences."

Tyler leans back and the laptop shifts view. His face is farther away, his eyes hidden beneath a shock of curls. "What's going to happen to her?"

"We'll have to wait and see." With any luck, this detective will overlook her driving without a license. "Tell me again what happened that night."

Tyler frowns. "I already told you."

"I need to hear it again. What time did your mom leave?" He says this casually, studies his son for a reaction. Tyler can't hear anything in his voice, can he?

But Tyler just shrugs. "Six-fifty-nine."

"Is that what time she left, or what time you got out of your room?"

"Okay. Then I guess she left around seven. What does it matter?"

"It doesn't." *It does. It matters.* "I'm just trying to get a sense of what happened. You watched her leave, didn't you?" Tyler always stood by the window and watched Eve drive away, as though fearful she might never return. "Which way did she turn?"

Tyler lets out his breath, looks up at the ceiling, and narrows his eyes. "Left," he says finally.

David's heart drops. "You sure?" Left was where Amy had been struck. Right was the way to the airport.

"I'm sure. She went left."

A knock, and he looks up to see Renée.

"Ready?" she says.

"He said he wouldn't be here," Renée says, unlocking the front door. They step into a tiny vestibule. She works the lock on the interior door. This one has a stained glass inset of red tulips. The window on the second-floor landing has purple asters and the one in the upstairs bedroom has white jonquils. She'd given him the tour the first time he came by for dinner. *Makes me feel like I'm living in a florist's shop,* she'd said, making a face, and Jeffery had shrugged. *I kind of like them,* he'd said.

The place smells faintly of woodsmoke. The floors are blond wood, the furniture pale ash and white leather. Jeffery had picked out the living room furniture, had waved around with his wineglass. *Just put in Bose speakers,* he'd said. *Wall-to-wall sound.* He'd seemed uncomfortable, laughing a little too hard at his own jokes. *He's a little jealous of you,* Renée had told David the next day. *I know, I know.* She'd rolled her eyes. *But that's how he is.*

"Need any help?" he asks Renée.

"I'll just get my clothes. A few other things. I'll be right back."

There's an ink drawing of a woman's naked back, her head turned to show just her demure profile, fringed wall hangings in maroon and black, a trio of tribal masks.

The first mask Eve had fashioned for Tyler had had a thick sheet of UV plastic hanging down from the brim of a sun hat. He had hated it, kept reaching up to tug it off. He wouldn't keep his socks on, either, or his gloves. Taking him to the doctor's had been a nightmare. David would take off from work and drive while Eve sat in the backseat with Tyler, who screamed and cried and kicked his legs. By the time they arrived, they were all exhausted. And then they'd have to do it all over again the following month.

On the mantel is a large silver-framed portrait of the two of them, professionally shot, Renée standing inside Jeffery's embrace, both of them smiling at the camera. *Our engagement photo,* she'd told him. *His mom insisted.*

He and Eve had rented a place downtown after they were married, a one-room apartment with a kitchenette, all they could afford. They'd sit at the counter to eat. He'd tell her what he'd learned that day in business school, and she'd regale him with stories from the hotel where she worked. *I placed the wake-up call to Malcolm Forbes,* she'd say, or, *Housekeeping found a briefcase filled with passports.* She was always interested in other people's stories, and talking with her always brought things alive for him. He misses that girl. He wonders if Eve misses the boy he once was.

He heard the sharp tapping of high heels, and Renée's back, rolling a suitcase behind her and carrying a shoulder bag. "Let me get that," he says, putting his phone into his pocket and taking both suitcases from her.

Renée looks around at the walls, the white furniture. When she looks at him, her eyes are shining with tears. "I guess this is it."

Tyler possesses an uncanny ability to recall conversations word for word. He's like that with stories he's read, images he's seen. He can remember walks they've taken, step by step, and where every house is and what every neighbor was doing when they passed by. His mind is always working, finding ways to challenge itself. So if Tyler had said that Eve had turned left, then that was what she had done.

FREAK

Something's happening on Facebook. Zach's posted a winky face on Savannah's wall. Does that mean they're dating? Tyler stares at Zach's avatar—the picture Tyler took of Zach leaping on the trampoline. Zach hasn't changed it, but he's unfriended him. As soon as Tyler figured that out, he did the same.

No one tells him not to, so at 7:51 he unlocks his bedroom door and swings it open. The hall stairs spill away into darkness. Silence ticks around him. His mom's at the hospital with Albert. Melissa's at Brittany's.

Beige carpet rolls down the stairs. He knows each riser, the third one from the top with the loose thread, the second one from the bottom with the tiny red smear of wax from the time he'd pretended to be a medieval knight. He'd tried to scissor it away and his mom had caught him. *It's all right,* she'd told him. *It's just carpet.*

Downstairs, he turns on the lamps—the tall brass lamp by his mom's favorite reading chair, the glass globe on the end table, the two smaller candlestick lamps on the server. He flips the switch in the kitchen, and everything jumps out in brightness. The dining room chandelier, the outside lights around the patio. At last he stands alone in the kitchen, with all the gleaming countertops. The whole place feels empty, like a balloon that's let out its air, leaving just a thin rubber skin.

Tyler shouldn't open the door. His mom would tell him no. She would want him to wait until she was home. He undoes the latch and twists the doorknob.

His mom had called him from the hospital. He'd heard the garage door rumble up then, and a while later, rumble back down. He hadn't even heard her drive away, and so when his phone rang, he was surprised to see her name on caller ID. *I had to take Albert to the hospital,* she'd told him. *I don't know how long I'll be.*

He could go to the park if he wanted to. He could check on that python in Dr. Cipriano's basement, to make sure it was still in its cage. He could go over to Holly's house, but Mark's car is in the driveway.

He sits down on the front step.

His dad had been full of questions. Tyler had sweated through every one of them, though none of them was important. They were all about his mom. His dad hadn't asked a single one about Melissa, though Tyler knew they were coming. And then his dad had to hang up, and Tyler had been saved from having to answer. But the one about which direction his mom had driven had been an important one. His dad's face had changed at Tyler's response. Tyler doesn't get why it mattered, but he tries to think now of that night, picture the way the rain had fallen and the thunder had boomed. He squints up the street, trying to picture his mom braking there before driving away, and then there she is, the dark shape of her car turning the corner and heading down the street toward him. He stands up. He's glad she's home. He never likes it when she's gone, especially at night.

The garage door rumbles up, but his mom's car stops in the driveway instead of pulling in. The engine is silenced. She climbs out and hurries toward him. "Tyler! Oh my God. Get inside this instant!"

"What happened?" Melissa asks when she gets home. She's staring in the refrigerator, holding onto the handle. She looks empty, like she's got nothing holding her up. She reaches in and pulls out a cherry yogurt.

"Albert broke his elbow," his mom says. He and his mom are playing Uno and he's kicking ass, but now his mom stops and looks at Melissa. She's been doing that a lot—watching Melissa as though she might vanish. "He might need to have surgery."

Melissa turns and looks at her. "Is he going to be okay?"

"He'll be fine, honey." His mom sets down an eight. "They're keeping him at the hospital overnight for observation. He was a little dehydrated."

"Who would hurt Albert?" Melissa takes a spoon from the drawer.

"He stumbled. No one meant to hurt him."

Tyler wishes he'd seen it, everyone standing around yelling at one another. Even Holly had been there, his mom had told him. Everyone had.

"Crazy." Melissa wanders away. His mom doesn't call after her to bring back the spoon when she's done.

Don't worry, his mom had told him, but she's been watching, getting up every so often to stand by the kitchen window and look between the gap in the curtains. Nine o'clock comes and goes. He discards a three. "Maybe she changed her mind."

"Maybe," his mom agrees.

"Uno." He sets down his cards and she shakes her head.

"How do you do that?" she says, scooping the cards together to shuffle them. "I never even see it coming."

She used to let him win, pretending not to notice what he was collecting, keeping the bad cards in her hand until she had no choice but to play them. But then Melissa ratted her out, and she had to stop. Now she has to work hard to win, and they can play for hours, slapping cards down and laughing. Tyler's dad shakes his head at them, and Melissa, who used to play with them, glares and tells them to keep it down.

Ten o'clock comes and goes, and ten-thirty. At eleven, they're working on their laptops when his mom gets up to look out the living room window. She stiffens, and he knows. He's always liked Sophie. He doesn't understand why she would do this to him. He feels trapped, a fly banging against the glass.

"Tyler," she begins, and he shakes his head.

"No." He won't wear that fucking mask. She might as well hang a neon sign over his head: *FREAK*. He closes his laptop and stomps upstairs. He doesn't open the door when his mom knocks.

THURSDAY, SEPTEMBER 11

SUNRISE 7:09 AM
SUNSET 7:49 PM

EVE

She paces from window to window.

She'd been pregnant with Tyler when she and David and Melissa drove into this pretty little street with its sloping lawns and mature trees. The moment she'd spotted the white house with the gray roof nestled at the bottom of the street, she had felt a spark of interest. The realtor had unlocked the front door, and she'd stepped inside to gleaming wooden floors and sunshine streaming through the windows. She had thought, *Here's where I want to raise my family.*

Around 2:00 am, she thinks about borrowing Albert's shotgun and taking aim. She almost laughs at the thought. She's already a felon. In for a penny, in for a pound. It was the glass of wine she'd had, though not the first one, which had only left her longing for more. The third one—that was the one she really felt. She'd have to hide the empty wine bottle before David came home. He'd be sure to ask her about it. He'd look at her with judging eyes. How would he look at her when he got home? Would he look at her at all? She wishes she could call him, but she doesn't trust herself to keep the pretense going. What if he saw through her?

At 5:00 am, the lights flare off.

There has to be something she can do. There has to be. Could they move to the country? They'd have to buy a property and make it safe for Tyler before they risked moving him. Which meant they'd have to pay two mortgages. Was that even possible? Melissa has told her that David's talked to her about moving to DC. *I don't want to go,* Melissa had said, crying, and Eve had reassured her. She had hoped that this was the beginning of a return to the way things used to be between them, but the confession's had the opposite effect on Melissa. Her daughter has retreated. She's licking her wounds. *She's just like you,* her mother had said, with a sigh of resignation, as if she were saying, *See what you put me through?*

She's walking across the basement floor, laundry heaped in her arms, when she stubs her toe against a sharp, hard corner. She curses, drops the jeans and towels in a heap. It's that dollhouse she'd been making for Amy. Somehow, it's been dragged away from the wall to stand directly in her path. A hammer and wrench lie nearby—so David had been down here working. She looks at the delicate wooden structure. That tall pointed tower, the curved bay window, all the cheerful gingerbread molding that had taken forever to tack into place. The tiny iridescent pink tiles painstakingly glued to form a kitchen backsplash, the hours spent cutting out and fitting pink-and-white-flocked wallpaper against each wall. Amy had clapped her hands with joy. *When will it be done?*

Now the dollhouse glares at her. It squats on her floor, angled precisely to draw blood. The gold wire and pink beads for the chandelier sit inside their glistening plastic pouches; the carpet she hadn't yet installed lies curled inside one room like a tongue. She reaches down and grasps the house by both sides, pushing her fingers through the windows she'd sliced open with a mat knife. It's heavy and rises slowly, resisting. She raises it up, stretches to stand on her tiptoes, and opens her hands.

It crashes down. The bay window crumples and floor tiles pop loose. She snatches up the hammer and swings. The chimney snaps off; the roof caves in. She pounds at the hole she's created, driving the metal head of the hammer into the floor below. There goes the master bedroom. There sinks the charming nursery. *Bam! Bam! Bam!* The rooms for the twins lie in splintered pieces.

She kicks the house onto its side so she can reach inside. Those shiny pink tiles dissolve into dust; the balsa banister shreds. If only she can reach the fireplace. She'll have to come at it from the other side, after she's smashed through the living room wall—

"Mom?"

Eve wheels around, panting, to see Melissa standing on the bottom step, staring at her, frightened.

Eve picks Albert up from the hospital around noon. He looks small and defeated as the nurse pushes him in a wheelchair out to Eve's car. "I got it," he says irritably as the nurse tries to help him up. He's not himself, either. Driving out of the cul-de-sac that morning, she had felt the change. Charlotte's curtains were closed. Neil's newspaper lay on the driveway, well past the time Neil usually carried it inside.

Eve helps Albert into his house. The emergency room doctor had pulled Eve aside the night before and confided that broken bones in the elderly were serious. All sorts of complications could set in. It had taken a lot of persuasion on Eve's part to convince Albert to listen to the doctor and stay overnight. He'd wanted to go home; he'd wanted to sleep in his own bed, surrounded by Rosemary's things.

"How about some soup?" she suggests.

"I'm fine. You don't need to mother me."

"You sound like my kids. Let me mother you, okay?" She goes into the kitchen and opens the pantry door. Her heart sinks at the sight of the few cans and boxes. "Pea soup or chicken noodle?" she calls into the family room, where he's in his recliner, a pillow propped beneath his arm.

"You choose."

"Chicken noodle it is." She pours some kibble into Sugar's bowl and checks the water level. When the soup's heated, she brings in a bowl on a tray. Her toe's throbbing; she'll have to change the bandage when she gets home. "I'm going to the store later," she says, though she hadn't planned on it. "You should make a list."

"It's not your fault, Eve."

She's in the process of setting down the tray. Her heart squeezes, and she looks at him, afraid to see the accusation she knows is there. But he reaches out and pats her hand. "I shouldn't have turned to Charlotte's boy for help. I should have known better. I could have gotten him in real trouble."

A shiver of relief, followed by dismay. He's admitting he gave the pills to Rosemary. Did Rosemary know, or did he hide them in her food? Did he have a chance to say good-bye the way he wanted to? "I think David's going to leave me," she hears herself blurting out.

"He say that?"

"No, but all we do is argue about every little thing. And all the big things, too." *He thinks I'm a murderer and he's right.* "I don't know what to do." Those early years, she slept beside Tyler, stretched out on a mattress on the floor, her days reversed to match his, to keep him from getting up and wandering out into the daylight. She and Melissa made a magical world, just the three of them. David would go to work and come home right as they were getting up. He would join them on their picnics and their little field trips, but then he would have to go to bed and it would be just the three of them again. Was that when she started to lose David? She didn't notice it.

She was too focused on Tyler and keeping him safe, on Melissa and giving her as happy a childhood as possible. And now she wonders if she's been kidding herself about how much time she'd truly given Melissa. Something had to give, in either case, and it had ended up being her marriage.

"Talk to him."

I can't. "I want to."

He's staring at her. "You've never been afraid to say what's in your heart. What's going on, Evie?"

Her mother calls her Evie. She feels disoriented. She doesn't think Albert's ever called her that. Is she imagining things? Is she losing her mind? She'd been on the verge of confiding everything. She pushes herself up. "I forgot to get you a napkin."

In the kitchen, she opens drawer after drawer. Silverware, cooking utensils. She can't remember where Rosemary kept the napkins. Here's the junk drawer, filled with rubber bands, takeout menus, batteries, pencils. She's about to push it closed, too, when she catches sight of the slim black flashlight, zipped into a plastic bag.

"Albert?" she says, going back into the family room. "Where did you get this?"

He pauses, his spoon halfway to his mouth. "That fellow dropped it, the one I caught snooping in Farnham's window."

It's an ordinary flashlight, sold everywhere. There's nothing the least bit special about it, except for the green duct tape she'd wrapped around the handle so that Tyler could grip it with his gloved hands.

THE BEAST

The message pops up on the corner of his computer screen. Someone's chatted him on Skype. Tyler minimizes his teacher's talking face and mouses over to the icon and taps it. It's from Dante: *Get on the Forum*. There's only one thing it could be. Tyler's hand is shaking as he clicks on the tab. The Forum opens and he sees the thread that Yoshi's mom posted just a few minutes before.

"Tyler?" His math teacher's looking at him from the classroom, her hands on her hips.

He taps on the Skype icon, makes the image full-screen. "Here," he says automatically.

"That's not what I asked. Haven't you been paying attention?"

Some of the kids are turning around to look at him. What do they see? He clicks the video button and the screen goes blank. Now he can't hear or see any of them.

A sharp knock on the door. "Tyler?"

He hadn't even heard his mom come up the stairs. She never interrupts while he's in class. She must have heard the news about Yoshi, but her voice doesn't sound weepy. "Hold on." He goes into his bathroom. "Okay." When he comes back out, his mom's there, holding up a plastic sandwich bag. Inside is a black flashlight. Where did it come from? How much does she know?

She gives the bag a shake. "What were you thinking? Why would you do something so dangerous?"

"I'm fine."

"You can't know that." She drops the bag and comes over, lifts up his shirt to see his back. "Let me check."

He squirms away. "I'm fine, I said."

"Did their lights go off? Were you anywhere near them?" She's got him by his elbow, holding fast. "Stand still. I have to check your head, too."

He yanks free. "Will you leave me alone?"

"I would love to, believe me, young man. Take off your shirt."

"I won't."

"This is serious, Tyler. I need to check you over."

"No."

She stands back. He's taller than she is. She can't make him take off his shirt, not if he doesn't want to. "You want to tell me what's going on?"

"Nothing."

"It had to be something. Why would you go out in the middle of the night? What on earth were you doing? The Farnhams', of all places!"

"It's no big deal."

"It *is* a big deal. How can you say that?"

"I was careful."

"You can never be careful enough. Never. You know that. Look what happened when you and Dad went to the park that night."

"It's my life."

"Yes, and I want you to live a long one."

"Stop it! Stop saying that. It's not going to happen."

"What's gotten into you? What's upset you? Is it Amy? Is it Yoshi?" Her expression changes. "Oh, honey. I didn't know."

She moves toward him, but he stumbles back. "You *don't* know. You just don't know."

"Tell me. Let me help you."

"You can't. No one can."

"What happened to Yoshi isn't going to happen to you."

"That is such a lie. All you do is lie." He's yelling. He can't help it. He's exactly like Yoshi.

"Tyler, listen to me. Remember that scientist I told you about?"

He wants to know. Does it hurt? Is there a place after, or is this it? Is this all he'll ever have? "I don't want to hear about your stupid scientists." His hands open and close. He wants to hit something. "Fuck your stupid scientists."

Her face is soft with sympathy. "Oh, sweetheart."

He doesn't feel anything anymore. Maybe this is what it's like to be dead.

He crouches in the darkness of his old fort littered with dead leaves and beetle carcasses, the planks soft and splintery, and watches his mom through the bright kitchen windows. She's talking on the phone, moving from stove to refrigerator to cabinet to pantry. She's called the doctor and asked if she could bring Tyler, *immediately*, on an *emergency basis*. She's made an appointment for him on Monday. Now she's talking to his dad. Every so often, she'll stop and look outside. She can't see him, though. To her, it's all blackness.

Next door, Holly's windows glow with light. Shadowy figures move around inside. They're talking, their voices coming out through the opened window. Holly's voice is low. It's Mark's voice that's loud. "You have to stop."

He remembers when this fortress smelled new, and the nailheads shone. He and Zach used to play war in it, hunkering down below the windows and pretending there were enemy soldiers approaching from all corners. Amy had whined about playing with them, so they made her their scout. She'd go off and come running back to report all sorts of lame things. After a while, they stopped listening to her, and then they'd stopped playing in the fortress altogether.

His mom comes out to stand on the patio. She's a dark shape against the brightness of the kitchen behind her. "Ty," she calls softly. "Aren't you hungry?"

He doesn't care if he never eats again. Everything's been chopped around him, slicing away big chunks until all that's left is a narrow tunnel only big enough for him. And who wants that?

"Ty?" she tries again.

But he still doesn't answer, and after a minute, she goes back inside. The sky's darker now. The stars are coming out. Smells drift across the air. Someone's barbecuing.

What if he could have a do-over? He'd have left the flashlight at home. He'd go back in time and stand behind the car so that Melissa couldn't back out of the garage. Maybe he'd go all the way back and not be born at all.

A sob rises up from deep inside him. He misses Yoshi. He never even got to say good-bye. He's crying, big choking gasps that roll through him, dragging everything up and up and up. She would be mad. She would tell him to cut it out, but he can't. He just can't. Furiously, he rubs his face against his sleeve.

Something's standing there on the grass, staring at him through the little door of the fort. They're only a few feet apart. The Beast.

He's gray with white patches on his chest. His bushy tail hangs down. He's just a coyote. A stupid, dirty dog. "What are *you* looking at?" Tyler hisses. He picks up a stick and hurls it with all his might. It clatters to the ground.

The dog whirls and runs away, melting into the darkness.

FRIDAY, SEPTEMBER 12

SUNRISE 7:10 AM

SUNSET 7:47 PM

EVE

She sits on the couch by the front door, lamps burning like sentinels on either side of her. She has a direct line of sight to the stairs that lead up to Tyler's bedroom. If she falls asleep—and the chances of this are remote, given how much high-octane tea she's consumed over the course of the past few hours—she'll be awakened by the click of the French door unlocking. If Tyler tries to sneak out the front door, she'll feel the air swirling around her, the heat from the night coming in and dispelling the coolness of the room. She's always been sensitive to temperature. If Tyler somehow makes it un-detected to the kitchen and goes out the door there, the garage door will moan and creak along its tracks, and alert her to full conscious-ness.

In the morning, she'll call a security company and have an alarm system installed. Cost be damned. She won't tell them she's not afraid of people breaking in.

Melissa's alarms go off and are smacked into silence. Ever since the dollhouse, her daughter's been avoiding her. She'd left early for the bus; she'd gone to Brittany's house after school. When she'd come home, she hadn't wanted to hear Eve's pathetic attempt at explanation. *Whatever,* she'd mumbled, and slammed her bedroom door.

Eve puts her feet on the cold floor and walks up to Tyler's room. He won't tell her why he'd gone over to the Farnhams'. He's remained stubbornly stoic about it. It makes her wonder if he's hiding something bigger, a deeper secret. She misses David with a piercing longing. He's always been her partner. He's always helped her find her way.

When Tyler slides into his chair at the table, he won't look at her. He doesn't answer when she asks if she can make him something to eat. He takes a banana from the bowl and peels it. With a pang, she sees the shadows under his eyes.

"Grow up," Melissa tells him, as she slides books into her bag. Her eyes are red, her lips pinched. It's hard on her, too, when another XP child dies.

"Mind your own business."

She slings her backpack over her shoulder. "How could you be so selfish? After all that Mom's done for you? She gave up her *life* for you."

This is terrible, that she would think this. "I didn't give up anything, honey. It's okay. Tyler knows."

Tyler pushes back his chair, leaving his banana half-eaten on the table. His footsteps thud up the stairs.

The phone rings as she's getting ready to go to the store. She lets it go to voicemail. She can't be sidetracked or distracted. This is how she gets through each day, by putting one foot down after another.

She'll be in the grocery store and stand there, wondering. Why had she made the trip?

The garage door rolls up on another relentlessly sunny day. She flips down the visor and slides on her sunglasses. She looks into the rearview mirror. Someone's there, blond hair flying. For a heart-stopping second, she thinks, *Amy?* But it's not Amy. How could it be? It's her older sister, Nikki, running barefoot down the sidewalk toward her.

Charlotte's in her front hall closet, going through coats, yanking them off hangers and dropping them on the floor. "Where the hell are they?" She doesn't look up as Eve and Nikki come in. Nikki gives Eve a look. *See?* As if Eve is the sane one. As if she can take control.

"They're not in your pockets." Gloria's picking each coat up, a bundle of black and tan and brown and red in her arms. "Tell her, Eve. Tell her to forget her car keys and sit down."

"Stop, Charlotte," Eve pleads. "Just stop for a minute. Tell me what's going on."

Charlotte shuffles through a pile of mail on the hall table, pulls open a drawer. "Detective Irwin's arrested *Robbie.*"

Which is what Nikki had said, but that makes no sense. "Are you sure he didn't just bring him in for questioning?"

Charlotte turns in a circle. "Where *are* they?"

"The police aren't going to let you see him, Charlotte," Gloria reasons. "What do you think you're going to do—hang around the police station until he's released?"

Charlotte pulls things from drawers, drops them on the floor. Batteries go rolling, coins. "I have to see him. I have to see his face when he tells me he didn't do it. Because that's what he'll say. That's exactly what he'll say."

"But maybe he didn't do it," Eve says before she can stop herself.

Isn't this what she wants, for the finger of suspicion to be pointed somewhere else?

"Let the police handle it." Nikki's huddled in a corner of the sofa.

"You need to try and calm down," Gloria says. "This isn't helping."

Charlotte upends the magazine holder. Magazines go sliding. "I never saw a thing, not one thing. What kind of mother does that make me?"

"It's not your fault, honey," Gloria says. "It's his fault. He tricked you. He tricked all of us."

"Not Aunt Felicia," Nikki says. "She guessed. She said Robbie was a creep. She asked me if he'd ever been alone with me. *God.*"

Eve stares at the girl in horror. Nikki's holding a pillow against her chest. Tears slide down her cheeks. Had Robbie *touched* Amy? Had he *hurt* her? She feels sick. "No," she says, shaking her head. It can't be true. It's impossible. She stops herself. Isn't that what people always think?

After Nikki's boyfriend comes to pick her up, Charlotte and Eve sit alone in the kitchen. Gloria's lying down in an upstairs room. She's aged these past weeks—the heavy way she goes up the stairs, clutching the banister, the measured click of the bedroom door. *Let me know if the police call,* she'd told them.

"Detective Irwin wouldn't come right out and say it," Charlotte says, "but I'd have to be an idiot not to put it together."

Eve takes Charlotte's hands, icy cold in hers. She tries to rub warmth into them. How could things be any worse? Somehow, they are.

"He asked me if I'd ever left Amy alone with Robbie. Of course I had! I wanted them to be close. Close!"

Eve had judged Charlotte for this. Privately, she had thought Charlotte didn't know Robbie well enough to be trusted watching a child. She had worried about neglect. She had never once considered *this*.

"He asked if Robbie had ever handled Amy's backpack. I said no. I'd just gotten it for her that afternoon." No need to explain which afternoon she meant. *That afternoon* would forever mean only one point in time. "Robbie hadn't come over that day. So why would he ask that?"

"I don't know." Eve doesn't. She can't imagine.

When Charlotte swallows, it's a hard motion, like stones sliding down her throat.

"He wanted to know if Robbie had ever driven Amy anywhere in his truck. I told him, all the time. He picked her up from soccer practice if I was with clients. He took her to the movies if I had an open house. He was trying to make Amy like him. He wanted us to be a family. That's what he said, and I believed him. What an idiot!"

"But you would have known if something was going on—"

"Would I? Would I really? I don't think so."

"Yes, yes." Eve believes this. "Amy would have told you."

"Our kids don't tell us everything. They don't. You know that. They keep things from us, secrets."

This is true. Eve had thought she'd made a safe place for her children to confide in her, but they had slipped from her arms and wandered away. Maybe, at some level, they had not been fooled by her. They had seen her for what she truly is.

"Remember when Amy begged me not to let Robbie pick her up from school? I thought she was just being stubborn and I had a closing. I told her that either Robbie picked her up or she'd have to walk home."

Is it possible that Robbie's determination to win over Charlotte was rooted in his secret desire to win over Amy? Eve's stomach roils. Her mouth goes dry. "Oh, Charlotte. I never saw it, either."

"I let him into my house. I let him near my little girl. She was just a baby, and he *killed* her."

"Wait." Eve needs to think. This doesn't make sense.

Charlotte won't stop. "Detective Irwin asked how long Robbie had played semipro ball. Years, I told him. He wanted to know if he had a temper. I had to admit it, sometimes Robbie could act like a little kid. He wanted to know if Robbie kept a baseball bat in his truck. Yes, I said. He did. An aluminum one. It's not there anymore."

None of this is true. *She* had struck Amy. *She* had gone down the side of the ravine and found her lying by the river. This had all happened. *She* had killed Amy, not Robbie. Hadn't she? She feels something green and growing inside her. It's been so long since she'd felt it, or anything like it, that it's a moment before she recognizes it. *Hope.*

Charlotte snatches back her hands and stands. "I went up to Amy's room. I thought that maybe she'd have left something behind, some clue that would tell me if this was true. But I just stood there. I couldn't go in. I couldn't know. God help me. Owen's right. This is all my fault."

Eve's treacherous heart lies heavy and inert in her chest. She gets up and goes to Charlotte. She faces her. She doesn't dare touch her. "No, no. It isn't."

"I can't live with this."

"Charlotte, look at me. I need to ask you something."

Charlotte's pupils are black as buttons, large and unfocused. "Tell me this isn't happening. Tell me my boyfriend didn't molest and kill my daughter."

Eve had felt that impact. She had seen the damage to her car afterward. "The medical examiner said Amy had been hit by a car." Say it fast, make it meaningless.

"No. He said injuries consistent with a hit-and-run."

Eve stares at her. The green and growing thing is taking root; it's reaching for the sky and spreading. Maybe she'd been wrong all this time. "How did Detective Irwin find out about Robbie?"

"I don't know." Charlotte's gaze is wandering, dragged away by the distant wail of sirens.

"Listen to me. Please listen to me." Eve has to know. She has to understand. She grabs Charlotte's arms, so thin within her grasp. "Why did Detective Irwin ask you about Amy's backpack?"

Charlotte looks at her with confusion. "I told you. I don't know."

The back door opens. Sirens shriek. Nikki comes in with her boyfriend, a gangly boy who ducks his head hello. The sirens are louder now, pulsing right outside. Eve turns her head to see.

THE FLASH

His teachers have been emailing short little notes asking where he is and if he's okay. Tentative, like they're afraid to know the truth.

He's got his vents wide open. He can hear *everything*. The rumble of a lawn mower starting up, whining away into the distance. The peculiar puttering of the mail truck circling around the cul-de-sac. Melissa had once videotaped it for him so he could see what it looked like when their mail arrived. She'd done it on a day when she'd mailed him something, a funny card with a pack of regular, full-sugar gum inside. *Shh,* she'd said. *Don't tell Mom.*

His mom can't keep him a prisoner forever. She can't stay awake all night, watching the door. He tells himself to be patient, but still he feels panic rising up in his chest and pushing into his throat. This can't be it. This can't be all he gets. His dad might understand. His dad's constantly wanting his mom to relax, take a few chances. But Tyler's always felt safer with his mom. He feels like he's split into two people—the one wanting out and the one wanting to be safe—which is why he's pacing.

At first, he doesn't hear it. It's a small sound, lost within the shuffling of his feet across the carpet, the buzz of a lawn mower, the faraway mutter of an airplane. His phone buzzes, letting him know he's got a text—it's from Zach: *Hey*—and when he stops to read and delete it, the small sound separates itself from all the other sounds and takes shape.

Someone's knocking on the front door.

He lies on the floor and puts his ear to the vent. The sound magnifies. Maybe his mom's left a window open. It's an unimaginable possibility. What if more than one window's open—what if they're all open? The doors could be hanging ajar, too, flooding the downstairs with sunshine. Tyler's bedroom could be floating on broad swords of sunlight. The thought makes him break out in a sweat.

Knock knock knock.

Maybe it's Detective Irwin, come to arrest Melissa. *Need anything from the store?* his mom had called through his door, and when he didn't answer, she'd added, *Text me if you think of anything.* Tyler will tell him Melissa was only gone for thirty minutes. He'll tell him that she hadn't been drinking at all. He's practiced his bored face in the mirror.

Knock knock.

He rubs on sunscreen, pulls on his gloves, fits the mask Yoshi made him onto his head. He imagines she's there, laughing at the crazy flames she's cut out of plastic. Quick, before he can change his mind, he undoes the latch and swings open the door.

Everything's in shades of gray. The stairs fall away, leading to the front door. Now he can hear the knocking more clearly. He goes downstairs and puts his mouth close to the wood. "Hello?"

"Mister?"

It's just Connor, Holly's kid. Not the police. Relief makes him tilt back his head and laugh. "Go home."

"Mommy needs you." Connor rattles the doorknob.

"You can't come in. What do you mean she needs me?"

"Tyler!" Connor wails.

This is strange. Why would Holly send Connor over? She knows Tyler can't come out. But maybe Connor had been sent to get Tyler's mom. Maybe Holly really is in trouble.

He should go back upstairs. Instead, he opens the door and steps onto the porch.

A flash of white makes him blink. Then the world blooms bright before him, blazing with color. His heart leaps. He's forgotten how things look in the sun. He holds out his hands, to touch the blueness of the sky, feel the green of the grass. He turns his head and sees Connor waving from his front porch.

The pavement sparkles with diamonds. No one told him treasure was buried there. Holly's house looms before him, gray and black and white. "Holly?" His voice is muffled behind plastic. His voice is puny.

Connor seizes his hand and drags him inside the house, where everything is dancing, so bright it makes his head hurt. Now he hears the baby crying. He sounds like he's upstairs in his room. "Where is your mom?"

Connor pulls him up the stairs and down the hall into Holly's bedroom. Tyler feels shy. What will he find? The room is dark with welcome, and there Holly is, a slight lump beneath the covers, her face turned toward him, pale, her eyes closed and her hand curled beneath her cheek. She looks impossibly pretty.

Connor pushes her shoulder. She doesn't move.

Tyler's suddenly afraid. Didn't Rosemary fall asleep one day and never wake up? "Holly?" But she still doesn't move. He leans close and sees the pulse in her throat. "Holly," he says, louder. He studies her face. Nothing. "It's okay," he tells Connor, who's sniffling and rubbing his eyes with his hands.

Tyler picks up the phone on the nightstand and presses the buttons: 9-1-1. He hears the operator's voice, distant and small. She won't understand him, not through the mask. "Tell her your mom needs help," he says, handing the phone to Connor.

Christopher's screaming down the hall. Tyler knows what to do. The baby probably needs his diaper changed, or maybe a bottle. He'd told Holly he'd never babysit again, but this isn't really babysitting. As soon as the paramedics come, Tyler will give them Christopher and go home.

Light falls on the carpet outside the baby's room. The shrieking grows louder as Tyler steps into the room, which is flooded with sunshine. The curtains are open here. The room is bouncing with UV, but Tyler feels none of it. Maybe he doesn't have to stay in his room the rest of his life. Maybe he can walk around just like everyone else. Maybe he's been stupid not to wear his mask, to follow all his mom's rules.

Christopher lies on his back in the crib, his hands in fists by his sides, his legs stiff. His mouth is wide open, his cheeks bright red.

"Hey, buddy." This is what his dad called him when he was little. He leans over the side of the crib and puts his hands around the baby's tummy. Christopher flails, his arms swinging. He knocks Tyler's mask from his head.

Tyler grabs at it, tries to fit it back on. *It's okay, it's okay.* Then it's not. An angry pain flames up his throat, zips along his cheek right to the top of his head. His hair stands straight up. His skin is on fire. He drops and curls up in a ball. He hears himself shrieking.

My hero, Holly had said.

EVE

Everyone walks to the window to see the ambulance race down the street. They push through the front door to watch it stop at the bottom of the cul-de-sac. When the siren silences, Eve hears an awful screaming coming from inside the Rylands' house. It makes no sense, but she knows. It's Tyler. She races down the sidewalk, shoving her way through the paramedics to pound up the stairs and run to her son, kneeling on the floor with his arms crossed over his head. She yanks the blanket from the crib and throws it over him, crouching beside her son, crooning. Her worst nightmare, throbbing in three dimensions.

The doctor meets them at the emergency room. The nurse has a cubicle ready, the lights doused. Eve holds her breath as the doctor removes the blanket. Until this moment, she hasn't seen the damage. The left side of Tyler's face is swollen and red, blazing with large white blisters. She doesn't gasp. She doesn't change the tone of her voice as she tells Tyler to hang on just a little bit longer, until the pain medication kicks in. But inside she begins praying.

I'm sorry, Tyler keeps saying. *I'm sorry.* It breaks her heart.

Hours later, she hears David's voice in the corridor outside. She turns as he draws aside the curtain and comes in, pulling his suitcase behind him. He'd gotten her message and come directly from the airport. She's so glad to see him. She's weak with relief.

David goes to Tyler and stands looking down at their sleeping son. Tyler lies propped up on pillows, his face bandaged and shiny with burn cream. "How is he?"

"It's mostly second-degree. It was just a second or two of exposure, but the doctor says there'll be some scarring." This isn't the worry, though. It's the damage below the skin, where creams and gels can't reach, that they can't fix. The horror of this catches her breath. It makes the room spin.

David pulls her to him. She presses against him, feeling his heart beat, and he kisses the top of her head. This perfect moment, unexpected. She has missed this so.

"What happened?" he murmurs.

"I don't know the whole story. For some reason, he went over to the Rylands' house. I found him in their baby's room. He'd already called the paramedics. He was worried about Holly. He kept asking if she was okay."

"Holly?"

"I didn't even know he knew her."

"I'm thirsty," Tyler whispers, and she turns back to him, reaches for the cup of water beside his bed.

Now that Tyler's awake and the sun has gone down, it's safe to take him home. She wants this very much. David helps Tyler into the backseat before climbing behind the steering wheel. She keeps up a cheerful monologue all the way home. She tells Tyler that Holly had just taken an extra sleeping pill, that she was in no danger whatsoever. She tells him how brave he was to check on the baby. Melissa comes running out the front door when they pull onto their street. Charlotte meets them in the doorway. She has kept Melissa company all this time.

"Thank you." Eve's teary with gratitude.

Melissa hugs Tyler, even as Eve warns her to be careful. But Tyler hugs her back, just as hard, and Eve feels something take flight within her. Joy. It's been so long.

"I don't want to go to bed," Tyler says after Charlotte leaves. "Can we order pizza?"

Eve laughs at this exquisitely ordinary request. She orders breadsticks and liter bottles of soda, too, and cuts Tyler's food into small pieces when it arrives. They sit on the patio. Night wraps warm around them. The stars are out, peppering the sky with brilliance. Sophie's lights blaze behind the fence. David notices and frowns.

They have talked about Robbie's arrest. Tyler has listened carefully. She wonders what he's taking in and understanding. The medication will make him woozy. Perhaps he's not picking up on the subtleties, but he's fourteen now. He may understand more than she realizes.

"Charlotte asked if Robbie ever made me feel uncomfortable," Melissa says.

"Did he?" Eve's stricken at the thought.

"No. Gross."

While David tidies up the kitchen, she helps Tyler upstairs. She and David have agreed—she'll take the early shift with Tyler and wake David to take over a few hours later.

Tyler goes into his bathroom and she wanders around his room. She picks up his digital camera, turns it over, and begins to look through his pictures. He hasn't said anything about his photography class in days.

The toilet flushes. "What's going to happen to Robbie?" Tyler calls.

"There'll be a trial." Everything will be brought to light, and she'll understand how the police had pieced it all together. She feels giddy with relief, Tyler's near miss.

"Will he go to prison?" The water's running in the bathroom.

"It depends on the evidence." That backpack, his baseball bat. What else?

"Like what they found in his truck?"

She's not sure what she's looking at, a picture of brown water? It's the river, she thinks. There are several in a row, with thin fronds floating beneath the surface. When did he take these?

Here's a picture of Holly Ryland, smiling directly into the camera, her arms around her little boy. Something cold spreads inside her. Tyler had known Holly. He'd gone over there with purpose.

"Mom?"

Here are pictures of Amy, taken outside her kitchen window, standing on a chair and reaching up. Then she's dragging the chair. Then she's entering the kitchen. Eve's eyes blur with tears.

"What are you doing?"

She looks up to see Tyler. He's reaching for his camera and she holds it up, out of his reach. "It wasn't just the Farnhams you were spying on, was it?"

"That's mine. Give it to me."

She hates to see him so upset. "You know we have to talk about this. How long have you been sneaking out?"

"Give me that!"

"You can't take pictures of people without their knowing."

"I didn't."

"You did of Amy."

"So what?"

Suddenly, something he'd said earlier registers. She looks at him, standing there defiantly, his eyes narrowed. She must have misunderstood. "How do you know the police searched Robbie's truck?"

"I saw it on the news."

But this detail hasn't been on the news. Her heart begins to beat faster. "So you know what they found." Or didn't find. It was Robbie's baseball bat they were looking for. But that's not what Tyler volunteers.

"A picture."

"A picture," she repeats. She looks down at the camera in her hand.

"So they know he did it. So he'll go to prison, right?"

Tyler's been wandering around their neighborhood for weeks, possibly months. She holds the camera, scrolls back to the image of Amy jumping down from a chair, her too-small nightgown revealing a little girl on the cusp of young womanhood. Charlotte had tried to get rid of that nightgown, but Amy had a way of holding onto things she loved most. So even though the fabric was worn so thin it was sheer, and even though it hugged her too tight, Amy kept digging it out of the ragbag. An innocent shot, and yet not. "This picture?" she says. Her hand is shaking.

Tyler looks away. "No."

My God. He's lying. She can't even swallow. "Did you put this picture in Robbie's truck?"

"No."

Her mouth is dry. "Why? Why would you do this?"

He still won't look at her. "I want my camera back."

"Tyler. Why would you do this?" She's whispering. She can't bear to say the words louder.

"I didn't."

"Please, Tyler. Tell me. Did you know what it would look like?"

"What what would look like?"

He knows. He knows exactly what the police would think when they found it. She's sick with dread. "We have to tell the police the truth."

"They won't believe you. That picture only has Robbie's fingerprints on it. Not mine."

She's icy cold, trembling. "Why? Tell me! Why would you do this?"

"They were going to arrest Melissa."

"No, no, they weren't. Why would you think that?" she cries, confused.

His mouth turns down, and there he is. Her little boy. "They were, too. Everyone knew it."

"Who? Charlotte? No, she was just upset. She didn't mean anything."

"They were going to arrest Melissa and I was never going to see her again." He's weeping. "She's my sister. My sister."

"Ssh," she says. He needs to calm down. "It's okay, honey. It's okay."

"You always say that."

"I know." She puts her arms around him carefully. "I know."

The first Christmas that they were a whole and complete family, Melissa got a toy kitchen with knobs that turned and cabinet doors that opened. Four-month-old Tyler lay beneath the Christmas tree, his little fist in his mouth, watching the lights blink above him. He'd reach up to bat at an ornament and Melissa would softly say, *No, Ty. No touch.* She would take his little hand in her little hand and he would coo at her. All those ornaments, the glass Santas and colored balls and tinsel-tailed birds, all of them, are wrapped in bubble wrap and tucked into sturdy boxes. They are protected, as much as they can be.

She stands in the doorway and watches Tyler sleep. All that sadness locked up inside him. She'd never guessed how deep it ran. He's growing up. His cheeks are hollowing out, his shoulders broadening. Her son's becoming a man. Isn't that what she's always wanted? Not just to be a man, but to be a good person. How will he get there if she doesn't show him how?

David's asleep in the bedroom down the hall. She won't wake him. Melissa lies tangled in her sheets, so many clothes discarded about her that she's lost among them. Eve leans close and puts her cheek alongside her daughter's, inhales deep, searching for the scent that is purely Melissa and not the shampoo or the body wash or the perfume. She closes her eyes. Yes, there it is. There's Melissa, warm and sweet and singular.

The moon hangs high above, sharp against the sky, a fingernail pressed against the black. All the houses are dark. Does Charlotte sleep? Amy's funeral's in a few hours. Almost everyone will be there.

She looks down at the vegetable patch, what remains of it, the exhausted tomato vines and oregano gone to seed. They've learned a lot from these few yards of earth. That asparagus needs three years to produce. That a single pumpkin seed can send out monstrous vines that overtake everything in its path. That Tyler hates beets, and that they can't produce enough strawberries to satisfy Melissa. The zucchini didn't take this year; she doesn't know why. David says it's because the soil is overworked, and so next year they had agreed to move it to the other side of the yard.

The darkness is lifting. It's getting lighter. The sun is coming. Everything will be revealed in the light of day.

SATURDAY, SEPTEMBER 13

SUNRISE 7:11 AM

SUNSET 7:46 PM

DAVID

The moment he'd walked into Tyler's hospital room and seen Eve standing by their son's bed, her gaze focused on his sleeping face and her hand resting on his shoulder, all the ugly suspicion had evaporated. Eve, who had been so selfless, who never once asked why, who instead simply accepted and moved on. She'd been so true. How could he have doubted her? She had looked at him and the gladness on her face filled him with emotion. They had come so close. He had pulled her into his arms and, despite everything, felt peace.

He finds her in the garden. She rises as he comes out the door, brushing her hands together. Her hair is loose, the way he's always liked it. She's wearing the same T-shirt and jeans she'd been wearing the day before. "I thought you were going to wake me. How's Tyler?"

"Still asleep. I gave him some more ibuprofen around three."

He pulls out her chair. "Come sit with me. I made you tea."

There are purple circles beneath her eyes. He'll have to encourage her to nap later. "Did you know Neil Cipriano was keeping a snake? Some sort of python, by the look of it. I saw Animal Control take it out of his house just now while I was getting the newspaper. Unreal. Can you imagine if that thing had gotten loose?"

She shakes her head and lifts her cup to her lips. She's clearly exhausted. Normally, this sort of news would have provoked some response from her.

"Mark Ryland came over last night," he continues, "while you were upstairs with Tyler. He wanted to thank him. He said his mother's coming to live with them while Holly's getting help. Our son's a hero."

"I don't want a hero. I just want my little boy."

"He's not your little boy anymore."

"He'll always be my little boy."

"Maybe so." Back when the children were little, Eve was always coming up with different activities—swimming by flashlight in the YMCA pool just after it closed for the night, visiting a neighboring farm at midnight to pet the small animals, hitting tennis balls by lantern on the clay court of a mansion undergoing renovation. The moonlight traipses through the park, daubing incandescent paint on rocks and trees, and making their own private art show. All those picnics under the stars.

Robbie. He still can't believe it. No doubt Eve's been beating herself up, trying to see what clue she'd missed. But it's not her fault. She'll realize it, with time. "They opened a new coffee shop in my apartment building. Remember me telling you the old one had been closed by the health department? I was reluctant to try the new place, but I finally did." He doesn't tell her it had been at Renée's prompting. "It reminded me of that place we used to hang out at in college."

"Gibson's."

"Gibson's. Maker of the best whole-wheat doughnut in the world."

They'd eaten a million of them over four years. "There was a girl working behind the counter. She had to be about sixteen or so. I asked if she had coffee, and she told me she'd start a fresh pot. So I wandered around while I waited. Do you know they make pickle-flavored potato chips?"

"Melissa loves them."

"No kidding." He shakes his head. "So, anyway, this old guy comes in. He reeked. He was bumping into things. I moved toward the counter, to let the girl know that I was there. He asks her for a sandwich and she goes to the display case and pulls one out. She gets a bottle of juice, too, and hands them both to him. He doesn't pay. He just turns and walks away."

She's put her cup down, watching him, absorbing the details he doesn't know to express. They used to sit like this and describe their days to each other.

"So I ask her if he's one of her regulars, but she says no. I told her it was nice what she did, and you know what she said? She said, *What goes around comes around.* And that's when I remembered." He pauses for dramatic effect, and she obliges by asking, "Remembered what?"

"The first time I met you."

"It was in my dorm," she says. "The girls across the hall were having a party—"

He shakes his head. "No, that wasn't it. The first time I saw you was that first week of freshman year. You said the same thing. Or close to it."

"I did? Are you sure?"

"You were in front of me in line, and there was this kid looking at the doughnuts in the case. He didn't have the money to pay for one, so you did. The clerk said something and you told him, *What goes around, comes around.*"

"You never said anything."

"It never clicked in my mind. At least not consciously. Remember how I felt like I'd seen you before?"

"You said, *Do I know you?* I thought it was some cheesy pick-up line."

"It worked."

"It did."

"Things haven't been right between us for a while."

"No." Her voice is low. "I pushed you away."

"It wasn't just you. It was me, too. I let you push me away."

"David . . ."

"It's not too late." He moves his chair closer. Their knees touch. "The firm's about to offer me a partnership. It's what we've been waiting for. I know you're worried about moving Tyler, but I think we can do it. We'll find a place somewhere in Virginia, or maybe Maryland, off the beaten track. I'll have to commute, but at least we'll be together. We can start over."

"David, I'm sorry. I'm truly sorry, but it is too late."

"No, it's not. We'll work it through." Nothing had happened with Renée, but it could have. He had been on the verge. Maybe Eve had been lonely, too. "What's important is we love each other."

Her eyes shine with tears. "I do. I do love you."

"Then we can figure this out. I know you're tired. I know I should have waited to say anything, but—"

"Stop, David. Please." The finality in her voice reaches him and he sits back.

"Are we talking about another man?"

She laughs, a short, brittle sound. "My God, I wish . . ." She scrapes her hands through her hair, shakes her head. "I've done something terrible, something unforgivable. I should have told you right away, but I didn't."

He can't imagine what she's talking about, and fear begins to make a place inside him. "What? Did you steal from the foundation?" He tries for the ridiculous, to lessen the panic in her voice. "Did you rob a bank?"

"I killed Amy."

He hears her say this. He sees her mouth form the words, but the sense of it slips right past him and into the air. *It's Robbie. He's in jail right now.*

"I was texting and I looked down. When I looked up, there she was. I tried to stop."

This is impossible. Why is she saying this? But then he remembers: *The fender.*

"I didn't realize it was her. At first I thought it was a deer. You know how they run across the ravine road all the time. That's all I thought. I went looking and that's when I found her, lying there by the river. She was just lying there. I tried to save her. I tried."

But you didn't call the police.

Until she replies, he doesn't even realize he's said this out loud. "I wanted to. I was about to, and then I realized . . . I couldn't." She's pleading, trying to meet his eyes, but he can't look at her. He's looking all around at everything else—the flowers beginning to wake up at the fence, the worn gray planks of the fence. If they stay here, he'll need to paint. "I couldn't. Don't you see? The minute they found out I'd been texting, they'd take me away. They'd lock me up and then where would Tyler be? Who would keep him safe?"

He looks at her, her bright blue eyes so startling against the paleness of her skin and the glossiness of her black hair. She's a stranger to him. Ice runs through him, a cold fury. "You're not the only one . . ."

"Yes. Yes, I am."

The whole weight of what has happened, of what is about to happen, lands beside him, shaking the earth. "Are you blaming *me*?"

She doesn't look away. "I blame myself."

"All this time. Charlotte. Your best friend. You put her through hell."

"I did."

"That's it? That's all you're going to say?"

"What do you want me to say? I'm done crying and feeling sorry for myself. I can't fix this. Nothing I can do or say will make any of this whole again. Who knows if I'll ever see Tyler again? Who knows if Melissa will ever get over this? Amy's dead."

"Why are you telling me this now?"

"It's Tyler. He framed Robbie. He put the photograph in his truck, called the police to say he'd seen Robbie creeping around Charlotte's house and taking pictures. None of it's true. Tyler made it all up. He was terrified they were going to arrest Melissa."

David looks at his wife, the woman he's loved. He thinks of their son. All the ways in which they've worked to protect this house from the sun had only allowed the darkness to creep inside.

The tow truck's long gone, and all the police cruisers that had lined the curb. Still, he stands in the empty place in the garage, staring up the dark street. It had taken all day, but felt so quick.

"Dad," Melissa says fiercely. "Come inside."

He presses the garage button and the door slowly lowers, sealing them off from the rest of the world.

The house looks like a great and terrible wind has swept through it, drawers opened, books pulled from shelves, clothes heaped on the bed. Eve's laptop is gone, her cell phone, her shoes. *What had she been wearing that night?* the detective had demanded, and David had looked at him blankly.

Melissa's crying. She can't stop. Sodden tissues lie in heaps beside her on the couch. Her face is blotchy and swollen. She looks so young. Tyler hasn't said a word. He pulled his hands from Eve's and pushed her away, locked himself in his bathroom until she was gone. This is what he was like after Rosemary died. He went silent for weeks. Eve had despaired, then wept with relief when he began speaking again. This is the same thing, isn't it, just a different form of death?

"My God, David," his sister says when she answers the phone.

"I don't know what to do with the children. I have to work." He's overwhelmed by all the things he has to do.

"I'll fly in. I can take them with me."

"To Arizona?"

"We'll figure it out. I'll let you know when my flight arrives."

"What are we going to do?" Melissa wants to know. "Are you going to make us move to DC?"

He thinks of his apartment. It would never work to move Tyler there, but what are his choices? "I want to."

"But Mom will be *here*, won't she?"

He doesn't know. All he knows is that his wife's been arrested and might never return.

That first night home from the specialist's office, having settled Tyler to sleep in a makeshift bed in the windowless basement, they sat at the kitchen table. Eve had a pad of paper before her, and she was already making plans to convert their house into a fortress. *We'll give him the second floor and move down into his room. I'm worried about the windows, though.* Her cup of tea had steamed gently before her. *What if we start a foundation to raise money to find a cure?* Her words had skipped around the room. They couldn't settle in his heart. Her hope, so pure.

"Are you hungry?" he asks his daughter now. Had they eaten at all that day? "Do you want me to make some dinner?"

She looks at him strangely. She walks down the dark hallway and goes into her room.

He walks heavily up the stairs to Tyler's room and stops in shock at the sight of the bare walls. Papers lie in shredded heaps all over the floor. Tyler himself sits on his bed, head buried in his folded arms. He doesn't answer when David tells him he'll be back in a few minutes.

He lets himself out of the house and into the cool night. The cul-de-sac is quiet, all the houses dark. Only Charlotte's blazes with light, every window throbbing bright. He doesn't know what to say, but he knows he has to say something. They've both lost loved ones, haven't they? They can help each other. The two families, so closely entwined all these years.

He walks onto her porch and glimpses her through the living room window. She's sitting there, holding a doll in her lap, her head bowed. She looks so forlorn. Where is everyone—her children, her mother?

He knocks softly.

A moment later, the door swings open and Charlotte stands there. He hasn't seen her since the night Amy disappeared, and he's horrified at how ugly she's become. Her orange hair stands up around her white face; her lips are colorless. Her clothes hang from her shoulders. "Charlotte," he begins. He'd thought she might be guilty. He'd warned Eve to stay away from her. "I wanted to see you. I wanted to say . . . I don't know. I don't know what to say."

"You don't know what to say?" She frowns. "You think words can fix this? You asshole. There's nothing you could say that could bring my little girl back."

Her fury shocks him. "I know. I'm sorry."

"Shut up. I don't want your apologies. You were never there."

Maybe this had been a mistake, coming here. He's only making things worse. "I should have been home more. This would never have happened—"

"Even when you were home, you weren't there. My Amy died in an instant. I have to think that." Red circles burn in her cheeks. Her eyes are feverishly bright. "But Tyler's been dying for years. You wrote him off, you fucking coward. Eve never did."

The truth of her words peels back his skin. How can she know this? Is this who he is? "I know you're upset. I get it. I'm a parent, too. I understand."

She steps close. The air around her wavers. "You still don't know, do you?" Her voice is quieter now, and it frightens him. "You don't understand anything. If it were Tyler lying there and Amy who needed saving . . . If it were my Amy—I'd have done just what Eve did."

She shuts the door behind her, and the porch light flares off, leaving him in a pool of darkness.

TUESDAY, APRIL 15

SUNRISE 6:55 AM

SUNSET 8:09 PM

TYLER

The sky's black and velvety, the full moon stamped bright, hovering behind the trees, the air cold and wet. Up and down the street, windows and porches glow pumpkin orange. A patch of dirty snow sits in the grass by the driveway. By tomorrow, it'll be gone. Tyler huddles on the top porch step and wraps his arms around his bent knees. If anyone asks, he'll say he's waiting for his dad to come home from work. *It'll be late, buddy,* his dad had warned him that morning. *It's Tax Day.*

It's also the day that Charlotte's moving away.

The moving van has sat outside her house all day. Tyler had heard the loud rumble early that morning and gone to see. Melissa and his dad had stood beside him, silently looking out the window. Then his dad had patted his shoulder and told him, *Time to go up.* When Tyler came out of his room, he ran down the stairs and saw the truck was still there as evening shadows fell across the men carrying things out of Charlotte's house and up a wooden ramp. But now they're getting ready to leave. One man rolls down the big metal door with a rattle. Another stands with Charlotte on her driveway, holding a clipboard, talking. Then he climbs into the driver's seat and the engine starts up with a noise like a belch that would have made him laugh any other day. The van pulls away from the curb and turns onto the ravine road, and a moment later is gone.

Charlotte stands looking after it. She's wearing a long, droopy sweater and jeans. Then she looks around at all the houses—the Farnhams' with its Easter Bunny flag hanging by a pole; Albert's, dark while he's in Florida visiting his son; Dr. Cipriano's with the two cars parked in the driveway now that he and Bob are together again; Sophie's with its bright lights gone, unhooked by her new boyfriend in one afternoon and taken down; and Tyler's house, sitting in the dark and invisible. If she were to keep turning her head, she'd see Holly's house with the hanging baskets of ivy her mom put there shortly after moving in, but she doesn't. She stands there, looking directly at him. Then she steps onto the sidewalk and walks down the street toward him.

What does she want? Should he get up and go inside before she gets there? When she reaches his front lawn, she just stands there. Her pale hair gleams in the starlight. "Hi."

She doesn't sound angry. The last time he'd heard her voice had been on TV, talking to the reporters after his mom's sentencing. She'd been really angry, her voice unforgiving and harsh. His dad had quickly raised the remote and silenced her, but still. The sound of all that rage directed at his mom made Tyler's stomach clench. "Hi."

"Mind if I sit with you?"

He thinks about this. Melissa's at the barn with her new boyfriend; his dad won't be home until after midnight. He's alone. But this is Charlotte, and so he says, "Okay."

When she comes closer, he sees that her hair's not the only thing she's changed. She's not wearing any jewelry, and her sweater has a long thread trailing from one sleeve. She sits down on the step beside him. She smells of dust and coffee and wet grass. She looks up at the spring sky, at all the stars there. "How are you doing?"

Is this a test? "Okay." He doesn't dare ask how she is.

"I meant to come by earlier. I've been meaning to come by, actually, for a while." She tilts her head and studies him. For a moment, he sees Amy in her eyes. "I hear you're trying a new ointment. How's that going?"

How does she know? Then he realizes she probably read about it in the newspaper. There've been tons of articles about his mom, and then the checks had started coming in, all for the foundation. Tyler's dad had sent them to Dr. Abernathy, thousands and thousands of dollars. "It's stupid, but my dad's making me do it."

He hates this new lotion. It's greasy and stinks like metal, but he has to put it on every day, all over. He imagines it sinking into his skin and knitting things together. That's not exactly the way it works, Dr. Abernathy's told him, but Tyler likes the idea of his skin cells armoring themselves up, getting ready for battle. *Just think,* Dr. Abernathy said. *If it works, you'll be able to play football, go to college. Visit Paris.* Tyler had asked, *What about learning to drive?* Dr. Abernathy had laughed. *That, too,* he'd said.

"I'm glad."

"Charlotte," he blurts out. "I'm sorry I lied about Robbie. I'm sorry I made you think that."

"I know. I'm glad you told the truth. I wish he had."

Robbie only confessed after the police found his DNA on the buckle of Amy's backpack. Tyler stares up the street, trying to picture the way the rain had hammered down that night six months earlier, Robbie pulling up his truck to make Amy see that his moving in was a good idea. But Amy had jumped off the porch and run out into the storm, away from him. The TV reporters said it was because Robbie had hurt Amy before, maybe done something to her that he shouldn't have, but Tyler doesn't know. He thinks Amy would have told him if that were true.

"I wish I'd seen him." He'd followed the path the two of them had taken—across the street and into the park, down to the bridge where Amy had swung her backpack and cut Robbie's hand. Then she'd made a sharp turn and run through the trees up to the ravine road. Robbie hadn't given up. He'd chased after her and grabbed her by the side of the road. But she hadn't given up, either: she pulled away and stumbled into the path of his mom's car.

"It wouldn't have made any difference, honey. It happened too quickly."

"I would have tried." Amy had tried. She had been brave. Tyler had stood among the trees and felt her heart beating like a bird's.

"I know you would have."

At least Robbie's in prison. *Involuntary manslaughter,* the judge had decided, because he was the reason Amy ran across the street to begin with. It's the same thing Tyler's mom had been charged with. She couldn't have braked in time, and so instead of getting four years in prison, she got two. Tyler's watched the TV shows that debated this, re-creating the accident. Always, his mom's face is a ghostly blur behind the steering wheel.

"How's your mother doing?"

"I miss her." His voice wobbles, like a little kid's. But he does miss her, not seeing her every day, not talking to her. It's like this huge hole in his heart, and he doesn't know how to fill it. He tries to force this sorrow away—after all, Charlotte must miss Amy, but she's never coming home. His mom will come home. His dad's promised that when she did, they'd all live together again, although maybe not here. He pulls off his sunglasses and rubs his eyes, determined not to cry.

Charlotte puts her arm around his shoulders and squeezes. "I miss her, too."

He looks at her, surprised.

"She never meant to hurt me. She was just trying to take care of you."

"I thought you hated her."

"I did, for a while. But I don't anymore."

She rests her cheek against his shoulder. After a moment, she says, "I think you'll like the new family moving in. They're from Michigan and they have twins your age, a boy and a girl."

"Where are you going?"

"I'm renting a condo near Nikki's school. Scott's going to live with us, too. Did you know he's starting classes again?"

"That's good."

"Yeah. I'm proud of him. He's trying hard."

"What about you?" It was a grown-up question to ask, but he felt that Charlotte was talking to him like a grown-up. His mom would like that, he thinks.

"Not sure. I might go back to real estate, or I might try something else. I don't know what my future holds. But that's what life's all about, isn't it?"

Tyler doesn't know what's going to happen for him, either. Maybe the ointment won't work; maybe it will.

The moon rises from behind the trees, fat and full, like a shiny coin. If Tyler reaches out, he could touch it. There are other kinds of vanishing points, he thinks, ones that reach into forever, carrying with them their deepest secrets. He leans against Charlotte and she holds him closer. "Look!" she exclaims, pointing to the bright yellow sparks that blossom everywhere along the cul-de-sac.

They sit there in the scented darkness, as the fireflies dance.

Acknowledgments

My deepest thanks to:

Kate Miciak, my editor, my champion, who spotted this story among the rubble and held it up to the light.

My remarkable team at Random House, dream builders all: Gina Centrello, Libby McGuire, Jennifer Hershey, Kim Hovey, Susan Corcoran, Allyson Pearl, Kelly Chian, and Kristin Fassler.

Dorian Karchmar and Alicia Gordon, agents extraordinaire, and my whole wonderful team at William Morris Endeavor.

Pam Ahearn, for years of support and guidance.

Liese Schwarz, my sister and my muse, gifted with brilliant insight and the generous willingness to share it.

Chevy Stevens, my friend and critique partner. I am so happy our literary paths brought us together.

Tim Buckley, my husband and the start of it all.

THE
DEEPEST
SECRET

CARLA BUCKLEY

A READER'S GUIDE

An Interview with Carla Buckley and Kimberly McCreight

Kimberly McCreight is the *New York Times* bestselling author of *Reconstructing Amelia*. She lives in Park Slope, Brooklyn, with her husband and two daughters, where she is hard at work on her second novel, *How I Lost Her,* which will be published in 2015. Her teen trilogy, *The Outliers,* will be published in 2016.

Kimberly McCreight: *The Deepest Secret* is a compelling family drama, but it's also packed with suspense. Which aspect of the story were you drawn to most?

Carla Buckley: Is it fair to say both?

I'm endlessly fascinated by how families behave under stress, how facing a crisis can bring some families together while others crumble. Being a mother myself, I want to know the answer to the nurture-nature question of how we become the people we are and, once we're shaped, whether we can change.

Parents are regularly called upon to make tough decisions, often with little warning and no assurance that they've made the right choice. What if we were confronted with a terrible dilemma and had only a moment to think—how would we know what to do and what if we made a mistake? Would we be able to forgive ourselves? I hope my readers recognize themselves in my characters and ask themselves what they would do if they had to wrestle with the same issues.

KM: You write with enormous empathy. Do you think that Eve is a good mother? David a good father?

CB: Coming home from the hospital with my first child, the one thing I wished for most was a how-to manual, some magical reference tool that could tell me exactly how to take care of this infinitely vulnerable, impossibly tiny new life with which I and my husband been entrusted. I'd lost both parents several years before and had no extended family to help me figure out my new role as mom. All I had was love and a fierce determination to do the best job I could.

My husband and I ended up having three children so I've had my share of emergency room visits and sleepless nights filled with worry and heartache. I've watched my children stumble but I've also watched them get up. I've made plenty of mistakes of my own, and the one lesson I've learned—and keep trying to learn—is compassion. To look around and understand that everyone makes mistakes. Everyone stumbles. Everyone's just trying to do the best job they can. There is no magical parenting manual.

So do I think Eve and David are good parents? I'm not sure I believe there is such a thing. Who gets to decide what constitutes good parenting? I'm more comfortable thinking of them as *real* parents. They're just trying to raise their children to be the best they can be, despite hardship and sacrifice, despite a world that offers them very few solutions.

KM: This is your third novel. How is *The Deepest Secret* similar to or different from *The Things That Keep Us Here* and *Invisible*? How has your writing process changed—if at all—over time?

CB: I would say that all my novels have the drumbeat of a thriller with the heartbeat of a family drama. I came to write this way almost by accident.

I'd written eight unpublished traditional mysteries when I decided to change course and tackle a question that had been haunting me for some time: how would I protect my family if the worst came to pass and the H5N1 flu strain in China turned pandemic? That story became *The Things That Keep Us Here,* a novel set entirely in one family's living room as a pandemic rages around them. In my second novel, *Invisible,* I asked myself how much hardship a family could sustain before it broke apart. I set that story in a fictitious northern Minnesota town reeling from a deadly environmental contamination.

In some ways, *The Deepest Secret* is like both of my previous works. In it, I also follow a family already in crisis forced to their breaking point by a devastating event. I explore the same themes of community and moral obligation; I ask, who are we when no one's looking—or when we *think* no one's looking? But in other ways, *The Deepest Secret* ventures into new territory for me. There's no global threat, no impending doom hovering overhead. I focused more sharply on a much smaller scale—eight suburban houses ranged along a cul-de-sac—and to my surprise, found my story expanding into something much bigger.

At heart, *The Deepest Secret* is about one boy growing up and the impact that one small life can have on so many others. It's a story about love in all its guises and in the end, love prevails—which is the happiest ending of all.

KM: I imagine the novel has sparked some intense discussion. Have you been surprised by readers' reactions? Does your own opinion about who is culpable dovetail with reader reactions?

CB: One of my biggest challenges in writing this story was making Eve sympathetic. I wondered whether some readers might not be able to get past the hit-and-run scene, but I hoped they would persevere, if for no other reason than to find out what happened next. What has surprised me, however, is how many readers have sided with Eve, understanding how isolated she felt. They've pointed to David's abandoning his family and Charlotte's letting her young daughter leave the house in the middle of a thunderstorm. What about Robbie, chasing a terrified young girl through the woods? Owen, for not answering Amy's plea for help? It's impossible to say, *There. That's the moment where everything started.* I believe that everyone in a community shares responsibility for what happens within it and I'm gratified to know that readers have agreed.

KM: XP is a relatively rare medical condition—what got you interested in this disease? Do you have any personal connection to the subject matter?

CB: When I began thinking about ideas for my third book, my son was fifteen and learning to drive, his first real step to growing up and leaving home. It occurred to me that this normal, turbulent, and always challenging period of a boy's adolescence would be complicated immeasurably if he had a medical condition. But which one? I turned to my sister, a writer and a physician, for ideas and she suggested xeroderma pigmentosum. It sounded familiar and when she explained that it was essentially an allergy to sunlight, all the bells in my head started loudly chiming.

How on earth do you protect a child from something as ubiquitous as sunlight? I began to imagine a mother whose sole focus was doing just that. Her son could never attend school or play a sport; he would be virtually imprisoned within his own house. I had recently read Emma Donoghue's *Room* and I saw the mother in my own story building her son a special world to compensate for the real one he could never investigate; I saw her fight passionately to help him lead as normal a life as possible. I wanted to spend time with a mother like that. I wanted to understand her.

KM: Your descriptions of the Lattimore family's day-to-day life are so vivid. What kind of research did you do medical or otherwise to so effectively capture their experience?

CB: XP is an extraordinarily rare disease passed on by both parents in which a person's skin and eye cells cannot repair the deadly damage done by ultraviolet radiation. Most parents don't realize they're carriers until their child is diagnosed, usually by the time their child is two years old. But by then, the damage has already been done. The average life expectancy for someone born with XP is twenty years. Though doctors understand what causes XP, they can't prevent it and there is no cure.

In order to understand the disease itself, I scoured online resources (there are two parent-run organizations, one in the U.S. and the other in the U.K. that offer general information to caregivers), read numerous medical research papers, and interviewed dermatologists and dentists. Combined, this gave me a basic foundation upon which to build. Then I began to put myself in Eve's place to imagine what I would do if I had to keep my child safe from sunlight.

KM: Secrets play a significant role in this novel. Is there one character whose secret you see as being the most significant—in other words, the deepest secret?

CB: In many ways, the titular secret is Eve's. Her decision to keep silent about the hit-and-run is what sets everything in motion, but as I wrote, my story evolved into something more than a mother's dilemma. It became about the terrible cost of keeping a secret. After all, we all keep secrets, even from those we love the most—sometimes, especially from those we love the most. We can have desperately good reasons for keeping something to ourselves. But secrets can nibble corrosively at a family's well-being. They can leach into the homes of our friends and our neighbors. They can rip apart a community.

KM: Did you know from the outset where the characters in *The Deepest Secret* would end up? Did the conclusion surprise you?

CB: I'm a plotter. Before I start any story, I structure it into four acts and figure out the turning points at each critical juncture, which for me occurs every fifty pages. Doing so keeps me focused as I write and helps me create a taut suspense through line. Therefore, I always know exactly where my story starts and ends.

Or at least I thought I did.

The ending for *The Deepest Secret* eluded me for the longest time. As I wrote, I realized that the ending I had initially decided on didn't answer the important questions about the characters I had begun to know. The first draft I submitted to my editor included the caveat that I was still working on the ending. I hoped her feedback would help me find it. Six drafts later, we did indeed uncover an ending that made me happy and one I hoped left the reader at a satisfying place.

KM: Can you tell us a little bit about your next project? Because I can't wait to read it!

CB: Thanks, Kim! My next novel, *The Good Goodbye,* is the story of two young cousins after they arrive at a burn unit following a devastating college fire, and that of their families and the mystery which ultimately brought them to that moment.

Questions and Topics for Discussion

1. How do you think Melissa's and Tyler's involvement in the crime (Melissa as a suspect and Tyler planting evidence) impacted Eve's actions? Would she have confessed if her children had not been involved?

2. Eve's efforts to guard her son from light are sometimes considered excessive—by her son, her husband, and her neighbors. Notably, Eve's determination to prevent Sophie from installing outdoor lights on her house leads to a neighborhood fight. What do you think of Eve's protective instincts? Does she take things too far, or is she behaving as any concerned parent would?

3. At one point, Holly asks Tyler "Do you think it's better to have dreams and lose them, or not have dreams at all?" How would you respond? What do you make of Holly and her relationship with Tyler?

4. David wants to move the family to Washington, but Eve

considers this impossible given Tyler's condition. Is David's desire to move selfish, or is he looking out for the family's best interests?

5. What sacrifices does Eve make for the sake of her family? Are they necessary? Is it worth it?

6. Describe the relationship between Tyler and Eve. In the end, Tyler's desire to protect his sister led him to make questionable choices. How are his choices similar to Eve's? How are they different?

7. Discuss the nature of secrets. Is it human nature to keep secrets? Do our secrets define us? Is it human nature to want to know the secrets of others and to confess our own? Do you believe that all secrets eventually come to light? What is *The Deepest Secret*?

8. Tyler learns some surprising truths about his neighbors during his nighttime wanderings. How do people change in the moments during which they believe themselves to be alone? During unobserved moments, are people more themselves? How much of life is a performance, and to what extent are we defined by the external perceptions and behavioral expectations of others?

9. How much did you sympathize with Eve? Would you feel differently about her actions if she had not been texting at the time of the accident? What if Tyler had not been burned while playing basketball with David? Would you have felt differently about Eve's behavior if Melissa had been the one to hit Amy?

10. How would you describe Eve's relationship with Melissa? Melissa's needs in her family are often viewed as secondary to Tyler's, given his illness. How do you think this attitude impacted her psychologically? How did it affect her relationships with Tyler, Eve, and David?

11. It seems clear by the end that a number of people played

some role in Amy's death, including Charlotte, Robbie, and Eve. Who, if anyone, do you hold responsible?

12. What do you consider appropriate punishment for the driver in a hit-and-run accident? Can there ever be extenuating circumstances, such as Tyler's condition, that justify fleeing the scene of a deadly accident? If so, what are those circumstances?

13. Toward the end of the novel, Charlotte says, "If it were my Amy—I'd have done just what Eve did." What do you think of this statement? If you had been in Eve's position, how would you have acted on the night of the accident? In the weeks following?

14. What did you think of the conclusion of the novel? Did it end as you expected it to? Were you satisfied?

If you enjoyed *The Deepest Secret,*
read on for a preview of Carla Buckley's next novel

The
GOOD GOODBYE

The first thing you should know is that everyone lies. The second thing is that it matters.

NATALIE

I keep a list of Arden's first words. *Banky, mimi, 'ghetti, daddy.* She'd been napping fitfully in my lap when I picked up the gas bill lying on top of the nightstand and groped for the pen inside the top drawer. *Mama, nana, milk, doggy.*

Everything else from those years is a blur of sleeplessness and the constant feeling of being pulled in too many directions. I treasure that list, keep it folded in my wallet. *Banky, mimi, 'ghetti, daddy, mama, nana, doggy, rainbow, juice.* All the important things in Arden's life—her threadbare pink blanket, her favorite foods, Theo and me. I miss her. I miss hearing her voice. That first night after she left for college, I lay on top of her tousled sheets, breathing in her apple shampoo and pear soap. Now I keep the door closed.

"So how do you want to celebrate?" my husband asks.

I thought Theo had forgotten. Maybe, if I'm to be completely honest with myself, I'd hoped he had. He squares off in front of the bathroom mirror to give himself his usual morning pep talk look, his eyes half-closed and his chin raised. Maybe, shocker, he'd remembered on his own.

"I don't know." I turn off the water and drop my toothbrush in the cup. There's nothing I feel less like doing than dressing up and spending money on our anniversary.

Just thinking about it makes me want to crawl under the covers and yank them over my head.

"Anything you want," he promises. "Sky's the limit."

We both know the sky is very much not the limit.

"I have that big party coming in tonight," I remind him. Eleven Homecoming couples, a giggling pack of kids, uncertain in their finery. The tips would be meager, half the food would go uneaten or end up on the tablecloth, and the restrooms would be a disaster. But any port in a storm. And these last six months had been so stormy they'd ripped the shingles right off the roof.

"They'll be gone by nine, right? We can do something then."

"You know I can't close early."

There's always the chance an after-theater crowd could wander by and decide to come in—though that's been happening less and less frequently. Why? Too many seafood options, not enough vegetarian? A food trend I haven't picked up on? We used to have a line snaking down the sidewalk. Now whenever I glimpse people pausing outside to read the menu posted by the window, I find myself catching my breath.

"Let Vince cover for you. You've done it often enough for him."

"Right. You want to ask him, or shall I?" I shut the medicine cabinet a little too hard, rattling the bottles inside.

"Look," Theo says. "We should do something, Nat. I don't know what. But I do know nineteenth wedding anniversaries only come around once."

I tug my hair back into its usual ponytail. "If it's so important, why didn't we plan something ahead?" Theo has no answer for that one.

Downstairs, the boys are waiting in the front hall. They'd rejected the bright, small backpacks in the back-to-school section, and like a team of matched ponies marched straight to where the adult-sized backpacks hung, the very same display from which we'd chosen Arden's. *Are you sure you don't want a Batman one?* I'd coaxed. *Or the Hulk?* Oliver had glanced tentatively at his brother, but Henry crossed his arms and pushed out his lower lip, and Oliver instantly followed suit. So here they stand, six-year-old boys huddled beneath enormous black carapaces each containing a slim folder of math homework and a single, sharpened pencil. Vince would applaud the twins' show of solidarity. I miss Vince, despite everything, but I can't tell Theo this. There are so many things I can't tell Theo.

"Did you brush your teeth?" Theo asks the boys, and both solemnly nod.

I'd heard them counting in their bathroom, mumbled shouts filled with toothpaste and spit . . . *eight, nine, ten!* Henry's the one who keeps the count, who makes sure Oliver brushes his tongue, too. *It tickles!* he shrieks. The differences between my sons are much vaster than the four minutes that separate their births. Henry had howled as the doctor held him up so I could see him over the draped fabric; Oliver had been terrifyingly silent. I hadn't even been allowed to see or hold him until the next day, Theo pushing my wheelchair up to the incubator to where Oliver lay, surreally tiny inside, his arms and legs extended and taped down, his chest motionless. Fear clamped down hard. Then Oliver had turned his head and, slowly, blinked at me.

This morning, Oliver grips his ant farm between two hands, a plastic frame holding a half-inch of sandy dirt sandwiched between two rectangles of glass and crisscrossed by tunnels. Our dachshund sits by Oliver's feet with his long nose lifted, sniffing. *Friday's Sharing Day,* Oliver had told Arden on Skype. *But I don't know what I'm supposed to take.* I'd stopped cramming things into my bag and listened. *What did Caleb bring,* I heard Arden ask. *A baseball,* he'd answered, dolefully. *You can do way better than that,* she scoffed. *How about one of your science projects?*

Like my ant farm? Oliver had suggested, his voice swelling with hope. Arden had led him there and now it was his idea. I'd walked over to where my laptop sat on the kitchen table and leaned over to blow a kiss at my daughter. *Sorry, honey,* I'd told Arden. *But I have to leave for the restaurant. Can we talk later?* DC traffic was unforgiving. I was already cutting it close. Used to be Gabrielle would run over to watch the boys until Theo got home, but those days are gone. Arden had paused, then nodded. *I'll call you tomorrow,* she'd said. Which was yesterday. The whole day had come and gone, and she hadn't called. A million reasons why—she'd been out with her new friends, she'd been studying and lost track of time, she'd forgotten until it was too late to phone. But still, that hesitation—had there been something there?

I crouch to pat the dog bed. Percy trots over. "You be good," I tell him, rumpling his soft ears. He lies down with a sigh.

"Want me to take that?" Theo asks Oliver, and I know he's thinking about ants crawling around the car. Oliver shakes his head, then pushes past his brother to race down the path to where our Volvo rusts in the driveway alongside our sputtering fourth-hand Honda.

"Remember when Arden stole your diaphragm?" Theo whispers, leaning close.

I laugh. At the time, though, I'd been mortified when the teacher called to let me know what Arden had smuggled in for Sharing Day. Theo had shaken his head and looked thoughtful. *We'd better keep an eye on that one,* he'd said, meaning Arden.

I have, haven't I?

Theo slides his arms around me. "You're right, sweetheart," he says. "I should have put some thought into it. I just assumed you wouldn't want to make a big deal out of it."

"We can't afford to make a big deal out of it."

"We can afford to make a little deal out of it."

I sigh, lean into the circle of his arms. "Like what?"

"How about a movie? There are some good ones opening today."

We haven't seen a movie out in ages. The ticket prices, the time. I tell myself I want this, and all of a sudden, I do. I want to sit in a quiet, dark theater beside my husband, our arms touching, a bucket of hot buttery popcorn nestled in my lap. No worrying about my failing restaurant and bills piling up, my little girl grown up and gone. I smile at him. "I'll see if Mom can babysit."

Theo kisses my temple, soft, but it tingles all the way through. He scoops up his briefcase. "Arden will call," he says. "Try not to worry."

I watch him walk away. Nineteen years.

Vince has left me a note on the desk we share at the restaurant. He'd gone home before me the night before and his car isn't in the lot now, so I have no idea how he'd managed this impossible feat. Too bad his magic didn't extend to the stock market.

I frown at the bold ink strokes, as familiar as my own hand-writing. All those hours poring over cookbooks, calling across the kitchen, teasing and laughing and working in happy synchronicity side by side have come to this.

We need to talk.

I'm done talking. I've heard the excuses and explanations, the countless reasons why he couldn't have seen it coming. But it doesn't change the fact that he took a chance and lost, trapping all of us in the downward spiral. That's Vince for you, always grabbing the shiny brass ring, never stopping to look below. I uncap a Sharpie and slash a heavy line through his words.

I pick up the waiting sheaf of invoices. The top one is stamped in red—our meat purveyor. I'm surprised he'd agreed to extend us credit in the first place. It must have been Liz's doing. What would I do without Liz? I'd had to let two more servers go last week. Vince and I haven't drawn a salary since March, and we're down from thirty-seven employees to eight. We can light the place with candles and cook over charcoal briquettes if we have to, but the one thing we can't run a restaurant without is food.

Vince shows up around noon. I'm mixing pasta dough at the steel table. The one part of the day when I feel truly myself, my hands measuring and kneading, feeding the thin sheets of pasta through the pasta machine, letting my mind wander. I hear the back door open and know without looking up, recognizing his footsteps going down the back hall. A minute later he joins me, tying on his apron.

The first thing Vince and I'd done when we'd taken over the building five years before was to knock down the wall between the kitchen and the dining room. We'd been absurdly happy, our dream realized at last. One big open space—no barrier between customer and chef. Who knew it would be the barrier between the chefs that would bring it all down?

He rolls up his sleeves. "You got my note, I see."

"Does it have anything to do with twenty-two teenagers who are going to be showing up in just a few hours?"

"No. I guess it can wait."

I sprinkle buckwheat flour on the mound of beige-gray dough and cover it with cheesecloth. "I need you to close tonight."

"No problem. Boys okay?"

"They're fine," I say. The twins adore their uncle Vince. They ask after him and Aunt Gabrielle all the time. *How come she doesn't play with us anymore?* Henry had wondered just the other day and I'd replied, *She's busy.* He'd scrunched his eyes at me. *Busy doing what, exactly?* he'd wanted to know.

"Hey, that's right." Vince brings out the double boiler and sets it on the stove. "Today's your anniversary. Congratulations. You and Theo have big plans?"

Last year, on their nineteenth wedding anniversary, Vince and Gabrielle had toured Napa Valley, a lavish six-day trip he later wrote off as a tax deduction. It should have been a clue.

"We're going out," I answer, and I hear how curt my voice sounds. He nods, heads toward the dry goods section. "Apple strudel," I tell him and he stops.

"Not raspberry mousse?"

Raspberries are six dollars a pint. "Not unless you've won the lottery." I turn away so I don't have to see his expression.

By seven-twenty, the Homecoming couples still haven't shown. I bend a wafer-thin slice of pickle into a curl and nestle it alongside the piece of grilled Kobe. Wiping my hands on the towel tied into my apron strings, I slide the plate beneath the heat lamp. I'd called that afternoon to confirm the reservation. *What?* the teenaged girl had said. I'd had to repeat myself. *Oh, yeah,* she'd said. *The restaurant. We'll be there.*

The restaurant. Not, *Double.* I glance toward the front door and Vince says, "They'll be here."

Friday night and we've had only five tables, a total of sixteen covers.

"What if they're not?" I'd ordered a supply of shrimp and filets— the two proteins teenagers most like to order, as well as the most expensive. I should've stuck with chicken.

"Then we'll run a surf and turf special tomorrow."

"For the crowds thronging the door?" Filet mignon doesn't keep. Shrimp turns in a day. Vince knows this as well as I do but he's always happiest with the easy solution, even if it makes no sense. He loops lines of pureed basil across the piece of flounder, a magical composition of confidence and artistry but right now, it looks all wrong. Too bright. Too hopeful. Just like Vince.

"Nat," he says. "We really do have to talk."

"About what, another wonderful investment opportunity?"

"Are you ever going to forgive me?"

Just then, the door opens into a swirl of laughter and gold lamé, yards of black tulle and a windstorm of Axe and perfume. For a moment, I see what they see: eclectic chairs painted purple, green, orange; red and yellow Gerbera daisies in their glass bowls; flickering candles and white linens stiff with starch but looking cloud-soft. *Come in,* it all beckons. *Be yourself.* Arden had helped pick the colors, her hands on her hips, frowning at the selection.

Vince hands me the plate to finish and, grinning, goes over to greet and escort them to their tables. They tilt their faces to him and giggle, take their seats and pick up their menus.

This is the Vince I miss. But this is the Vince who betrayed me.

Theo arrives as the Homecoming couples are leaving. There is chaos by the door as kids push past in a happy clamor and then Theo steps through. "Hey," he says. He looks tired, but he's taken the trouble to put on a jacket and tie, and slide cuff links through the cuffs of his shirt. "You look nice."

"My Spanx's cutting me in half," I confess, and he laughs. I'm covered chin to knee in heavy bleached cotton; my feet are encased in dumpy clogs and I must reek of grease and garlic and onions. But Theo's smiling at me and I feel the heat of his affection. "Ready?" he asks. He doesn't look around for Vince.

I go back to the office to get my bag and drop my apron into the laundry bin. I tell Liz I'm leaving. "I'll let Vince know," she promises.

The night air's breezy with an impending storm. The weather forecasters have been warning us all week. *Gonna have a wet weekend, folks. Better move those cookouts inside.* I shrug out of my chef's jacket and fold it over my arm. "How was soccer?" I ask Theo.

"Fine. Henry still likes the coach."

T-ball had been a bust, Oliver ducking every time the bat was swung and Henry looking confused when the ball soared into the air. Soccer had been our compromise. "What about Oliver?"

"He fell and scraped his knee. He refused to go back onto the field."

"Shoot."

"Don't worry, sweetheart. It's all part of learning to play a sport. He'll be fine tomorrow."

I glance up at the clouds massing overhead. "What if we're rained out tomorrow?"

"It might blow through quickly. Even—"

My phone is ringing inside my bag. "Hold on," I say. "It must be Mom." Or maybe—at last—Arden? I pull out the phone and don't recognize the phone number. "Hello?"

"I'm looking for the parents of Arden Falcone." A man's voice, a stranger.

Trouble. Arden's in trouble. I know it instantly. "This is her mother," I say. "Is she okay?" I've stopped walking. My heart is trip-hammering, panicked. "What's going on?" Theo says and I shake my head. I press the phone against my ear.

"Your daughter's been in an accident," the stranger says, and everything slides away.

ARDEN

Someone's shouting in my ear. "What do we have?"

"Eighteen-year-old victim found unconscious."

"Where are the lines?"

"We got two. Eighteen gauge line in her right arm running saline . . ."

"Which room?"

"CAT scan."

A jolt. I open my eyes. Ceiling tiles swim past. A purple sleeve patterned with red hearts over my face. Above that, a hand gripping a metal pole. The light blinds me.

I am rolled, then lifted. A face leans close. A man. He needs to shave. "I'm Dr. Saunders. You're in Salisbury Hospital. You're going to be all right. Do you have any allergies?"

I can't remember.

"Does anything hurt?"

Panic rises in a huge wave.

"Is it possible you're pregnant?"

His face is gone. I feel cold air against my legs, my belly. The smell of something sweet and burned, then a pain so awful it carves a huge hole inside me. I hear moaning. It's me.

". . . push more," the man says.

A new face, a woman's hovering above mine, worried. "We're giving you some medicine that will make you feel better."

The whole white world telescopes to a black dot and blinks into nothingness.

Buzzing. A fly looking for a place to land. I try to lift my hand but my arm won't move. I'm so sleepy.

I'm in my bed. It's early and peaceful; the twins aren't up yet. I feel Percy on the covers by my feet. I try to move my foot to find him.

That fly won't stop whining. And there's something else, a soft whooshing. The ocean, rolling in waves to the shore. So I'm not in my bed at home. I'm at Rehoboth, with Mom and Dad, Oliver and Henry, and Percy.

The buzz is too loud to be a fly. A bee?

I can't open my eyes. I feel darkness pressing down on me. Something brushes my cheek.

". . . eight milligrams."

"When was her last morphine?"

Who are they? Why are they in my room? Fear. I want my mom. I want my dad.

". . . think she's awake."

"I'm Dr. Morris. I'm taking care of you. Are you in pain?"

Yes.

"You were in a fire, honey. Do you remember?"

So hot I can't breathe. Flames and greasy, awful smoke. Rory twists away, her hair swinging out in a glowing circle, shrieking as Hunter flails around. I can't help him. I'm going to be sick. I gag, scrabble at the sheets. Something's stuck in my throat. I'm choking on it. My heart gallops, faster and faster. I'm screaming. Why can't they hear me? Where's my mom?

"It's okay. Don't worry. That's just a tube helping you breathe. You're going to be okay." The doctor turns away. "Increase the drip."

Wait! A swoosh of heat. Flames leap across my bed, race up the walls. They claw at me. They hiss. Screaming so animal I feel my skin rip.

You were in a fire, honey. Do you remember?

Why was I there? Why didn't I get out? Why can't I remember?

Carla Buckley was born in Washington, D.C. She has worked as an assistant press secretary for a U.S. senator, an analyst with the Smithsonian Institution, and a technical writer for a defense contractor. She lives in Chapel Hill, North Carolina, with her husband, an environmental scientist, and their three children. She is the author of *The Deepest Secret, Invisible,* and *The Things That Keep Us Here,* which was nominated for a Thriller Award as a best first novel and the Ohiana Book Award for fiction. She is currently at work on her next novel, *The Good Goodbye.*

www.carlabuckley.com

About the Type

This book was set in Garamond, a typeface originally designed by the Parisian type cutter Claude Garamond (c. 1500–61). This version of Garamond was modeled on a 1592 specimen sheet from the Egenolff-Berner foundry, which was produced from types assumed to have been brought to Frankfurt by the punch cutter Jacques Sabon (c. 1520–80).

Claude Garamond's distinguished romans and italics first appeared in *Opera Ciceronis* in 1543–44. The Garamond types are clear, open, and elegant.